"Bad Boys on the Starboard Side!" the pilot clicked in.

"Thanks, boss man!" Snakeman yelled back, and glanced over to the right-side hatch. It was smeared with blood, the door gunner hanging limp from his monkeystraps—killed by twenty rounds of dink tracers.

"Eat shit, motherfuckers!" he screamed, unloading over one hundred rounds of hot lead from his hatch-60 at a VC platoon huddled near the east perimeter wire on Fire Support Base Belinda. They scattered and left their dead behind.

"You going the record, bro'," Warrant Officer Gabriel clicked in to the door gunner.

"Fucking right, man! Bring us lower, now!"

The pilot brought the gunship *Pegasus* around for another sweep, this time neare̶r̶ ̶.̶ ̶.̶ ̶. VC troops assaulting the ̶.̶.̶.̶.̶.̶.̶.̶.̶.̶.̶ ort base.

Snakeman ̶.̶.̶.̶.̶.̶.̶.̶.̶.̶.̶ rd and let loose ̶.̶.̶.̶.̶.̶.̶.̶.̶ r station near a ̶.̶.̶.̶.̶.̶.̶.̶ y flew back, thei̶r̶ ̶.̶.̶.̶.̶.̶.̶ by the big shells. The fourt̶h̶ ̶.̶.̶.̶ ran for the tree line.

"Damn!" Fletcher grunted. Quickly adjusting pitch, he aimed his glowing red barrel and cut the guerrilla in half with thirty rounds.

Includes a complete GLOSSARY
of military jargon.

Other books in the **CHOPPER 1** series:

CHOPPER 1

#8 DEATH BRIGADE

Jack Hawkins

IVY BOOKS • NEW YORK

Ivy Books
Published by Ballantine Books
Copyright © 1988 by Butterfield Press, Inc.

Produced by Butterfield Press, Inc.
133 Fifth Avenue
New York, New York 10003

Library of Congress Catalog Card Number: 87-91049

ISBN: 0-8041-0078-0

Manufactured in the United States of America

First Edition: May 1988

This novel of American gunship adventures during the Indochina War has been compiled in honor of Quan Van Truong—the warriors' God (for those whose faith was forged in the Orient). And for all the door gunners, both Occidental and Asian, who died defending South Vietnam—especially under a black moon. The stars were not uncaring after all, dear brothers, for legend has it they are the ghosts of the countless brave soldiers and other patriots who fell before you.

It is also dedicated to Colonel Vo Dai Ton, Hero of the Vietnamese Resistance and currently imprisoned in Hanoi.

And to the million boat people who have perished in the South China Sea during their quest for freedom since the fall of South Vietnam 30 April 1975. Heroes without a homeland, they are truly "the lonely birds at dusk. . . ."

The Lonely Birds at Dusk

In the dark sky at dusk
The cloud was seen mourning.
And the lonely bird
was wandering. . . .

The sun in agony
Reddened the hills of pine.
There was not a breeze
To bring soul to life.

The lonely bird stopped its flight
In vain it searched for its nesting place.
The cold evening covered the plain
With clouds that warned of stormy rains.

The night that sank the sun at last
Denied a nest for lonely birds.
Amid the ocean full of fog
The bird vanished like a trace of smoke.

The night stood still after it'd gone
Homeless, in exile it carried on
With tiny wings and burdened grieves
An endless flight without a nest. . . .

—VO DAI TON

Hero of the Vietnamese Resistance
Currently imprisoned in Hanoi

AUTHOR'S NOTE

Two North Vietnamese Army Divisions—the First and the Tenth—were making the western Central Highlands plateau a dangerous place for Americans and other global policemen in early 1967. Dug in on South Vietnamese territory-treacherous terrain known as the *Chaine Annamitique*—the NVA were more than willing to sacrifice large numbers of their own troops rather than surrender strategic positions overlooking Pleiku and Kontum provinces.

The *Chaine Annamitique*'s mountainous spine rose both majestically and menacingly where South Vietnam's western border met the Cambodian frontier. The region was made up of some of the most insurmountable tropical obstacles on the planet, much less Southeast Asia: vast rain forests with huge, hardwood trees, topping out at 275 to 300 feet high and some six to eight feet in diameter, often defied clearing explosives and chain saws. Valley slopes cut through the maze of dense jungles, rising sharply into jagged, silver mountaintops six thousand feet above the green, triple-canopied ceiling. U.S. artillery "fire support bases" often dotted such visual vantage points, where temperatures could reach 110 degrees in the shade during the day, yet drop to 45 degrees overnight.

The artillery fire support bases were some of the few stretches of real estate semisafe from enemy annihilation and were used to lend cannon fire cover for American troops searching the dense, enemy-infested jungles below.

January 1967's Operation Sam Houston saw two brigades of the American Fourth "Ivy" Division hustled into the rugged wilderness and steep-walled valleys dropping between the *Chaine Annamitique*'s mountaintops. Some of the peaks were blown away, to build fire support bases directly onto the new "flattop," which overlooked miles and miles of jagged land. By February U.S. commanders had allocated certain units of the 173rd Airborne Brigade and First Air Cavalry Division for standby emergency in the event Ivy's grunts radioed in a Brass Monkey call for assistance.

One of those urgent cries for help is what this episode in the *Chopper-1* archives is about. Fire bases Belinda and Buffy may be literary devices created by flashbacks of stories or events vaguely recollected by participants and archivists some twenty years after the fact, but the lower Plei Trap and Nam Sathay River valleys existed then as they do now, and the dusty, isolated mountain village of Plei Djereng was indeed witness to the death and destruction that descended upon the steep slopes all around it the week thirty-one B-52 Arc-Light bombing runs "saturated" the area. Plei Djereng and the men and women who defended her will never be the same because of the events of that March 1967.

Though "Neil Nazi" Buchanan, Vance "the Victor," "Snakeman" Fletcher, and Brody "the Whoremonger'' may remind readers and Air Cavalry vets of ARP Team Blues they knew in The Nam, the following chronicle is more or less a work of fiction, with liberal doses of adrenaline juice injected whenever I deemed it appropriate. Other than well-known public and historic figures, any semblance of its characters to actual persons, living or killed in action, is purely coincidental.

Jack Hawkins
1 August 1987
In the shadow of *Wat Arun*,
Bangkok, Thailand

CHAPTER 1

Western Banks of the Nam Sathay River

There was shadowy movement across the endless carpet of black-and-silver mushrooms. Beneath an orange crescent moon, the rotting jungle floor had seemingly come alive, but there was more than the usual assortment of centipedes, lizards, and snakes slithering about in the razor-sharp reeds and elephant grass: Men prowled the darkness tonight.

Low-crawling shapes slick with greasepaint, their limbs burdened with long knives and short rifles, their necks adorned with *Yarde* trinkets from the Central Highlands or lucky charms that had dangled between the breasts of Saigon bar girls only days earlier. These were white men—charcoaled along the faces and forearms—grunts and heroes of the U.S. Green Machine.

The elusive phantom at the head of this pack was Sgt. Don "the Brick" Wickman. A big, powerful man, Wickman commanded respect as a fierce jungle fighter.

1

But his knuckles were what really impressed most chopper crewmen. Deep, purple scars crisscrossed every single one of the knuckles. Brody the Whore-monger once watched those very fists turn a marine's face to pulp inside the Ding Dong Club—a dead-end dive at Subic Bay in that clusterfuck of Filipino islands anchored a mere five hundred or so klicks off the east coast of Vietnam. It was Brody who first christened Big Don "the Brick." The handle had stuck ever since then.

Wickman was first out of the gunship *Pegasus's* star-board hatch. He was hard to keep up with, until a wall of nearly impenetrable vines and bamboo stopped him cold. "Been a tour or two since I happened down this way," he'd whispered to Treat Brody before breaking out the machete. The dry, matter-of-fact statement told Whoremonger his fellow NCO was blaming the unex-pected obstruction on rain forest regeneration.

Crouching in the dim shafts of moonlight as storm clouds raced across the sky, they'd sent out two scouts in both directions, but, fifteen minutes later, both troopers returned with bad news: the wall of bamboo extended as far as the eye could see in this inky vac-uum. "Damn river," Wickman had commented.

Wickman began hacking away at a series of wait-a-minute vines, thick as his thighs. Riflemen hastily spread out behind him, careful to remain low profile or even proned out as they sought cover. There was no way this job could be done silently. Ripping through dense jungle growth with a two-foot blade always sounded like all hell was breaking loose. Especially during the predawn silence. And now they were in bon-afide Injun' country. Luckily, the Song Nam Sathay's rushing waters masked the disturbance somewhat. The mountain walls rising up before them were an ominous landmark: the Cambodian border.

It was either that or turn back and hump to the insertion point, radio in a no-go, and drop down into the reeds for a couple of leech- and mosquito-infested hours, waiting for the first free extraction bird to return for them. And that was *if* there were even any slicks available on such short notice. Unless they were calling in a Brass Monkey, the team would just have to wait their turn, settling into a slot as low men on the life's-tough-then-you-die totem pole. The colonel would have their butts, but that was not what worried Wickman. He just wanted to mix it up with Charlie more than he cared to play games of mindfuck with Neil Nazi. "The Brick" lived for shoot-outs with those bad boys in black pajamas.

"Neil Nazi" was the "affectionate" label the men of Echo Company had tagged onto their sometimes beloved Col. Buchanan—who, more often than not, could be found circling high above the kill zone in his C&C Loach, monitoring their progress, radioing down pep-talk chatter.

Brody listened to Wickman's thick blade slicing away bamboo stalks. His eyes scanned the other three men who'd dismounted the chopper with them. All crouching back in the shadows or squatting, Asian style, in the waist-high elephant grass, their eyes were scanning the landscapes of the night, searching for movement. But Charlie appeared oblivious to the fact that they'd trespassed on his block. Or else Charlie was just waiting silently for the right moment to spring one of his wily traps. Charlie was bookoo good at after-hours ambushes. Not a man in The Nam would argue with you about that.

There were only five of them in the boonies tonight. Brody felt better when they had *two* chopperloads of grunts—even if half were newby pogues, fresh up from

3

Camp Alpha with mosquito wings for rank and bug bites dotting their pale arms like measles.

It might be just as well, he thought. Tonight was one of those weird ones, with a cemetery silence greeting their arrival. Less might be best. Quick in, quick out. It should have been an ash-'n'-trash mission, anyway.

Buchanan didn't like the fly-over technique. "Charlie's no fool," he would say. "Ol' Ho Chi Minh's bastards mighta been born at night, but not *last* night, gentlemen. You take the easy way out by air-droppin' booby-trapped parcels into the trash heaps, and the VC know what you're up to before the sound o' yor flappin' roto' blades done faded in the distance!"

Brody was head of the Boob Squad tonight. It was a shit detail, plain and simple, but some gung-ho fool had to do it, and Whoremonger's number happened to come up again. It didn't matter how many *joss* sticks he'd lit that week. A lifer was a lifer, no matter *what* the D.O.B. on his military ID card read. A man's gotta pull his weight.

The Viet Cong were notorious scavengers. They rarely littered their bivouacs and never discarded items that could be used in the war effort. The Americans, on the other hand—and even many of the South Vietnamese units—were well known to leave behind all sorts of items the enemy could fashion into weapons that would later be used against them: empty C-ration tins, lost ammo magazines, even an occasional misplaced weapon.

The Boob Squads' missions were to sneak into these dumps shortly after the main element of GIs moved on—and before the Communist insurgents located the "prize"—and booby-trap certain items, such as a discarded boot or empty LAW tube. Brody's favorite trick was to transform loose ammo into bolo beans.

Bolo beans could be M-16 or .45-caliber bullets that were tampered with prior to abandoning them again for Charlie to find. The lead was removed, and some of the powder was replaced with a small charge of plastic explosives, or pliers were used to recrimp the brass cartridge around the bullet so tightly that the shell would blow up rather than discharge hot lead through the weapon's barrel—damaging the firearm and injuring or even killing the shooter. But Charlie was quickly catching on, as he had with the grenades-under-the-old-boot and C-4-in-the-rations-tin traps.

Brody's people were constantly being challenged to improvise, and it was even becoming more commonplace to return to a unit dump for the body count only to find one's own traps double-boobied.

Brody the Whoremonger loved his work, though. *Pegasus* was his girl—riding the gunships into Void Vicious his first love—even the despised ash-'n'-trash details and Boob Squad missions. Vietnam was where it was at for Treat Brody. The faces of Sgt. Leo "the Lionhearted" Zack and First Lieutenant Vance flashed in front of his face momentarily with the thought as he listened to Wickman's sparkling blade hack away at the wall of bamboo. . . .

Focusing his concentration on the task at hand, he stared long and hard at Sgt. Wickman as the Brick tore into the last few feet of vines and bamboo separating the team from their target. He would have liked to have Sgt. Zack along for the ride, too, but Wickman didn't seem to get along well with Leo. He didn't think it was because Zack was black and Wickman white—both men were often part of interracial crews. Brody had worked with all the teams before, and he'd never heard either man seriously address a fellow soldier by any derogatory name. Racial slurs were rare. "Howdy, honky" and "No shit, nigger" didn't count, of course—especially when bright, gleaming ear-to-ear grins were in place on such occasions.

His purple vision was suddenly snatched away by a lightninglike bolt of fire and flames erupting from the high bamboo wall.

Brody's first impression upon seeing the shower of white sparks was that Don "the Brick" Wickman's machete had just struck a live power line. But that was a ridiculous thought, of course—there were no power lines within ten or twenty klicks of here—and then his gut instincts and field experience kicked in, and the young NCO realized a Viet Cong tracer had smashed against the sturdy blade. Charlie was using white tracers more and more lately, straying away from his usual green.

"Everyone down!" Brody shouted, but the three pogues behind him were already eating mushrooms. A burst of three more tracers passed through the air where Wickman had just been standing and slammed into the tree line on the other side of the river.

Wickman was rolling to the left. His machete was gone now, and he'd pulled the slung M-16 down from across his back and fired short three- and four-round bursts from the hip with a controlled confidence.

Brody searched for muzzle flashes, but now the swirling wall of black mist beyond the bamboo was silent. Charlie was out there, though—waiting. This was obviously not the "eight-and-skate" mission Lt. Vance had anticipated. Lucky Jake was air mobile, however, actually manning a hatch-60 for the first time as *Pegasus* returned to camp for another cargo of grunts eager to dance with danger. It was something the officer had always wanted to do, and Sgt. Zack turned his back on the man's antics, making no sign he cared one way or the other. Odd Vance picked a quiet, cold LZ run to play door gunner, though, Brody thought.

Screams left the throats of two newbies proned out behind him, and as he turned to check their status, Brody's night went white with discharges—the entire tree line seemed to explode with hot lead!

"Claymore!" he heard Wickman yell as dual blasts sent rolling concussions in on the Americans from opposite directions.

And then Brody spotted the sparkle. The orange crescent moon had set between two shadowy peaks in the west, but by starlight he could not miss the evil gleam approaching through the mist. *Bayonets!*

Charlie was swarming in to finish them off. He and Wickman had unknowingly led a team of inexperienced pogues in through the Void to their doom. Undaunted, the Brick continued firing. They were dead meat—of that he had no doubt—but he was a soldier, and he would go down fighting . . . taking as many of the dink bastards with him as possible!

The newbies were directing long bursts on full automatic. Their instinctive actions made him proud—even in so short a time, he'd instilled in them a few of the basic battlefield tactics necessary for survival.

Wickman was yelling something, but he could not make out the words above the crescendo of approaching muzzle blasts. Brody turned to find the Brick leaning over a dead corporal—their radio man. Blood trickled from countless puncture wounds along Wickman's own chest and both arms where shrapnel and lead splinters had been stopped by rock-hard muscle or bone.

Sgt. Don was screaming cords into the hand-held mike as green-and-white tracers arced in all around him. Artillery! Brody could make out the directives now: the big bear of an NCO ignoring several upper-body wounds was going to make heroes out of every last one of them.

The Brick was calling cannon fire in directly on top of their position!

CHAPTER 2

Two Miles to the West

U.S. Army Captain Sandeki stared at the jagged outline of mountains rising in the inky blackness along the Cambodian frontier. The First Cavalry officer was himself standing atop a mountain—highest in the immediate vicinity, in fact—but the monstrous *Chaine Annamitique* rising in the predawn distance dwarfed even this position. He was glad Charlie had no artillery pieces powerful enough to reach them from those insurmountable crags far away.

Hands on his hips in mild awe, Sandeki surveyed the fire support base extending out around him for one hundred yards in a crude, shaved-off circle. The shallow crater in which he now stood had once been the tree-cluttered peak of a mountain range, but Uncle Sammy had flattened it more than level and cleared the surrounding trees away for another hundred yards down the slopes on all sides.

Stumps rose in the misty starlight here and there, reminding the captain of tombstones rising in a grave-yard killing ground at another recent firefight not so very long ago. Other than that, the support base was a barren moonscape, with old NVA bomb craters every-where. Movement in the inky distance made Sandeki freeze—only his gunhand moved, and it slowly dropped toward the holstered .45 automatic on his hip. The of-ficer relaxed as the shifting of shadows became a sen-try's helmet bobbing along the rim of an LP fifty feet down from the western edge of camouflaged foxholes and reinforced fighting trenches.

Concertina wire marked the circular perimeter, and 50mm cannon barrels cut into the night all around San-deki—silent for now but as menacing looking as during any daytime inspection or fire mission. He was im-pressed by the versatile guns but didn't like the tree stumps. Someone should lead a detail of men down to clear them out, he decided. They would make good cover for any team of enemy sappers attempting to breach the perimeter and overrun the camp from below. The officer made a mental note to talk with Buchanan about that as soon as he had his first cup of morning brew. Sandeki checked his Rolex—that would be in about an hour and a half, now: zero six hundred hours.

His ears perked slightly—he thought he heard the distant rattle of gunfire down in some box canyon or river valley far beyond the nearest walls of sheer gran-ite. But then the muffled clamor was covered by a slowly growing sound of helicopter rotors. Huey gunships were approaching.

He caught the silver glow of a winged horse painted across the snout of one of the Hueys. Below the mural, two words: WIDOW MAKERS. *Pegasus*. Gabriel's ship. He spotted crossed sabers on many of the birds and the word HEADHUNTERS emblazoned across the belly of one craft.

A smaller, sleeker Cobra brought up the rear, and he focused on the mean-looking sharks' teeth painted along both sides of the two-man craft's snout. Below and slightly behind the cockpit was a zipperlike line of dents, punctures, and peeling paint. Fresh bullet holes.

Sandeki could tell by the manner in which some of the birds swerved gently from side to side—their pilots obviously bored with regulation flying—that the team was light, empty of cargo. The insertion had been successful.

One door gunner in particular caught his eye. Lt. Vance.

Sandeki was unable to keep his manufactured frown intact, and a sly grin slowly worked its way across his features as his thick, sunburned wrists toyed with a drooping handlebar mustache. "Fucking Jake Vance," he muttered under his breath as the Huey passed overhead with a frame-numbing roar. "If only Neil Nazi could see you now—" Sandeki spat a wad of chewing tobacco into the mud at his feet—"he'd have your ass stuffed with tracer glow, boy. . . ."

Vance was standing in the port hatch, feet braced apart in a businesslike stance. Even this close to the relative safety of camp, with no targets of opportunity presenting themselves below him, he was still leaning into his cord-suspended M-60.

But Sandeki was still smiling. That ol' Jake! he said to himself. Always trying to impress his men.

Another Huey passed low overhead, and this time the cavalry captain could hear rock and roll music blaring from the unmanned hatch. It sounded like Dion, singing "The Wanderer," but Sandeki couldn't be sure.

A third gunship roared past, and he locked eyes with

two troopers sitting in the open hatch, their legs dangling outside, boot soles just above the skids, M-16 automatic rifles balanced across thighs covered in torn and shredded fatigue trousers. One of the soldiers flipped him the thumbs-up. He tipped his helmet slightly in reply, impressed anyone could see him in the shifting glow of a solitary flare.

"Enjoying the sights, Captain?" A deep, authoritative voice sounded from behind him in the dark somewhere just as the last chopper's downblast began to fade in the distance.

Sandeki recognized Col. Buchanan's voice automatically, but oddly enough he felt no chain-of-command-instilled fear. "Uh . . . ." he stammered only slightly, "good evenin', sir. . . ."

"What's so fuckin' good about it, Captain?" A tall, barrel-chested man, sporting a gray crewcut and Hitler-style mustache, chomping on a cigar, and carrying a slung MP-40 across his paunch, emerged from the shroud of blackness that had been pressing in against Sandeki.

"Well, I just meant that—" Sandeki began, but Buchanan's good-natured chuckle cut him off.

"I know, I know." The six-foot-one, big-biceped commander approached closer. "No incoming makes it a good fuckin' evening, eh?"

Sandeki's smile returned. "Uh, right, sir. . . ."

Buchanan's forefinger flipped the embers from his cigar, and his callused thumb ground out the smoldering stub. He knew the rules: no smoking out in the open, especially at night. Sandeki watched him place the cigar into a waist pocket of his fatigue blouse.

"That Echo Company comin' in?" His eyes rose to the silver glow of rotors appearing in the distance.

"Uh, right, sir . . . Echo and Delta." Sandeki stared

at the horizontal, two-inch scar running under Buchanan's left eye. He'd heard the story about this Congressional Medal of Honor winner: souvenir of Korea. But, the rumor said he got it from a beer bottle–wielding bar girl in Wanchai, Hong Kong.

"You didn't go out with them?" Buchanan seemed only mildly interested.

"Lt. Vance took the teams out tonight, sir. It was just a cluster of Boob Squads."

"I'll bet *he* told *you* to kick back and stay here at the FSB, right?" Buchanan chuckled again.

"Something like that." Sandeki did not sound happy.

"Was he civil about it?"

"Very." But civility did not seem to be the issue here, and both officers knew it.

"Don't let them clowns in Echo Company get to you, Captain." Buchanan still sounded amused, though. "You've only been with 'em a couple weeks now. . . ."

"But I've been in The Nam going on ten *months*, sir. That should make a difference."

"It does, son, it does. . . . They haven't booted your 'occifer' ass out a chopper hatch, have they?" Buchanan sensed Sandeki's lower jaw dropping, and he didn't give the young captain time to respond. "You're still green, son. They have to get used to you. They've been without a captain for a long time. Vance has babysitted them since Ia Drang, and Leo Zack before that. . . ."

"*Sergeant* Leo Zack?"

"Right. They're all probably a little standoffish because Rumor Control had it Vance was going to get his captain's bars after that clusterfuck along the Quang Ngai coast a little while back. . . ."

"Some of us thought he was, too."

"I put him in for it, but MACV came back with a

13

thumbs-down, saying he doesn't have enough time in grade, but 'soon.' "

" 'Soon' could be permanent around here, sir." Sandeki did not sound optimistic. "The way Vance keeps extending, he's pushin' his luck."

"I told him long ago he oughta rotate back to Benning or Bragg." Buchanan nodded almost somberly. "They'd make him a captain in ninety days."

"Ain't that the way it always works out?" Buchanan's low, wavering chuckle floated on the humid night air again.

"I just hope my assignment to Echo doesn't interfere with—"

"You've got to be patient, son."

"I was before I came to The Nam."

"Hmmph. . . ." Buchanan folded his arms across his chest, electing to change the subject, if only somewhat. "Speak of the devil, was that Vance I saw leaning on a Hog-sixty aboard . . . which one was it? *Pegasus*?"

An odd sense of Lou-'n'Cap loyalty hit Sandeki. "I couldn't tell you for sure, sir."

"No way to impress your men, playing gunnie. . . . Distracting to ground troops here, too!"

He motioned toward the battery of antiaircraft cannon in the middle of the mountaintop fire support base. "After all, we wouldn't want Charlie sneaking up here, gettin' his grimy hands on these babies, now would we?"

Sandeki nodded solemnly as he stared at the line of 50mm cannon behind Buchanan's broad shoulders. "Do you think Charlie's gonna move on this mountain, Colonel?" he asked.

"Charlie?" Buchanan's chest expanded as he thought the remark over. "There's hard-core NVA out there,

14

Captain. North Vietnamese Army Regulars, eager to make mincemeat out of us. Don't let anyone tell you it's just *Charlie* crawling around out there in the night. . . ."

"I know that, sir." Sandeki cleared his throat as they listened to lizards exchanging a set of guttural mating calls in the distance. "I just meant that—"

"You've been fraternizing with your men too much, son. To the grunts, everyone's Charlie. But believe me . . . there's a big distinction. Victor Charlie are the indigenous Commies. The NVA are northern imports, and have been a real pain in my—"

"Do you think Major Minh is in the area?" Sandeki felt suddenly confident enough to tread on dangerous ground.

Buchanan hesitated. He did not like discussing the notorious Lam Van Minh with subordinates. The subject was taboo. They had a special thing going—the Air Cav colonel and North Vietnamese major . . . a personal relationship—he and Minh. Once, near Dong Tre, he'd nearly had the bastard in the palms of both hands. But the winds of fate were not blowing at his back that campaign. It had been an embarrassing episode for the colonel—one he'd just as soon forget, though he knew someday he and Major Minh would meet again. . . .

"How much longer we gonna be stuck on this godforsaken sliver o' rock, sir?" Sandeki watched a starburst cluster of red, green, and gold flares burst a mile or so in the distance—well below their own level in the mountain range but slightly above the layer of mist clinging to the lower slopes.

"Until we get the mission done, Captain." Buchanan sounded suddenly irritated as he, too, focused on the arcing orbs of multicolored light plummeting back down toward the rain forest canopy. A starburst

15

like that usually meant some trooper on night watch was bored with combating only mosquitoes and fatigue. No discharge sounds reached either officer's ears. "Until we get the mission done. . . ."

It was Sandeki who frowned this time. . . . They had been living on artillery fire support bases for only a few weeks now, but he didn't like it all the same. A cavalry officer's place was always from the mountains and valleys where sudden and unexpected shifts in turbulence could down a craft as quickly as some giant, invisible hand swatting a dragonfly. Sandeki preferred the vast plateaus of the Central Highlands or, better yet, the Mekong Delta marshes, but it appeared they would be here for a while to come.

Buchanan's battalion had been ordered, along with the 173rd Airborne, with assisting Ivy Division infantrymen as they scoured the *Chaine Annamitique* for two elusive North Vietnamese divisions. The fourth was not having much luck. The NVA was out there, but they were engaging the Americans only on their own terms, often laying down bait that led the search-and-destroy teams into steep valleys where they were expertly cut off and ambushed by teams smaller than their own—but teams that held the high ground and tactical advantage. The infantry usually ended up calling for artillery support from the mountaintop fire bases—*if* they knew where the hell they were and could radio in the proper coordinates. And no sooner did the artillery teams fire off their barrages then separate NVA units were mounting unexpected sapper assaults on the cannon positions themselves, necessitating an arty call for infantry assistance to repel the attacks. It was a vicious, never-ending circle. The War Room brass hoped the introduction of airborne troops and Huey gunships would help bring the fray to an accelerated conclusion.

16

Less than half a mile west of Fire Support Base Belinda, where Sandeki and Buchanan now stood, a larger mountaintop encampment—which actually combined a rare, interconnecting and rather level plateau with two-shaved-off peaks—was being used to house a small contingent of cavalry troops and seven gunships for immediate, close-in support. It was known as Fire Support Base Buffy. The younger soldiers told each newby arriving in-country that it was named for folk singer Buffy Sainte-Marie, but Buchanan claimed he was thinking of the knee-high ceramic elephants, popular in Saigon souvenir stalls, when he came up with the handle. He'd never heard of any Sainte-Marie singer and was still slightly upset that person—or persons—unknown made off with his own matched pair of white-and-gold Buffies from his CP bunker when the division was kicking ass in the Ia Drang Valley. Larger contingents of helicopter ARP teams were based in Kontum and Pleiku proper.

"It sure would be nice to run into old Minh again, though," Buchanan mused. "And I'm not referring to Ho *Chi*. . . ."

"Though *that* might be doubly delightful." Sandeki produced an unexpected giggle.

"You can say *that* agai—" the colonel began, but both officers dropped into a sudden squat as a dull pop erupted nearby, and a projectile spouting sparks and a loud *whoosh!* streaked toward the heavens from only a few meters away.

"What the fu—" Sandeki fell silent again as a flare popped high above the valley separating Fire Support Base Belinda from the nearest mountain peak shadow jutting up ominously from the valley floor half a mile away.

Edgy sentries along the southern perimeter began firing sporadically in the direction of the sputtering flare, but neither Buchanan nor Sandeki could see any movement on the slopes below the drifting silk parachute.

"You notice any movement in the tree line down there?" Buchanan whispered as both officers rose slightly into a cautious crouch, eyes scanning the stumps and moonscape that lay between their encampment's ring of concertina and the upper limits of jungle growth reaching toward them.

"No." Sandeki drew his pistol anyway as one of the privates in a forward LP sent a ten-round burst of white-hot tracer gliding down into the rain forest's misty edge. "Nothing resembling genuine targets, anyway. . . ."

Buchanan knew what the man meant: nothing but shifting shadows, created by another cluster of flares drifting down along the mountainside.

Someone threw a grenade, and as the explosion's echo rolled out to the far wall of cliffs and started back, Buchanan uttered a low curse. "Those idiots are buckin' for a mad minute," he muttered as garbled chatter from a PRC-25 reached his ears from the command post bunker thirty feet behind the two officers: something about "bookoo WIAs" and an arty request near the border LZ the choppers had just returned from.

"What the fuck is everyone shooting at?" Sandeki shielded his eyes from the multitude of zigzagging flares and eerie tracer glow. "Just what the fuck is—"

And then both men saw them, creeping backward into the bamboo a hundred feet down the mountainside: countless crouching shapes clad in black, no doubt carrying satchel charges and a bangalore torpedo or two.

" 'Welcome to my foxhole,' said the cobra to the shack rat." Buchanan pointed at a figure lying frozen halfway through the vast coils of sparkling concertina wire on the encampment's southern edge—right where the shaved-off peak began to drop toward steep, debris-

18

covered slopes. A woman! Naked, flat on her back, and unmoving.

Her skin was oiled down in an attempt to make breaching the perimeter barbs easier, but she had still managed to hit a tripwire somehow, sending up the first flare. Her limbs seemed frozen against the fragments of activity all around her—she was trying to blend in, go unnoticed amidst all the shouting and confusion a few meters above her head, no doubt.

Buchanan could not see her face clearly from this angle and distance, but there was no mistaking the long straight hair. Even as she lay there inside the coils of concertina, he could see that the jet-black strands reached down well below her haunches. Poor field discipline, the military half of his brain was thinking: she should have braided it. The hair was what probably snagged one of the flare traps. Then he suddenly remembered Major Minh and the woman who had helped effect his escape at Dong Tre's LZ Bird. Could this be the same VC bitch—the same cunt who'd nailed a Viet Cong flag to Sgt. Patterson's back as well? Movement from Sandeki registered suddenly in his peripheral vision, and he found himself knocking the captain's pistol up in the air just as he fired.

"*Sir!*" the officer protested, but Buchanan was already off and running through the red-and-green ricochets and golden flare'chutes, headed for the woman lying beneath the barbed wire.

CHAPTER 3

Near the Cambodian Border

Don "the Brick" Wickman knew he was wounded, but the emotion that was strongest in him just then, as flares drifted overhead and "friendly" artillery slammed down mere meters from their position, was blatant anger and self-rebuke. The small of his back was wet with his own blood, and the injury had been a stupid accident.

They had all jumped up and charged the enemy, and someone had sent an entire banana clip of rock-and-roll rounds into a slab of granite instead of NVA flesh. The bullets bounced back, of course, only to ricochet once more off the sheer walls of stone jutting up from the riverbanks several meters behind the team. And two large slivers of lead tore into Wickman's lower back. They struck nothing vital, however—a handful of slugs also flattened out between his shoulder blades but were stopped by an ancient flak vest cavalry troopers had been passing

21

around since Christ was a corporal. Wickman was fuming because the incident had occurred in the first place. "Aim at the dinks, not the rocks!" he yelled past Whoremonger to the two newbies still standing.

Brody glanced back at the third green recruit. His head appeared shrunken—the facial bones seemed to have collapsed in on themselves. His eyes were already swollen shut from the blunt trauma, his tanned features streaked with crimson. Brody recognized the result of an AK-47 burst immediately.

He dropped to one knee as another barrage of shells slammed into the ground between his small team and the larger contingent of Communists that had sought to ambush them en route to the company dump.

Either Wickman knew his trade, or he'd been lucky calling in coordinates—because cannon blasts were forcing the NVA back into the bamboo while failing to harm the Americans themselves. Actually, perhaps the Brick *had* been a bit off, Brody reflected as he rammed a fresh magazine of ammo into his M-16. Wickman had called the rounds in directly on top of their position— that's how bad the situation had looked, initially.

Brody sent fanning bursts from the hip—left to right, then back to the left again—as he followed Wickman toward a clump of tree stumps that would afford them better cover. He could sense the two newbies following in his shadow.

The night air was alive with screams from the wounded North Vietnamese. He could hear a dozen separate casualties crying their lives away before he stopped counting. The sensation of so many men wailing beneath the stars was eerie.

The artillery had definitely been right on the mark: there were more casualties than survivors who could drag them away.

"How you wanna end it, Whoremonger?" Wickman grumbled in his direction as the last artillery barrage played itself out and the swirling mists seemed to settle back into a ground-clinging and surrealistic haze of silver and gray.

" 'End it' ?" Brody found himself firing a couple of bursts in the direction of the closest wailing voices.

"Yeah!" Wickman nodded, his eyes glowing faintly against patches of rain forest luminescence in the distance. "You wanna drop back and lie low . . . wait for extraction? Or you wanna go in after 'em?"

"Go in after them?" whispered one of the recruits.

"Do our job" the Brick affirmed. "Go in an' *get some*!"

"I don't know if we could watch that many wounded zips until Python-Lead got some slicks in here and—" Brody began, but Big Don cut him off.

"Take no prisoners." He seemed to be imitating a favorite movie scene, but John Wayne wasn't in the cast of characters racing to their rescue.

Brody's eyes seemed to glow slightly as well now, as the adrenaline began to flow, snuffing out the fear, and the two newbies sensed the change in both soldiers. "Yeah." Whoremonger nodded solemnly. "Let's do it to it . . . 'fore it's too late." He noticed Wickman's blood-soaked fatigue blouse for the first time. "That is, if you—"

Wickman gritted his teeth and growled like a bear. "Ashes to ashes, tongue to twat," was his peculiar reply. Then, "Follow *me*!" Brody waited for the crescendo of dramatic music to reach his ears, but there remained only the screeching of tree parrots and angry gibbons in the branches overhead. And, of course, the screams of the dying.

Two helicopter gunships rushed past overhead at

treetop level just as they started through the brush, searching for NVA wounded. *"Pegasus!"* A startled Brody pointed skyward as three more Hueys roared above the palm fronds, and they spotted the silvery mural of a winged horse painted across the craft's broad snout. They could all see the door gunners crouched inside each bird's hatches, but none of the gunnies were firing.

The lead ship was circling back now: they would pinpoint the Boob Squad's position before dumping any ordnance on top of Charlie.

"That was *Peg*—" Brody started to say, but Wickman was already gone—had disappeared through the same wall of vines and bamboo he had been chopping away at before they were fired upon. "Let's go!" Brody yelled at the two recruits, who were already clinging to his shadow like flies on a body bag.

When Brody caught up to him, the Brick had his pistol against the temple of a sobbing NVA lieutenant. The North Vietnamese was suffering several gunshot wounds to the chest but still seemed coherent. "What unit you sons-of-dogs with?" Wickman yelled in pidgin Vietnamese, but the enemy officer only responded by gagging on his own blood.

The Brick was holding his M-16 pistol fashion, with one hand. The rifle's barrel was still pressing snugly against the side of the lieutenant's head as he coughed and puked. "*Ice* his Commie ass!" One of the newbies shocked Brody with the high-pitched demand.

Wickman glanced up but did not look amused by the request. He rattled another question off as Brody swung around to poke and prod at other NVA bodies lining the clearing's gore-splattered edge. "Who told you we were coming tonight?" Wickman screamed. "How did you *know* we were coming tonight—or did you just

24

stumble across us? *Talk* to me, you zipperhead son-ofabitch!''

Wickman had been holding the soldier's upper torso off the ground by the front of his shirt. He now let him drop back down into the moist carpet of blood-soaked mushrooms.

The NVA lieutenant mumbled something unintelligible and fell face first into the rotting jungle floor.

''Do it!'' The FNG closest to Wickman stepped between Brody and the Brick.

Teeth bright as ivory now as they flashed an ear-to-ear death's-head grin, Wickman rushed toward the eighteen-year-old baby-faced recruit, grabbed the front of *his* shirt, and hurled him toward the vomiting Vietnamese. ''*You* do it, son!'' he yelled back as two helicopters flared into a tense hover directly overhead. ''Go ahead! Prove you're a man.''

Shaking noticeably, the private lifted his M-16 and aimed from the hip. He was still a good five feet away from the NVA lieutenant. He glanced back at Brody, but the Whoremonger was busy checking other casualties and was paying him no attention. He looked toward Wickman again, but the Brick was now aiming at fleeing shadows in the opposite direction and firing off first two, then three rounds on semiautomatic—also ignoring the recruit's actions. The private glanced up at the two gunships. Neither was using its spotlight, nor was either actually directly overhead—they were both off to the side somewhat, slowly drifting farther and farther away, it seemed.

He stared over at his fellow newby. The teenager looked like he was about to faint or throw up but had no energy to drop and nothing left in his gut to vomit. Like he wanted no part in any of this but had no choice in the matter—was stuck with this trio of insane troopers for another 350 days and counting.

The outline of three crumpled pith helmets a few feet away—at the clearing's edge—caught his eye, and he dropped to one knee, removed the lieutenant's sidearm from its holster for a souvenir, kicked the bullet- and shrapnel-riddled AK-47 away, then started over toward the other bodies to do his part in searching the dead and wounded.

As if condoning or approving his decision, one of the choppers hovering overhead ascended suddenly. Its tail boom swinging around as it rose toward the fading stars, the Huey disappeared beyond the clutter of palm fronds like the fading memory of an elusive dream. The second ship drifted to one side, and he lost sight of it beyond dual columns of thick black smoke rising into the night sky.

The three North Vietnamese soldiers seemed dead as they come—each man missing several limbs and an entire head in one case. He slowly turned them over, one at a time, careful to feel beneath their bodies for Chi-Com stick, or even captured American M-33 or M-26 grenades, before moving them.

As he pushed the last one back, the sparkle of a lone strand of fishing wire caught his eye. It was a tripwire, his mind told him—probably to an Arvin or even one of their own booby traps. The NVA had fallen onto it but not detonated the claymore. Now he suddenly saw his epitaph emblazoned across the purple sky in blood red: BOOB SQUAD RECRUIT KILLS OWN TEAM.

He grasped the third North Vietnamese soldier like a lover, holding him tightly in his arms, stump where its head had been decapitated oddly against the hollow of his underarm, as the blast erupted, snuffing out his cries of warning.

26

CHAPTER 4

Fire Support Base Belinda

"Private Rogers! Rogers, wake your no-account ass *up* or I'm gonna toss it right back out that gunship hatch!"

The newby recruit shook the fog from his head and woke to find Sgt. Don "the Brick" Wickman, eyes bulging almost insanely, staring down into his own.

"You fucking low-life *skate*!" The Brick was screaming into his face now as he slowly rose from a position flat on his back, up onto his elbows. "You nearly got us all killed!"

Rogers glanced over a right shoulder—saw that he was inside one of the gunships. The door gunner was blasting away at the jungle smothering them as the ship slowly ascended, nose dropping slightly as the tail boom rose with the pulling of pitch.

Wickman slapped his face forward again, but then Second Lieutenant Vance was crowding closer. "You okay, pogue?" He actually had the gall to bump shoul-

27

ders with Wickman, knocking the Brick slightly off balance.

"I'm . . . I'm . . ." Rogers took in a deep breath of air, waiting for Big Don to react, but the huge NCO sounded like he was snickering lightly as he rose to his feet only to drop back into a crouch behind the gunny.

"Spit the jizz outta your mouth, boy!" Wickman shook his head from side to side slowly as his eyes scanned the blur of motion outside the gunship hatch.

"I'm . . ." Rogers watched a steady stream of empty brass pour from the hatch M-60 as spurts of red tracer flew out into the trees.

"Yeah, you're all-fuckin'-right!" Vance slapped him on the shoulder and whirled around to join the two troopers squatting in front of the other hatch.

Rogers glanced over the opposite shoulder. Against the cockpit bulkhead lay the body of Sherman—the newby he arrived with . . . the recruit whose first name he never learned.

"Was that *dinky-dau*, or what?"

His head slowly turned again at the sound of Johnson's excited voice. Johnson. The other man in their trio of FNGs. Already into the local lingo. He was kneeling behind Wickman now, trying to get a better look at what the door gunners were firing at.

"Yeah . . ." Rogers said slowly as he ran his fingers down along all four limbs—the legs first, then, as if to reassure himself he was really seeing his hands move unhindered, his forearms. "To the max, Johnny-san." The words continued to leave him matter-of-factly, without any tonal inflection whatsoever. "There is no way I'm going to be able to make it through twelve months in this hellhole. . . ."

But nobody heard Private Rogers complaining. Shells were coming in again as the helicopter rose above the

28

jungle's triple canopy. He stumbled through the piles of empty brass shells, and Brody the Whoremonger was laughing about something the Brick had said. Rogers sensed movement above and behind him, and just as he was about to look up, something heavy dropped against his head and the stars returned. He lay back into the vast field of black cotton.

Wickman jerked his head around to see what happened. "God*dammit*, Elliot!"

"*I* didn't do it!" Snakeman stared at the bolts and rivets of the fiberglass shelving that had come loose from the wall of the ship, dumping two ammo boxes as well on the newby recruit, Ricky Rogers. "It's this goddamned equipment Uncle Sammy gives us"—Fletcher was down on one knee, gently slapping the pogue back to the present—"expectin' us to go out and fight a war with it. Shee-*it!*"

"Cut the shit, you two! Rogers is okay!" Vance barked back at the two door gunners.

Rogers's head rose slightly, his eyeballs rolled, and the color of his skin turned suddenly pale. "Don't go up-chuckin' on us, sport!" Fletcher returned to his hatch-60 duties as *Pegasus* rose above the thousand-foot mark and out of the immediate kill zone.

"I'm okay. Help me up." Rogers was not all that steady on his feet, however, as Brody grabbed one of his elbows and hoisted him off the fiberglass floor-boards.

"Asshole Pogues," Wickman was muttering now. He turned his broad back on the fiasco and moved forward toward the cockpit as Rogers dropped to his knees again, still stunned.

Brody tried to help him back up. "Maybe you better

just sit this one out," he said as the chopper swung around for another pass over the extraction point. "We'll be headed back to the hilltop soon, kid. . . ."

"Buffy?" Rogers's eyeballs did a pinball roll again.

"Yeah." Treat nodded. "Buffy. Just gonna make another flyby . . . drop the last of our ord' and try for a body count. . . ."

"It's too dark for a fuckin' body count!" Snakeman called back over his shoulder as *Pegasus* roared along the western riverbank, only fifteen or twenty feet above the mud and muck. "Man, I *love* this *lima-lima*!"

"Just do your best!" Vance yelled from up front as the ship slowed suddenly, flared into a hover above the pall of gunsmoke, and began drifting to the side.

"Fucking NVA done already dragged all their boyfriends back into the bamboo," Fletcher grumbled as the gunship floated above blood trails. "Ain't no way I'm gonna be able to—" But the Snakeman suddenly fell silent. He rose up on the balls of his feet slightly and leaned into his monkeystraps until his upper torso was a couple of feet outside the protective sphere of the hutch. "One, two, three, four!" he began yelling as he released the M-60 and strained to get a better look down a certain angle, then another. "Five . . . ten . . . shit, fif*teen*, brothers . . . fifteen and counting. There's more dinks down there than you can shake a stick grenade at!"

"All KIA, right?" Vance yelled, leaning over his shoulder for a better look.

"Yeah!" Snakeman yelled loud enough for every man on board to hear him. "We musta blasted so many o' them mothers outta their Ho Chi Minh sandals there was no one left to drag the bodies away! Twenty . . . twenty-five . . . thirty-five . . . *shee*-it, we *sac-Mau'd* the little cocksuckers!"

30

"Those boys back on the first base creamed 'em!" Brody corrected his best friend as he left Rogers's side and scurried over to the hatch himself for a look, but *Pegasus* abruptly pulled up, swung around, and then, nose dropping, accelerated back toward Fire Base Belinda. "Hey!" the Whoremonger protested as he was knocked off balance and tumbled onto his haunches.

"Gabriel, you motherfucker!" Fletcher screamed as he flew out the hatch and was left dangling in the air, upside-down—suspended by his lifeline a few feet above the landing skids. Wickman was already struggling to pull him back in. "I'm gonna *kill* that no-account sonofabitch!" Fletcher sounded only half-serious as the ship began gaining even more speed.

"Sorry, ladies!" Warrant Officer Cliff "the Gunslinger" Gabriel clicked into the ship intercom. "Just received a Brass Monkey from some Agency spooks on the other side of the mountain. Now hold on to your assholes, 'cause its already Lima Zulu in dirty sex, and they tell me it's gonna be hot!"

"What about the other—" Fletcher was leaning out the hatch again, trying to eyeball the other ships, but they were already ahead of *Pegasus* several hundred meters as the seven gunships darted up through the crags, racing toward the access pass between Fire Bases Belinda and Buffy. Snakeman had assumed at least one of the gunships would remain in-station—surely they didn't need the whole gang for a close-in Monkey, but it seemed everyone was humping on this one.

"We're the only bird responding on the Bravo-Mike." Gabriel seemed to read his thoughts. "The others are returning to Belinda. Neil Nazi called 'em in! She's under sapper attack right now. . . ."

"Belinda's bein' attacked?" Vance yelled, eyes wide as they passed over the fire support base and he leaned out the hatch, but further words from the cockpit were unnecessary as he watched several gunships spiraling down toward the besieged mountaintop encampment.

Flares floated in a crude, flickering ring around the barren hilltop, five hundred feet below *Peg*'s landing skids. Brody and Vance watched outgoing red tracers crisscross with incoming green ones as more and more flares popped above the escalating battlefield. Black pajama-clad sappers in teams of one or two dozen were still climbing up the steep slopes, despite the arrival of gunship support. "Suicide squads. . . ." Brody whistled under his breath as Belinda passed below them, already enshrouded in smoke along the edges. Fire Base Belinda had always been thought to be impenetrable, and now here were a hundred or more Viet Cong sappers attempting to breach the wire!

Brody strained against his monkeystraps as the peak disappeared beneath the expanding cloud of black gunsmoke and *Pegasus* shuddered from the turbulent impact of blasts rising from below. He shook his head and rubbed his eyes and leaned into the M-60, fighting the urge to unload on the target of opportunity.

The entire base was hidden by thick smoke. Flares bursting inside the black cloud looked like heat lightning flashing within a roaming blanket of storm clouds, and Brody thought of the monsoon downpours that had flooded Ia Drang Valley two years and a lifetime ago.

And now *Pegasus* was dropping again, spiraling down toward the jungled slopes on the other side of the mountain range . . . shooting almost straight down into the Void in a dive so steep Brody thought he might lose the bellyful of C-rations remaining in his gut.

"Welcome to Void Vicious, you animals. . . . Your target's approx' five zero straight up the nose on tiptoes. . . ."

Gabriel's parting words struck Big Don Wickman as an echo chamber of mixed emotions as the Brick flew out through *Peg*'s hatch while the gunship was still a good six feet above the rain forest floor. Brody and another trooper—Martinez—were right behind him. Rogers and Vance stayed aboard the ship to help Snakeman, the door gunner, with ammo.

Gabriel set them down alongside a dry creekbed meandering snakelike at the bottom of two steep slopes. Its banks were unstable, and too narrow to support the ship anyway, so Gabe kept *Pegasus* in a steady airborne hover until a slight tipping vibration signaled the pilot the last man had jumped out the hatch lip. The helicopter then continued on down along the creekbed, rising swiftly back up out of the valley's oppressive shadows.

CHAPTER 5

LZ Fang

As the small team stopped beside a clump of tall mangroves to catch their breath—he'd much rather have had a six-man squad for something like this or even a full platoon—he watched *Peg*, blacked out but her outline still visible against the glow of a pending sunrise, disappear beyond the nearest mountain ridge. No tracers arced up after her. Perhaps a good sign, but maybe not. He was getting no other good vibes about this Romeo foxtrot so far.

The three of them stared up at the high trees rising all around on both banks of the creek. Gabriel had picked the one spot where he could bring *Peg* down without having her fifty-foot rotor span clipping limbs and endangering the crew with a crash. It was probably the same spot the CIA Loach pilot had chosen to insert his team of Agency spooks.

"Let's do it to it," the Brick muttered as they routinely checked their weapons and scanned the terrain for the easiest way from point A to point B. Speaking to the rain forest ghosts of Void Vicious, he added, "Welcome to Donald Wickman's world, assholes." It was a challenge that made Martinez's skin crawl.

Brody nodded. Martinez remained silent and shadowy. He was low man on the rank totem pole but a veteran of several firefights nonetheless. He'd seen a lot of death and destruction, but Whoremonger and the Brick had wreaked more than he would ever know firsthand, so he bowed to their skill and experience. Martinez stared at Wickman's collar. The soldier wore no rank tabs. Never had, never would, he claimed—especially when blazing trails through the bamboo for Neil Nazi on some hush-hush, clandestine mission into the sticks.

There were no trails here, but the path the CIA assassination team had forged through the dense brush was clearly evident. Wickman dropped to one knee and checked depressions in the evergladeslike marshland, wondering only briefly how Gabriel had known exactly where they would find their quarry. He smelled no crash-marker smoke on the air. Perhaps the Loach pilot had radioed in exact cords when calling for help from the Cav CP, but even specific numbers were only good for triangulation down to a certain sector. There was no time for mental debate, however. "Over a day old," he whispered to Brody, running his thumb and forefinger along the inner groove of a boot mark. "Panama soles."

"Inserted downstream?"

"Yeah . . . I'd say so. Came up through this creekbed"—he motioned back over a shoulder—"and picked this spot to blaze a trail toward their target . . . whatever, or *who*ever it was."

36

"Think they were going into Cambodia?"

"Maybe . . . Maybe not. There's a ville back in there 'bout a mile or so, but it's ninety-nine percent Arvin-symp. I can't see the Agency messin' with 'em 'less they ID'd a double agent or some such shit. . . ." He was already moving through the waist-high elephant grass as a blue-green glow along the eastern mountain ridge behind them brought out more deadly shadows.

The land was a flat sliver of dense jungle that ran between the two mountain slopes—about a mile and a half out, just beyond the ville Wickman had spoken of—and rose again toward rolling hills below the opposite peaks' sheer cliffs. The village could be the only target, unless they were using this valley for access into some long-range mission. It would have been easier for the chopper to drop them into one of the isolated fingers of rain forest and let them hump in from there. Why waste time on RVN soil blazing a trail through thick bamboo? Brody shook his head from side to side: they were not really even sure what they were up against.

Martinez stared at the back of Sgt. Treat Brody's head as they moved through the dense brush one step at a time. Had the CIA spooks left booby traps behind to cover their flank? A definite possibility, but with Whoremonger and the Brick leading the way, he wasn't worried. He hadn't worked with Big Don Wickman before, but the NCO's reputation had preceded his final arrival at 7th Air Cav headquarters after several transfer requests from 9th Cav's Flashing Saber Blues had been turned down. Big Don had been a machine gunner for the longest time—even after earning his sergeant's stripes. He preferred carrying the heavy weapon to an M-16 and earned his place in the cavalry annals by killing one *thousand* Viet Cong and NVA soldiers during a multiyear stint in The Nam.

The one thousandth hit had been made at Plei Me, during the last week of Wickman's tour in-country. Buchanan had refused to let him extend again—even when it appeared he might not make the semihistoric kill. But Single Digit Fidget Wickman managed to come through prior to DEROS and, as an encore, sweet-talked his way back to the First Air Cav at a reup tent in Okinawa.

Brody, on the other hand, was someone Martinez had worked with on numerous past occasions. He seemed to be a haunted man, constantly driving himself to the limit. He was one of those warriors who could never leave The Nam—even if he wanted to. Martinez knew Brody would surely be one of those GIs who remained behind, with an Annamese maiden in every port and a hundred kids with blue-green eyes and Amerasian features as his Vietnam legacy.

Martinez stared long and hard at the back of Treat Brody's head as they moved silently beneath the canopy of trees, leaving the first shafts of dawn behind them and entering a dark, gloomy, and forbidding world where things creeped and crawled underfoot and in the latticework network of vines overhead, yet there seemed to be no life but the trees . . . green everywhere . . . a smothering, multihued collage of greens and misty blues. It was an uncaring place . . . an evil place. Unlike Brody, who seemed to thrive on the power emanating from the rain forest, Martinez hated it. His chest was pounding now as they moved catlike through the razor-sharp reeds and clumps of banyan ferns.

"Holy shit," Marty heard Wickman whisper back to Brody the Whoremonger. Big Don sounded worried, or surprised, or both. Martinez didn't like the cracking sound in the giant NCO's voice.

He rose from his cautious crouch, gazing over Treat's shoulder, and saw the black Loach lying on its side in the small clearing. The bodies of four white men, clad entirely in black, lay motionless around the crumpled wreckage. Marty could smell fuel on the air—kerosene was still leaking from the light observation helicopter's fuel cells.

The pilot's body was torn almost in two and had been ejected halfway out the front bubble of Plexiglas. A tiger sat in the cockpit beside the dead man. Eyes glowing a warm green in the rain forest gloom, it stared directly at Brody and Big Don and Marty Martinez, watching their every move.

CHAPTER 6

Fire Support Base Belinda

Warrant Officer Lance "Lawless" Warlokk brought his flying metal predator down out of the dark, looming storm clouds and pounced. His sleek Cobra, the sides of its snout decorated with bristling sharks' teeth, dove toward the west slopes of Fire Support Base Belinda, darting in and out of the smoke columns rising from burning foxholes and smoldering bodies in the cratered moonscape that was home to nearly a hundred besieged GIs.

With the rising sun at his back, it was easy for Lawless's gunner to unload on the waves of Viet Cong sappers with his minigun and rocket pods. They watched black-pajama-clad insurgents, one after another, somersault down the slope after each projectile impacted. But many of the enemy managed to break through the perimeter defenses. American artillerymen were abandoning their trenches and foxholes and engaging the enemy in hand-to-hand combat as the fighting escalated despite the arrival of airmobile support. The Americans all wore olive-drab jungle fatigues, or just the trousers and flak vests, or just the trousers alone.

Warlokk spotted a section of the eastern perimeter, on the other side of the peak, that seemed crawling with Cong. There were no Americans visible—none on their feet, anyway. He fired a single rocket into their midst, and half a dozen VC were blown back out over the ridge as a greenish-orange fireball rose with the first sliver of a sizzling sun above the eastern crags.

"Not bad, honcho-san," said the gunner.

"Yeah, and we ain't through yet!" Warlokk replied, gliding back along the eastern ridge.

Sandeki and Buchanan sprinted between sand-filled oil drums, crouching each time they reached another point of cover. Both officers had their pistols out.

Walls of dense smoke drifted past in front of them like giant black-and-gray bedsheets flapping in the humid morning breeze. There was so much smoke now, in fact, it was hard to tell the sun had ever made an appearance. But Buchanan was determined to get to the southern edge of the perimeter, where, from his privileged vantage point beside the CP, he'd spotted the female sapper frozen in the wire.

More and more Viet Cong bodies littered the edges of foxholes the closer the two officers got to the perimeter, the air seemed alive with cries of the wounded. Cordite on the breeze made Sandeki gasp—it was a sweet, licoricelike phlegm lining his throat now. He did not think they would find the woman. He was not even sure they would survive the day.

She was long gone, the captain was convinced. Either she retreated down through the concertina, back to the sparse tree line midway down the steep slopes, or into some tunnel complex somewhere—if indeed there was one. Rumors were rampant at Fire Base Belinda about a mysterious maze of underground tunnels honeycombing the mountain.

Sandeki hated all the scuttlebutt at Belinda. It got progressively worse from week to week as 7th Cav companies pulled alternating duty with the fire base artillerymen manning cannon stations along the vast string of mountains separating Vietnam and Cambodia. And now Charlie, or the NVA, was scaling the wire in black pajamas to mount a full-blown ground attack on Belinda. Sandeki still couldn't believe it. Belinda was supposed to be impenetrable. Some of the other, less defensible fire support bases might risk sapper attacks from insurgent suicide squads now and then, but Belinda was *supposed* to be different.

He'd heard stories about the woman, too—the Viet Cong vet with a gorgeous body but defiant glare everpresent in her icy, hate-filled eyes—and Buchanan's obsession with capturing her. It was almost as bad as this thing he had for Major Lam Van Minh, the men told him. He wanted Minh bad. But he wanted the bitch worse.

A ricochet yanked Sandeki out of his own thoughts, and he rolled opposite Buchanan as a grenade exploded several meters away and two wildly rolling forms—an American and a Communist—flew past, fists pounding on each other, boots kicking.

Buchanan's right foot pivoted as if he were going to swing around and assist the cavalryman, but then another stick grenade went off—this time much closer—and the concussion knocked both officers back to the ground, stunned.

Blood trickling from his ears and nose, Sandeki glanced up to see both a Huey and Cobra helicopter floating sideways between several columns of smoke as the sun once again broke through, casting a gold-and-silver glitter of sparkles off their rotor blades. The Cobra pilot was holding his fire, but the Huey door gunner was sending a steady stream of M-60 rounds down into the earth all around a squad of five sappers who'd breached the wire. The Huey was drifting too fast to the side, however, and before the gunny could compensate, bringing the bullets into the group of VC, the head sapper pulled a Chi-Com grenade from a chest satchel and brought his arm back, eyes locked on the two American officers lying beside a pile of torn and shredded sandbags. The instant he armed the stick grenade, however, it exploded.

Sandeki glanced up to see a severed arm flying, end over end, through the air as the sapper disappeared behind a blast of smoke and shrapnel. The Huey drifted closer to the Viet Cong, its rotorwash fanning the smoke away nearly as fast as it had appeared, and the captain could see that all five Communists had been wounded by their own grenade. Two were down on their hands and knees, necks arched, heads shaking from side to side as blood poured from head wounds. One of the Vietnamese was still clinging to his AK-47. A satchel charge of plastic explosives dangled from a strap around the neck of the other man. Their three comrades lay face down in the dirt, unmoving, numbers for the body count.

Sandeki glanced over at Buchanan—the colonel was himself rising to one knee, eyes glued to the ground as he fought to shake off the rolling blast that had disoriented everyone. The "old man" would make it okay. Sandeki patted him on the shoulder, rose to his own feet, sprinted across the fire base the twenty or twenty-five meters to where the enemy was also recovering, and grabbed one of the shattered AK-47 rifles.

He rammed its bayonet into the closest Viet Cong temple, thrashing viciously—just as they'd taught him in AIT and OCS years ago. The man's lower jaw was ripped loose as the three-edged blade snapped down through bone and brain matter.

The captain watched the soldier's fractured skull a short minute, then he whirled again, his right boot connecting with the face of the second soldier trying to rise to one knee. The Communist's skull flew back, a spray of blood filled the air, and he dropped flat on his back, unconscious and dying from the shards of nasal cartilage forced up into the frontal lobe of his brain.

"Yo! *Get some*, Captain!" The Huey was hovering forty feet above him and just off to the side now, its door gunner waving both a raised fist and thumbs-up.

Sandeki heard the trooper's cry despite the helicopter's deafening rotor blast, but he didn't recognize the gunny. The man was Brody the Whoremonger and Snakeman Fletcher and Corky Cordova and even that goofy Elijah Mohammed or whatever he was calling himself this month, all rolled into one, yet he was none of them.

Sandeki flipped the rifle's safety off, aimed at the other three Viet Cong, and jerked the trigger in, expecting to spray the trio with whatever ammo was left in the banana clip. His shoulder went back instinctively, but there was no kick, no recoil. The weapon was even more damaged than he'd expected. He threw it down and drew his pistol again, whipped the slide back in his excitement, ejecting a perfectly good round, then quickly, almost frantically, lined the sights up on the back of the nearest close-cropped head.

45

When he pulled the trigger a burst of green light filled his eyes. He yelled out in severe pain, his chest suddenly collapsing as the five carbine slugs tore through the zipper of his Arvin flak vest.

Sandeki heard that horrifying little sound that comes when blood and lung fluid mix with air leak from your chest with every breath. A sucking chest wound, the medics called it, only every time he'd heard it before, the mortal injuries had been sustained by somebody else. Sucking chest wounds were the worst—or almost, anyway. The captain felt himself dropping back, down into the bottomless pit of pain and confusion.

"Dammit!" Buchanan started toward his junior officer but immediately knew the captain had been killed. His left ankle pivoted, and, ducking low as another burst of tracer flew toward him from the sagging coils of concertina, the colonel charged toward the kneeling naked woman holding the Soviet-made SKS carbine.

"Check that out!" Warlokk yelled, and brought the gunship around. Gliding sideways through the drifting clouds of smoke, *Sharkskinner*'s tail boom swung around—but not in time.

Lance Warlokk backed off. "Is that who I fucking *think* it is?" his gunner yelled into the mike.

"Buchanan!" Warlokk dropped down closer to the fire base's circle of perimeter wire as he watched the stocky officer zigzagging through the bodies toward the naked Vietnamese woman. The downblast was blowing her long black hair up out of the dust, into the air, but she did not glance up at the Cobra. Her gun eye was narrowed as she concentrated on the rapidly approaching target. Buchanan was almost on her. Arms outstretched, he was screaming like a banshee. Warlokk

46

could not risk using his ship's nose cannon because the colonel was so close now.

"What's she waitin' for?" His gunner clicked in as both men's eyes shifted from the kneeling female to the charging soldier and back again. Warlock's eyes focused on the shapely woman's shoulders tapering down to a flaring swell of hips. It was a truly unforgettable sight: the smoothness and innocence of her amber features contrasting with the jutting rifle barrel's cold steel . . . the roaring colonel charging like an enraged bear, closing in for the kill. *What was she waiting for?* And then, with Buchanan less than ten feet away, he saw her right elbow jerk frantically. She was struggling with the bolt.

She had waited until the last moment, coldly, with cunning and calculated precision . . . waited for a certain forehead or heart shot, and the rifle had misfired. Or possibly, in her excitement, even she—the veteran VC sapper—had not realized the weapon was empty, that she had fired off her magazine's last burst or rounds at Captain Sandeki, until it was to late.

"Jesus!" The exclamation escaped Warlokk as the two pilots watched her drop prone and roll to the side, abandoning the rifle just as Buchanan was upon her. She rolled hard, back down into an opening in the barbed wire, and Buchanan stumbled forward, arms out, into the coiled concertina.

Warlokk's gunner brought the minigun into position as Sharkskinner dropped even lower. Buchanan's hands had shot out, but his forward momentum still took him into the bristling, razorlike barbs. Both warrant officers watched blood spurt from the palms of his hands and then one forearm clear to the elbow.

Lawless could read his lips as their eyes locked: *Get that bitch!*

He nodded as Sharkskinner's snout dropped, but then the gunship's tail boom was flipping completely over, and he heard the lightninglike whipsnap of a blast ripping out its underbelly as the rocket-propelled grenade exploded somewhere between the landing skids.

Warlokk struggled with the controls, but he'd lost all hydraulics, and the ship was flying out of control—dropping like a stone toward the steep slope below.

He jettisoned both rocket pods, watching the projectiles streak down into the jungled valley in the distance as his world turned upside down. Sharkskinner was sputtering and groaning now as fiberglass and magnesium began to warp and collapse. Warlokk just hoped none of the broken rotor blades struck Col. Buchanan when they crashed into the side of the mountain.

Big Don Wickman started toward the black CIA Loach despite Brody's hand on his forearm. Other than the silent, nearly unnoticeable gesture, Whoremonger wasn't about to bring further undue attention to himself: if the Brick wanted to take on a tiger, that was *his* business.

"It's okay, kitty. . . ." Wickman held out a hand, palm up, as he approached the tiger sitting in the crumpled Loach cockpit. Almost casually, Sgt. Wickman glanced at the four bodies lying haphazardly around the crash site. No visible signs of bullet or knife wounds. No evidence of a land mine or even death by fire. His eyes roamed the wreckage again: the Loach had not burned, though fuel was still leaking and an explosion was a distinct possibility.

His hand slowly went to the throat of the dead pilot. The man's head and upper torso were sticking halfway out the shattered bubble of a windshield. His face was shredded and unrecognizable, but Big Don knew the man. Or at least he thought he did.

When the tip of his forefinger pressed against the pilot's jugular, checking for a pulse, the tiger sitting beside the dead man let out a terrifying roar that sent the hairs along Brody's and Martinez's backbones rising.

He had spotted the pilot's necklace immediately— even before smelling the tiger. And he knew. The pilot was Weston. Career Agency, CIA to the core. Weston was the only spook he knew who was corny enough to wear the necklace. It was a live 7.62 machine gun round, hanging from a thin gold chain. Weston had had some 'Yarde tinsmith carve an inscription across the brass cartridge, and then he had a *mjao*, or Highlands witch doctor, cast a good-luck spell on the damn thing. Weston had claimed he was the next best thing to being supernaturally indestructible, and that that was being protected from the evil clutches of Void Vicious.

"Nice kitty. . . ." Wickman reached under the dead pilot's chin, took hold of the personalized M-60 bullet, and pulled the necklace free with a quiet snap.

The cat's jaws parted again, and it leaned back, preparing to scream, but one paw rose sluggishly off the cockpit seat. It tilted its massive head to one side and locked eyes with Wickman for a moment, but the greenish-gold orbs darted up into their sockets, then fell again, coming to rest on Brody and Martinez, who were still lying-dog in the distance.

"Nebbah mind dem, kitty." Wickman's own eyes scanned the cat's chest and front limbs. He could see no injuries, but the animal obviously seemed in some kind of pain. Its head began to sway slightly from side to side as if it had sustained a concussion, and then, with little further warning, the tiger collapsed onto its side.

Big Don Wickman did not move immediately. He listened to the sound of urine flowing from the cockpit seat, down onto the helicopter's floorboards as the dying tiger lost control of its bladder and abdominal muscles.

"What the fu—" Brody and Martinez both rose from their crouches upon spotting Big Don's slow-motion wave up to his position.

While Marty stood in the middle of the clearing, slack-jawed, eyes roving with a bewildered glaze, Treat rushed from body to body, checking the men clad in black. "All dead," he whispered to Wickman after a few moments. "And Brick . . ."

"Yeah?" Wickman appeared with the huge tiger in his arms.

"There's no blood or injuries. Nothing, man. . . ."

"Right. None on the cat, either. . . ."

"What does it mean?" Martinez was suddenly beside them, but he kept his back to the two sergeants as training dictated, discipline returning to the private. His own eyes resumed scanning the tree line in all directions.

"You wanna bury it?" Brody watched the Brick pull a small plastic vial from the first-aid pouch on his web belt. The vial was empty. It looked to Treat like the type of container used to carry rolls of film.

"Fuck no." Wickman nodded his bowed head from side to side as he concentrated on the tiger's rapidly beating chest. With his other hand, he removed the commando knife sheathed to his calf.

When the tiger's heart finally stopped, he ran the blade along the cat's inner thigh, and blood spurted

50

forth. He filled the container with the warm crimson, capped it, and glanced over at one of the dead men.

"Guess we better call in for a pickup." Brody stood and pulled the receiver from the prick-25 on Martinez's back. "What about the Loach?"

"We blow the sucker in place." Wickman's eyes were darting about the jungle's edge now. His chest and arm muscles tensed visibly. The sun was up over the mountains, but here, deep in the heart of the valley's rain forest, with a double- and, in some parts, triple-canopied ceiling of branches and vines concealing the sky, little if any light was getting through. It would remain dark until high noon, and even then only a few solitary shafts would pierce the dense floral ceiling, shooting down through the green mist like weak flash-light beams.

"Thermite charge?"

"Yeah. There's no way we could recover it . . . get it up through those trees . . . even with a shit-hook. Even if we had more time and *two* shit-hooks, which we don't."

Brody focused on the Brick's eyes. They had narrowed to black slits. The soldier sensed something. Danger? Trouble? "What is it?" Brody's voice dropped to a harsh whisper.

"We've got visitors. . . ."

And Treat Brody heard the first twig snap a dozen meters outside the dark clearing. Wickman rushed back to the Loach. In silence he searched the cockpit, but it was empty. The already shattered windshield exploded beside his head, and a second burst of tracers roared into the clearing as the squad of North Vietnamese Regulars rushed within the tree line a few meters away.

Brody and Martinez were already firing back, and several of the NVA were catapulted off their feet by chest hits—others dropped prone into the reeds at clearing's edge.

"What's the plan!" Brody yelled above the rapidly growing din of discharges, slamming bolts, and screaming injured. A grenade went off somewhere in the enemy's ranks: an NVA private must have dropped the Chi-Com stick before he could throw it. There came more death cries.

Wickman had not fired a shot yet. He was trying to rejoin Brody and Martinez but taking his time doing it—eyes concentrating on the ground around the Loach chopper, it seemed. "We back off!" he replied finally, carefully pushing the vial of tiger blood into a thigh pocket. But then, instead of rejoining the other two cavalrymen, he produced a second plastic container and was kneeling beside one of the dead Agency spooks now.

"What *are* you!?" a ducking Martinez screamed as more and more bullets bounced in around him. "A fucking *vampire* or something? Let's *go*, Sarge!"

Frowning, Wickman waved him silent and was quickly on his feet again after running the knife blade across the corpse's wrist. Brody watched him cap the container and bite down on the seal as he crawled, crablike, back through the reeds to their position.

"Mighty fucking strange, Whoremonger." The Brick winked at Brody as both men proned face-in-the-dirt flat against an onslaught of RPD machine-gun rounds sweeping the clearing now.

After the thirty-round burst, Treat glanced over at Big Don Wickman. An evil, ear-to-ear grin creased the cavalry sergeant's otherwise grim features. "No shit." Brody stared at the drop of blood clinging to his lower lip.

CHAPTER 7

Over Fire Support Base Belinda

Lt. Jake Vance leaned out the gunship hatch, clutching his bungee-suspended M–60, unable to believe what he was seeing: Col. Buchanan was elbow deep in some concertina wire, Captain Sandeki had just been shot in the chest by the leader of a suicide sapper squad, and his sometimes-buddy Lance Warlokk was scrambling from the Cobra helicopter he'd just crashed into the rocks. "Holy shit!" The lieutenant felt suddenly guilty and embarrassed for insisting on manning a gunny slot when he knew he should be down on the ground, "leading the charge" and all that "officer stuff."

Holding the mouthpiece of his headset against his lips, Jake clicked in. "Did you see *that*?" he yelled, unsure what incident to refer to specifically. "Take us down, Gabe! Take us fucking down!"

Splintered rotor blades from Sharkskinner were still floating lazily through the air, end over end—pieces came down all around a slack-jawed Buchanan, but the colonel was miraculously not injured by any of the flying debris.

As *Pegasus* spiraled down toward the fire base's smoke-enveloped edge, Vance watched two blood-smeared enlisted men rush up from a nearby trench to help Buchanan free himself of the nasty concertina barbs. Warlokk and his gunner were sliding out of the crumpled Cobra cockpit, bruised and battered but appearing to have sustained no major injuries.

Sharkskinner's upended landing skids pointed toward the sky in muted defiance—the chopper lay on its top on a rocky ledge fifty feet down the slope below the lowest rings of concertina and punji stakes. Smoke was pouring from the craft's underbelly and swash plate assembly, but Vance could see no fire. He smiled at Lance's good luck: Sharkskinner had not exploded upon impact.

The lieutenant's eyes shifted from Buchanan—his entire face and chest soaked in blood now as the privates worked frantically to free him from the concertina wire—to Warlokk and his gunner as they stumbled up the slope frantically, their own faces constantly glancing back over their shoulders to see if they were being pursued by any enemy ground troops. The mountain's steep slopes seemed suddenly deserted of Viet Cong sappers now, however. In the tree line, a lone VC rifleman was taking casual pot shots at the American chopperjocks. Vance watched puffs of dust and smoke rise here and there every few seconds as the bullets ricocheted off nearby rocks all around them.

His eyes shifted to the group of soldiers huddled around the unmoving captain a few yards away from Buchanan. "Take us down on that helipad closest to Sandeki! He's gonna need a Dustoff out, Gabe!"

"Rodg . . ." *Pegasus* was already flaring in above the bunker-top plates of metal tarmac.

But Sandeki was dead.

As Vance stared down at a dead man on the moonscape of Fire Base Belinda, only smoke—the black blanket of smoke drifting past a few feet overhead—was reflected in the captain's glazed eyes.

"Did you get her?!" Col. Buchanan was suddenly screaming in Vance's ear as the young lieutenant stared down silently at Doc Delgado's back. Echo Company's best medic was working frantically to bandage the captain's wounds, to pound life back into his chest, but it was all in vain.

"Forget it, Doc," Vance whispered down to the corpsman, ignoring Buchanan.

He reached down and nudged Delgado's shoulder when the buck sergeant continued the resuscitation efforts without letup.

"Did you waste that bitch, Lou?" Warlokk had somehow made it through the punji stakes and claymores and concertina wire without a scratch and was also beside him now.

Vance glanced back over a shoulder, down toward the perimeter where Warlokk's gunner was still tiptoeing through the fire base's mine field—he hadn't even gotten to the barbed wire or urine- and feces-soaked punji sticks yet. "Huh?" he said finally after Warlokk took hold of his shoulders and began to shake. "*What* bitch, Lawless?"

"You didn't see her, *Lieutenant*?!" Buchanan was in his face now as well, nose to nose. Vance focused on the blood-streaked face. "Buck naked—firing an SKS!" Spittle from the colonel's lips flew out at him.

Unfazed, Vance stared down at Sandeki again. He had liked the captain.

"Goddammit!" Buchanan was yelling and waving his arms in the air. Drops of blood splashed against the faces of every soldier standing there or crouching around Sandeki. "Move your asses out! I want a search team scouring this mountain, top to bottom! I want that cunt here before high noon—you *got that*, Lieutenant?!" Buchanan towered over Jacob Vance now. Vance just stood there, stone-faced and silent, staring past Sandeki's body, out over the edge of Fire Base Belinda to the mist-enshrouded valleys far below.

Smoke still drifted between him and the sagging line of concertina, but there was a sudden silence gripping the raped flattop of a mountain. The Viet Cong had melted back out of sight, back down the slopes, beyond the stumps and craters and debris . . . into the tree line of scrub oak and bamboo. Had they retreated for good, or were they just regrouping for a counterattack?

"Let's go." Vance motioned for several of the enlisted men to follow him toward *Pegasus*. "You boys know what to look for."

"I want that twat stuffed and mounted, *gentlemen!*" Buchanan added.

There was no grunting, psyched-up acknowledgment from the weary troopers. Their faces streaked with ash and soot and powder burns, the men complied silently—some dragging their rifle butts in the dust.

"Screw it!" Vance said.

Pegasus had been up in the air only two minutes when he and Gabriel both concluded that theirs was a lost cause. The VC had all disappeared, and that included Buchanan's bitch. They would not return before dark. "Swing back around by that drop point where we inserted Brody and the Brick," he clicked in, but Gabe was already taking the gunship up toward the clouds in a steep, gut-flopping ascent.

Fire Base Belinda loomed below them, refusing to disappear—the mountain was just too big—the highest, most heavily defended fire base in the province, and the most powerful as well, with its prized battery of 50mm cannon.

"Tango-Charlie just got Brick's transmission," Gabriel advised Vance. "They're taking on bookoo hostile fire and are requesting immediate extraction. Gonna be a hot LZ, ladies. . . ."

"We goin' in alone?"

"Rodg! Neil Nazi's keepin' all the other ships back at Fire Base Buffy, or in a holding pattern around Belinda in case Charlie launches another surprise attack. . . ."

"Shit. . . ."

"But then it wouldn't hardly be a fucking *surprise* twice in one sunrise, now, would it, Lou?"

Vance turned to the six privates sitting back to back—two cramped ranks of three apiece—in the center of the cabin. Each rank was facing out one of the hatches. None of the privates looked eager to mix it up with Charlie again so early in the morning. They'd been breathing cordite and black powder grit since zero four hundred hours as it was. "Prepare to unass!" Vance told them, motioning the smallest enlisted man over to the starboard hatch. "When was the last time you fired a fucking sixty?" he demanded.

"About five fucking minutes ago!" the PV2 shot back sarcastically.

"Good!" Vance grabbed his arm and whirled him into the hatch hog. The private would have flown out into empty space had Vance not grabbed on to the back of his trousers. He snapped the monkeystraps onto the trooper's web belt. "Now I wanna see that baby's barrel glowin' hot pink like elephant pussy the second we prang in!" he ordered.

"No sweat!" The soldier still sounded semidefiant.

Good! Vance was thinking as he turned to face the others again. *That shitty attitude just might keep him alive!* "How come I don't hear no gruntin' from the grunts?" he demanded, forcing himself back into the swing of things, the intoxication of the descent. "Let's go!" He pounded his chest, apelike, as his eyes stared past the men, out to the blur of lima-lima greens and blues as *Pegasus* dropped below treetop level. He began stomping up and down, motioning the troopers to rise to their feet. "Now . . . let's . . . *get some!*" He sensed the ground rising up to meet them, and suddenly they were sliding across vines and tree roots and boulders and bodies.

Pegasus pranged sideways through the field of mushrooms and rotting plant and animal matter, sending a cloud of purple dust into the fanlike shafts of sunlight that penetrated the clearing's edge. Vance winked at Snakeman Fletcher, who was on the opposite hatch-60, then turned to leap out the hatch.

Pegasus bounced several times as she struck small hills and dips hidden from view by the shoulder-high elephant grass, and then she was flaring sideways, rising completely up off the ground again. Gabriel obviously sensed trouble or didn't like the feel of the terrain.

Vance was surprised he'd risked setting down at all—they'd been prepared to drop down the five or six feet off the landing skids if necessary. But Gabe knew Vance was going in with a squad of green troopers—or semigreen, anyway, after that morning's predawn skirmish with Charlie.

"Kill some Commies for Mommy!" Snakeman

yelled, shaking a fist. He was not firing his M-60, as his hatch was pointed away from the direction they'd been humping, and he'd received no hostile fire yet. The private Vance had thrust to the opposite hog *was* busy unloading on the Void, however. His barrel was already beginning to glow slightly, and the lieutenant slapped him on the back as he flew past.

"What the fuck ya shootin' at, boy?" Vance leered like a demon preparing to pounce on unsuspecting prey.

"I don't *know*!" the door gunner yelled back. "I'm just fuckin' firin'."

The first Cong tracer entered the cabin, a glowing green flare that hung between their faces for a microsecond, pixielike, then vanished out the opposite hatch, missing Snakeman's nose by inches.

Vance surveyed the hostile terrain unfolding outside: dense trees thirty feet away, then nothing but jungle and muzzle flashes. "Just don't hit any friendlies!" he screamed as he leaped down into the swaying sea of elephant grass, wondering if Gabe had pointed them in the right direction and how long it would take to find Big Don and the others. And then he was gone—a blur of olive drab, followed by five more airborne cavalrymen.

The private leaned into his M-60, directing a steady stream of hot lead out toward the cluster of enemy muzzle flashes. "Whatta I do? Whatta I *do*?!" he screamed back over a shoulder at Elliot Fletcher.

"Just do what you're doin'!" the Snakeman yelled back as a slug struck the rim of his helmet, knocking it out of the hatch. He grabbed at his throat, where the chinstrap had torn free, leaving a nasty bruise but no cut. *"SHEE-it!"*

CHAPTER 8

LZ Fang

Well, fuck me till it hurts!'' Brody the Whoremonger pulled the pin from his last smoke grenade, but this third one was also damaged and refused to ignite.

"Forget it!" Wickman rose to one knee from behind the fallen log and sent a ten-round burst out at the VC in a brisk, fanning motion. "They're already down!"

Treat glanced back over his shoulder, as if he expected to see *Pegasus* rising up through a break in the canopy somewhere. "How could you tell?" His ears were ringing from the clamor of nonstop discharges.

"Take my word for it!" Big Don ejected a spent magazine, twirled the clip around, and rammed the opposite end into his M-16's feeder well. The Brick always kept his magazines doubled up: two taped together, side by side but slightly off center with open ends opposite each other. That way he didn't have to bother with ammo pouch snaps as often: only every forty rounds instead of every twenty.

Then the sound reached his ears. Topside. High overhead. Somewhere above the oppressive canopy of interlocking branches and leaves. Rotors flapping at the sticky, humid air. Chopper blades. The sweet sound of *Pegasus* circling the kill zone, waiting for the word to return and pick up her boys, bring them out of the Void. A rush of relief filled Brody's veins. They might make it out of this one after all.

His eyes fell to Wickman's back as the broad-shouldered sergeant sent several more bursts of lead in Charlie's direction. The lower edge of Big Don's flak jacket rose up several notches on his backbone, revealing dark brown, leathery skin. But it was not the tropical tan that caught Treat's eyes, nor the dried blood from his recent shrapnel hits. The tattoos were what he noticed despite all the shooting and all the noise and all the activity.

Skulls. Skull-and-crossbones tattoos, actually. VC skulls, each the size of a nickel and wearing tiny straw conical hats were lined up in neat rows along the Brick's lower back, between the maze of crisscrossing scars left by Cong bullets or bayonets at countless past battlefields across the whole of Indochina. A dozen or more of the grinning craniums. The first two rows were in blue, but there were also three skulls a crimson shade of red.

And Brody remembered the stories he'd heard. . . . About how Wickman had been shot so many times, he'd had to stop getting a single blue skull-and-crossbones tattoo each time because he was running out of space. These days he waited until Charlie had been lucky enough to leave five more pieces of shrapnel in his hide or five more slivers of bullet lead—be they ricochets or direct hits—before getting a new tattoo. Five hits rated a *red* tattoo. It was not unlike the gruesome tally chopper pilots kept on the sides of their gunships.

Big Don Wickman did not keep score on the amount of Cong he killed anymore. That had stopped when he reached "Numba-One-Thou," as the Kit Carson Scouts called it. Now the Air Cav sergeant only spent time, *piasters* and *dau* on tattoos in honor of the occasions Charlie managed to succeed in shooting *him*.

"Breathe *deep*, bro'," Wickman suddenly yelled as he brought an arm back. Brody did not have to be warned twice. It meant to duck down into the jungle floor. The Brick was about to lob a frag.

He threw five in rapid succession.

Viet Cong soldiers were blown back through the air like rag dolls, but their numbers did not seem to be seriously depleted, and a chorus of ricochet whistles kept the three Americans pinned down behind their own thirty-foot-long log.

Pegasus was circling lower now—the jungle canopy overhead seemed to hum and vibrate each time she passed overhead. Branches shook and leaves showered down, but the VC remained entrenched even as several bursts of red tracer tore down through the ceiling of mahogany and vines, peppering their position.

"Throw your frags!" Wickman yelled at the two men beside him. Pointing, he added, "Right over *there*!"

"I'm out!" Martinez replied, and when Brody and the Brick both glanced at him, the reason clicked in their minds at the same time: he'd thrown them all back at Fire Base Belinda. Brody had half a rucksack full, and after heaving two toward the VC's ranks, he divided another twenty up between the three Americans.

"Why the hell you carry so many?" Martinez asked.

"I like the feeling," Treat grinned.

"Yeah, one sniper round in the right spot and pieces of you would come floating down in Pleiku City next week!" Wickman forced his own smile.

Brody didn't answer, throwing another frag in an underhanded, softball fashion. The three of them, eyes barely clearing the log's top layer of bark, watched the grenade sail too far over the Viet Cong's position. But it bounced off a tree and back down among the enemy soldiers, some of whom yelled and tried to scatter. Too late.

"Eat shit and die, you French faggots!" Big Don threw another grenade.

"We screwed your kid sisters while you were humpin' rice sacks down the Ho Chi Minh Trail!" Brody heaved a third.

All three exploded swiftly, and Martinez cheered as an NVA sergeant flew head over heels out of the ravine where most of the Communists were taking cover. "Yeah!" he yelled. "Ho Chi Minh sucks water buffalo dick, you *du ma* creeps!"

Most of the VC probably had no idea what a "creep" was, but *du ma* was a grave insult to their mothers and grandmothers, and definitely fighting words. In angry reply, a barrage of stick grenades landed all around the three Americans, and they pressed their bodies as close to the rotting log as they could, moments before the explosions went off.

"Cut that shit, Marty." Sgt. Wickman glared over at the private after the concussions rolled off down the hillside, ripping leaves off branches in the rain forest. He was rubbing both his ringing ears and throbbing temples, and Martinez, nodding in anticipated compliance, started to say something.

Treat Brody's sudden yell startled them both. Whoremonger rolled away from the log as if he'd just leaned

64

into a nest of scorpions. Instinctively Wickman and Martinez both jumped a few feet back as well, though they remained proned out on hands and knees, one eye on Brody, the other on Charlie.

"What is it?" Marty yelled, but then he spotted the huge spider clinging to Brody's lower jaw. It was a bark dweller—green and hairy, with bent, wiry legs seven or eight inches long.

Martinez watched Brody roll through the ankle-deep field of mushrooms, bashing his face and neck against the earth each time his head came down. It would have looked almost comical had the circumstances not been so dangerous: bullets were still zinging in all around the three Americans.

Wickman began low crawling toward Brody with lightning speed, but by then it was already over. The Whoremonger had rolled to a stop in a deep grove of mushrooms beside a man-high anthill. He lifted his face out of the small black-and-gray umbrella-shaped fungi.

"You tryin' to gross us out, Trick-or-Treat?" Big Don was not laughing as he and Marty stared at the spider's squashed remains dripping from Brody's chin.

Two sets of long, clothes-hanger-like legs were still clinging to his left earlobe and sideburns, and, like someone who had just walked around the bend of a cave into a giant spiderweb, the cavalry sergeant began batting them away with the palms of his hands.

"Suck eggs, you assholes!" he finally replied after ridding himself of the spider. Brody sat back against the anthill, bent knees pulled up against his chest, arms wrapped around his legs, and let out a long, gut-cleansing shiver. "Damn!" he screamed, shaking his head violently.

"And you better get your butt away from that mound

before some fire ants take a likin' to your *ying-yang*, troop!'' Wickman warned.

''Fuck it!'' Brody did not seem concerned about mere ants after dealing with the big bark dweller, but he dropped back down and began crawling over toward Big Don and Marty Martinez anyway.

There was a flurry of motion behind the three soldiers, and they whirled, preparing to fire, but it was friendly faces they recognized. Their trigger fingers relaxed considerably.

''We accept your invitation to join the party!'' Jake Vance and five enlisted men dove into the dirt on either side of Wickman, taking cover behind the log. The privates were ignoring the pleasantries and directing every ounce of firepower they had out into the surrounding tree line. But enemy resistance had already subsided upon their arrival, and it appeared Charlie was pulling his classic move when faced with what could potentially be overwhelming reinforcements: melting back into the bamboo.

''Do we pursue?'' One of the pogues' helmets was a foot above the fallen tree now, moving out from behind cover even as he changed magazines. Wickman latched on to the back of his web belt and jerked him back down just as a burst of green tracers passed through the space where he had been standing. It was Vance who spoke.

''Negative!'' he yelled above the roar of four other M-16s rock-and-rolling on full automatic. ''The colonel wants us all back at Fire Base Belinda, and pronto!'' His eyes scanned the Loach wreckage and dead bodies. And then they came to rest on the unmoving tiger. ''What the fuck, over?''

''Long story, Lou,'' Wickman muttered.

"How many chapters?" Vance remained straight-faced.

"Bookoo!"

"I'll wait for the movie!" He motioned for the five privates to each pick a corpse. Brody read the plan in his eyes and was already hustling over to the helicopter, breaking the thermite packs out of his ruck.

Less than a minute later the Loach was consumed in flames, and each cavalryman under Vance's command had a dead body hoisted over his back. Big Don Wickman was nowhere in sight, however. "Move it!" the lieutenant whispered harshly, pointing back in the direction through which they had just come as *Pegasus*, her door gunners, Snakeman and Cordova, unloading unceasing streams of machine-gun rounds down into the enemy positions, passed low overhead, returning to the pickup point.

He and Brody looked around the wreckage for Brick. They found him down in a shallow gulley behind the burning Loach. He was on his knees, examining tracks in the dust. Vance's eyes darted up and down the ravine in both directions. "What is it, Sergeant?"

Without speaking, Big Don waved him over, and Vance dropped to one knee in the rain forest gloom. A solitary shaft of sunlight shot down through the jungle's thick ceiling just then, illuminating the tire tread marks.

The tracks had been left by a jeep. A U.S. Army jeep. And the tracks were as fresh as the crater made by the downed Loach.

CHAPTER 9

Over the Rain Forest, South of Fire Base Buffy

"Man, when I get back to Buffy, I'm gonna get my tubes oiled and lubed!" Snakeman Fletcher boasted after he and Sgt. Wickman's three-man team had dropped off the bodies atop Fire Base Belinda and *Pegasus* returned to pick up Vance's extraction squad. Big Don had vanished among the artillery base's many bunkers, and since it would be a tight fit, only Brody and Fletcher accompanied the ship back to LZ Fang.

"Is that so?" Vance's eyes looked exhausted, but he still managed a smile as he dropped into a squat.

"Yes, sir!" Snakeman grabbed his own crotch affectionately. "You know Captain Buck? The Strick Force officer?"

Vance nodded but immediately began shaking his head from side to side in mental reprimand. "I'm afraid to hear the rest." He sighed.

"Well, ol' Buckaroo's got this fucking harem . . ."

"Yeah, I'll just *bet* they fuck." A short but stocky corporal dropped his hand in front of his own groin and stroked an imaginary erection. Brody stared at the name tag: STYX.

"Hidden out back behind the helipads," Fletcher continued, "and he always manages to stock it with some fresh pussy from Pleiku City or Kontum . . . *special rates* for Air Cav troopers, *gentlemen*! Who wants to join the Snakeman in a little beaver hunt when we get back?"

"Yeah, you mean *cunt*-tomb, don' ya, Fletch?" Another corporal crouching beside the first spoke up now in reference to Kontum. "Nothin' but *dead* pussy down in Buck's bunker. Touch the stuff, boy, and your whanger'll fall off! Doc Delgado'll have to med-evac your young ass off to the Philippines, where they keep all the terminal syph cases, man. Haven't you heard about the incurable crud makin' its rounds in the Central Highlands?" He bared his teeth for emphasis.

"Naw." Snakeman's smile warped into a frown as the ghostlike faces of two dead men floated in front of his mind's eye for an instant: Stormin' Norman and Nervous Rex. The images fell apart in misty fragments just as abruptly, and Elliot was staring out the hatch again at shards of fog lacing the rain forest. He continued to rub his crotch, but more slowly now, and with considerably more respect. "Buckaroo guaran-fuckin-*tees* his bitches, man."

"I shit you not. They'll have to quarantine your young ass . . . keep you in a compound on Roxas Boulevarde in Manila until well after the fucking war's over, man."

"Until they find a *cure*." The first corporal produced an ear-to-ear grin, and Elliot swallowed loudly, causing both junior NCOs to crack up, slam shoulders and foreheads, then bash each other's knees with glee.

Brody stared at the second corporal. This man's name tag read STONE. Unbelievable. He shook his own head now: Styx and Stone, sitting side by side on the same gunship. And they looked mean enough to break bookoo bones: both short but stocky, with close-cropped brown hair, big chins, and bulging biceps.

"Well . . ." Snakeman was not sure how to react. "All I can say is my balls are draggin', guys. The Snake needs to unload into the warm, fleshy folds of a hot crotch. Any crotch—of the female persuasion, of course."

"And the indigenous variety?" Brody smirked.

"Damn straight!" The Snake nodded. "Gotta be Oriental pussy, right, Whoremonger? Oriental pussy's the best."

"You're so full o' shit, Snakeman." Vance chuckled. "Look at you there, squattin' behind your big gun like Luke the Good, strokin' its barrel like some pervert an' talkin' 'bout Cong cunt like it's something to look forward to. You plannin' on goin' native on us, Elliot?"

Fletcher flashed his teeth at the lieutenant, but his eyes shifted to Brody for support. "Tell him, Treat! Tell him Viet broads know how to fuck a man silly—way bookoo better than round eyes."

"*Fucked* is the word." Styx laughed. "They'll stab you in the back every chance they get, and *then* they'll screw you again for good luck!"

But Fletcher was ignoring the corporal. "Tell Jake about 'em, Brody!" Snakeman's eyes pleaded. "Tell these disbelievers about zip pussy . . . 'bout how they got this way about 'em."

"Your breath's beginning to smell like *nuoc-mam*,

Snake." Stone waved his finger at Fletcher in mock reprimand. "Brush your teeth with some LSA, and before ya knows it, you'll be half-human again."

"It's the legs," Brody admitted, eyes gazing out the hatch as if searching his memories for the good times.

"Yeah! Tell these dumbfucks about their legs, Treat. *Magic* legs, Treat calls 'em!"

"Comes from squattin' the way dinks do all the time," Styx said matter-of-factly.

"Huh?" Fletcher tilted his head to one side slightly, as if waiting for fightin' words.

"Squattin', man. Firms up their thigh muscles . . . tightens up their twat. Nothin' magical."

"Well, that's plenty!" Snakeman lifted his chin. "Now fuck *you* very much." He turned to Vance. "Just get some cherry girl to sit on my face, Lou, and I'll be happy. The Snakeman'll reup for another fuckin' six, man!"

"Cherry girl?" Styx was laughing again. "There ain't no cherry girls left in The Nam, man—ain't you learned *nothin'* yet?"

"Ha!" Fletcher laughed louder. "A lot *you* fuckin' know, *troop*! The Snakeman's got it all arranged."

"Got fucking *what* arranged?" Stone challenged him.

"A young, virginal-type maiden who's never been touched by the hands of man, dude."

"Where?" Stone glanced out the hatch as *Pegasus* tipped nearly onto her right side and began banking sharply to negotiate the steep mountain valley.

"Nam Dong, brother." Elliot smiled proudly, and Brody's eyes narrowed suspiciously. Snakeman had never revealed this secret before . . . had never told him this story. Was he putting these jerks on, or was he serious?

"Nam Dong?" Styx challenged. "Where the fuck is Nam Dong, man?"

"See?" Fletcher leaned forward again. "You've never even *heard* of it, have you? That's where the cherry girls come from, man: places GIs and Arvins never *heard* of. . . . Little ville up by the DMZ." Snakeman's chin rose another inch. The man was beaming now, but both Styx and Stone erupted into laughter again.

"The *DMZ*?" Styx was shaking his head from side to side.

"Nam Dong?" Stone cocked an eyebrow at Elliot. "Nothing but Communist bitches up at the DMZ, man. Nam Dong? Them bitches gonna cut off *your* dong, brotha!" And both cavalrymen resumed laughing.

Snakeman Fletcher calmly folded his arms across his chest. "Go ahead and laugh." He gritted his teeth. "You dickheads just wait and see. I've already got her picked out." He slipped a bruised and battered hand down into his thigh pocket, pulled out his wallet, and flashed a color photograph at Styx and Stone. Styx was quick. He reached out and grabbed the wallet, and both corporals huddled around the picture for a closer inspection.

Staring back up at them was the likeness of a young, innocent-looking maiden with an infectious smile and large, dark eyes. Her tight-fitting sarong did little to conceal jutting, perky breasts. "You stole this off some dead VC soldier, right?" Styx sounded skeptical.

"My ass," Fletcher replied loudly.

"Okay, I bite, what's the story?"

Glancing over at Brody with a confident wink, Fletcher reached down into the same thigh pocket and produced an airtight, waterproof plastic holder. He unzipped the cover and withdrew a tattered and yellowing

73

piece of paper of legal-form size. "She's guaranteed me." He threw an arm out, holding the notarized document a few inches in front of Styx's face. "I've got a *contract*!"

"What is this, a mail-order bride?" Stone's head fell back skeptically. "Come on, let us see it, asshole."

"No way anyone can guarantee untouched pussy, man!" Styx snatched the contract as Fletcher was about to argue.

"It's got Buck's signature on it!" Stone fell over on his side laughing.

"*That* motherfuckin' pimp?" Lt. Vance was shaking his head now, too.

Fletcher frowned at everyone's reaction. "Well, so maybe she won't be pure as the driven snow. But Buck guarantees me I'll be happy. He knows I better not be disappointed, man. He knows I *know* where to find him."

"How much did you pay for this worthless piece of—" Vance's eyes narrowed.

"It's notarized!" Fletcher pointed to the fancy multicolored seal.

"In *Saigon*," Vance observed.

"Don' mean shit," Stone advised him.

"How much?" Vance asked again.

"Nothin'." Fletcher looked over at Vance, and if no one else there believed him, the lieutenant seemed to. "Buck owed me one."

"From when?" Brody couldn't remember Captain Buck ever risking his life for anyone or anything.

"That night I bailed him outta Chi Hoa prison, man. The time we got him drunk on thirty-three and he bopped a *canh-sat*. The white mice thought he was VC. They were gettin' ready to wire the field phone to his nuts."

74

"Oh, yeah."

"You'd have better luck payin' the goin' price for a Hue City whore, man," Styx maintained. "Them DMZ cunts, man . . . they're nasty bitches . . . Cong to the core, brother, I'm tellin' ya."

"I think you guys are pullin' my pud," Fletcher said skeptically, causing Brody and Vance to erupt into laughter this time. The lieutenant started to say something, but Gabriel, up in the cockpit, interrupted him with an intercom blast.

"Hate to break up this intellectual circle jerk," he said, "but Buck's hookers at Fire Base Buffy's gonna have to wait. . . ."

Pegasus was already pulling pitch, and suddenly they were staring down at the multihued greens of Void Vicious as the gunship turned onto its other side, banking sharply to accommodate an unplanned course change. The gut-flopping maneuver was met with knowing groans of protest from the grunts sitting back to back in the cabin.

"Have a Huey down-'n'-dirty coupla klicks south of Fire Base Belinda," Gabe continued. "Sensitive cargo. The colonel's sendin' in a whole shitload of choppers to secure the area. Unknown if it's gonna be a hot LZ, but expect the worst."

Vance frantically slipped a headset on and clicked in. Now, only the pilots and door gunners could hear the conversation. "What *kind* of cargo, Mister Gabriel?"

"Tango-Charlie advises it was a reinforcement slick full of crates of that fancy new XM one forty-eight rifle, Lou . . . you know: the double-decker M-sixteen with grenade launcher attached underneath the rifle barrel."

"The one we had so much trouble with in Quang Ngai Province?"

"Same-same, boss. But new and improved."

"Where was it destined for?"

"Buffy."

"Our guys?"

"Rodge. The Brass don't want Charlie getting their hands on it."

"Man, this really sucks the big one! What's the status of the crew?"

"Unknown. Also unknown is whether Charlie shot the bird down, or if she experienced mechanical difficulty, but the crash site is definitely in the heart of the local VC sanctuary, Lieutenant, and it don't look good."

"Tell me about it." Vance seemed to reconsider the sarcastic remark. "Tell me something good, Gabe. . . ."

"It gets worse, Jake. Belinda and Buffy are both having trouble with their commo after this morning's sapper assault. They're unable, so far, to call off the attack."

"What attack?" Vance sounded puzzled but not overly concerned.

"Arc-Light, Lieutenant."

"B fifty-twos?" *That* grabbed his attention.

"Yep. Headed for the valley separating Fire Bases Belinda and Buffy."

"Can't we relay a cancel code using ship-to-ship frequencies?"

"That's what they're tryin' to do now, but with the high-altitude peaks and all the interference . . . well, you know the trouble they're running into."

"Fucking mountains! How much time do we have?"

"Between six and seven hours."

"That should be plenty."

"Except that the colonel's not allowing any of the ships outside the AO, Lieutenant. He wants all available firepower at his disposal . . . told everyone we'll just have to hump and get in there and recover the weapons before Arc-Light arrives."

"Shit. . . ."

Gabe the Gunslinger terminated their private conversation with a static-laced pop. His voice boomed over the cabin intercom again. "Tighten up your garter belts, ladies!" he warned. "Lima-Zula comin' up in dirty sex, and she's a hot bitch!"

As the treetops began rising up above them on both sides, Stone stared out the hatch, breathing in the sweet-and-sour jungle scent. Void Vicious was calling to them . . . she was singing her siren song of doom and glory. "Fucking-*A*!" He slapped his partner hard on the back as the rotting carpet of mushrooms and dragonflies rose up to meet them, "Ya love it, and ya know it!"

Kim, the twenty-five-year-old VC sapper, was known by many names, among them Vu Y-Von, Kha Thi Xinh, and Xuyen Thi Vau, but she preferred Kim, for most of the American soldiers she had killed knew her by that name up until the moment of their death. Kim studied herself in the small, cracked PX mirror. She glanced down at the jagged scar along her right breast, and the usual shudder swirled through her. The shudder always came whenever she forced herself to stare at the scar, as did the flashbacks of that night on a dark hilltop overlooking Dong Tre, when the one they called Two-Step sent a crossbow arrow slamming into her chest.

Kim had been lucky—the aluminum shaft struck a rib after penetrating the fleshy portion of her right breast. No vital organs were damaged, but the impact had catapulted her back off a steep cliff, down into a

77

river below, and she was dragged several miles downstream before making her way to the banks.

The river rapids had slammed the shaft around inside her chest as she tumbled and rolled downstream. They had twisted it and pulled at the arrowhead, then pushed it back in, twisted and pulled again, until the muscles along the right side of her chest were like shredded meat.

And now the First Air Cavalry Division was back . . . home from the Mekong Delta. They had returned to the mountains and highlands Trinh Thi Kim knew so well.

Kim stared long and hard at the jagged scar, where what might have been a simple puncture wound had been opened into a tear running from her nipple to her throat. It was a brand, really . . . evidence she would never be anything but a soldier of Ho Chi Minh.

Kim leaned her head back against the cave's cool limestone wall and shifted her shoulders within the fishnet hammock. She closed her eyes, trying to imagine what it would feel like to have a man kissing her breast again, after so long, but the image refused to form. Instead she saw castrated bodies and headless corpses and severed limbs. She saw a black soldier repeatedly rape a young idealistic revolutionary and then tie her naked, tortured body to a stump.

And then she saw Fire Base Belinda, and the confrontation with the Bull. Another shudder racked Kim's slender frame at the haunting recollection. How stupid and careless of her! She had allowed the excitement of the kill to overwhelm her and neglected to keep track of her rounds. Before she knew it, the SKS was no longer so powerful—and she was left with an empty chamber as the cavalry officer stormed toward her.

Luck had been with Kim this morning, however, and

she had managed to duck away and slide back down through the concertina as well as some deep and hidden crevices the Viet Cong cadre leaders had outfitted with a bamboo network of ladders and planks during the hours of darkness preceding the surprise attack.

They would just have to try again. Fire Base Belinda—which the VC called *Cai Doi Cau Dau*, or "Mount Pain," because of the sacrifices they had made trying to retake the hilltop artillery fire bases of the region—could be conquered. Every fort had its vulnerable point. Kim and her team would find it, and they would capture the camp. She would personally execute every officer and NCO there. Her friends could dispose of the enlisted men in whatever manner they chose. All of them except one. Broken-Arrow.

She wanted Chance "Two-Step" Broken Arrow for herself. The soldier who had disfigured her body would pay dearly.

Kim winced as Hang, sitting upright in the hammock suspended beside Kim's, applied more ointment to the deep cuts along her thighs and knees. "I am sorry, sister." The younger woman recoiled slightly at hearing the sharp intake of breath. They were not related, but it was common custom for one female to address another as "sister" if there was great respect involved with their relationship. "Never mind." Kim's voice remained low, her eyes closed. "Complete the dressings quickly."

Closing her own eyes for a moment in embarrassment, Hang said, "The wounds run deep. The Americans are using a new type of wire."

"Yes." Kim nodded, her tone still clear. Her eyes rested, but she could not sleep. "The barbs were a half inch long. Like little axes. And low against the earth—

79

very difficult to crawl beneath. I do not look forward to trying it again.''

"Then *don't* go, sister!" Hang's features creased with deep concern. "We have no chance in the daylight. They will pick us off like empty cans and bottles on an old target range. The Americans have so many helicopters.''

Kim's eyes opened slowly. She stared hard into Hang's. "You fear the battle," she said simply. "You fear killing the long-noses . . . or having them kill you, perhaps?''

Hang's gaze dropped to the bloody wounds she was treating. And then her hands stopped working, and the eyes closed altogether. Hang's fingers fell to her own belly, which Kim noticed had been swelling steadily over the last few weeks, though Hang was clever at hiding it.

"You are with child.''

After a moment of silence, Hang nodded meekly.

"Thieu?''

"I think so.''

Hang began trembling violently, broke into tears, and began sobbing silently.

Kim's grin faded. Ignoring the pain that lanced across her shredded thighs with the movement, she leaned forward and grasped Hang's arms tightly. "What is it, girl? You do not want the child? I can understand if you fear injuring the baby in battle, or even if you are scared that the child will have no mother to raise it if you yourself are killed, but we all have our duties to perform, Hang . . . our sacrifices.''

The woman did not respond immediately, and Kim's fingers took hold of her chin gently, lifting her face. Hang's eyes remained closed. "Perhaps I can talk to the major," Kim whispered. "You were allowed to remain here in the caves these last few missions because of your malaria. Perhaps I can persuade the major to let you take charge of the supplies and munitions cache, or—"

The sound of footsteps reached both women's ears. Hang was wiping her eyes when the overweight papa-san in baggy shorts and black T-shirt waddled up to their hammocks.

"What is it?" Kim snapped at the old man, but he did not appear offended.

"Huey." He winked before switching back to Viet-namese. "We have shot down one of them."

CHAPTER 10

South by Southwest of Fire Base Belinda

Glancing out the open hatch at the steep mountain slopes rising up on both sides of the narrow valley, Chance "Two-Step" Broken Arrow tapped the rifle's magazine with the edge of his hand. Confident it was seated firmly in the M-16 feeder well, he joined the other troopers in grunting, pounding his chest, and stomping his boots: time to psych each other up.

Pandora was flaring into a hover above the dense ceiling of tree branches. Three additional choppers swooped in on either side of her. But none of them were able to land. The canopy was just too thick. They could see the blackened latticework of tangled vines and broken limbs where the downed Huey had impacted, but the hole it left in the canopy was not large enough for *Pandora* or any of the other ships to negotiate. The men would have to lower each other down on rope ladders.

He watched Corky Cordova and Abdul Mohammed

throw the coiled rope ladder out the port hatch, then lead three newbies down into the green hill below. He started after them, eyes still roaming the tree line and rocky crags rising above, seeking out someone or something . . . searching. Then he saw her. Two or three thousand feet out: approaching fast from the northwest. Mohammed saw her, too, and hesitated in the open hatch.

Pegasus. Two-Step nodded. He felt better taking on Void Vicious knowing that Brody the Whoremonger and Snakeman Fletcher would soon be covering his tail.

"When's he gonna say it, bro?" a slender, big-boned black soldier, wearing dark sunglasses, no helmet, and clinging to the rope several rungs below Two-Step's boots, shouted up against the ship's deafening rotor-wash.

"When's *who* gonna say *what,* Abdul?" Two-Step yelled back, and stared at his own grim reflection in the other trooper's sunglasses.

"The pilot, my man. And it's Elijah, bro . . . Elijah, if ya don' mind. When's the pilot gonna tell us we's 'headed for a hot Lima Zulu, ladies, and she's gonna be hotter—' "

" 'Than a whore's hole on Saturday night. . . .' "

"*Yeah!* Right. . . ."

"Maybe it's gonna be a cold one, Mo." Chance glanced back at the dozing door gunner. "Maybe Charlie called in sick today, and all we olive-drab fools are gonna find down there is one totally fucked-over Huey helicopter, *bro.* . . ."

"Yeah!" Mohammed stared back down at the vast canopy below again. "Yeah, I can dig it!" And he was gone.

Broken Arrow waited a few seconds, but nothing flew up in their faces. No smoking shrapnel or glowing tracers. He started down after Mohammed, his M-16 slung upside-down across his back like the black GI's.

Void Vicious was dozing like the door gunner, though Broken Arrow knew the door gunner wasn't really dozing at all, but just acting as if he were—acting *cool,* man. . . . Cool for the newbies. "*Shee*-it"—Chance could still hear his words as *Pandora* lifted off from Fire Base Buffy to answer the scramble siren—"don' you pogues sweat it . . . you boys is with a good team now . . . a *tight* team that's been into the bitch's cunt and back. You assholes stick with us: John Wayne ain't got jack*shit* on us, gentlemen!"

The kid had used just about every in-country cliché available, but it never seemed to get old. The memory brought a tight grin to his lips.

Broken Arrow stared at the gnarled branches reaching out to him, and a sudden fear surged through his chest. Was it just wind from the helicopter's powerful downblast, or was the Void awakening . . . the jungle coming alive?

Broken Arrow concentrated hard on overcoming the fear, but it only got worse. Today was the day: Void Vicious was going to devour him. Not Mohammed. Not any of the others. Not even the pogues. Just him. Just Chance Broken Arrow. He could feel it in his gut—the knot kept tightening until his chest felt like it was going to burst and his throat suck itself shut. He was suffocating, yet he kept climbing down—down, down the rope ladder toward the ceiling of endless green, thirty, twenty, ten feet. . . .

He heard more rotors, bigger blades growing closer, and then a giant shadow passed over Two-Step. He glanced up to find a monstrous, twin-rotored Chinook floating into position above.

Already it was lowering a thick cable, equipped with

a hook the size of his ruck. A crewman was riding the steel hook down. Whatever was down there, Uncle Sammy obviously wanted it back bad.

"Come on," he muttered under his breath as the first jagged limbs rose up around him. "Come on, Whoremonger . . . you and Snakeman get your no-account asses over here, *pronto*!" Ol' Chance needs some backup, boys . . . he needs some rea*ssur*ance!"

Broken Arrow glanced back down at Mohammed again. He was just now dropping down out of sight below the second level of vines and interlocking branches. Chance nodded to himself: at least he had Crump. Born Clarence Crump III, anyway, but who had gone by the names of Abdul Mohammed or Elijah—depending on his mood—ever since that first month in Nam. Mohammed was one of the experienced vets Two-Step could count on. He wasn't a jive megaphone anymore, but dangerously close to becoming a lifer—a career soldier.

Elijah had completed his first Tour 365 shortly after the Ia Drang Valley campaign and returned to The World with clenched fists. There was also a Dear Clarence letter in his back pocket and an ammo box of smuggled grenades in his duffel bag, which he somehow managed to get past the overworked and undermanned MPs at Military Customs.

Mohammed had received a letter from his stateside girlfriend during the bitter fighting at Ia Drang. It came from the man she was seeing, complete with a Polaroid snapshot of the two of them in a rather compromising position. That the Don Juan was white only fueled the fires of hate Mohammed had been tending since a card-carrying Ku Klux Klan member burned a small cross in front of his tent at An Khe's plantation. The incident had also been the catalyst that made Crump change his name to Abdul.

But when the black militant made it back to Hometown, U.S.A., he found that his cheating high school sweetheart had blossomed to hippolike proportions. She was eight months pregnant as well, and outweighed Clarence Crump III—a.k.a. Abdul Mohammed—by a good hundred and fifty pounds. Grinning ear to ear in pleasant if not startled surprise, Elijah shook the hand of the man who had moved in on his princess during the soldier's patriotic absence and took a taxi back downtown to check out the employment agencies. During the slow cab ride through hubcap-deep snow and heavy, bumper-to-bumper inner-city traffic, he counted his blessings and good fortune, block by barrio block.

Life in the ghetto quickly began eating away at Abdul. He joined the underground BLA movement but found his heart wasn't in the all-night, chest-expanding rap sessions. All anyone ever did was *talk* about killing policemen, *talk* about overthrowing the United States government, *talk* about hustling white women and Latinas. Abdul wasn't into talk. He was a man of action—the only army vet in the group; the only one experienced enough with firearms and explosives to know what it really felt like to kill.

The "Movement" became a joke to him: all talk and no action. And, before you could finish a bottle of antimalaria pills, Mohammed was back among the gunship troopers, considerably more mellow and surprisingly dedicated to the Green Machine and Uncle Sammy.

Elijah's screams jerked Two-Step back to the present.

The jungle below had suddenly exploded with enemy tracer fire. And the men on the rope were sitting ducks.

Chance frantically directed a circular motion up at

the pilot, who was already ascending back out of the fiery funnel of lead. Holding on tight with both arms, he stared down between the toes of his jungle boots. Mohammed was still clinging to the rope ladder as well.

The newbies were all the way down to the bottom rungs but had failed to reach the ground before *Pandora* roared back up, away from the charred canopy and hostile fire. Two of them were bleeding bad but appeared wild-eyed, alert, and coherent.

In his peripheral vision, Two-Step noticed that the huge Chinook helicopter was also swinging away from the area, the lone soldier hanging on to its shit-hook, a black speck against the gray sky. *Pegasus* shot past, too, circling wide, staying out of the way. He did not bother trying to see who was working the gunny slots— they'd all be slapping backs and exchanging war stories soon enough, *if* Neil Nazi didn't have them reinserted a klick or two down-valley for a rubberband, two-pronged ground assault on the crash site.

Two-Step stared down at the tracers arcing skyward, mostly toward the men clamoring up the rope ladders of other gunships. The Cong bullets were flying not straight up, but at an angle. The enemy was not directly below the American troopers, within the crash site itself, but it appeared they were nearby. In all the excitement, Chance was not able to see the downed Huey at all—only a large bomb crater where he'd expected to find the usual carpet of mushrooms or waist-high elephant grass.

It was surely going to make retrieving the cargo more difficult than originally anticipated, and now it appeared the race was on to see *who* made the retrieval first. The men clinging to the bottom rungs of nearly every rope ladder were firing their M-16s down into the trees on full automatic, eating up the encounter. Two-

Step was up on the higher rungs, where no one was firing because it was too dangerous for the soldiers holding on below.

The pilots had obviously gotten the word on Echo Company's next move. Chance glanced up and saw the tiny black C&C Loach circling high above the crash site and Huey gunships. Buchanan was up there, directing the operation. Good men would die before he'd allow Charlie to have whatever was down there. But at least he'd be leading the charge—Broken Arrow had to hand him that much: the colonel had guts. He was one of the few officers Two-Step respected, one of those who didn't expect their men to do something *they* wouldn't do first themselves.

He concentrated on the direction *Pandora*'s pilot was taking as the ship banked gently to the right and the long rope ladder swung in the opposite direction. They were quickly out of the direct line of fire, and the ship's landing skids were dropping toward the treetops again as every bird in the formation headed down-valley. Due to the dense forest growth, Charlie was having a hard time sending long shots after the retreating craft.

A Cobra gunship remained behind, however. Two-Step watched him dart about the opening created by the crashed Huey, his gunner sending bursts of minigun fire down at the glitter of VC muzzle flashes. No rockets flared from their pods. It would be too dangerous for any American survivors on the ground.

The trees parted suddenly below *Pandora*, and before Two-Step could reinforce his grip on the rope ladder, the gunship was gliding so low that men on the bottom rungs tumbled from the rope at high speed, rolling through elephant grass twelve feet high, trying to avoid boulders and stumps.

A small clearing at the winding bend of a dry creek

opened up as *Pandora* continued down-valley at a much slower rate, and then it was Broken Arrow's turn.

He watched the ground rise up faster and faster, and when the reeds began slapping at the rope five or six rungs under his boots, he released his grip and rolled, curling as much as his rifle and rucksack would allow. His ears told him *Pandora* was already ascending again, and the gunship behind her was coming in to drop off its troops as well.

Someone slammed into Chance, and he heard the trooper apologizing in a gruff voice, using more profanity than diplomacy. And then two soldiers were pulling him up out of the mushrooms, helping him onto his feet. "Jesus, Two-Step! You gettin' soft or something?"

It was Abdul Mohammed. Mohammed and Doc Delgado. He glanced up in time to see *Pegasus* swooping low overhead, then abruptly rising, getting out of the way for one of the approaching Hueys that was still dragging a rope ladder full of men under its belly.

After they rolled free, Gabriel brought his ship around again. Two-Step watched him prang it sideways through the reeds, striking tree roots, small boulders, and a rucksack someone had lost. Snakeman and Brody, Lt. Vance, two corporals, and three pogues jumped out the starboard hatch.

Pegasus began ascending with only Gabriel and his peter pilot aboard, but two cavalrymen from one of the first ships in rushed up in front of her snout, waving the tail boom and landing skids back down. An instant later two more troopers emerged from the high elephant grass, carrying an injured buck sergeant. Blood oozed unabated from one thigh, where the pants leg of his fatigue trousers had split from crotch to ankle.

Two-Step didn't recognize the man, but he'd seen that kind of wound before: a compound fracture. The bone jutted out an inch or so above the knee like a crimson-streaked splinter of bright ivory.

The four troopers lifted their wounded squad leader up into the hatch, then two of them climbed aboard as well. As if they'd practiced the maneuver a hundred times before, one manned the port hatch-60 while the other attended to the groaning NCO.

"Bummer," Snakeman muttered.

"It's a Purple Heart." Styx shrugged.

"And a million-dollar wound, amigo," Stone added. "Freedom bird, here comes the sarge. . . ."

"Rodg." Vance remained edgy as well: they were only two or three hundred yards down-valley from the crash site. He knew there were probably more than a few VC sprinting toward them through the tree trunks at that very moment.

He waited for Leo Zack, the ranking NCO, to trot up with a squad of disoriented newbies before holding his hand straight. He pointed directly at the center of the clustered cavalrymen, then swept his hand to the left. "You men will go with Sgt. Zack," he directed the twenty troopers. "The rest of you stick with me," he advised an equal number, speaking fast but clearly. "My people remain on *this* side of the creekbed. Sgt. Zack's on the opposite. We sweep back toward the crash site and secure the area. Now spread the fuck out! One lousy Chi-Com'd take the whole circle jerk of us out!"

"What if Charlie outnumbers us, Lou?" Corporal Styx asked, stone-faced.

"You're fucking Air Cav, soldier!" Vance shocked himself as well as Snakeman and the Whoremonger—he could not believe the words were coming out of his own mouth. "You are a superior fighting force! Now get in there and *sac mau* the bastards. *Get some* for Captain Sandeki! Any more stupid questions?" But he

91

was already off and running toward the clearing's edge before anyone could speak.

Pandora assumed Python-Lead's position as the head of the pack while Gabriel used *Pegasus* to transport the injured sergeant back to Fire Base Buffy. The flapping of six sets of rotor blades was heavy in the air as the remaining gunships returned to the crash site in anticipation of providing the ground troops with escort cover fire.

Zack took his men to the other side of the creek, and the contingent of Americans melted into the bamboo.

CHAPTER 11

Fire Support Base Belinda

Col. "Bull" Buchanan stood atop Artillery Fire Support Base Belinda, along her southernmost rim, overlooking the mist-enshrouded valley thousands of feet below. The mist was turning silver in the center and black along the edges as smoke from the crash site firefight increased. He glanced up as two more helicopter gunships swooped past, dropping suddenly as they began their descent down through the steep mountain slopes, their pilots hoping to come in on Charlie's blind side, surprising him with M-60 machine-gun blasts.

Shortly after they disappeared down beyond the crags, two other ships rose from the murky rain forest gloom, their rotor blades glowing with bright blue flashes along the edges, appearing almost halolike from this high vantage point above them. The choppers slowly rose, growing larger and more noisy, then were suddenly passing over him, too, the bottoms of their

93

landing skids gleaming as they headed the opposite direction, back to Buffy—back for more fuel and ammo.

There were bustles of activity all across the fire base's flat top peak as they anticipated Lt. Vance's radio call for a fire mission. But the net remained strangely quiet. Echoes of long series of discharges down below, thundering up through the gulleys and ravines with an eerie regularity bordering on an apathetic calmness now, reached his ears every half minute or so. Vance's people were still shooting it out with the contingent of enemy soldiers dug in near the downed Huey.

Buchanan resumed pacing back and forth above the ring of concertina wire as he watched the cloud of gunsmoke growing far below. His Command & Control Loach had been struck by a lucky AK shot from the ground. His crew chief advised him it would be a half hour at least before they were airborne again, while the pilot patched up the tail boom.

The grating sound of heavy brass slamming together turned his attention to one of the nearby cannons. A cursing soldier was struggling with the loading mechanism of one of the guns.

Buchanan stared past the battery, less than a mile up-range, where Fire Base Buffy rose a few hundred yards above Belinda, overlooking the smaller camp—well within rifle range but, thankfully, in friendly hands.

Lighting up one of his trademark cigars, Buchanan watched another helicopter roar past, low overhead. He inhaled deeply, feeling a pain suddenly, deep in his chest. It brought the news he'd received from Nurse Maddox a few days earlier.

Lt. Lisa Maddox was running the MAST detachment up-valley, at Fire-Base Buffy's small, Quonset-hutted, mobile surgical team. The X-rays from third Field Hospital were back, she had told him, forced grin crumbling into a sad half smile that saw her lower lip tremble ever so slightly. It was confirmed, Colonel. Lung cancer.

Buchanan stared at the gunship. He thought about his Congressional Medal of Honor—from Korea, the cold Asian war—his nation's highest award. Now there was not even retirement to look forward to. Just death. A lingering, shriveling, grotesque death, if what the army doctor down in Saigon told him last month was even close to semiaccurate. The captain had almost seemed to delight in informing Buchanan he was overdoing life: his drinking, smoking, eating, womanizing. The Bull was going to have to slow down, or the China store was going to collapse on top of him. It would be messy, and there would be no survivors, the captain had maintained.

All Buchanan really wanted was Lam Van Minh's head atop a bamboo stake outside his command bunker before he bought the farm.

He knew the scrawny little bastard was somewhere in these mountains . . . hiding right under his nose, waiting for the right moment to strike. He could *feel* it . . . could taste it on the muggy morning breeze. Minh was somewhere in the *Chaine Annamitique*. An intelligence team had triangulated his last three operations and placed him somewhere in Pleiku or Kontum Province. He wanted the NVA major more than anything in Asia right now—more than the VC cunts, even more than a pardon from the death sentence Lisa Maddox had handed him. Somehow he knew Minh was involved in all the crap taking place down there in the jungle.

Two artillerymen trotted past him. Both out of breath, they still managed a tight grin as one saluted for both himself and the other. Buchanan returned it with a sluggish lift of his gun hand that only came up halfway. The two soldiers were already gone—had their backs to him, anyway. He heard them laughing over a private joke or something.

Buchanan's eyes shifted up for some reason, and he stared at three wisps of white vapor, high in the sky. He knew the vapor was being produced by the heat exhausts of some massive B-52s, headed on a mission unrelated to Buffy and Belinda, farther north. The planes themselves flew too high to be seen from the ground. How long until ''his own'' fleet of stratofortresses arrived, pulverizing the valley below? Buchanan checked his watch: five and one-half hours before the big bombs began to fall on the slopes of the mighty *Chaine Annamitique,* and there was little he could do to stop them.

The fire bases were safe, of course. Virtually impervious to close-in air strikes—friendly or enemy—but not due to any overhanging rock outcroppings or other natural cover. They had once been nearly the highest peaks in the *Chaine Annamitique*'s immediate range. Blasting, grading, and sawing their tops level had not changed any of that. These two fire bases were protected by an odd combination of downdrafts, atmospheric turbulence, and what some ace pilots claimed even amounted to a weird form of wind shear. Fixed-wing aircraft had a terrible time flying through the pass and generally avoided it altogether. Only the helicopters were able to negotiate the freak wind currents without much trouble.

Buchanan's eyes took in the battery of cannon again. Sappers had succeeded in destroying the northeast set a few weeks back, using a barrage of RPGs fired from below the perimeter in the middle of the night. The deployment configuration had to be temporarily reduced to a crude square, though the artillery commander was assured by his junior officers that they still had the entire area of responsibility covered. Fire Base Buffy still had all of its guns intact.

Recoilless rifle teams, M-79 thumper operators, and machine-gun nests were deployed around Fire Base Belinda's perimeter, but they were down to half strength because of DEROS rotations and casualties, and the camp's M-42 battery was out of commission altogether due to self-inflicted damage: a shell had exploded inside one of the gun barrels only yesterday, badly injuring several artillerymen.

"It would be a damn sight more pretty if it wasn't for all that smoke down there, wouldn't it?" A low, animallike growl from nearly followed the question.

Buchanan did not turn to confront the officer intruding on his thoughts. He recognized his pilot's voice immediately. "Yes." The colonel took one last look at the string of olive-drab gunships climbing up out of the valley below. "It certainly would. . . ."

Someone or some*thing* was tugging at his unbloused boots as well, and he glanced down to see Brody's dog, *Choi-oi,* his chops full of trouser cloth, staring up at the colonel, daring him to try and break free.

"Your Loach is back in business, sir."

After a slight pause Buchanan said, "I guess that means we have to coax it back into the air again, eh, Captain?" He turned, finally, and winked at the short, slender pilot, before dropping his cigar on Choi-oi's forehead and turning to leave.

"Yes, sir . . . I suppose it does. Of course, we could always call off the war. Or call a truce, anyway. . . ." The captain watched Choi-oi roll out from under the cigar, clutch the soggy stub between his grinning jaws, and run off toward a group of artillerymen.

The breeze against Choi-oi's ugly mug made it appear the dog was actually puffing out crude smoke rings, but Buchanan did not appear as amused as the other men. He and the pilot rejoined the crew chief, who was wiping grease from his bruised and scraped hands with an oily rag.

"Maybe we could fly down to Vung Tau for a couple weeks," the pilot continued, ignoring the crew chief's quizzical look.

"Let's cut the shit, soldier," the colonel replied more sharply than he'd intended. "Shove as many ammo boxes o' seven sixty-two int' that fucker as it can lift-off the ground. We got a job to do."

CHAPTER 12

Nam Sathay River Valley

Vance paused to glance back over a shoulder, but it was an unnecessary gesture: Sgt. Brody was still right behind him. They exchanged glances, and he continued onward, into the rain forest gloom.

They had been walking a good five minutes now, since the six helicopter gunships dropped the two platoons of men onto the valley floor. Vance's eyes darted the thirty or forty feet to the other side of the dry gully. Zack's group was still where it ought to be: directly across from his own team and slightly back a few meters or so. They were encountering no resistance, either—only silence.

Vance glanced up as a scurrying sound in the branches overhead made the men freeze in place. There came an irate squealing high overhead, in the second or third layer of canopy up above, out of sight, and then what almost sounded like an angry exchange of primal fist blows. Vance caught sight of one of the tree monkeys falling several meters through the branches and vines before regaining its footing and bounding off into the multihued greens and yellows shifting brilliantly beneath the elusive glimmer of sunlight suddenly poking through here and there.

But it continued to get darker the farther they creeped along the ravine, away from the clearing where the gunships had set down. The ceiling of branches and vines overhead—its lowest level only five or six feet above the men's helmets—weighed down on them like the walls of a cave. They had entered the Void.

A thrashing in the deep reeds at the bottom of the gully sent every man into a cautious, unmoving crouch again, and Brody's rifle barrel swung around to confront the movement. His eyes locked on to the glowing orange orbs of a huge cat slinking through the bamboo ever so slowly, one paw at a time, shoulders moving independently, black fur glistening as the panther continued on through the ravine, seemingly unintimidated by the gang of gun-toting, two-legged intruders.

Vance's fist shot out, motioning for restraint. The men watched the panther disappear into a clump of shoulder-high bushes, headed away from their target; headed in the direction of the clearing several hundred yards back.

Jake brought up two fingers, pointed at the last man in his column as well as the trooper walking point, then at the bushes where the cat had vanished. They nodded and kept watch on the platoons' flank, in case the big cat was feeling brave this silent Sunday morning and had plans to circle back around in a crude attempt to ambush and drag the last man from the column.

But the panther made no further appearances. Probably lying-dog, Vance smiled to himself. Waiting for

100

the battle to begin and end. Waiting for easy meat, heated by hot lead and smoking shrapnel. Waiting for the games to begin. . . .

The smell of molten magnesium and singed fiberglass reached the Americans' noses then, and they knew they were close to the Huey wreckage—very close. Waves of hot air were rolling out from the heart of the jungle, hitting their faces like blast furnace heat. But there was no crackling sound, no licking of flames nearby, no distinctive popping of loose, burning ammo rounds—only the sporadic discharges now and then from AK-47s in the distance as the enemy troops fired up at helicopters passing overhead.

By the sound of rifle fire, Vance and Zack estimated they were still a hundred yards or so from the crash site. Both soldiers wondered what the scene would look like—how close Charlie would be. Perhaps the Cong were already forming a long line—a human chain—from the mangled Huey, up the slopes and into the trees, as their raw recruits and ville slaves began lugging crates of the new rifles up out of the crater, into the walls of bamboo and mahogany, where it would disappear without a trace.

The crater was going to pose a problem. Vance had gotten only a fleeting look at it from aboard one of the cruising gunships earlier, but the damn thing had looked deep and difficult to negotiate.

Moonscape, his brain whispered as they entered a barren clearing hundreds of yards wide and filled with several of the bomb craters.

They were getting closer.

The two men in front of Vance stopped suddenly. Both soldiers dropped to one knee to investigate something blocking the maze of blackened, fire-gutted trails through the bamboo—trails blazed by the rolling fireballs of the bombing run, no doubt. Sgt. Brody brushed past him without so much as a word and was quickly crouching between the two corporals, one eye on the tree line closing back together up ahead, the other on the pile of fur before them.

A slack-jawed Lt. Vance joined the three soldiers after waving the men behind him into defensive squats. Using the blade of his survival knife, Brody was just turning the animal's body over.

"Fucking King Kong *Junior*," Corporal Styx whispered back at the officer.

Brody nodded. "He's a *big* one, ain't he?"

"Killed by fire?" Vance noticed the swift manner in which Brody was examining the stiff carcass.

"Don't look like it, Lou. . . ." A stream of worms and maggots poured from the mammal's mouth as Corporal Stone pulled its long fangs apart, and Vance recoiled in disgust.

"Doesn't appear to have been shot, either." Brody gently pulled its eyelids apart, unsure what he was searching for. The monkey's eyeballs were bulging beneath the lids, their centers an unseeing, milky white.

"Baboon?" he asked.

"Looks like a fuckin' gorilla to me," Stone answered for the Whoremonger again. "Or maybe an orange-tango."

"No way," Styx argued softly. "He's big, but he ain't *that* fucking big."

Brody's eyes kept shifting back and forth from the dead monkey to the trail ahead, but no VC were rushing out from the bamboo just yet. "Something bookoo weird about all this, Lou." He was speaking only to Vance now, sealing the others out.

"You think this monkey died from the same thing that killed the tiger and those CIA spooks back at the downed Loach?'' Vance scratched at the stubble turning dark along his chin.

''I don't know''—Brody started down the trail again, moving ahead of the two corporals—''but that's beginning to sound like a good guess.''

As they moved past the craters, the trees came together again, the greenery returned, and at a bend in the narrow trail the stench of melted plastics, molten metal, and burned corpses became almost overpowering. They still could not see the crash site up ahead, but when the bend straightened out again, widening into another narrow clearing, they found it was blocked by a scattered pile of bodies.

The same thought raced through the minds of Vance, Brody, and Zack simultaneously: ambush. The uniforms were Viet. *North* Vietnamese. But their backs were all turned to the Americans—hardly a clever position for a surprise assault.

Vance and Zack both motioned their men to prone out, and the lieutenant started to wave Brody up to investigate, but the cavalry sergeant was already low-crawling toward the bodies, M-16 across his wrists, bruised fingers clutching its sling at either end. It was the only cover for his face in the event this short recon of his hit a tripwire.

An odd, primitive fear seemed to surge through Whoremonger's veins as he reached the nine bodies blocking the trail ahead. There were no bullet holes in the bodies—no blood oozing down through their uniforms from puncture wounds or jagged lacerations or severed limbs, the way it always was at ambush sites or mass graves.

Slowly he reached out and pressed a forefinger against the temple of the nearest man. Nothing happened.

103

Cold to the touch and unmoving. No pulse whatsoever.

Brody sniffed at the air as flashbacks of the CIA Loach crash creeped back to haunt and harass him, but there was nothing that could account for this mystery. Just the stink of burned corpses drifting down the trail from up ahead. *Other* corpses—not these bodies, Brody had to remind himself. *These* NVA had died from something strange—something unconnected with the hostilities around the next bend in the bamboo.

He reached out and took hold of the nearest soldier's arm, turning it over to examine the wrist. There appeared to be no discoloration, nothing that would indicate cholera or smallpox or even—

A hand appeared at the edge of his peripheral vision without warning. It grasped his own wrist gently. The faint smell of peanut butter reached Brody's nose.

"What is it?" The lieutenant's lips were beside his right ear as he whispered, and Brody remembered the C-ration tin of crackers, jelly, and peanut butter they had all shared on the tense gunship ride in.

"They're dead," he whispered back. "Every last swinging dick."

"No shit." Vance would have chuckled were it not for the seriousness of the situation. "What *caused* it, numb-nuts? Friendly fire, or—"

"They weren't bombed, and they weren't blasted, Jake. . . ."

"Huh?"

Brody locked eyes with the officer. "*You* check the bastards," he said. "*I* ain't fuckin' touchin' 'em again!"

"What's *that*?" Vance pointed at the shadowy outline of an object down the trail.

Brody had not noticed it before. He rose up higher

on his elbows and glanced down at the bodies again—aware he would have to low-crawl over them to get to the car-sized shape beyond the bamboo.

"Howitzer?" he whispered.

"Hope not." Brody could see Vance's teeth grinding as mosquitoes buzzed between their faces. "If Charlie's got a cannon set up this close to Fire Base Belinda, it could mean—"

"They're hard-core NVA, sir. Check out these uniforms."

"But the bastards we surprised in the wire this morning back at Belinda were Cong," Vance shot back. "Would you argue with that?"

"No but . . . aw, fuck it." He started slowly creeping over the tangle of Vietnamese arms and legs.

"Be careful, Sergeant," Vance whispered after him, but Whoremonger was already one with the mist.

The shadow turned out to be a U.S. Army scout jeep painted over in dark blue. No bumper markings. A metal top, but no glass in the windows.

"Look familiar?"

Brody nearly jumped through his flak vest again. Vance was right beside him. Refusing to look at the officer, he concentrated on the small striped snake slithering up over his knuckles.

Swallowing the bile rising in his throat, Treat nodded as calmly as he could. "Graves." He counted the snake's red stripes, then the yellow ones, and finally the blue. It wasn't a coral snake—one of the smallest but most deadly serpents roaming the rotting floors of the earth's jungles. But the snake had dropped back into the piles of dead reeds and dragonfly wings anyway—no longer a threat.

He looked up at the abandoned and bullet-riddled jeep again. John Graves. CIA agent extraordinaire. Had been one with the rain forest since his old OSS days, running guns to Ho Chi Minh when the Viet Minh leader was fighting the French instead of the Americans . . . before the Viet Minh had become VC. Friend of all cav troopers and infantrymen, blood brother to many a Montagnarde, the local Agency spook. Chunky Caucasian sporting a powerful frame and Asian manner of thinking, Indochinese way of doing things—accomplishing the impossible most of the time.

John Graves. A funny sight every time Treat Brody happened across him—usually when the Langley spy was emerging from a skirmish in the sticks, a firefight in the rain forest. His face almost always was smeared with charcoal or black powder, o.d. green T-shirt torn and bloodstained, one of the lenses in his thick black glasses a spiderweb of cracks. Your typical professor type except for the dark tan and the scar. It ran ugly and deep across one side of his chin. He appeared to be in his late forties, but the man had been living and working in the Orient for so long, his true age was a mystery to most. The kind of "old Asian hand" who squats when offered a chair, refuses Winstons or Marlboros or Salems—preferring to smoke Viet cigarettes or Cambodian cigars—speaks several area dialects almost fluently, yet often slips into the local pidgin slang when back among fellow Americans, particularly GIs. The resident, card-carrying psy-ops expert.

Brody low-crawled under the jeep, coming up on its driver's side. He rose slowly to his feet and peered in through the rear window. The cab was soaked with blood.

"Any sign of Graves?" Vance was Brody's shadow again, but this time Whoremonger expected him.

"Nope. But ol' John musta have put up one hell of a battle."

106

"Maybe it's not his jeep. Maybe it's some other spook's jeep."

Brody waved the rest of the platoon up closer to their position. Out the corner of one eye, he watched Corporals Styx and Stone reach a point in the trail where it started to bend before motioning for the men to stop and drop back against the bamboo until he and Vance gave further signals.

On the other side of the creekbed, Zack's people kept a low profile as well, keeping behind cover and inside the shadows. There was still that telltale clank and rattle of web gear now and then, though, from the newbies who didn't yet know how to tape things down or discard altogether the equipment issued to them back at division that they didn't need out here in the boonies in the first place.

His eyes scanned the bullet holes. Some were old. He found the four-round group he was looking for. "See that?" he whispered.

"Yeah. . . ." Vance was not really looking at the metal punctures. His eyes kept watch on the trail up ahead.

"Ia Drang," Brody muttered. "Ia Drang Valley. That's where Graves got *these* four. I was there. . . ."

"So was *I*." Their eyes meshed momentarily.

"I *remember*." Brody winked.

"Fuck it." Vance, turning away, surprised him.

Brody's eyes dropped to the jeep's wheels, and he remembered the earlier Loach crash site and the tire tracks Big Don Wickman had been examining. "Wait a minute." His whisper was harsh as he grabbed the lieutenant's arm.

"What?" Vance whirled around, ready to unload on the trail up ahead.

"Graves and this jeep of his. Graves was back at that

107

first crash site, Lou. Where the Loach was downed. The one with the tiger. . . ."

"So?" The officer did not seem interested in puzzles today—only in finishing this mission and getting his men out alive. "He's always into everything. Whatever's going on involving clandestine crap or secret shit, you're bound to find John Graves cuttin' farts somewhere nearby."

"But don't you *see*?"

"See *what*, Whoremonger?" An irritated look crept across Jake's face.

"Those bodies we found back at the Loach crash site. They were CIA spooks, right?"

"Tell me something I don't already know, soldier."

"They bought the farm without any sign of physical trauma to their bodies, *Lieutenant*—no bullet holes, no knife wounds, no shrapnel injuries. Just like that pile of NVA corpses back there!" He pointed in the direction of the ripening North Vietnamese bodies they had recently passed.

Vance locked eyes with him for a silent, contemplative moment. Corporals Styx and Stone were suddenly behind him, eyes darting up and down the trail, ears tuned in to everything the two men were saying. "CIA and NVA?"

"Yep. . . ."

"No wounds?"

"None."

Styx spoke for Brody and Stone both. "Gas!" he said. "Poison fuckin' *gas*!"

Both Styx and Stone backed away from the Agency jeep. The two corporals sucked in lungfuls of air, then held their breath, hands clamped over lips. Brody's eyes widened: it would have been comical if the situation wasn't so serious.

"I'm too short for this," Stone said after he couldn't hold his breath any longer. "Me and Styx here are *both* too short for this shit, Lieutenant! Ten days each, and we fuckin' *DEROS*, man! This ain't fair, Lou! No way! Poison gas? CIA? Chemical warfare? This is against the fuckin' Geneva Convention, man!" He took in another lungful of air and tried desperately to hold it.

The tense silence was broken by Stone's inability to hold his own breath longer than a minute. "I'm writin' my fuckin' congressman, Lieutenant!" His lips fluttered as air rushed out through them, and Vance turned away slightly so the corporal wouldn't see his grin. "We don't even have *masks*, man!"

"I'm too short for this shit," Styx muttered again as his oxygen supply ran out.

"You'd already be dead if—" Brody started to explain as semihysteria began to filter back among the ranks of nervous cavalrymen, but then there came an unexpected snapping of branches beyond the bamboo, and the four soldiers dropped flat against the earth, faces in fungi, the colorful umbrellalike tops of the huge mushrooms blocking their view.

Brody lined up his rifle sights on the broad-shouldered shadow emerging from the tree line.

CHAPTER 13

Nam Sathay River Valley

"Sorry, Sarge. . . ."

Big Don Wickman glanced over his right shoulder at a blushing Ricky Rogers. "Fucking new guys." He shook his head, only half-serious. The Brick's huge hand came up when he spotted all the rifle muzzles pointed at them.

"Whoa!" He backed up as if pulling on the reins of a runaway horse. "We're the *good* guys."

Brody knew Sgt. Wickman had not been startled to stumble across their two platoons in the middle of nowhere but had no doubt been aware of their positions all along. He glanced beyond Rogers, but the two appeared to be alone.

The dry creekbed narrowed to a mere three or four feet here, and as Vance waved Zack's people up to their position, Brody said, "Don't *tell* me you two beat feet

111

all the way out here just so Rogers could rejoin his unit.''

"Not quite.'' Wickman pulled a vial of blood from one of his shirt pockets, held it up for all to see, then nodded his chin back in the direction of the dead North Vietnamese soldiers. The vial was only a quarter full.

"A blood sample?'' Vance tilted his head slightly. "No way you already got to that group back there.'' He shook his head this time. "We would have known, Brick—''

"From the downed Agency Loach.'' He winked at the lieutenant. "This is what's left of the samples I took, anyway.''

"Sgt. Wickman had them flown over to Fire Base Buffy,'' Rogers revealed. "Where Nurse Maddox ran 'em through the wringer.''

"Lisa?'' Brody and Jake both asked.

"She ain't no Einstein''—Wickman's grin grew slightly—"but she told me way back during one of our''—he winked at Vance this time—"*midnight chow* coffee break chats that she *did* spend an eighteen-month tour at Fitzsimmons Army Hospital in Colorado as a lab technician.''

"Well?'' Vance folded dust-caked arms across his chest skeptically.

"She couldn't come up with any specifics, being out here at Buffy and all with nothing better than a regulation nerve gas detection kit, but—''

"Nerve gas?'' Styx sucked his chest in again and held it. His eyeballs rolled skyward for Vance's benefit.

"Can it, asshole.'' Wickman's own eyes grew stern: he didn't want a panic out here in the middle of a combat patrol.

"Aw, fuck me till it hurts,'' Brody muttered. Chemical, biological, and *germ* warfare weapons. Just the

112

thought of going up against all that made him want to puke.

Wickman held the small vial of blood up over his head again. "Definitely some kind of poison gas," he said.

"I told you the CIA was behind this shit." Brody was surprised at his own tone: he usually supported everything the Agency was trying to do in Indochina.

"But the first victims we came across were American," Wickman said.

"And those bad boys back there are NVA Commies." Styx nodded. "So we've got victims on both sides of the fence. So what? Who gives a damn? Let's all go fucking AWOL, what do you say to that, Lieutenant? We could cut across the Cambodian border, get laid in Phnom Penh, hump up into Thailand via the Mekong River, and hire a longboat to Chieng Mai. Then—"

"Shut up, Corporal," Brody snapped.

"Yeah, get serious." Stone was losing patience in his partner as well.

" 'Shut up, Corporal'? 'Shut up, Corporal'?" Styx turned to Wickman. "Did you hear how he talked to me, Brick? NCOs can't talk to corporals that way . . . *we're* fucking NCOs, *too*, ain't that right?" He fixed an intimidating glare on Stone, who shrugged meekly.

Brody rushed forward, nose to nose with Styx. "And I could blow your fucking head off right here and now for suggesting, during a combat patrol, that my men desert the ranks! Now with all due *respect*, Corporal . . . what do you fucking think about *that*?"

"I dare you." He grinned stupidly at Brody, chest expanding with self-importance.

A loud, cracking discharge exploded in the tree line nearby, sending every man there into a combat crouch.

113

The soldiers acted out of reflex. No one was hit by the whistling ricochet of a bullet, but the vial Sgt. Wickman had been holding over his helmet exploded.

Brody and Vance both watched the blood inside it spray down onto the Brick's shoulders before he disappeared from view behind a fallen log.

Abdul Mohammed was the only man to spot the sniper. He saw a shadow in the distance—movement so slight it could have been vines or branches swaying in the breeze.

But Abdul was no pogue. He kept his eyes pointed in the direction of his suspicions—slightly off to the right, actually, for a good infantryman will train himself to counteract visual phantoms floating about. The same held true for stalking your prey or standing guard at night. Purple vision could play tricks on a man. Staring straight at an object was not a task the human eye was well designed for, especially in the dark. But concentrate on the blank blur just to either side of your target object, and it worked wonders.

Mohammed's rifle was up. "I saw her!" he yelled, sending a ten-round burst into the bamboo. "A VC bitch, man!" He jacked off another five rounds, fanning left to right. "*Got* you, you VC cunt!" he screamed louder, directing his hopes at the female insurgent he'd barely caught sight of—not at all sure he'd really hit her.

Mohammed glanced around. Everyone except Brody was taking cover. Mohammed scanned the bamboo field thirty meters distant again. All he could remember now was the outline of long hair and a woman's hips. And black pantaloons! He could remember black pantaloons, now, as she climbed up over the slippery tree roots to flee.

"Come on, Whoremonger!" he yelled, waving Leo

114

Zack's platoon into the pursuit as well. "It *was* a bitch, man! I know it—maybe the same one's been fuckin' with us since them Ia Drang days, brother! Let's *bag* 'er young ass!"

And Abdul "Elijah" Mohammed was gone. Brody stared at the puffs of silver smoke converging where the black GI's M-16 barrel had been poised an instant earlier, and then he, too, gave chase.

"Come on!" He glanced back over his shoulder to find a worried Leo frozen in step, hesitating halfway through the dry creekbed. "You don' want Crump to have her all to himself, do you?"

There was a general commotion that followed as over forty American boys took off after Brody the Whoremonger.

He chased her, sprinting the entire time, a good hundred and fifty yards before Pvt. Mohammed found himself out of breath and no closer to catching the woman. When he stopped for air, chest heaving and side aching, the black soldier found himself standing on the rim of a huge bomb crater.

Glancing down, he saw the crashed Huey lying on its side at the bottom. The creekbed, deeper but still narrow, ran through the bottom of the crater here, making it even more difficult for troops to get down to the craft. Large sections of the red clay walls were crumbling before his eyes, dropping to the bottom in dusty funnels.

He also expected to see the place swarming with Cong, but the gunships darting about along the break in trees overhead had kept the enemy back somewhere beyond the tree line on the other side of the bomb crater. And there were survivors of the crash. Mohammed could see at least two Americans crouching behind debris from shattered weapons cases, their backs to him as they peered up at the crater's opposite rim.

"Yo!" he yelled down at the three cavalrymen. Mohammed listened to his voice echo back up impressively, and when the startled white faces glanced toward him: "The Black Blade has come to your rescue, white boys!" Lifting his chin, Mohammed pulled a subdued commando dagger from his calf sheath and held it up toward the triple canopy.

One of the soldiers raised a clenched fist above the rebel flag glued to the front of his helmet and yelled back, "White on, brother! Now get us the fuck outta here!"

"We need a med-evac, too!" the soldier beside him advised. "AC's dead as they come, but peter pilot may stand a chance if we can get him to—"

A rattle of discharges rang out, silencing the two Americans—sending them back facedown into the crater's red dust. Brody arrived behind Mohammed just as the burst of AK rounds tore bark from the tree beside his head.

"What is it, man, whatta ya got?" The words were leaving Brody's lips with rapid-fire speed.

"There she *is*!" Abdul crouched slightly as he pointed, leaning to the side so Treat could follow his eyes. "There's the VC *bitch*!"

Pith helmets were popping up now, and as a dozen rifle muzzles erupted with bright flashes on the other side of the bomb crater, Vance's platoon arrived behind the two cavalrymen. A dozen privates were already unloading on the enemy, and Vance, spotting the AK-toting female, nodded to Brody and Mohammed. "Go!" he yelled over the growing din of rifle fire. "Drop the hammer on that cunt!"

"Waste her, Abdulla-san!"

116

"Blow her back to Cockbang, man!"

Brody turned to gauge Mohammed's reaction to Vance's "permission to kill" directive, but the black GI was already gone.

CHAPTER 14

Nam Sathay River Valley

"Not you, Brody!"

Vance called for Two-Step and the twin corporals. Styx and Stone rushed up. Broken Arrow and Martinez were behind them.

"Shadow Crump!" the lieutenant ordered between semiautomatic shots from his M-16. "Sgt. Brody, I need you here to help me with the pogues!"

Though he tried to slow himself down, pace himself, so the two corporals and Martinez could keep up, Two-Step found himself losing sight of Mohammed in the maze of winding trails up ahead, so he poured on the speed again, leaving the other three cavalrymen behind.

Was she leading Mohammed into a trap? Broken Arrow wondered as he sprinted through the jungle, vines slapping at his face, thorny branches whipping at his hands, forearms, and chest. That these interlocking trails were even here, in the middle of what appeared to be dense forest far from any supply lines or dwelling centers, worried him. Places like these were usually overflowing with booby traps. She *had* to be baiting him.

But Two-Step ignored the pangs of caution rumbling in his gut, urging him to slow down, to pay greater heed to the sparkles of light here, the black threads of vine there. They'd easily covered two hundred yards already, and no claymores had gone off, no spring-activated planks filled with spikes had swung around, slamming into him. It was only a matter of—

He practically somersaulted over Mohammed in his haste.

The black soldier was down on one knee at a fork in the trail, examining the dust for any sign indicating which way the woman had gone.

"Jesus!" Two-Step muttered, flying past Abdul, rolling off the side of the trail, but quickly regaining his footing.

"Yeah?" Mohammed trained a tolerant smile on him.

"Let the bitch outrun *you*, Clarence?" Two-Step wasted only a glance at the sandal scuffs and grooves before distinguishing which tracks were old and which belonged to the woman.

"It's *Elijah*, clit-breath." He glanced over at the ditch Two-Step had rolled into. "And you're lucky you didn't impale thouself on some honorable piss-soaked punji sticks, Comanche-man." He rushed to catch up with the American Indian, who had already started down the right fork.

"Come on!" Broken Arrow's whisper was harsh but distinct. "She's close, man!"

"I want a piece of that ass, Two-Step!" Adbul growled, and he was not speaking in sexual terms.

120

"She's *really* close, man!" Chance added, but he didn't seem to be slowing his pace any.

"Where's Whoremonger?" Mohammed called after him.

A teakwood plank suddenly shot out from thick vines on the right. It was not filled with spikes or razors or glass shards, but it knocked the wind out of Two-Step.

Mohammed watched the Indian flop over the heavy plank and collapse in a groaning heap at the side of the trail. A woman's defiant laugh pierced the air. Mohammed fired a short burst from his rifle before spotting the three Vietnamese women squatting in the smoke-laced distance twenty feet away.

They all wore loose-fitting, black pantaloon trousers. The woman in the middle also wore a khaki shirt that swelled along her belly, but the other two were topless, their amber bodies glistening with perspiration from the jungle heat. The girl with the swollen belly let out a catlike cry, then flopped back into the bamboo from the impact of Mohammed's M-16 rounds.

Abdul recognized one of the women as the long-haired VC bitch he and Two-Step were chasing. She had no weapon, so Mohammed relaxed slightly. "Momma, get ready to see Buddha," he said as he raised his weapon.

The woman bent down quickly and grabbed something at her feet. In one smooth, powerful motion, she lifted the ivory-tipped spear and hurled it at Abdul before he could fire.

Trinh Thi Kim grunted her approval upon hearing the heavy spear impact against flesh and bone. The tip tore through the back of Abdul "Elijah" Mohammed's throat with a dull wet sound, killing him instantly.

The black American dropped straight back into a clump of gnat-infested ferns and dead palm fronds.

121

Oozing down into the blood-slick elephant grass, his thoughts and dreams and memories were now nothing more than food for the centipedes and cockroaches.

Kim stared at the toes of Mohammed's jungle boots, rising from the edge of the trail. Shifting her gaze, she glanced down at an unmoving Hang and her lifeless child. The woman beside Kim grabbed her shoulder gently, urging her back to reality . . . back to the present. They locked eyes. "Perhaps it was for the best." Kim motioned toward Hang's ghastly wound. "Perhaps it was for the best."

"Come." The older woman, her hair piled atop her head but legs still long and sleek, took hold of Kim's wrist as the sound of Two-Step's groaning stopped and there came a commotion down beyond the trail's bend. "Come, Kim . . . we must go!"

"Holy shit!" Martinez and the two corporals skidded up to the scene, rifles blazing. But Kim and her comrade were gone. They left Hang's body where it had given birth to a bullet-riddled baby.

Younger troopers were moving past Brody, trying to get nearer the bomb crater's rim for a better shot at the enemy. Brody dropped back behind a tree trunk to catch his breath and reload his M-16. Ricochets bounced past his position, arcing out into the bamboo rising behind the cavalrymen. He rolled around the tree trunk, spraying an entire clip of bullets at the enemy troops dug in on the other side of the bomb crater, then slammed his back against the stump again, content to let the newbies experience the blooding factor. He chuckled: they deserved everything they fucking got.

"How much time we got left, Lieutenant?" someone yelled over at Vance from behind several fallen logs.

122

" 'How much time we got left?' " Vance mimicked him. "What are you, fucking late for a bus or something?"

"The B fifty-twos, Lou!" The private was not laughing. Not even close. "Arc-Light! How much time we got before Arc-Light pounds this valley into mushroom juice—"

"And us along with it!" added a soldier beside him.

A deep frown creasing his features, Vance glanced at his wristwatch. "Five hours, dildo-nose! Now don't fucking bug me while I'm tryin' to—"

His words were drowned out by a roar of rifle fire from the other side of the crater. Twigs and dirt clods and lead ricochets bounced about between the Americans.

"Jesus!" yelled a newby, lying proned out behind several low boulders only a few feet away from Brody, as he witnessed a chunk of shrapnel rip part of the bulletproof collar from Whoremonger's flak vest. "*Jesus*, Sarge! You all right?"

Brody felt the sting and buzzing pain, but, strangely, he felt no fear. He knew that the wound was only superficial.

"No sweat." he turned his back on the PV2. "Just keep your goddamned eyeball on the NVA, kid!" He sent a five-round burst sailing out over the bomb crater for effect, and the younger soldier shrugged, then resumed shooting as well.

Brody slowly moved around the edge of the wide tree stump. A bullet struck bark inches from his face, sending a lead sliver into his cheek. He'd better get his act together, he told himself, or this valley bomb crater could very easily become his tomb.

Brody rose up several inches above the cover of the tree stump, firing off magazine after magazine of bul-

123

lets on full automatic without even managing to knock a single Communist out of his tire-tread sandals, before a bouncing Chi-Com stick grenade came to rest beside his tree trunk, and he proned-out beside two privates who'd moved up to watch the Whoremonger at work.

"They're making a run for it!" He heard what sounded like Snakeman's voice, and he found himself running after a sprinting North Vietnamese soldier who was zigzagging through the bamboo stalks.

Treat gained on the NVA soldier and tackled him. They both tumbled through the reeds for several meters—the North Vietnamese smashing the side of his head against a boulder. Brody rose up on his knees swiftly, commando dagger raised in both hands high over his head, but he resisted plunging the blade down into the dazed and semiconscious enemy's heart.

Slowly he lowered the knife, sheathed it, and roughly dragged his prisoner to his feet.

The NVA force had not been making a break. Only this one man. Vance and Wickman rushed up to assist him.

He slung the man's AK-47 over his shoulder, lifted a leather rain flap, and withdrew a Soviet-made revolver from its holster. Brody stuffed the barrel into his waistband and bound the prisoner's wrists behind his back with another, then led him back toward the bomb crater.

"How much time we got left, Jake?" he asked the lieutenant.

Vance did not have to check his watch. "Less than five hours," he replied somberly.

"That should give us enough time to get some answers out of this asshole."

CHAPTER 15

Crash Site Sierra

"We need more firepower in here, Sgt. Zack!" a soldier with three months in-country under his belt called to Leo the Lionhearted as a shower of lead rained down on his position. "Artillery or something!"

"Yeah! *Arty*! We need some arty in here, Sarge!" A PFC nearby agreed.

NVA muzzle flashes seemed to be increasing as they spoke, but Zack appeared undaunted. "No arty until I get a better idea of what's goin' down!" The stocky master sergeant waved the suggestions aside. "Not until I know just exactly where that chopper's crew stands, and where *we* stand with Charlie! I don't want no shells crashin' down on the cargo, either!"

"Aw, come on, Sarge!" the PFC protested. "*Screw* the cargo, man!"

"We're gettin' the shit pounded outta *us*!" The first

soldier was trying to disappear beneath his steel pot, turtle fashion. "Call in some arty!"

"Aw, you girls just better eat it and swallow!" Zack wiped the beads of sweat from his shaved crown. Despite his enormous size and expertise with light weapons and small arms, the NCO almost always sported a contented smile, prompting more than a few South Vietnamese Arvins to nickname him the Black Buddha. Zack preferred "Leo the Lionhearted," of course. Most of the men just called him "Sarge," or "Leo," if they'd been around as long as Treat Brody. The original Echo Company troop.

"Fuck." The PFC exchanged irritated glances with his fellow grunt.

"Fuck me till it *hurts*." The other enlisted man imitated Brody the Whoremonger's cast-fate-to-winds tone, but neither soldier chuckled—the North Vietnamese machine gunner was directing another sustained burst. A small cloud of dust grew around the PFC as bullets dug into the ground on all sides.

"Sad Sap!" Zack called over to a Vietnamese Kit Carson scout cowering between two massive tree trunks.

"Yes, Sgt. Zack?" the scrawny scout screamed back without lifting his face from beneath his crossed forearms.

"Get back there and help the lieutenant interrogate that dink!"

"*Yes*, Sergeant!" The scout's head shook up and down furiously. He was obviously relieved at having been ordered back from the front line—where it just *had* to be safer.

"*Now!*" Zack yelled after glancing over a second time to find the scout had not moved. "Or I'm gonna shove a frag up your no'count ass!"

126

"Right, Sergeant!" The scout disappeared in a puff of dust and gunsmoke as incoming bullets danced on his heels but failed to strike flesh.

The staccato roar of enemy discharges smothered his words with sharp, ear-ringing claps.

Brody stared up through a break in the canopied ceiling of branches and vines at the dark storm clouds billowing black and menacingly overhead like an omen of things to come.

Treat directed his vision back toward the ground as two South Vietnamese troopers kneeled on the prisoner's biceps, effectively pinning the man down on his back. The prisoner locked wide eyes with him. Brody looked at him, then folded his arms across his chest.

"Fucking queer!" the prisoner screamed, shocking them all with his sudden and unexpected bravado.

The two South Vietnamese troopers and several American soldiers glanced over at Treat, but Lt. Vance was down on one knee beside the prisoner now. "Shut the *fuck* up!" he hissed. Turning to confront the shuffling sound of approaching feet, he told Sad Sap, "Blindfold the bastard!"

"Yes, Lou!" Sad Sap nodded vigorously, happy to be finally out of the enemy's direct line of fire.

Vance crouched with Brody and about half a dozen Americans in a shallow bomb crater a dozen meters behind Zack's defensive line of grunts. The crater's rim behind them formed a dikelike wall separating the cavalrymen. The original B-52 bombing run that had created the crater, perhaps weeks or a month earlier, had also destroyed huge sections of the jungle, leaving behind barren rings of thirty and forty meters where the shells had exploded. Before, immediately following the horrible blasts, breaks in the canopied ceiling above had been left behind, but dense foliage had since grown back.

Unaware the NVA prisoner was still watching his every move, Brody surveyed the countless hues baking beneath a simmering sun overhead. "You a god*damn* queer, soldier boy!" the prisoner spat at Brody just as the scout finally came up with a blindfold.

"Shut up!" Sad Sap's earlier timidity had vanished. Brody watched him unload on the prisoner with a flurry of dark brown fists.

"Knock that shit off!" Vance lunged forward, pulling the Kit Carson scout off.

"He say Brody fag!" Sad Sap protested, an intense look of hurt in his narrow eyes. "Brody not fag, Lou!"

Vance's eyes shifted to Brody's, down to the resisting prisoner, then back to his sergeant. He found it amusing the man would zero in on Whoremonger with such slurs. "You two know each other?" He chuckled grimly.

"What do *you* think?" Brody's tone was sarcastic as he brought up his M-16. Turning his anger on the Vietnamese, he added, "This is the only *butt* stroke you'll get from *Whoremonger,* scumbag!"

"Mellow out, Treat," Vance said without emotion before Brody could connect the rifle butt with their prisoner's forehead. "We need answers from this slimeball."

"Commie motherfucker." Sad Sap was prodding the POW's chin with the tip of his bayonet—not drawing any blood, just causing the Vietnamese to wince. Sad Sap lowered his nose to the prisoner's. He lowered his voice, too—switching to Vietnamese when he began the threats.

"Just find out why I got a goddamned infestation o'

128

NVA crawlin' through the sticks this close to Buffy and Belinda," Vance told the scout. "No bullshit threats."

Brody stepped closer to the prisoner and suddenly forced his barrel's rifle between his lips. "Want a blow job, *faggot*?" he asked the Vietnamese. " 'Cause I'm gonna fuckin' blow your head off."

The enemy POW did not appear intimidated. He twisted his head to one side, trying to withdraw his mouth so he could hurl more insults at the American sergeant, but Brody kept a firm grip on the M-16.

"Come on!" Vance grabbed Brody's arm and turned him in the direction of increasing gunfire. "Go help Zack. I've got this end covered!"

Nodding slowly with a mixture of relief and irritation, Brody had no sooner jerked the rifle's muzzle free than Sad Sap stuffed the prisoner's mouth with an empty ammo bandolier. He tied the sling in place snugly behind the man's head, effectively muting him.

Brody left without another word.

"He says the enemy strength is limited to one platoon!" Vance's elbows slammed down into the red dust beside Leo Zack after he dove to avoid a haphazard collage of NVA ricochets.

"*Who* says *what*?" the stocky NCO sergeant said, proned-out flat behind a log as the lieutenant spoke. A string of RPD rounds ripped bark from the fallen tamarind.

"The prisoner!" Using one hand, pistol fashion, Vance lifted his M-16 above the chewed-away bark and sent a ten-round reply back at the enemy riflemen. "Claims they're here to link up with a caravan coming down the Ho Chi Minh Trail—now whatta ya think about *that*, Leo?"

"Caravan?" Zack responded by throwing a fragmentation grenade at the enemy's dug-in positions.

"Yeah!" Vance risked great bodily harm by rising an inch or so above the top of the fallen log. His eyes rose and fell as they followed the M-33's gentle arc across the bomb crater. A deafening blast rocked the ground as soon as the grenade disappeared beyond the tree line, and he watched three NVA enlisted men, dazed and smoking, rise to their feet, stumble backward, and vanish from view. Zack's hand grabbed his shoulder like an iron vise a few seconds later, pulling him back down, and the earth trembled hard as the North Vietnamese detonated an American-made claymore.

"I *hate* when they use our own weapons against us!" Zack was glancing around, but he could spot no casualties among his men. "There oughta be a law!"

Vance threw one of his own grenades. "It's covered under the Geneva Convention." The lieutenant wasn't sure if he was talking about using stolen armament or something just as ridiculous.

"*Screw* the Geneva Convention, and Sweden as well—all them Icelanders are fuckin' Communists, don' you know?"

"Geneva's in Switzerland, Leo."

"Samo-samo, Lou. Fuck 'em all!" Zack was wishing he weighed *one* hundred and fifty instead of nearly twice as much as he tried to flatten out beneath a wall of moving shrapnel that crashed past over them, keeping low to the ground and nearly disintegrating their log.

Vance lifted up his M-16 again, fired off ten rounds rapidly, then ejected the spent magazine and slammed a fresh banana clip of thirty rounds into the feeder well of his rifle.

130

"What about that caravan, Lou?"

"Supposedly carrying some new, hot-to-trot anti-helicopter, shoulder-fired rockets."

"Bullshit." Zack spat onto the ground between them, and Vance watched a small puff of dust rise innocently, like a miniature mushroom cloud.

"I shit you not, Leo." Vance waved a hand in front of him as a sign of his sincerity, then rose up on one knee and sent the entire thirty rounds out over the bomb crater's rim.

Zack watched the lieutenant flop back down into the red dirt, uninjured, chest heaving, a wild sparkle in his college-boy eyes. "Not you. The dinks, Lou. They wouldn't feed you that much info 'less'n they had a reason. I think they're tryin' to jerk us *all* off."

"That scout seems to have some pretty good . . . 'interrogation' techniques."

Zack's grin had returned. "Taught the little zipperhead everything he knows," he said.

"The prisoner said the whole gang was supposed to link up around here somewhere, bypass Belinda and Buffy entirely—"

"*Bypass* them?"

Vance nodded. "Without firing a shot. Supposed to tiptoe through the tripwires and beat sandals on down toward the Iron Triangle, so they could test the new devices closer to the capital—where the Western Press Corps can provide expanded evening-news coverage for the voters and congressional constituents back home. Or some such shit."

Zack pulled the pins from two more grenades. He threw both with one hand, and both men ducked, listened for the explosions and whistle of shrapnel ripping the acrid air, then resumed their conversation almost casually. "Uncle Ho's goons ain't got no antichopper

131

rocket, Lou," said Zack. "They weren't meeting no larger force in these mountains—that would be shit tactics. And if they were, the NVA wouldn't waste the chance to flex some muscle and lob a couple dozen satchel charges at U.S. fire bases."

"What about—"

" 'Sides, ain't no way any NVA gonna be all that open with ya, *suh*!"

"But I thought you just said you taught Sap everything he knows, and—"

"Yeah, but them NVA suckahs are hard-core, Lou. When it comes to torture, some of 'em can outlast a whole swing shift of interrogators—even Kit Carson scouts. NVA hate the ex-VC scouts. Hell, I seen scout interrogators clamp vise grips on balls and ram bamboo slivers up—"

"Can it, Sarge!" Vance succeeded in waving Zack silent only momentarily.

"I'm tellin' ya, Lieutenant. That dink is only tellin' you what he thinks you want to hear! Just tryin' to save his own ass for a couple more hours—till his buddies arrive to liberate him."

"Well, I still think we should play it careful and—"

As Vance lifted his rifle pistol-fashion again, sparks fell from the carrying handle like an arc welder's overflow. A burst of orange tracers slammed against the weapon. Zack watched the M-16 sail out over Treat Brody's helmet ten feet away.

"Woo-*wee*! You all right, sir?"

Vance stared at his gunhand. He wiggled his fingers—all five still seemed to be intact. His eyes locked on to Zack's after both soldiers stared at his mangled M-16, smoking in the elephant grass behind Whoremonger.

Suddenly, a loud roaring *whoooosh*! rose up through

132

the trees to their right. It came from a distant tree line that had not been involved in all the recent hostilities up to this point. Zack and Vance watched a tiny white fireball shoot skyward, about two hundred yards away. Trailing a silver plume of smoke, the projectile rose up through the trees toward a Huey gunship.

They watched the sudden aerial pursuit. The chopper had been banking hard to the left, circling back around to return to the bomb crater crash site, when its pilot obviously spotted the small, surface-to-air rocket and tried to take evasive action.

"That sucker's locked on to the heat trail by the ship's exhaust!" Zack said as the foot-long rocket rapidly gained on the craft.

"Is it *Pegasus*?" Vance called out.

Zack paused, waiting for the explosion. A bright, golden fireball appeared where the Huey's tail boom was last seen dipping for a sudden dive. The explosion seemed to float up slightly, at an odd angle, and then everything disappeared beyond view behind the high trees. "No, I . . . don't . . . think . . . it was *Pegasus*," Zack whispered in awe.

The North Vietnamese must have paused to watch as well, for the shooting ceased. And then the sound reached them, jarring the ground slightly as a muffled blast rolled forth with it.

A wild cheer went up from the NVA side of the bomb crater, and then one of the Communists unloaded on Zack and Vance's log with his AK-47, nearly burying the two cavalrymen in chipped and flying bark.

Jack Vance could not take his eyes off the floating column of silver smoke that still remained along the clearing's far edge, marking the rocket's path through the air.

"Guess I was fucking wrong," Zack said without shame, "about the rocket-totin' caravan. . . ."

"Take a goddamned bead on that smoke!" Vance was yelling at several enlisted men. "Triangulate the damn thing from points of reference—you know how to do it! And Leo"—he turned to Zack, a semisincere apology in his eyes—"I want you to—"

"Beat feet over there with a gaggle load o' pogues and ice the NVA reinforcements."

"I love it when you read my mind, *Sarge!*" The lieutenant was not smiling.

"It's what I get paid for!" Zack slapped Jake's shoulder before inserting a fresh magazine and low-crawling back toward Brody and the others. Halfway there, he hesitated and glanced back over a shoulder. "How much longer, Lou?" He couldn't resist the question.

Vance glanced at his wristwatch. "Four hours until Doomsday, Sergeant!"

Zack nodded. He was not smiling either.

CHAPTER 16

Nam Sathay River Valley

Trinh Thi Kim's coal-black eyes remained narrowed as they scanned the surrounding terrain. There was no sign the Americans had been successful in pursuing her. The two Vietnamese standing beside her carried a bulky, inert object wrapped in what appeared to be a camouflage-colored rain poncho. They stood unmoving, watching Kim.

Kim's calm stance and their own open nervousness indicated she was obviously their leader. She scanned the trail in both directions again, then met their eyes. "*Tien hanh,*" she nodded softly. *Proceed.*

Without dropping their soldier-sized bundle, the two-VC cadre stooped to one side, pulled several bushes away, and whipped up a gunnysack containing a half-inch-thick layer of cement. Beneath the cover, a spiderhole tunnel entrance was revealed.

Both young men glanced at her again, and Kim nodded a second time. They dumped the bundle unceremoniously down the narrow, web-filled shaft and climbed in after it.

Kim heard a branch snap. Then the flutter of leaves. The sound of men running swiftly through the trees. The American GIs were still hot on her trail after all, apparently.

Kim sensed she had some time left and took the extra few seconds to whisper a few additional commands into the underground tunnel. Then she covered the entrance over again and ran.

She sprinted away from the sound of approaching cavalrymen. A forty- or fifty-foot straightaway had to be traversed before reaching the trail's next bend. She could not simply sidestep into the brush and foliage—there were too many booby traps and punji stakes hidden along this stretch of trails, and even she was not familiar with them all. Kim ran silent as a panther and nearly as fast. But the female VC cell leader was not quick enough.

"There's the bitch!" yelled a familiar voice with exhausted excitement.

Kim recognized this voice, and when she whirled, the Comanche's grin was obscured by the puff of smoke rising from his M-79 thumper. She dropped to the ground and rolled hard to her right, her face filled with dust and twigs and spiderwebs as she tumbled toward a pit hidden behind the trail's shoulder-high reeds.

The grenade Two-Step fired at her struck a tree trunk several dozen meters beyond where she had been standing, but the storm of shrapnel that resulted posed no direct threat to her.

She attempted to stop her descent down the steep ravine wall by grabbing on to weeds and roots, but the soil was too damp here, and everything she clung to either broke free or split apart. Broken Arrow's words echoed in her ears as she approached the punji stakes rising lancelike at the bottom of the slippery hill.

A scream ripped free of her throat as she reached the bottom of the hill and a single punji stake struck her right calf, slicing all the way through. It was not a clean wound—though bone had not been fractured in the fall. Kim could smell the stink of excrement all around her—where the Viet Cong had hung from tree limbs and emptied their bowels onto the three- and four-foot-long bamboo slivers after planting them at angles pointing up toward the trail's edge.

The stench of feces and urine was heavy in the ravine's stifling air. Kim flopped over rapidly—like a rat trap slamming shut—from her right side to her left, allowing herself another scream as the polished skewer was roughly withdrawn by the movement.

"She's down there!" someone was yelling, though she could not see the Americans, and she did not think they could see her yet.

"Where?"

"Did you get her, Two-Step?"

"I got her, man!"

"He didn't get her! That frag flew way the fuck over her head!"

"I told you I fucking *got* the cunt, man!"

Kim listened to the snapping of branches and dried-up palm fronds as the cavalrymen started down through the brush.

"Naw, she plain dropped outta sight on you," someone argued. "She's long gone, man, tits to the wind!"

"I ain't goin' down *there,* you guys!" a younger voice protested.

"Keep an eyeball open for punjis and tripwires!" Two-Step's voice.

"I heard a scream!" The younger trooper again. "*Two* screams, matter o' fact!"

"Parrots, man! You heard parrots pissed off up in the trees."

"Don't look up!" Someone else was actually laughing as the sound of a soldier stumbling in the thick brush reached Kim's ears. "Or it's total white-out, kid. And if ya do, keep yo' slack-jawed mouth shut!"

A general sprinkling of laughter went through the group as they reached the halfway mark down the hillside.

Kim stared at her calf through the long tear in her pantaloons. The wound was not bleeding much yet, but it was painful, and she could already see where it was swelling from an ugly infection setting in. Cursing under her breath, she bit into her lower lip.

She rose into a low crouch, whimpering slightly as sharp pains rose up past both knees, along her thighs, into her groin. But she began moving. Slowly. Catlike. Through the dense reeds and vines, between the punji stakes rising at odd angles above her shoulders. She tiptoed through the puddles of human and water buffalo urine, nostrils wrinkling with nausea.

"Hold it!" a voice yelled close behind her.

She recognized the American's voice. Only the one with the crossbow could have moved so fast and silent down through the plants and punjis without her noticing. The American fired his grenade launcher again, and by the sound of its discharge, she realized he was not so close after all. Perhaps twenty meters away, up beyond the line of punji stakes. But he was firing low. Low and close in, putting himself in the grenade's kill zone. The big GI must want her bad—bookoo bad! Kim's mind raced frantically. It would be better to die than be captured.

She dodged to the left, ignoring Two-Step's commanding voice. There came a dull *thud!* and cracking hiss as the projectile impacted against the muck where she had just been crouching. Gray smoke poured forth from the crater. Kim glanced back over a shoulder long enough to see the urine, displaced by the blast, flowing back in over the foot-wide crater's rims. He was firing smoke at her. Shells that could maim and kill if they struck you, but probably wouldn't dismember. A direct hit would knock the target down and out, dazed and helpless, stretched and prepped for capture.

"Did you get her?" someone yelled.

No answer from Broken Arrow.

"Fuck no, he didn't get her! Drop a frag into that blooper, Two-Step—a fuckin' frag, man!"

"He's too close in, you idiot! Want him to blow his own balls to the wind?"

"Quit jawin' and get a move on! Catch up to the bastard 'fore he leaves us *all* behind in this smoke screen, goddammit!"

Broken Arrow was swiftly leaving his fellow teammates behind. His ears ignored their fading shouts as his eyes and jungle boots followed the blood trail zigzagging down the now gentle incline, deeper into the valley's tangle of dense trees and foliage.

Kim tried to ignore the pain lancing through her entire lower torso now—throbbing with each footfall. There was no doubt in her mind she would lose the leg if she didn't make it back to base camp for treatment by nightfall. At the base camp, she would summon the aid of one of the medical cadre. And if they were not available—if they were away, busy with the fighting echelons—she would treat herself from the cache of first-aid supplies purchased on the Saigon black market and stockpiled in the underground tunnel complexes

139

honeycombing the entire region. But there was presently a threat more immediate than losing one of her legs—forfeiting her life would be the penalty for allowing the Indian to catch up to her. He would never waste time and resources simply taking her prisoner.

Yet she could not outdistance him today. Her wound was opening up with each score of yards traveled—she was unable to stem the flow of blood.

An M-79 discharged with an ear-numbing blast twice as loud as the last time. Bits of black powder residue flash-burned into her face and chest, and a shroud of silver smoke billowed past her as the round missed her cheek by inches and struck a tree in the distance.

Kim darted to the right, ran a few meters and stopped. Almost out of breath, she leaned against a large tree and waited. She knew her strength was nearly gone. She could not run much longer. *I am Trinh Thi Kim, trained VC warrior,* she said to herself. *I will die an honorable death.* As she turned away from the tree, she saw a huge shape hurtling through the bushes.

"*Dung-lai,* cunt!" Two Step yelled just before he jumped.

Kim whirled, and her heel connected with Two-Step's jaw with blinding speed. The startled American, knocked off balance by the unexpected blow, dropped his grenade launcher and tried to land on his forearm with a martial-arts slap against the ground, breaking his fall, but his elbow struck a protruding root instead. His whole right side went numb with an odd tingling sensation.

"Damn!" He rolled the wrong way, coming face to face with the woman he wanted to kill—the woman he had *thought* he *already* killed, long ago, at a place called LZ Bird. The woman slid forward on her knees, tiny

140

fists flying back and forth in front of his eyes, and then he realized she was punching him repeatedly.

Broken Arrow tried to regain his footing, but then she was slamming the butt of his own M-79 against his forehead, knocking him down again, back into the plush carpet of rotting mushrooms. She rammed the barrel against Broken Arrow's lips, forcing several front teeth in. Two or three inches of the barrel disappeared before she jerked in the trigger, but nothing happened.

The sound of distant voices reached Kim's ears.

"Where is he?"

"Goddammit, Two-Step!"

"Which way did he go?"

"Two-Step, goddammit! Give us a fuckin' hint, man!"

Kim listened to their voices, approaching nearer, then abruptly fading as they took a wrong turn in the nearby maze of interlocking trails. Above, the constant drone of prowling helicopter gunships hovering above the triple canopy . . . always the choppers, seeking her people out, pouncing without compassion.

Bitterly shaking these thoughts clouding her vision, Kim fumbled with the grenade launcher, vaguely familiar with its breech break-down lever, but this one was not cooperating. She could not pop the barrel open. It had been jury-rigged with wire somehow.

She bashed the metal butt plate against his face several more times, knocking him senseless. She dropped the M-79, grabbed his right elbow, twirled him over, facedown in the mushroom juice.

And there it was.

She grabbed at the crossbow strapped upside-down to the back of Two-Step's ruck, where his E-tool should have been. She snatched at it like a rabid tree monkey, trying to steal fruit from a canopy snake without getting

141

bitten—but the short, customized stock would not break free from the pack.

Her eyes focused on the canvas straps holding it in place, and she fumbled with them frantically, her ears hearing movement nearby again. A rustling in the reeds approaching this bend in the narrow trail.

Finally Kim pulled the crossbow free, an inner pain scraping at the ugly scar over her right breast when she found the aluminum shafts taped to the bottom of the weapon's smoothly polished teakwood frame. For a minute, time seemed to stand still, and as her thumb and forefinger rubbed the rough, unyielding guidance "feathers," she saw a vision of herself standing on the edge of a cliff overlooking a valley much like this very one.

Below, Comanche-man confronted frail, innocent Vietnamese maiden, fighting for her Cause. Vietnamese maiden had just killed the GI who raped her—a turncoat traitor to both the Americans and Viet Cong. Comanche-man had just cornered them both. And the crossbow bolt flew free and strong, impaling itself in her right breast with a terrifying *thud!* that knocked the air from her lungs and her feet out from under her. The woman dropped back out into the black abyss, her fall broken by a ledge thirty feet down. But the river still claimed her as the momentum carried her down the steep hillside in the uncaring night . . . a steep hillside not unlike the one that had brought her here now. . . .

The mental image fragmented like glass crumbling after an explosion, and Kim returned her attention to the matter at hand—fumbling with the crossbow shafts only a moment before learning how simple it was to arm the weapon. Then she propped Two-Step up against a bullet-scarred tree trunk and placed the metal tip against his heart.

She hesitated, remembering something, and then, grabbing the semiconscious soldier's hair along the back of his head, she forced his face upright. "Kiss the widow maker!" she hissed, pressing her lips against his mouth violently, forcing her tongue between his blood-caked lips, probing roughly, then suddenly, viciously, biting down on his tongue.

A parrot sitting in a high branch behind the Viet Cong woman, its fluffy white head cocked to one side curiously, watched with considerable interest as Kim's fists beat the soldier's sluggishly flailing arms down and continued the kiss. The parrot squawked with noisy displeasure and disappeared amidst a wild flapping of wings when she finally pulled her lips away and slapped Chance viciously. Kim watched the bird soar up into the tangled canopy above.

Wiping the blood from her own lips with bruised knuckles, Trinh Thi Kim smiled and dropped to her knees before the cavalryman and began unfastening the belt holding up his trousers.

"Where the fuck is he?"

"I don't know, semen-breath!"

"Eat it, bro'," a third voice mimicked Leo Zack.

"All you assholes shut up before I—" a commanding voice began.

"Hey!" One of the soldiers, whispering harshly, pointed at the shadows moving across the trail up ahead.

"Yeah! I saw 'em, too!"

"It wasn't her! It wasn't Two-Step and the bitch he was chasing!"

"No, it wasn't!"

Three male Vietnamese had darted across the trail

about forty meters up ahead, keeping to the brush. They all appeared to be wearing civilian attire and carrying small black satchels. The kinds of satchels Viet Cong agents favor for loading plastique explosives into.

It did not appear they had seen the Americans, though Martinez didn't know why not—his group was making enough racket as they rushed through the overgrown trails, trying to catch up with Broken Arrow.

"Two-Step can handle the cunt!" Styx hissed, evil intentions in his dark eyes. "Let's ass-kick them three bastards back to Binh Dinh! They just *gotta* be VC!"

Stone was already off and running without Marty's approval—not that a corporal needed any thumbs-up from a mere E-2.

"Shit." Martinez, chest already heaving, fell in step behind the others.

They didn't have far to go.

A loud pop greeted them around the first bend in the trail. Styx skidded to a stop, Stone slammed into the back of him, and Martinez knocked the two corporals to their knees just as the tripwire bounced back against Styx's groin.

There was no devastating explosion to follow—no bouncing betty popped up out of its hiding place—just a loud hissing as two black satchels hanging from tree limbs up ahead began releasing a tear-gas-like mist. They hung four feet off the ground and were not unlike those the three Vietnamese were seen carrying.

"Aw, fuck!" Styx tried frantically to untangle his legs from Stone's. "I'm too fucking short for this shit, you guys! I'm too motherfucking, ever-lovin' *short*!"

"See you guys in never-never land," Stone muttered, trying vainly to raise his rifle with both hands as the odorless gas quickly overpowered the Americans.

144

Before he too passed out, Martinez thought he saw a set of unblinking almond-eyes in the distance, staring back at <u>him</u> through the leaves.

CHAPTER 17

A Few Kilometers to the Northwest

NVA Army Major Lam Van Minh slowly lowered the Deg-4 rocket tube from his shoulder. With a satisfied smirk in place for the benefit of those subordinates watching his reaction instead of the plummeting Huey, Minh chuckled lightly. "Not bad," he muttered in a Northern Vietnamese dialect.

The two captains squatting on either side of him clapped softly—soft as hummingbird wings, Minh found himself thinking as he watched the American gunship disappear beneath a billowing fireball. The men around him listened to the ship's wreckage crash down through the trees several hundred meters distant.

Minh's eyes followed the drifting plume of white smoke from the midair point of impact, back to where he now stood. He stared down at the empty rocket tube. "Very nice indeed," he decided.

"You say we are getting many more of them, Major?"

One of the captains risked the question, fear and respect in his squinting eyes as he examined the one remaining prototype. "They would come in quite handy when we attempt the capture of the Americans' fire base."

"Many, many more." Minh nodded without looking up. "That is what brings us to this valley here today, young man. That is why we venture so close to the enemy fire bases ahead of schedule. . . ."

"Not to attack the Americans' mountaintop camps themselves?" The captain sounded suddenly disappointed.

"The fire bases can wait." Minh's eyes rose with a reprimanding intenseness to them. "Today we meet a caravan coming south, off a tributary of the Trails. They will have probably more antigunship rockets than we will be able to carry back—"

"But—" The other captain's tone was inquisitive as he tried to interrupt respectfully.

"But we *will* manage to carry them all back to our camp." Minh's eyes dropped again.

He ran the edges of his fingers along the seams of the three-foot-long tube. Like the U.S.-made LAW launcher, the disposable tubes would come in handy for constructing booby traps after their rockets were fired. Nothing was left to waste.

The Deg-4 was a Soviet-made antihelicopter surface-to-air rocket. Fired from the shoulder, it packed an explosive payload large enough to penetrate fourteen inches of armor but was also equipped with a device specially made to home in on the large amount of exhaust heat produced by Huey and Cobra turbines. Produced by Degtyarev—which also made the deadly RPD (Ruchnoi Pulyemet Degtyarova) machine gun found in so many NVA assault forces—it would be the North

Vietnamese Army's first portable "heat-seeking" missile that could be easily carried in the field.

The prototype that Minh had just fired proved to be extremely accurate. He had winced immediately after launching the rocket, for the Huey was faster than anticipated and was nearly gone before he had been able to pull the firing mechanism trigger. But the projectile quickly locked on to the Huey's heat trail, swerved after the aircraft in a deadly cat-and-mouse game of catch-up, and eventually blew the ship out of the sky.

Lam Van Minh chuckled to himself as one of the captains remarked they'd better leave the area before the Americans skirmishing nearby sent a probe out to the launch site. Let the Americans come. The caravan could wait. He had one more sample Deg-4 left—the one his senior captain was holding. And if the 1st Air Cav attacked, Colonel Buchanan could not be far behind.

Minh had held a personal grudge against the battalion commander for nearly three years now—all starting when their troops first engaged on the highlands outside An Khe prior to the famous Ia Drang campaign. The grudge festered like an open wound and would not heal until Buchanan's head was mounted atop a tall bamboo pole in front of Lam Van Minh's command bunker high in the hills.

There was no rush, Minh nodded at his own thoughts. There was plenty of time. This war would last a thousand more years, and their two ghosts would remain in the Void, dueling for all eternity, trying to win the successive stages of the ultimate game. He would wait for the big American's C&C Loach to float into view. And then he would fire the second prototype.

* * *

Styx and Stone both woke within spans of the same wheezing coughs. Vomiting, Marty Martinez rolled over as well, his head throbbing, his vision blurred.

"What the fu—" Corporal Styx began. All three men were missing their weapons, rucks, and boots but still wore the issue fatigue trousers and shirts.

Stone glanced down below the beads of sweat coating the hair of his chest: the dog tags chain was still there, as were its two aluminum data tabs—taped together to prevent a clinking sound in the bush.

"Any theories, *Corporal*?" Martinez stared long and hard at both soldiers, trying to focus on their name tags.

"The enemy did this to us," Styx muttered.

"No shit." Dumbfounded, Stone wiggled his toes.

"Why didn't they kill us?" Martinez asked.

"Beats me," Styx replied. "If I knew the answer to that, I'd be fuckin' occifer material, wouldn't I?"

"Why didn't the *gas* kill us?" A cool, out-of-place breeze rustled through the rain forest clearing as he spoke, and Stone wiggled his toes as well. That was when he noticed the twine. A long, taut strip of it. One end tied around his big toe; the other disappearing into the trees several feet away.

"What the fu—" Martinez began again, but Styx cut him off.

"Stop wiggling your goddamn toes, idiot! You wanna get us all blown to bits?"

"Tripwire?" Martinez whispered for his own benefit.

Stone glanced over at Styx's toes, then his eyes shifted to Martinez's, but it was obvious his own were the only toes so "honored." The gas had left Stone with a bewildered twitch to his grin. He tilted his head to one side, toes still wiggling. "Ain't no goddamn

150

booby trap, Corp! Just hold on to your oats while I figure this all out, okay?"

"Then just what the heck do you figure—" Styx began, but his partner waved him silent.

Stone's eyes followed the twine as it rose higher and higher off the ground every few feet, finally disappearing over a low tree branch at the clearing's edge. He squinted for a moment, then dismissed the fleeting fear as movement in the murky distance became a large white parrot watching them from behind a quilt of thatched leaves. No one else was spying on them.

His eyes fell to the red dust around on either side of his hips. Footprints. Narrow soles, barefooted. A woman's, he decided, watching his mind's eye's re-creation of events immediately prior to the gas bomb explosions. The three Vietnamese men in civilian attire had all worn sandals. Stone didn't know why, but his memory was clear on that one point.

His chin motioned toward the nearest print. "The women," he muttered with distaste.

"What?" Styx's palms checked the dirt around his own frame for booby traps before scooting closer through the dust.

"The women Two-Step was after are behind this. I don't know how, but them cunts is fuckin' with us, boys!"

"What!" Martinez stood, wavered on unsteady legs for a moment, then pointed at the twine disappearing into the foliage and trees. "Just *what* is *this*?" He grabbed the twine and jerked on it without warning.

"Don't!" Styx yelled, proning-out flat against the earth.

But nothing happened.

The twine did not break, nor did it give much.

151

"Something tells me we're supposed to follow the damn thing," Martinez decided aloud.

Styx stood now. He was shaking his head from side to side. "I'm gettin' bookoo bad vibes about this one," he said, staring at a company-strength contingent of black army ants headed straight for his toes. Styx glanced at the twine again, his eyes following it to the tree branch. "*Powerful* bad vibes, gentlemen. Reminds me of my childhood days—"

"*Shee*-it, you're still a kid." Stone began brushing his trousers off.

"Wait, I hear something," Martinez said.

In the distance there came the flapping of helicopter rotors, but the pull in pitch faded abruptly—the gunship was flying away from their position, not toward it. Martinez felt tears welling up in his eyes: the chopping sound made him think of rescue, and then all hope was instantly gone. He lowered his eyes so the others wouldn't notice. "Too bad we got no prick," Styx said. "We got to hump through it now."

"Yeah, with no equipment," Martinez answered. "Why did they take all our—"

"*Equipment*, exactly!" Stone replied. "Boots and bullets, rifles and rucks, for the Resistance, dude. Don't you know nothin'?"

"Oh. . . ."

Tiptoeing carefully through mushrooms and spiders and snakes, the three soldiers followed the twine down through the interlocking maze of trails for nearly a hundred yards until they came upon a small, mist-enshrouded hilltop rising up slightly above several circular pathways.

"I don't like the looks of this," Martinez whispered to Styx.

"Shut up!" came the corporal's answer.

"Is that *smoke* rising up through those branches . . . that tree on top of the hill?" Stone asked.

"It looks bad, man," Marty maintained.

His persistence was matched by Corporal Styx's determination to reach the top of the hill by a route other than that suggested by the trail of twine becoming baseball-sized in Stone's hand.

The soles of his feet were bleeding after climbing straight up through the bushes and other dense foliage, but Styx's efforts proved to be a waste of time.

The hilltop was not booby-trapped.

"Oh, my God!"

Stone and Martinez rushed up along the trail, both pulling in the twine, upon hearing Styx's startled cry.

They found Two-Step, arms outstretched, armpits propped up over two punji stakes impaled in the thick tree trunk. His hands were open, palms stapled to two gnarled limbs by his own crossbow shafts.

"Jesus." Martinez crossed himself as he stared at the soldier's head. It was tilted to one side and unmoving, blood dripping freely from the hideous cuts.

"Looks like we got here just in time," Styx muttered. "Musta scared the bitch away before she finished off the crazy Comanche."

"You think Doc Delgado can fix him up?" Stone was beside his partner now.

"No sweat. You got some butterfly bandages?" Styx grinned.

"What about his hands?" Martinez started to pull at one of the arrows but froze when Chance groaned loudly.

"Superficial," Styx declared, running his two forefingers along Two-Step's wrist and following the outline of his finger bones. "Right between the fuckin' phalanges, gents. Cunt knew what she was doin'."

153

"Don't move him anymore!" Marty suddenly shouted. His eyes had dropped to the length of twine Stone was still holding in one hand. "Look!" He pointed to Broken Arrow's trousers. The zipper was down, and the free end of the twine disappeared inside.

Styx was still smiling. "Think she tied it to his dingdong?" he snickered. "Hopin' one of us would tug on the twine, jerkin' poor old Broken Arrow's wanger off?"

"Or at least puttin' a sprain on the ol' family jewels." Stoner dropped the ball of twine as Styx unfastened Chance's web belt.

"Christ," Martinez gasped as the trousers fell to Broken Arrow's knees and they discovered the rusty straight razor taped to the soldier's penis—tied at just such an angle that the slightest pressure on the twine would have severed the organ's head.

Styx pulled a commando dagger from an ankle sheath and commenced working on the tangled twine with the delicacy of an EOD expert defusing a land mine.

Looking pale as a rain forest ghost, Stone suddenly bent over and threw up on Martinez's bare feet.

Kim stood patiently in the drifting cloud of gnats and mosquitoes, remaining stone silent. She did not have to fight the urge to slap at the buzzing pests—the discipline came naturally now. She did not have to wait long, anyway.

"There it is, sister. . . ." The woman who was present when Hang was disemboweled by Clarence Crump's M-16 bullet pointed to the far side of the wide, tree-cluttered valley. High up the opposite mountain slope, a flash of light, then another. Nothing, as the panorama of brilliant greens and browns seemed to close back in,

154

swallowing the sparkles, then two more flashes. Kim wanted to be sure. She brought the small set of folding binoculars to her eyes and focused carefully. It was indeed a signal mirror, flashed from just below the perimeter rim of Fire Support Base Buffy.

"Spread the word," Kim whispered to the woman as she eyed the thunder clouds passing low overhead. Soon they would blot out the sun. A giant shadow would be cast across the land. The reflection of sunlight had not come too soon. "We wait five minutes after the rifle fire has begun. Then we attack."

"Yes, sister." The woman hesitated, eyeing Kim's heavily bandaged calf. "Your leg . . . it will be okay?"

"Never mind the leg," Kim responded firmly, but not without an expression conveying thanks for her concern. "Now go." The wound was painful, but one of the NVA nurses attached to her cell had managed to stem the blood flow.

"Yes, sister." She hesitated, though, as both women stared back over their shoulders now, up at the peak rising above their own positions and the gleaming ring of deceptive and deadly concertina wire that began another two hundred yards up the steep, rocky slopes: Fire Base Belinda.

The plan was a simple one—so simple Kim was positive it would not work. Something *had* to go wrong. Using the binoculars again, her eyes scanned the opposite gorge. The agents moving slow and ratlike up the crevices there were heavily camouflaged, but she found herself able to count some twenty of the forty-five or so snipers. She hoped the American sentries above did not notice them as easily. If one alert GI spotted any of them, a routine mortar and artillery barrage would be called down on the slopes beneath both artillery camps, and her plan of attack would be squashed.

Her eyes shifted as she watched the woman moving along the vast assemblage of Viet Cong soldiers squatting just within the tree line. Above this point, the trees ended. The enemy had cut them down long ago. A few stumps and boulders remained for cover between timberline and the first coils of concertina and barbed wire, but the open space should not pose too much of a problem.

The mine field would be the worst obstacle.

Hopefully, the riflemen on the other side of the gorge would prove effective, and the team she herself was a member of—numbering nearly five hundred local hardcore VC—would be able to take their time, cautiously negotiating the obstacles before even being noticed. Comrade Minh of the NVA would be quite pleased.

The plan was simple.

Fire Base Buffy stood slightly higher in altitude and up-range from Belinda. From their positions overlooking Belinda, Minh's forty-five snipers would each zero in on different, predesignated targets moving about below, in the smaller artillery camp—mainly soldiers manning the guns, and perimeter sentries. Initial shots would be crucial. Kim hoped they would take out half the guard force and most of the artillerymen before the crack of sniper rifles even reached them. A majority of the Americans would be dead before they even knew what hit them.

Two dozen mortar teams would then go into action, along with a squad equipped with four RPG-7 rocket launchers and a wheel-mounted 75mm recoilless rifle—dragged up the slopes with ropes—and the remaining survivors would start running for bunkers in anticipation of a routine enemy mortar barrage. Before they

156

could emerge, Kim hoped to have most of her sappers through the wire and waiting outside the bunker entrances to greet the GIs with bayonets once the smoke began to clear.

That was her plan. Major Minh's own NVA troopers waited in the wings, preparing to sweep through the fire base after the Viet Cong breached the deadly perimeter. At least the southern guerrillas and North Vietnamese Regulars were cooperating for a change. This would be a unique opportunity to show the major how well she commanded her own platoon of forty suicide sappers.

It was too late now to worry further about tactics and strategy. It was starting. Kim felt a staticlike ripple of energy tickle the fine hairs along the nape of her neck. Her people's faces raised simultaneously to a sudden din of cries erupting high overhead. And then the rifle discharges from across the gorge finally reached their ears. Echoes like low thunderclaps bounced back and forth off the high gorge walls and nearby box canyons.

"Let's move!" she cried, urging her people out of the tree line and toward the concertina. Binoculars against her eyes again, Kim scanned the barbed perimeter above and the defensive positions beyond.

The Americans were dropping like flies.

CHAPTER 18

Atop Fire Support Base Belinda

Colonel Buchanan jumped back, startled, when the sandbags at his feet began exploding under the impact of hot lead slugs. He glanced to the left, saw two soldiers knocked off their feet by terrible head wounds, and dropped back automatically into a low-profile crouch.

Then the sound of distant rifle discharges reached his ears.

"Incoming!" A young private was running from a gun pit toward the CP.

Buchanan's ears pricked up as he dropped down behind the cover of several sand-filled oil drums. His eyes rose toward the source of the gunshots: Fire Base Buffy!

The enemy had infiltrated up through the densely forested slopes below Buffy's artillery camp, bypassing or perhaps even eliminating the modest security contingent patrolling at its base, and was now firing down on the lower artillery compound. His eyes focused on the black calico pants and camou shirts of local VC. And NVA pith helmets farther below!

"Get on the horn!" he yelled to a nearby RTO. "I wanna know if Buffy is receiving fire as well!"

"Yes, sir!" The corporal turned away and began running toward the CP.

"And gimme a scramble siren for imminent enemy ground assault!"

"Ground assault, sir?" The corporal slid to a stop and turned back again to make sure he'd heard the officer correctly. Eyes rising in vain as he tried to spot a barrage of mortars whistling down toward them, the soldier dropped into a low crouch, too, one palm across the top of his helmet as his other hand hastily fastened the chin strap.

"Right!" Buchanan snapped as he sprinted past the RTO, headed for the CP himself now.

The corporal's eyes were still darting around wildly as he ran to catch up with the colonel. "Any idea where it's all coming from, sir?" His expression told Buchanan he'd always thought they were semisafe nestled atop a mountain fire base.

"Just get on the horn"—Buchanan didn't have time to explain as he grabbed the soldier's M-16—"and button up that flak jacket, soldier!"

"Yessir!"

"Then check yourself out another rifle from the armory, and do it *rikky-tik,* son!" Buchanan's eyes scanned the perimeter wire below them with worried concern. His best troops were down in the valley bottom, trying to retrieve cargo from a downed Huey. Most of his airworthy slicks were up-canyon at Buffy or circling the AO below. And now Charlie had picked this sunny afternoon to leave the mist-enshrouded rain for-

est for the relative safety of the rocky cragged slopes—
a few hours before Arc-Light was scheduled to unload
on the valley. It was beginning to look like the only
troops ready to be pulverized were his own—and the
dwindling contingent of VC fighting to take the gre-
nade-rifles cargo away from them.

Buchanan dove flat against the ground as the first
wave of mortars came crashing down. The alert siren
began honking its irritating hi-lo racket. "Right on
schedule," he muttered, not proud his prediction had
panned out. The air was filled with the hiss of flying
shrapnel, and a thin blanket of gray smoke began covering the fire base's central hilltop as the VC mortar
team compensated for wind and distance. They were
aiming for the command post.

If the snipers had been firing from the slopes below
Fire Base Buffy, the mortar team was somewhere on his
own slab of land—somewhere in the trees below Belinda's very perimeter, he thought.

Buchanan's eyes rose past the countless dead Centaur
bodies, and those of his men littering the trenches of
defensive perimeters, and locked on to the staggered
line of black-pajama-clad insurgents emerging from the
tree line.

They were making their move!

Buchanan jerked back the M-16's charging handle
and chambered a live round. He flipped the fire selector
from safe to semiautomatic, wishing he'd grabbed the
bandolier of extra magazines hanging around the corporal's neck as well. Within thirty seconds he had
smoothly fired off fifteen rounds.

Eleven of the sappers fell dead with chest or head
wounds before they even made it to the mine field.
Three more staggered backward and dropped out of
sight behind tree stumps with leg wounds. "Not bad,

Buchanan," he muttered to himself, electing to save the last five rounds for self-defense. "But you shouldn't have missed that first one." *Wish the kid kept a thirty-round banana clip in his weapon,* he was thinking as his eyes scanned the nearby gunpits.

Both AA-gun crews appeared dead from rifle shots to the upper body. "Jesus. . . ." He felt a sudden chill drop from his backbone to the pit of his stomach. There appeared to be little activity at the defensive pits on the other side of the fire base as well. Only at the main bunker in the center of camp were men scurrying about for cover, unsure what they were supposed to do without a fire mission other than defend their guns. The attacking force was too close for the antiaircraft weapons to be used effectively at such short range. Even Fleschette rounds—which could be fired low and "point-blank" at the enemy—could not be used without taking a great risk. They delivered a devastating shower of thousands of little steel darts, which would no doubt slaughter friend and foe alike, scattergun fashion. "Shit. . . ." His eyes surveyed the defensive trenches along the perimeter.

Half the main-line force appeared dead—victims of both the snipers nearly a mile away and the ensuing mortar barrage. Buchanan was still amazed the Viet Cong were able to field such skilled riflemen—he'd been unaware they possessed any snipers that good in their ranks.

Puffs of muzzle smoke erupted here and there along the perimeter wire. Not all the sentries had been fooled into thinking this morning's attack was an assault by air only. The LPs had spotted Charlie the instant he emerged from the timberline below and were unloading on the Communists with everything they had.

Explosions began sending geysers of red dust into

the air as unlucky sappers ran across land mines hidden in the barren stretch of open space between the trees and first coils of barbed wire.

Buchanan was up and running toward the CP now. "Blast 'em with the claymores, guys!" he yelled. Deafening explosions began erupting below as the surviving soldiers seemed to anticipate his commands.

The mortars had stopped as more and more of the VC rushed the perimeter. The barrage's unearthly whistle was replaced with screams from the wounded as claymore after claymore blew roaring walls of steel ball bearings into the enemy's ranks.

The VC were hitting the bunkers with RPG-7s now. Fewer and fewer of the defensive positions were firing back as the powerful antitank weapons penetrated many of the sandbagged fortresses, killing the soldiers inside. The unearthly chorus of screams and groans grew, however, fueled by the pain of survivors . . . those who hung on—dismembered, gut-shot, blinded, or burned.

"Christ!" Buchanan was knocked backward off his feet as a rocket-propelled grenade slammed into the CP's fortified entrance when he was only twenty feet from reaching it. Multicolored plumes billowed forth up the sandbagged steps as a footlocker full of smoke grenades and CS went up.

Coughing and choking, the RTO and two lieutenants stumbled from the command post just as several shoulder-fired rockets slammed into the bunker's opposite wall. They escaped as the entire structure collapsed.

"There goes the main fuckin' radio!" one of the officers yelled, unaware Buchanan himself was rising to one knee beside the dazed radio-telephone operator.

"Well, we still got the prick-twenty-five!" The colonel grabbed the receiver from its snap on the portable radio the corporal wore on his back.

"No way you can get through to Division on that piece of shit!" the lieutenant argued, wiping dirt and debris from his eyes.

"Not with these mountains in the way!" the second officer agreed.

"Not Division!" Buchanan replied. "The gunships running cover fire down along the valley floor! They probably aren't even aware we're under attack up here!"

Both lieutenants gazed toward the distant flickers of light two or three miles below—reflections of sun off the tops of helicopter rotor blades circling the rain forest crash site. Then their eyes shifted up, closer to home.

"Holy shit!" the RTO gasped as two or three hundred insurgents, all clad in black and carrying AK-47s, emerged from the tree line and began walking casually toward the mine field and perimeter wire.

"They got the mine field figured out." Buchanan drew his pistol and fired eight rounds over a pile of American bodies, dropping four VC before he ejected the empty clip and slammed home a fresh magazine of seven hollow points.

"By hit and miss," one of the lieutenants added: bodies of the Viet Cong who were unlucky enough to step on a land mine were now being put to good use as they were lined up where they fell. Ducking the dwindling and intermittent M-16 fire, their comrades were then able to run, hunched over, across the corpses' backs all the way to the barbed wire without fear of detonating additional mines.

"This situation is rapidly going to hell." Buchanan nodded to one of the lieutenants as he called for three of the gunships to return to Belinda.

"You mean we're going to surrender the camp?" One

of the lieutenants fixed a disbelieving glare on Buchanan.

"Not surrender it." The colonel's face grew even grimmer. "*Abandon* it!"

"*What?!*" The other lieutenant could not believe his ears, either.

"It's either that or die heroes!" Buchanan returned the receiver to the RTO and resumed firing with his pistol. "Now see if you can get to a field phone and advise the LPs and whatever defensive positions are left that they are to immediately prepare to pull back. I want an orderly retreat on my starburst cluster!"

When both officers hesitated, Buchanan pointed down toward the tree line and added, "You gentlemen see what *I* fucking see?" No response was necessary: hordes of VC sappers were still emerging from camouflage.

"But abandon the camp, sir?" The nearest lieutenant seemed petrified now. "That's *desertion*!"

"Desertion my ass! We pull back, regroup, and counterattack."

"Counterattack?" The other officer's eyes pleaded for a miracle.

"Somehow! We'll figure out a way . . . somehow! In the meantime, *I'm* the C.O., *I'm* in charge, and *I* fucking-well figure I don't wanna die at no godforsaken dump called Fire Base Belinda!"

"But the AA-guns!" The first lieutenant pointed at several sandbagged pits rising like irritated blemishes above the blanket of gray gunsmoke.

"Fuck 'em!" Buchanan masked his own concern with unconvincing bravado.

"If Charlie captures those guns, they control the valley! Hell, they'll control this whole damn mountain range, Colonel! I don't want a defeat like that goin' down in my file, sir! I respectfully request that—"

"If we don't take a hike, *Lieutenant,* and take it fucking *rikky-tik,* the only thing that's gonna end up in your two oh one is a posthumous Purple Heart!"

"But—"

"Duly noted! Now move the fuck out!"

Rolling blasts from the bangalore torpedoes exploding in the concertina sent them all diving against the ground again. After the echoes moved on, another sound reached their aching ears: rotors flapping. Buchanan's ears distinguished three sets.

Gunships!

That should be enough to extract whatever survivors remained along the perimeter or in the gun pits. "Give the command to move back!" He pointed at a field phone lying off its hook at a nearby foxhole. "Advise all personnel to regroup behind what's left of the CP. Advise 'em to regroup at the helipad where my Loach is parked!" He struggled back to his feet, ignoring the dozens of minute puncture wounds peppering his belly, rushed over to what had once been his CP bunker, and dragged a half-visible footlocker from the debris. He kicked the lid open, withdrew a flare gun, checked its load, and fired high into the wind.

Moments later a red, green, and gold starburst exploded several hundred feet above the fire base's western slopes. "Well, what are you waitin' for?!" He turned to find one of the officers still gawking. "Tell my boys to pull back!"

"You got it, Colonel, but I want it down on record that I think this truly sucks the big one, sir!" The lieutenant exchanged nods with his fellow junior officer.

"I already fucking noted it, kid!" Buchanan stamped his approval on the comment by pounding the officer's back with an open palm as they both turned toward an undamaged field phone. The gesture sent him flying toward the foxhole as an RPG round exploded where he'd just been standing.

"Goddammit!" The colonel stared at the lieutenant's decapitated body flopping about in the dust. Finally feeling a sudden sting of pain from the minor shrapnel punctures all across his own chest, Buchanan wiped blood from his palms onto his trousers, shook his head in resignation, and started for the Loach. He hoped that, unlike the dead officer's corpse, his chopper was still in one piece.

Treat Brody glanced over his left shoulder along with several of the other soldiers curled up beside fallen logs scattered along the bomb crater's ridge. Their eyes followed the three choppers ascending beyond the tree line, climbing through the smoke screen, heading back to Belinda.

"Where the fuck do those guys think they're going?" someone yelled.

"Just when they started doing us some good, they hightail it outta here!" another grunt commented as bullets zinged in all around them with an increasing and most-sickening regularity.

"Probably headed back to the fire base for more ammo and fuel!" Brody said in an attempt to allay their fears. After the current wave of enemy gunshots seemed to lessen somewhat, he risked rising above the bullet-riddled bark of a long log most of the troopers had been using for cover.

On the other side of the bomb crater, the Viet Cong, supplemented by North Vietnamese Regulars, were holding their own—and keeping the Americans from climbing down the steep, barren walls to the helicopter crash site below. The Americans were doing their best to keep the enemy soldiers away from the valuable cargo as well. It was a stalemate—one that had been tipping slowly in favor of the cavalry after several gunships pounded the enemy positions with rocket and minigun fire for over an hour. But now half the choppers left without explanation.

"See if you can raise someone on the prick," Brody directed his RTO. "Find out for sure."

"For sure?" A shell-shocked enlisted man's lips moved numbly in reply.

"For fucking sure where the hell them birds went and why!" Thinking he was being sarcastic, Brody cast an irritated glance back at the Spec-4, then dropped his eyes upon realizing how demoralized and afraid the man really was.

He concentrated on the ravine below again, eyes scanning the deep gash in the earth from one end to the other. It ran directly through the middle of the bomb crater, though he could not tell if it had been created by recent monsoon rains or the B-52 bomb just happened to drop onto it. That fate dropped the downed helicopter where it did only made matters worse. There was no way he could send a team down to the Huey without risking total annihilation from the enemy RPD nests, and little chance that the trapped flight crew could make a run for it without being gunned down in their tracks. The only hope was air support, and now that seemed to have been cut in half as well.

"Sgt. Brody!" someone called behind him. Treat's hand was out when he turned, expecting to be given the radio, but he found two of the men pointing back up at Fire Base Belinda instead.

His gaze followed theirs.

168

"What the hell?"

He watched a starburst cluster arc out over the distant camp's western perimeter and plummet down to the steep, rocky slopes below.

A black column of smoke was rising from the mountaintop. Billowing wisps of gray gunsmoke clung to the barren slopes between timberline and what Brody recognized to be the camp's lowest perimeter defenses.

"Belinda's under attack!" The gasp left him like a death rattle. He shivered and turned away, refusing to believe it. The two fire support bases were always believed to be impenetrable. Now one seemed to be burning to the ground.

"It's—"

With the others, he watched a dark speck rise from the besieged encampment, ascending rapidly and pursued by a burst of yellow-and-orange tracers. "It's Neil Nazi's Loach. . . ."

They watched the other three helicopters circle Fire Base Belinda once, then drop in for sudden, steep descents at different angles and from opposite sides of the artillery camp. "The slicks are goin' in to extract the Centaurs and whoever's left from Air Cav Command," someone whispered. "Those poor bastards . . . the ones that didn't make it—"

"Shut up," the man beside him hissed at the omen. Words had power in The Nam. You didn't say what you didn't want to happen. You didn't even *think* it.

After less than a minute, the gunships rose from mortared helipads again, one by one, heading up-canyon toward Fire Base Buffy.

As Brody's people watched, two stick grenades came sailing over the bomb crater from the enemy side, and his men—distracted by events unfolding up on Belinda—nearly missed the flying Chi-Coms. Catching their smooth arc out the corner of his eye, Brody called out, "Hit the ground!"

The men dropped against the earth, shielding their faces and upper torsos as best they could. Dual explosions rocked the fallen log, showering everyone with fragments of bark.

"You think they'll blow 'em in place?" a private curled up in the fetal position beside Brody asked the enraged NCO after the debris settled and the deadly waiting game resumed.

"Them? The antiaircraft guns?"

"Yeah!"

The last chopper was rising above the mountain peak's jagged crags now. "Don't look like that's what the colonel had in mind," he muttered finally.

"They're gonna fall back and regroup, right? The colonel'll come up with a plan to save the camp, right, Sarge?" An eager-eyed PFC nearby locked eyes with Brody.

"If I was dumb enough to come up with an answer to that"—Brody was not grinning—"I'd be wearing butter-bars instead of chevrons, chump."

"Oh. . . ."

Brody glanced back at the two peaks rising majestically above the valley floor, but he was staring between the mountaintops, toward a third rocky crag that jutted out from the *Chaine Annamitique*. He had stood atop that peak only five days before—during one of the uneventful patrols through the treacherous gorges shadowing the Nam Sathay River Valley—and he would never forget the feeling of tranquillity he had felt to the core of his soul.

CHAPTER 19

Over LZ Sierra

Colonel Buchanan checked his wristwatch: two hours until the B-52s arrived. He leaned against the Loach's port window, eyes scanning the smoke-laced terrain below. The helicopter crash site and bomb crater were clearly visible, as were the two opposing forces dug in on either side of the steep clay rims, but from this altitude he could not spot Sgt. Zack's squad or the second element of Communists rumored to be sweeping the valley.

"Did you hear that, sir?" his pilot called out against the engine roar above and behind them.

"Neg!" Buchanan shook his head from side to side.

"It's Black Buddha! Says he lost the contingent that downed the second chopper. Says he reached the second chopper, and it's nothing but molten magnesium and piles of ash!"

171

"No survivors?" The color seemed to drain slightly from Buchanan's features.

"That's affirm: *no* survivors! Says the enemy rocket squad just vanished—and right when he thought he had 'em cornered or something!"

Buchanan glanced straight ahead, and his eyes went wide.

"Holy shit!" The pilot's hands and feet went to work, and their tiny light observation helicopter swerved to one side, banking sharply to the right as the white plume of smoke rising rapidly through the skies veered directly for them, changing course as well.

"Can we outrun it?" Buchanan fought to remain calm as the wasplike projectile gained steadily on them.

"Nope." Beads of sweat had instantly broken out on the pilot's forehead. "But we might be able to out*maneuver* the damn thing!"

The Loach zigzagged through the air, rising nearly vertically at one point, then dropping in a sudden descent and swooping down between treetops before gliding to its side between two rows of palms—the surface-to-air rocket closing on its tail. It was now less than fifty yards behind the Loach. "Well, it's been nice knowin' ya, Zeke." Buchanan sounded prepared to die, but "Zeke" was not paying attention.

"Aw, *fuck*!" he grunted, hands instinctively forcing the Loach to roll nearly upside-down as a Huey roared past only a few feet above their upended landing skids. Zeke was not upset about the near miss. He was mad at not having spotted the bigger gunship sooner—and avoiding it. Now it would be nearly impossible to keep the slick out of the gloomy picture.

Too late for regrets: the Deg-4 locked on to the Huey's exhaust and quickly overtook the craft.

Wincing and shutting his eyes against the rising fireball, Buchanan braced for the secondary blast that would roll out from the explosion, possibly blowing their Loach from the sky as well.

The smaller three-seater bucked and bolted, but Zeke was able to keep it under control as the shockwave struck them. Immediately he swung around to check for survivors.

"Well, at least we know the North Viets got their cargo of anti-Huey toys." Buchanan shook his head in resignation.

In ten seconds they were hovering over the latest crash site. The triple canopy burned brightly where its upper layer was in flames, but the leaves and branches were too green for the fire to make much progress before being snuffed out by the heavy humidity. There were few raging infernos in the damp rain forest.

Buchanan's eyes locked on to the bodies of two men who'd been thrown from the falling Huey's hatches. Both door gunners, they hung from the treetops, chests impaled by jagged limbs thick as a dancer's thighs. The sight made him think of Madame Nhu, South Vietnam's so-called Dragon Lady. He heard her infamous words as his mind made mental comparisons: *Dancing with death is sufficient. . . .* Actually, there was no comparison. None whatsoever, yet her words kept ringing in his ears.

"Damn," Zeke muttered as they watched the pilot stagger from the crumpled wreckage fifty feet down below the branches. He was totally engulfed in flames and made it only a few yards before flopping over, already charcoal black from head to toe. "Poor fucker. . . ."

"What about the—"

Buchanan didn't have to ask about the peter pilot. As Zeke brought the Loach around for a frontal view, they spotted the man's head protruding from the Huey's Plexiglas windshield. The top half of his skull was gone.

"No cargo?" Buchanan was referring to a crew. He wanted confirmation there could be no other survivors wandering around down there somewhere before they headed for a safer altitude.

Zeke's eyes focused on the melting tail boom numbers. "Not in *that* ship." He checked his clipboard. "Just gunnies and chopperjocks. Her Blues unassed at first light—are down augmenting Brody's people."

"Right." Buchanan nodded. "Take us up, Zeke. Take me up outta this goddamned hellhole before I fuckin' upchuck on the army-issue upholstery."

"Thanks for the warning, honcho-san."

"Do it. *Now!*"

"Your wish is my command," the ever-sarcastic Zeke replied gratefully.

"The colonel can't be serious." Brody stood nose to nose with Leo Zack after the platoon of American cavalry men pulled away from the bomb crater—back to the depression where they had interrogated the North Vietnamese POW earlier. "I just don't believe it."

"Believe it." Leo nodded firmly.

"But what about us?" Snakeman Fletcher's right shoulder rubbed against Brody's left as the two friends calmly squared off against Black Buddha.

"You two and your pogues get to hold down the fort here." Zack waved a meaty arm out to encompass the smoking battlefield. An occasional tracer still passed by overhead now and then.

"*What* fort?" Brody did not sound optimistic.

"You got a log back there, don't you?" Zack produced an ear-to-ear grin.

174

"What *platoon*?" Fletcher added, referring to their current manpower shortage, but Zack ignored the Snakeman.

The big sergeant had just returned from his attempt at locating the enemy rocket team. He was relaying what Buchanan's pilot had informed his RTO, and Whoremonger was not enjoying what he heard: the colonel wanted a platoon of men to remain in place along the crater's eastern rim, while Leo Zack rounded up every last available "swinging dick" so he could mount a counterassault against Fire Base Belinda's new tenants.

"Even if we *were* able to muster every troop not on casualty status," Fletcher argued, "it still wouldn't be enough to go up against the number o' grunts Charlie fielded today. Did you *see* that swarm o' sappers crawlin' up Belinda's slopes, Leo?"

"Slopes is slopes, ladies." Zack's chest expanded menacingly. "Are youze pussy, or *what*?"

"We ain't stupid, that's for goddamn sure!" Brody replied, though the plan had potential. He was in one of his feeling-immortal moods, too, but that lining of caution kept most of the adrenaline juice from being absorbed into the meat of his gut instincts.

"I'm in!" A private switched from Brody's side to Zack's.

"You're in if I say you're in." Leo did not appear impressed.

"We'll go with you, too, Sarge." Three more privates low-crawled from one side of the depression to the other.

"That's fine." Zack nodded, apparently experiencing a sudden change of heart. "Who else?"

"Christ!" Snakeman wiped beads of perspiration from his upper lip with the back of his hand. "What

175

are we doin' here, pickin' sides for a basketball game, or *what*?''

When it was all over, Brody was left with six men under him, including Elliot. ''Not much of a platoon,'' Elliot observed. ''That's for sure.''

''Barely enough for a *squad*.'' Brody's eyeballs rolled skyward. Would the combat zone challenges never cease? They didn't pay him enough to face these kinds of odds! Seven troopers total, to maintain the status quo at crash site number one, which was definitely numba *ten* on Treat's All-Time Chart of Misfortunes. Zack, on the other hand, had assembled four gunship loads, or just about twenty soldiers.

Wickman stepped forward from Brody's small group. His hand was clamped on Corky Cordova's bicep. ''What about Martinez?'' He directed his question to Leo Zack, who outranked him by three stripes this month. ''We're gonna go looking for him.'' It was a statement of fact, not a request. The Brick did not often make requests.

''What about Styx and Stone?'' asked Cordova.

''And that goofy Crump,'' Big Don added. ''We just gonna let 'em fend for themselves out there?''

''They're on their own,'' Zack affirmed.

''What?'' Cordova's eyes bulged slightly.

''Me and the Cork'll go lookin' for 'em while you guys play games o' mind-fuck with the pogues.'' Wickman released Cordova's arm as if setting loose a mad dog.

''Listen up, Sgt. Wickman.'' Zack turned his back on the two cavalrymen. ''Belinda and Buffy are our first concerns right now. They *are* the mission. Martinez is in good hands. Styx and Stone will look out for him. It still takes more than acorns-for-brains to rate corporal stripes in this man's army, believe it or not.''

"We'll go looking for them," Wickman repeated, and Zack whirled around as a second gunship appeared overhead. "You've got enough men to stuff four birds," the Brick continued undaunted as the two NCOs faced off. "Whoremonger can handle those assholes pussy-footin' around on the other side of the crater over there. Styx and his boys don' know the territory. . . ."

"And you do?" Zack's tone remained calm despite bulging eyes.

"I know it well enough to track 'em down and—"

Leo waved Wickman silent. "I just remembered, Big Don. That goofy Indian, Two-Step, is with 'em. They'll be okay. . . ." His use of the name "Big Don" quickly brought down the Brick's defenses. The fight-or-flee surge of adrenaline was no longer pounding at the inner walls of his gut, trying to get out in the form of a thrown fist. Zack further ruined the moment by changing his mind on the spot. "Shit, go ahead, Sergeant," he said. "Do what you think you gotta do to prove your manhood and maintain the Big Don legend. Just watch your lily white ass, brother."

"I think you oughta split those two up," Brody challenged as he grinned at Cordova and the buck sergeant. "Leave Corky here with us—I could use a good machine gunner."

"You've got plenty of firepower as it is." Wickman turned to leave. "We'll be on our way. . . ."

"But Sarge—" Brody called after him with false affection.

"Aw, eat it like a man," Leo responded to Whoremonger's complaint.

"Someday I'm gonna ask him just what the hell he means by that." Brody turned to Fletcher as they prepared to return to the bomb crater's rim to check on the three men holding a vigil there.

"Sounds like faggot talk to me," Snakeman said loudly.

Zack's shadow fell over him. "Would you believe I'm referring to ham-and-motherfuckers, asshole?"

Feigning a meekness that wasn't there, Fletcher nodded and, in mock terror, hurried to catch up with Brody as the first helicopter flared into a hover beyond the tree line. Zack let out a bellow of a laugh as another burst of tracers flew past, missing the top of Snakeman's head by less than a foot and passing through the open chopper hatch without hitting either of the ship's door gunners. "You two don' need three extra men to hold down the fort." His words were cast after Fletcher with respect and a renewed sense of admiration. "Send 'em over to that Huey!"

"Nothin' doin', Leo!" Brody did not look back. "You gave me four men to do the job, and it's gonna take every last one of them—to hold . . . down . . . this . . . fort!"

Zack did not take time to fire off another reply. He was too busy waving his people toward the hot LZ.

Fire Base Belinda

Kim finished tying the pressure knots on her leg bandage before allowing herself a rare luxury: surveying the spoils of war. Coils of concertina wire, streaked with blood, encircled the artillery base. Already her people were scrambling about the defensive trenches, executing the last of the wounded GIs. Her eyes scanned the AA-gun pits—a few men were looting the American bodies of valuables and equipment. She memorized faces. They would be duly searched and face disciplinary action later. Finishing off the casualties was allowed, but Minh had given specific orders there would be no corpse-robbing. The GIs were fast learning from the VC about booby-trapping themselves while they took their last breaths.

A dull explosion broke the tense calmness. Kim recognized the blast of a U.S.-made M-26 fragmentation grenade as she dropped into a low squat. Her ears listened to the screams of one of her own men—briefly, from the corner of one eye, saw him dashing past, staggering, blood spurting from the stumps where both his arms had been severed at the elbows. She turned her back on the sapper as two comrades ran him down in an attempt to apply first-aid. "Fool," she muttered in English.

Kim's eyes shifted to the haphazard collage of AA-gun barrels rising up behind her through low clouds of gunsmoke. The VC cell leader had never seen such magnificent weapons up close before. She had been on the receiving end of several in the past. American grunts loved to lower the barrels downslope and fire at anything that moved in the mist-enshrouded valleys below—they rarely had enemy aircraft to aim at. Memories of the guns' devastating firepower sent a shiver through her, and she turned to a nearby insurgent. "Find someone who can operate them." Her chin motioned toward the twin fifty-caliber weapons as she spoke in low-key Vietnamese this time. "I want them manned now. Major Minh will be here any minute."

She surveyed the steep slopes dropping away on the mountainside below. Several thousand feet down, she could see helicopters circling a break in the jungle canopy along the valley floor. "They will be coming soon," she told the woman standing at her side as she withdrew the banana clip from her AK-47 and began filling it with ammunition.

179

"The GIs?" An odd mixture of fear and excitement seemed to dance in the female guerrilla's jet-black eyes as she watched the columns of NVA infantrymen climbing through the rocks now.

"Yes." Kim's hips shifted slightly as her stance became a defiant one. "They won't give up this flattop without a fight."

"But they fled in their helicopters." The other woman found it hard to understand the Americans' tactics.

This surprised Kim, and she stared down at the older Viet Cong, irritated by the remark. "Again, the longnoses learn from we VC," she said. "When outnumbered, they flee. They regroup. They return."

"In the night?"

"Perhaps. But maybe sooner. We should be prepared for a counterassault within the next few hours. They do not like to work their gunships after dark."

"But they have been known to. Often."

"I feel today it will be different. They will not want us to become too comfortable on what they fancy their property. Their commander . . ."

"Buchanan."

"Yes. He is a stubborn one. He will be trouble."

"What about Major Minh?"

Kim's lips pursed in mild annoyance again. "The major has a personal grudge against Buchanan. He has assigned his junior officers the task of taking this mountaintop"—she nodded toward three NVA captains giving directives nearby—"while he spends all day on the valley floor, trying to capture a chopper that will never see airmobile days again."

"One of his men told me the Huey carries a cargo of new weapons aboard. Rifles that shoot grenades as well. It would be a fine prize. . . ."

180

"And they claim to be meeting a caravan from the Trail, loaded down with Soviet-made or Chinese-block rockets that can be fired from the shoulder. Such important missions for such a small contingent."

"But you yourself saw the two Hueys downed by rocket fire. Those were not RPG-sevens, sister. Can you explain to one as ignorant as I what—"

Kim interrupted the woman even though there was no disrespect or sarcasm in her tone. "It was a U.S.-made LAW. Nothing more."

"One of the Americans' antitank weapons?"

"Yes."

"But it followed after the helicopters. It *chased* them, sister. You *saw* that with your own eyes. A LAW follows the straight path."

"You think too much for a woman with little rank." Kim lifted her nose slightly, upset she had no better explanations to give. "Hanoi would not honor Lam Van Minh with a mission so important and vital as—"

"You believe—"

"I believe Hanoi is tiring of the major's failures south of the DMZ. *My* contacts advise me it is possible Hanoi is planning to eliminate Lam Van Minh."

Binoculars to her eyes now, the older woman scanned the perimeter for signs of movement among the many enemy bodies, then said, "You are wrong. And you should not talk this way, sister. Not even to me, though I assure you I will keep your views secret."

"See that you do," Kim said firmly. "Now go and deploy the men along the perimeter." She motioned toward several privates who had started toward their designated trenches only to gather around the bodies of three Americans. One of the guerrillas was going through a corpse's pockets and rucksack, while another was running his fingers back and forth through the hair on one GI's forearm. "They are beginning to loiter and—"

"Your injury. How is it?"

"It will not prevent me from carrying out my duty." Kim eyed the woman suspiciously.

"And just what exactly is our . . . *duty* here today, sister?"

Kim hesitated before answering. Bringing the binoculars back up to her eyes, she spent a good half minute scanning the slopes of Fire Base Buffy, up-valley, before saying, "To secure and hold this camp. At all costs."

"The GIs will surely return. They will bring many reinforcements. I am surprised they have not already pounded their own compound with artillery from the other base up there." She pointed at Buffy. "We will suffer many casualties. We should destroy the quad-fifties, then run."

"With *that* one"—Kim's rigid forefinger rose toward an AA truck near the center of camp—"we control this entire string of mountains. We retake control of the *Chaine Annamitique* from the Americans. They will have to pay a very high price just to recapture a single hilltop."

"I fear this hilltop will become a graveyard for our people, sister."

"Go and deploy the men, as I instructed." Kim turned her back on the woman, instantly regretting it. But she did not whirl back around when the sudden, instinctive warning surged through her gut. And the older woman made no hostile moves against her.

CHAPTER 20

Nam Sathay River Valley

Big Don Wickman's gunhand rose in the murky gloom. Fingers motioning Cordova up to his position, the stocky NCO remained a shadow amidst the towering trees.

As soon as Corky reached Wickman's place of concealment, Big Don was gone again, moving forward through the creeping mist, one eye scanning the overgrown trail for tracks—the other watching the silent but ever-hostile rain forest up ahead. Void Vicious had a bad habit of lunging when you least expected her to.

It was still midday. High above the triple canopy overhead, the merciless tropical sun beat down on a tangled latticework of vines and branches two and three layers thick. But here, below the fronds and ferns and mosslike vines, it remained dark and damp. An odd twilight in a surrealistic stretch of jungle. Corky Cordova found it unnerving. Big Don, who had served in

Panama and the Dominican Republic before the wilds of Southeast Asia, loved it. Ate it up with a passion. There was only one thing he enjoyed more than hiking through the woods . . . and that was hunting other warriors through the woods. The dog tags around his neck did not contain the usual name, service number, blood type, and religion. Those could be found tied to his bootlaces. The set around his neck were customized tabs he'd had made in Pleiku City. *There is no hunting like the hunting of men*, read his favorite Hemingway quote. *And those who have hunted armed men long enough, and liked it, never care for anything else thereafter.* . . .

The Brick's eyes locked on to the telltale heel mark again: three horizontal gashes below a crude arrow. Two-Step's jungle boots. Wickman glanced back over a shoulder. *This way!* His eyes winked at a hesitant Cordova. Corky was obviously nervous in the service—an affliction that could prove fatal under the wrong circumstances. The wary soldier examined every set of tracks, though he could not easily distinguish them and wouldn't be able to tell you there were four distinct groups present—as Wickman noted on first glance.

The men of Echo Company played a peculiar game, though it was a deadly serious game indeed. They spent their idle hours carving sometimes intricate "brands" in the rubber soles of their boots so that they could be identified by friends, who for some reason or other, had to follow them or were trying to locate them. Twice a week, after constant humping through the sticks wore many of the soles down slightly, the brands were deepened again, and information as to the shape and reasoning behind each was exchanged with other members of the group. Broken Arrow always chose three horizontal gashes below a crude arrowhead.

At a bend in the trail, Sgt. Wickman waved Cordova up again, and both men paused as the sound of movement in the distance reached their ears. Big Don pointed down at another shuffle of footprints in the red dust under their boots.

Constantly scanning the trail up ahead, Cordova nodded with a grin as he finally recognized the second set of prints. They looked like narrow bare feet. A woman's set, perhaps. Slender, but curved in the center, as if the woman were bow-legged. The second set of prints was heading in the opposite direction from the group Wickman identified as Broken Arrow's. Yet Big Don and Corky knew they were actually made by someone walking alongside or behind Two-Step.

"Corporal Styx?"

"Yep." Wickman nodded.

"That goofy fucker."

Big Don nodded again.

Corporal Styx had had a cast of bow-legged old mama-san's feet made up last time he was in Quang Ngai City. The footprints were then molded onto the bottoms of his jungle boots, but backward: female toes where his heels should have been. That way, Styx reasoned, the only tracks he would leave in the woods would be those of a woman. Walking the other way. Any Cong trying to track him would ignore the footprints, fooled into thinking they belonged to some old, bent-over mama-san trudging back to her nowhere-ville.

"You think that's them up ahead?" Cordova moved back into the hollow of a lightning-charred tree trunk as Wickman's grin faded and he shook his head from side to side: the noise was fast approaching their location.

Heart pounding, Cordova watched Big Don's M-16 slowly rise to his shoulder. The noise was close, now—

185

very close. And something was rushing toward them down the trail. It—or they— was making an awful lot of racket. Charlie would never break so many rules of silence.

Silently imitating Wickman, he brought his rifle up, too, remembering suddenly that Big Don usually carried a Hog-60 but was without it this mission. Cordova wished they *both* had the heavy machine guns.

And then the hip-high forest furies charged past: wild boars.

"Damn," Wickman muttered, pulling up on his aim just as he was about to shoot.

"Little monsters." Corky Cordova dropped back against his tree trunk, rifle muzzle in the air, as a mother hog trotted past. It was followed by a troop of nine or ten hungry little baby hogs chasing after her. The adult was gnashing at the bushes and vines with her long tusks as if irritated by the mischievous and energetic piglets she was unable to lose in the maze of interlocking trails.

A full two minutes passed before the jungle again fell silent. Wickman used the time to confer with Cordova in low whispers. "Styx and Stoner." He pointed down at the four sets of prints.

"And Broken Arrow?"

Big Don nodded in the affirmative. His fingers broke the ridges of a new set of jungle boot treads. "Panama sole design," he mused. "Martinez." But his brows came together in annoyed contemplation. "Where would a newby get Panama-issued jungle boots?"

"Maybe he served in Central America before coming here, Sarge."

"And still carry mosquito wings for rank? No such shit, Corky."

"What about Crump the Third?" he asked, referring

186

to Abdul Mohammed. "Any sign o' that apprentice Black Panther?"

"None." And Big Don had been searching for some. An odd, perplexed look coated his features as he checked, rechecked, and triple-checked where different sets of prints covered others, but he could find nothing comforting.

"None?"

"None whatsoever." He was talking more to himself now.

"Any signs of the women they went after?" Cordova answered.

The NCO's head shifted from side to side this time as he carefully inspected the trail's edges. "But I can smell 'em."

"The women?" Cordova's eyes lit up.

Wickman nodded again.

"We could spend all fucking day following these tracks and never catch up to them."

"Agreed." Wickman's thumb flipped his rifle's safety back on noiselessly. "But there's little else we can do. I wanna find those clowns before Arc-Light arrives."

"Ain't that the ever-lovin' truth!"

"If I know Styx and Stone, they forgot all about an upcomin' and inevita-fuckin'ble bombing run."

" 'All else aside in the pursuit o' pussy.' "

"Somethin' like that. I don't really give a rat's puckered ass about Stone and his sidekick. But Martinez don't deserve to die because of their antics, amigo. And Two-Step's too valuable a trooper. I can't just leave his fate in the hands of those two jokers."

"Rejects from some REMF battalion." Corky sighed.

"It never fails."

187

"Then let's get it over with, Brick. I'll lead for a while."

"Forget it." Wickman started down the trail, but Cordova grabbed his wrist.

"No. Really! You've been blazin' trails since we started, two dozen tripwires ago. It ain't fair. I'll take my turn, Sarge."

Grinning again, Wickman ignored the offer. "I wanna *survive* this Lurp, Corkasaurus," he said, jerking his arm away. And then he was gone.

Cordova had to hump hard to catch up with the cavalry sergeant.

They found them fifteen minutes later, trying as gently as possible to bring Chance Broken Arrow down from his bloody crucifix.

"You worthless pogues don't put out no fucking sentry?" Wickman's powerful voice boomed out at them suddenly, and Martinez whirled—M-16 slung over one shoulder and riding his hip. He fumbled with the pistol grip for a full three seconds before realizing the words had been spoken in English.

And they had belonged to Big Don Wickman.

"*Jesus*, Sarge!" Corporal Stone glanced back over his shoulder, eyes wide. "Scare the shit out of us next time, will ya?"

Wickman's eyes focused on the crossbow shaft protruding from the groaning Indian's palms. "Better than some Charlie Cong sneakin' up on your no-account asses," he muttered as Cordova, rifle still poised for some gunplay and gut spilling, emerged from the tree line and followed him into the clearing.

"Greetings and salut*asians*." Styx locked cold eyes with Corky as he jerked one of the arrows from Two-

Step's hand. The Indian's right arm and upper torso flopped down over Styx's shoulder as Stone continued to work on the other hand, to no avail—the mahogany tree trunk was protesting stubbornly, though silently.

"What happened to my Comanche?" Wickman's voice was lowered now, but he sounded twice as angry as he moved leopardlike through the sharp reeds.

"Charlie got him, Sarge. . . ." Stone pulled and twisted on the arrow's shaft, but hard as he tried, the bolt refused to pry free of the tree trunk.

"Did *I* give you fucking permission to die, Two-Step?" Big Don was abreast of the body drooping over Styx's back now. He grabbed Chance's chin and lifted the blood-drained face. "*Did* I, brother?"

"He's still alive, Brick," Styx muttered. "We saved him for you . . . knew you'd wanna kill him *personally*."

Styx and Stone exchanged worried glances. Big Don Wickman ignored them both, directing all his attention to the Indian. "Did *I* give you fucking permission to *screw up*, Two-Step?" He nudged the Comanche's cheek roughly with bruised and battered knuckles. "Huh? Did I?"

But Broken Arrow was not responding. He was out of it. Totally.

"He's unconscious, Sarge." Marty's words emerged as a cautious whisper.

Wickman glanced over at the private, fire in his eyes. "I fucking know that, *pogue*!" His hand shot out without warning. The palm struck Martinez in the chest, knocking him backward and off his feet.

Both Styx and Stone gasped silently at the sudden movement, and then slow-motion reality set in again as Big Don resumed talking to his old buddy. "Tell me who did this to you, Two-Step. Give the Brick some message, man. Speak to me from fuckin' never-never land, skate. Was it the bitch? The bitch who wore black?''

Stone resumed tugging at the aluminum shaft holding one of Chance's hands to the tree trunk, and, irritation flaring, Wickman reached up, brushed the corporal aside, and ripped the arrow shaft out of the tree trunk, freeing Chance's hand with a sickening, gushing noise.

Stone's eyes dropped to Two-Step's bloody hand. ''Jesus, Sarge,'' he whispered, his tone telling the NCO he felt Big Don had treated the Indian's body irreverently.

''Fuck it.'' Wickman pounded the crossbow arrow over with his fist. ''Two-Step didn't feel nothin', man. Two-Step's up in the clouds on a pain and adrenaline-induced peyote high.''

''But—'' A weak protest started to leave Stone's lips, and Wickman waved him silent.

''Tell me who did this to you, Two-Step.'' Big Don dropped to one knee beside the Indian's trembling frame as Styx laid it on the plush carpet of elephant grass and mushrooms. ''Give the Brick a sign. Which way did the cunt go, brother?''

''He can't tell you, Sgt. Wickman.'' Styx backed away a safe and respectable distance. ''The Comanche's out of it for now, wanderin' through limbo . . . checking the price of real estate in the Happy Hunting Grounds.''

Seeming to ignore him, Wickman reached down and took hold of a small leather pouch hanging from Broken Arrow's dog tags chain. He knew it was the Comanche's good luck charm—his medicine man's bag o' tricks and magic, Chance had called it.

190

"I thought you said he wasn't that badly hurt," Stone said.

"Shut up, Stoner," Styx and Martinez both replied.

"The broad didn't do this to him," Wickman decided. "She would have taken this pouch. And she would have cut his head off instead of just toying with his ying-yang." He glanced beyond the hilltop clearing.

"And *I* think you've gone over the edge on us, Big Don," Styx remarked with a jab. "I think you've gone *dinky-dau* native on us, man."

"Fuck you!" Wickman rose, and, in rising, broke the leather pouch free of the dog tags chain. He slipped Two-Step's medicine man's bag into a breast pocket, eyes shifting to Martinez, who was still sitting in the sticky pool of blood that had formed at the foot of the massive oak tree. "What can you tell me about this clusterfuck, Marty?" His tone became suddenly friendly as his hand waved to take in the entire clearing.

"The broads did it, Sarge." Martinez's words became a rapid-fire torrent of relief as his theories exploded forth. "The bitches cut up Two-Step! They left him his head because they knew it would blow our minds, man!"

"Yeah, these aren't your typical breed o' gooks, Sarge! These people are monsters! They did Two-Step *bad*, man!"

"Crump." Wickman's eyes rose to lock on Corporal Styx's. "What about Jivedude?"

"They got him back on the trail," Stone answered when Styx remained silent. "Zapped him real royally."

"How?" Wiping blood from his palms onto his trousers, Wickman pulled a thin green towel from the bottom of his ruck and draped it over Broken Arrow's bulging eyes.

"A spear, man." Styx spoke now.

"Spear?" Wickman did not look up this time.

"The broads chucked a goddamn spear into the jive fucker's throat, man. You should have seen it. I wish I hadn't pawned my Polaroid back in Pleiku City last month."

Wickman lunged.

Stone tried hard to intervene, but the Brick brushed him aside like some weightlifter elbowing the paper boy. Grabbing Styx by the front of his shirt, Big Don lifted him into the air and slammed his back against the blood-streaked tree where Two-Step had been hanging only moments earlier. "Crump was one of us," he hissed.

"Don't you mean *Abdul*, Sarge?" Styx grinned down at the NCO, unimpressed by the show of force and obviously caring little about what Big Don did to him. "Don't you mean Abdul *Elijah Mohammed*—the troublemaker?"

Quick to realize cheap theatrics would be a waste of time on this battle-hardened warrior, Wickman let him drop back to the ground. He turned his back on Styx, muttering, "Crump was one of us. Don't forget it. I'm green. You're green. Crump was green. Olive drab, dammit. There's no black and white in this fucking war, you got that? Now which way did the cunts go?" He did not give Styx a chance to respond. He did not cast a wary glance back at the corporal, and Styx made no attempt to counterattack. "We'll come back for Two-Step's body later."

"The only way out of this clearing is that trail." Stone pointed at a break in the bushes they'd all used to get to Broken Arrow and the oak tree. "But there's no sign of her entering or leaving. No footprints. No nothin'. We already checked."

"There's always something."

"I just told you: we already checked. The bitch is a phantom. A rain forest ghost, Sarge."

"He's right." Cordova spoke up for the first time, getting a strange inner feeling as he watched Sgt. Wickman walk along the clearing's edge, checking for broken vines and upturned leaves. "He's right about the bitch."

Big Don did not pause in his search. He did not look up but said, "What's on your mind, Corky? Spit it out, bud."

"She's the same one Two-Step killed back at LZ Bird, Sarge."

"Say again?" Wickman cocked an eyebrow skeptically at the trooper. "The one he says he blasted in the boobs with his crossbow?"

"Same-same."

"What makes you think so?" Wickman paused beside a broken wait-a-minute vine that was oozing sap down onto an upturned leaf.

"Just a feeling I got. A feeling in my gut. It's the same smell on the air, man. . . ."

"All *I* smell on the air is burned flesh." Wickman glanced at the protruding outline of a nose in the sweat towel covering Broken Arrow's face.

"I used to think he made up the whole story." Cordova was obviously speaking to Wickman alone. Wickman and the Indian, it seemed. "About blasting her in the boobs with his crossbow . . . you know, knocking her out over that cliff, down into the raging river below and all that—yet we never found a trace. Nothing at all. No blood trail. No bits o' flesh or bone. Jackshit."

"Sgt. Brody and the Blues sweep *did* find some blood," Big Don reminded him.

"Shit, Sarge. . . ." Cordova's laugh was hollow.

"They found blood *all over* that plateau. Dong Tre was truly a beast, remember?"

The Brick's reply was that of an old soldier, tired of the chase. "She went this way," he gave in. "There were two of them. Headed toward Fire Base Belinda."

"Aw, man . . ." Styx was shaking his head from side to side. "I'm too short for this shit."

"As short as your pecker?" Cordova elbowed the corporal hard but playfully.

"There's something else we gotta tell you about, Sarge." Martinez was not holding a grudge about being pushed, it appeared.

"I don't wanna hear it." Wickman started through the trees, grim-faced.

"You *gotta* hear it," Marty said. "The Cong are usin' chemical warfare on us, man! Some kinda poison gas!"

Big Don glanced back at the private. "Are you a ghost, too, Marty? Did this poison gas zap you into never-never land, only to have you come back to haunt ol' Sgt. Don?"

"But—" Stone joined in. Styx waved them both silent.

"Fuck it," he said. "Don' mean nothin'. Tryin' to figure it out only gonna warp your brains, boys. . . ." He tested the seal on his rifle's ammo magazine, then fell in behind the Brick and disappeared into the swirling silver mist.

"This sucks the big one." Stone turned to face Cordova and Martinez before joining the patrol.

"Don't it truly." Corky removed the twenty-round mag from his M-16 and replaced it with a special thirty-bullet banana clip filled with multicolored tracers, which he kept in reserve at the bottom of his ruck for "special occasions." "Let the floor show begin." Cordova stormed between the two. ''Gonna play some Colt rock and roll.'' He fingered the rifle's fire selector, moving it from safe to full auto. ''Gonna make some dames dance with death tonight. . . .''

CHAPTER 21

LZ Sierra

Snakeman Fletcher hated last-minute changes, unplanned events—even in The Nam. And the last one had truly increased his pucker factor tenfold. Leo Zack and his four gunshipsful of cavalry troopers hadn't been airmobile from LZ Sierra ten minutes when *Pegasus* suddenly returned. Snakeman and Brody had both low-crawled from the crash site's eastern rim to the depression where the North Vietnamese POW was questioned earlier. Zack did not bother jumping out of the gunship's hatch. "I need Snakeoil on board!" Elliot could still hear the big NCO's fateful words ringing in his ears over the rotors' angry flapping.

He and Brody had watched a blood-caked newby's lifeless body flop into the elephant grass beside *Peg's* landing skids. "But I need every last swingin' dick right here, Leo!" Treat had countered without anger. There was desperation in his eyes instead.

"The rifle fire hasn't increased much," Fletcher had told Zack, "but the zips are up to something, Sarge! We've noticed a growin' head count in hostiles gatherin' on the other side of the bomb crater."

"You'll be fine!" Leo the Lionhearted had not appeared impressed with their escalating dilemma. "My pogue gunny"—he had pointed down at the unmoving corpse beside the skids—"done got himself blasted beyond Bien Hoa before we were even halfway back to Belinda. The rest of these FNG's don't know their port from their starboard or their aft from their assholes!"

"We sympathize with ya, Leo, but—"

"I need a gunny who knows his shit!" Zack's tone was not a compromising one. "I need a fuckwad like Fletch there!"

"But Sarge—"

"Now get yo' ass *on board,* slick!"

And after a helpless exchange of nods with Whoremonger, Eliot had complied.

"Well, fuck me till it hurts," Brody had muttered as Snakeman handed him two M-16 ammo bandoliers, then turned and sprinted toward *Pegasus,* fleet of foot and light-headed.

"Sorry, Trick or Treat, but we'll be back to get ya soon as we save Belinda from the dinks!"

"Watch your worthless, no-account ass, Snakeshit!"

"Roger-wilco!" Fletcher had also responded with a good-natured obscene gesture.

He stared down at the green blanket of treetops racing by below as *Pegasus* lima-lima'd up-valley toward Belinda. Fletch was unable to shake the terrible feeling of foreboding closing in on him—darkening his world and his outlook and his attitude despite the pleasant and almost blinding shafts of sunlight bursting through the hatch. It wasn't often he and Treat Brody were separated. And he didn't like it. They worked well together as a team. Apart, he felt suddenly vulnerable and alone. It didn't matter that Zack crouched directly behind him, trying to psych up the five pogues seated back to back in the middle of the troop cabin. This run definitely had the feel of a Romeo-foxtrot: a mission doomed from the start.

Fire Base Belinda

An odd vision danced before Kim's eyes as she exchanged rifle fire with the air cavalrymen circling the encampment in their roaring gunships. She saw Broken Arrow's face just as she had aimed the crossbow.

The Comanche had remained in a daze their entire "discussion," and she had been disappointed. She had watched the American's eyes roll up into their sockets—but without fanfare . . . without an emotional scene. No helpless gasp—no heaving chest. It was as if he'd simply resigned himself to his fate . . . accepted the pain he was to endure.

Kim bit softly into her lower lip as she remembered viciously slapping Two-Step, trying to bring him around . . . trying to make him participate . . . to *feel*. But the Indian had regressed . . . retreated into his own mind.

Mind over matter. . . .

That Two-Step had not outwardly appreciated her technique angered the Viet Cong guerrilla more. "I should have chopped his damn head off," she muttered as another gunship cruised past several hundred yards out—level with the perimeter line, but far from the mountainside itself. "I should have remembered to keep the leather charm pouch, too." She thought of the medicine man's pouch now. "It contained his power." Kim was a superstitious sapper.

A burst of machine gun rounds danced along the bank of sandbags in front of her, and Kim responded by spraying an entire magazine after the Huey. But it was swooping down too low and fast.

She watched the three or four tracers fan left, struggling to catch up with the craft, but to no avail. *Pegasus* was suddenly gone, and the glowing green rounds were arcing out into space, plummeting toward the steep crags below.

Another helicopter appeared before her eyes, replacing the first as it circled around the fire base flattop, port door gunner spraying the Viet Cong intruders with relentless streams of hot lead. Kim watched black-pajama-clad bodies dropping left and right. Some were blown clear out across the concertina. She watched a few fly backward through the air after dual air-to-ground rockets left a chopper pod, arms and legs flailing wildly, before vanishing from view beyond the marauding walls of gunsmoke.

Another Huey crisscrossed the first ship's path, and both door gunners' front sights seemed to be centered on *her*! The MG blasts were just too much—Kim dropped against the ground behind her pile of sandbags as broken rocks and chips of lead created a firestorm all around.

After the choppers had passed, she found there were tears in her eyes. She was trembling violently, and numerous minute puncture wounds covered her arms and legs. The wound on her calf had reopened as well, and her ankle and sandal below it were drenched in bright crimson as wide shards of sunlight suddenly dropped across her position through a break in the cloud cover, illuminating her dilemma.

"Are you all right, sister?" The older female cadre was beside her somehow, firing a Soviet-made SKS at one of the Hueys as it banked hard to the left without warning, passing directly over them.

Kim did not answer as both women dropped onto their backs, firing straight up. Forty-odd rifle rounds sliced through the muggy air, mere inches behind the craft's tail rotor.

As if its tail boom had been grabbed by a giant, invisible hand, the Huey was whirled around now, dropping several dozen meters with a gut-wrenching suddenness—but the gunnies remained braced behind their M-60s, their faces detached and calm, as the Huey's landing skids came down nearly on top of them.

"They are landing!" the woman beside Kim screamed as she struggled to reload her weapon. Hands numbed with excitement, she was having trouble feeding the fresh magazine into the rifle. "They are going to *land . . . right . . . ON . . . US*!"

"No!" Kim yelled back even as she rolled away, beyond the protective wall of sandbags. "They are only trying to—"

Bluff. She had wanted to say *bluff you, girl!* But then the Huey—its walls bloated, insectlike, under the pressure of sudden descent—was bouncing through the dust, landing skids crushing the woman with the SKS.

"You die, *du ma*!" Kim screamed as she rose to one knee and brought her own rifle butt back against a shoulder. She fired off a five-round burst—watched two tracers pass through the port cabin hatch and out the starboard one—then rolled in the opposite direction as one of the ship's door gunners leaned into his Hog-60.

She seemed to remember the face as dust and gunsmoke blurred her vision, but then the chopper was whirling around again—turning in a wild and complete, nearly 360-degree flare as the pilot spotted a squad of rifle-toting insurgents rushing toward his ship. The last thing Kim saw was a dark-skinned American crouched in the chopper hatch behind the gunny, reaching down, latching on to her comrade's leg . . . jerking hard, losing his grip, grabbing again—this time with both hands . . . ripping so hard the woman's black, billowing pantaloons tore free, leaving her kicking at the air. The medic grabbed her again, latching on to an ankle, hoisting the woman halfway off the ground as the gunship rose out of the dust funnel, rotors flapping, the woman screaming as blood poured from her chest wounds . . . screaming for Kim to help her.

The big bullets chased Kim across the trench line as she rolled like a circus tumbler through rings of fire—and then she was dropping down through a rain poncho used for shade, dropping into one of the gun pits, dropping onto her head and into the lap of a dead American artilleryman.

Her ears filled with the roar of rotors pulling pitch as she stared into the unseeing eyes of four corpses sitting in the gun pit with her, their backs to the earthen wall, entry holes in their foreheads where VC sniper rounds had found their mark. But then the Huey was floating overhead again—haphazard reality rolling back in place atop the nightmarish fragments—the woman dangling beneath the landing skids by one leg as a soldier behind the door gunner held on to her twisted ankle.

The Huey's whirling blades filled her eyes with more dust, and Kim swallowed her fear, rolling back from sight, out of view . . . rolling between two of the dead men . . . grabbing their rigid arms . . . pulling their bodies down onto her as the prowling gunship passed low across the gun pits, searching. . . .

"I lost her!"

"You *missed* her, Snakeman!"

"Bullshit!"

"Admit it, Skate: you're just gettin' rusty in your old age, papa-san!"

"My ass!"

Snakeman. She remembered the face now. The one they called Fletch. The ugly one. The one with the disgusting habit of carrying a helmet full of scaled and squirming, tangled serpents tied upside-down to his web belt. *The Snakeman.* Another one she thought she had killed.

"In the pit, man!" Their voices drifted down to her as the gunship hovered beside one of the quad-50s, its flapping rotors lower even than the gun's dual barrels.

"Naw, man!" another crew member was yelling in competition with the downblast and turbine whine. "Nothin' but KIAs down there, bro! *Sorry!*"

"My ass! I'm gonna unload on that gun pit, goddammit!" A short burst of rounds struck the wall of sandbags rising up above Kim's unmoving head. "I'm gonna clean it out!"

"Aw, have some respect for the dead, Snakeman— them's 'mericans down there, troop!" The voice of the one they called Doc Delgado—yelling over the screams of the dying woman hanging upside-down below him. "Help me drag this VC bitch up through the hatch, asshole! I'm losing my fuckin' *grip*!"

"Shit, Doc, let the cunt *drop*!"

But as if the pilot had ben monitoring the entire argument, *Pegasus* jerked away from the fire base now, and the woman dangling beneath the port landing skid, still alive and screaming, arms and legs flailing helplessly, fell to the mine field below.

Two more gunships quickly took its place and began strafing the Viet Cong positions only twenty feet away.

Kim took a moment to compose herself. Chest heaving, heart pounding, she concentrated on catching her breath and, for the first time, smelled the odor all around her. It was the stench of death—corpses baking in the hundred-and-thirty-degree heat. Bloating already. Swelling up. The whites turning black or blue—the Negroes paling to a ghostly hue. And all of them leering at her, it seemed—flashing their teeth. Laughing in grotesque silence at her predicament.

She attempted to hold her breath, felt her temples throbbing, ready to explode, and tried taking smaller and smaller breaths instead—but the foul odor had become overpowering as her mind went to work on her, exploiting the surroundings, forcing the dead flesh in on her.

Another gunship passed above, low overhead, and she felt the ground shake and shudder under the fury of three, four, then five rockets slamming against the earth.

The sandbags were even jumping up and down now, reinforcing the reality of it all, but Kim continued to scream. She beat at the dead faces with her little fists— brought up her knee many times, too, as best she could. But the ground only continued to dip and sway, popping up and down, back and forth, with the rolling concussions.

Screaming, Kim struck out at the dead man, fists and feet, but most of the corpses outweighed her by a good seventy or eighty pounds. With an almost superhuman effort, the VC guerilla finally clawed her way up out of the dark, suffocating pit.

CHAPTER 22

LZ Sierra

Brody the Whoremonger threw a banana clip to the private on his right, then rolled closer to the one on his left. His ears picked up the telltale *click*! of a magazine locked properly into the rifle's feeder well. He waited for the sound of the first private's palm slapping against the mag's bottom, testing the seal for a tight fit, before asking the second private, "What's your name, soldier?"

"Pasco, Sarge!" Nearly a dozen VC bullets slammed into the log shielding them, as if to accent the reply with hot lead. All three soldiers ducked slightly.

Using one hand, pistol fashion, Brody lifted his rifle above the top layer of bark and fired off a ten-round response without aiming. The M-16 muzzle fanned left to right. Additional screams on the far side of the bomb crater were the reply. A satisfied half grin across his feature, Treat then asked, "Where ya from?"

The look in Pasco's eyes reflected mild annoyance at all the questions. "Detroit!"

"Detroit?" Brody unleashed the remaining ten rounds and switched to a thirty-round magazine with blinding speed.

"Do I stutter?" Pasco did not seem worried about respect mandated one's NCO. Apparently he didn't think rank was important since it appeared doubtful they were going to survive this mission anyway.

"*Mo*-town?" Brody imitated Abdul Mohammed's best jive accent.

Pasco nodded with a deep frown. Irritation laced the lines along the edges of his eyes.

"But you're a white boy!" Brody stared at the slender eighteen-year-old's protruding jaw, clean-shaven cheeks, and overabundance of freckles.

Pasco pulled a grenade from his canvas ruck suspenders and, eyes locked on to Brody's now, viciously jerked the pin free. "We got *white* folks makin' a living in *Dee*troit, too, you know!" When the cavalry sergeant did not flinch or even swallow hard, Pasco heaved the frag out over the bomb crater.

Brody's head rose slightly above their log, eyes scanning the kill zone to make sure the M-26 didn't drop into the bomb crater, wounding the Americans taking cover at the helicopter crash site below. The grenade sailed past the opposite rim with room to spare. He watched several of the enemy scatter from cover as the frag bounced among them and quickly brought up his rifle in an attempt to finish them off. But before he could get off even a few rounds, North Vietnamese Regulars positioned within the Viet Cong's ranks were triangulating a devastating SKS response from three different positions. "Shee-*it*!" He dropped down beside Pasco. In the same gasping breath: "Nothin' personal''—he grinned—''but I just thought *soul singers* like Diana Ross or Bobby Vinton came from Detroit.''

''Bobby Vinton's a white boy, Sarge.''

''Naw . . .'' Brody fixed a you're-shittin'-me look on the private.

''They call him the Polish Prince.''

''Well, son-of-a . . .'' But Treat's words trailed off as his grin grew.

Pasco gauged the odd seriousness in the sergeant's narrowed eyes. Dark rings dipped below them like shaded crescent moons. He looked like walking death, the private decided—like he'd been hunting men in these jungles since the war started. ''My pop and his pop and *his pop* before him been workin' in the auto factories since before I can remember.''

''Ahhh.'' Brody nodded as if he had completely forgotten that Detroit was the car capital of the country. ''Right. Ford or—''

''General Motors.'' Pasco cast him a reprimanding glare, then rose slightly to fire off a couple of rounds on semiautomatic. ''You aren't allowed to say the 'F' word around our house, although you *can* joke about what it stands for.''

''What it stands for?'' Brody spotted a fist-sized rock at his feet and, in a rare moment of chuck-it-all desperation, heaved the stone at the enemy's positions.

''Fix or Repaid Daily.'' Pasco winked.

Before Brody could laugh, there came a loud warping sound—like someone dropping a sledgehammer against hollow tin. ''Hey!'' came an aggravated voice from the bomb crater below. ''You cocksuckers got a problem?''

''Whose fuckin' side you on, anyway?'' another soldier yelled below.

Brody's head sunk between his shoulders with embarrassment. The rock had not made it across to the bomb crater's opposite rim but had slammed down onto the Huey's bullet-riddled roof or tail boom instead.

"Charlie did it!" he called out shamelessly, hiding the blush coloring his cheeks by throwing his shoulder into another rock-and-roll burst. Pasco joined him, as did the private lying behind Whoremonger.

"Yeah, *sure*!" came the same voice again as the chopper crew survivors sent a burst of red tracers up toward the enemy positions. "Just watch it next time, asshole!"

Brody did not reply but turned to the other private. "And what's *your* handle, kid?"

"Grove! Alexander Hamilton Grove!" And as if to punctuate the importance of his family's standing in the military community, the private rose up on one knee and began firing rapidly. Rapidly, but still on semiautomatic.

Five seconds passed before he had gotten off fifteen rounds, and a lone NVA bullet sent his helmet flying. Grove flopped back onto his buttocks, a dazed look in his eyes.

"Welcome to The Nam, General!" Brody stared at the bruised welt already rising on Grove's forehead. The kid was as innocent looking as Pasco—the same whiskerless face, close-cropped brown hair beginning to bleach with streaks of dirty blond in the cowlick and along the top. Just the way Uncle Sam liked his troops: semi-identical. Blood trickled down between his eyes from the superficial scalp wound caused by the bullet denting his helmet.

"You okay?" Pasco yelled, lunging toward him, but Brody reached out, latched on to Pasco's arm and yanked him back as a stick grenade came sailing

208

through the air. It bounced off Grove's forehead and rolled to a stop directly in front of them.

"Grenade!" Pasco and Grove both yelled simultaneously, scooting backward on their haunches as Brody dove forward. Both privates were sure their sergeant was going to sacrifice his life for them by covering the frag with his body. But such was not the case: Brody calmly scooped the Chi-Com up in his palm and heaved it back without even getting a good hold on the grenade.

He was flat against the earth even before the two privates could duck.

The grenade exploded in midair, high above the helicopter crew cowering on the bomb crater floor below.

"Gonna go back to Detroit after your tour of duty?" Brody asked, making combat zone conversation again.

"Yeah!" Pasco couldn't believe he was actually answering with a matter-of-fact tone equal in its lack of emotion as discharges exploded in the distance and ricochets bounced about their own position. "In the Chevy plant. I wanna make Cameros. I wanna customize my own—really soup it up, you know?"

"Yeah, I know!" A mental picture of his own convertible, sitting in a garage back in Los Angeles, flashed before Treat Brody's eyes. Suddenly he wished he was on Broadway, cruising through Chinatown, the most beautiful Asian actress from Hollywood beside him.

A solitary mortar round left its tube on the far side of the bomb crater, and its distinctive *thump*! on launch plucked Brody the Whoremonger from his gunsmoke-laced daydream. "Incoming!" he shouted just as the mortar slammed into treetops several dozen yards away. It detonated high above ground. Shrapnel sprinkled down on them as if mischievous Viet children hiding in the tree line were merely pelting them with stones.

"I wanna go home!" Grove yelled. It was a lighthearted plea, designed to elicit laughter from the others, but they were not in an accommodating mood.

He was yelling out something else, too—something equally as desperate, but the words were drowned out by RPD machine-gun fire on the North Vietnamese side of the crater.

"And where's home?" Brody finally asked after nearly a full minute face flat in the dirt and reeds. His eyes kept darting along the log's rotting bark, and he wondered if he feared another spider attack more than enemy-induced injuries.

"New York!" came the reply. "You *bic*, GI?"

"Yeah, we *bic*," Pasco answered for both cavalry-men.

Grove sounded exhausted, and Brody wondered in awe at how fatigued men could become merely from lying on the ground, exercising their trigger finger.

"Upstate!" Grove corrected him. "Albany."

"I thought that was in Georgia!" Brody screamed against the roar of gunfire directed at them.

"Everybody does!" Alexander Hamilton yelled back.

"You must be the product of a long-line military family!" Brody began the required taunt.

"Yeah, *right*! Five generations . . . all the way back past the Civil War. How'd you know, Sarge?"

" 'Cause only lifers' brats and jungle bunnies get tagged with the names o' presidents and old army generals!"

"And fuck you veddy much, Sarge!"

"You're welcome, newby!"

Grove and Pasco both rose to one knee and fired off entire clips at the enemy. Brody was popping up again, busting caps long and hard in the direction of the pith helmets bobbing on the far side of the bomb crater.

210

Ten rounds later the thump of lead against skullbone and the satisfying cry of someone dying as a direct result of his sharpshooter's skill reached Whoremonger's ears. He dropped back against the fallen log, nodding at the score. "The ultimate orgasm." He glanced over at Pasco. "You ever felt such fucking job satisfaction, kid?"

Pasco did not reply verbally, but he did rise up and fire another burst at the North Vietnamese and Viet Cong—searching, perhaps, for the same rush . . . the same high Sgt. Brody seemed to be getting out of all this. His ashen features told Treat he was no longer a kid at all, but a vet—tested in battle. Forged under fire. Branded a boonie rat.

Six months, Whoremonger was thinking. *Six months under fire before you can wear the combat infantryman's badge, kid. Six months o' hell on earth, then hog heaven and maybe even the Dirty Thirty Fraternity. Think you can last six lousy months, much less an entire Tour 365?*

"With all due respect, Sgt. Brody," Grove said, "you are one of the most *dinky-dau* motherfuckers I've ever seen. . . ."

"Since arriving in-country." Treat's eyes shifted to his as he corrected the enlisted man.

"Right. *Since* arriving in-country."

Brody's grim features cracked slightly as another grin formed beneath his bushy mustache. "Then no sweat," he said, " 'cause we *all* loco as loony-tunes after a tour or two humpin' the loins of ol' Void Vicious." Throwing back his head, the Air Cav sergeant let out a hideous laugh that sent chills down the spines of both Grove and Pasco.

The two privates exchanged concerned looks but immediately glanced away when Treat's face came back down. "Fuck it," the Whoremonger said simply, and lifted the M-16 over his head with one hand, pointing it backward, and held the trigger in until nearly two dozen rounds sprayed the opposite rim.

"That's another thing I like about this war." He lowered the weapon again and patted its black fiberglass handgrips. "Almost like playin' cowboys and Injuns back on the block, don't you think? Only *these* Mattel toys pack a powerful punch . . . and this really *is* Injun territory!" Again, chuckles from the pit of his gut escaped Brody as he reloaded.

"I'm just glad they issued us some sixteens that can shoot a couple times without jammin' up!" Grove glanced down at his own rifle.

"Oh?" Brody stared through him. "And *you've* had a shitload o' experience with your M-sixteen jammin'?" he asked skeptically.

"Well, no . . . but we all read about the problems . . . back in boot camp and AIT . . . before comin' over here. We all read that the rifles were—"

"We *fixed* the problem," Brody hissed, turning away as memories of dead men piling up because they'd died in close quarters, mud-and-muck fighting after weapons jams returned to haunt him like butterflies fluttering deep inside his stomach. "Wasn't the motherfuckin' M-sixteens at all, kid—was the ammo."

"The ammo?" Pasco fixed an inquisitive look on Whoremonger.

"Yeah. Goddamned ammunition was defective. Same old story: arms and ordnance people back in The World don't give a shit about us foot soldiers humpin' in the boonies, man." He glanced up at one of the high-tech gunships floating past beyond a sagging line of palm fronds. "No-account death merchants sent us shit

212

that got caught up in the breech on full auto—even semi-automatic mode sometimes. Neck problems, kid.''

"Neck problems?'' Grove tilted his head to one side.

"Yeah! The cartridge's neck wasn't crimped right. Sometimes the shell'd get fed into the weapon too fast, and a nick or dent in the brass crimp would hang up, jamming the feed.''

"Fuck.''

"Yeah. Made survivin' the Void a losing proposition. I shit you not. But we took care o' the problem, little kiddies.'' Brody slammed another magazine into his rifle and fired several rounds at the enemy. "The Professor wrote his congressman after too many pogues bought the farm. The vets . . . the vets could usually unjam the suckers as soon as there was a problem, but bookoo newbies panicked on first jam, man. Next thing they knew, Charlie was sittin' on their head, scramblin' their brains with his three-sided bayonet.''

"Jesus.'' Grove glanced away, looking like he might actually throw up. The drill sergeants back at Advanced Infantry Training had shown his recruit class one of the captured bayonets: triple-sided so the wound would refuse to close, bleeding more.

"Who's this 'Professor' you mentioned?'' Pasco asked after shooting the pith helmet off a North Vietnamese soldier trying to sprint across a clearing in the distance.

M-16 balanced across his forearms, Brody clapped as the helmet flew end over end through the air, then brought the rifle up and placed a single shot between the NVA's shoulder blades. After the soldier went down face-first into the reeds, he said, "His name was Shawn Larson. Only guy in First Cav I ever knew—draftee, that is—who packed a master's degree in his back

213

pocket. Not that it did him any good out here in the boonies, of course.''

"Well, it gave him enough brains to contact his congressman." Pasco winked. "I bet none o' you guys even knew your congressman's name, huh? I'll bet none o' you even knew what a congressman does!''

"Go ball a water buffalo, okay, Pasco? Sure we knew. Most of us. But I figured they were all just a bunch o' no-good Comm-symps anyway, and—"

"Comm-symps?''

"Communist sympathizers, you douchebag. See, whole lot *you* know. Bet you got a big-deal degree, too.''

"Workin' on my associate's, matter of fact—"

"Lotta good it's gonna do you out here in the sticks, chump. We both get the same amount of combat pay.''

"We'll see." Pasco nodded with a confident smile and tapped his PV2 stripes.

"*Shee*-it." Brody spat into the elephant grass. "Promotion, my prick! Anyway, the Professor got a newsworthy-type congressional investigation going, and we got good ammo. End of story. Maybe someday we'll really make some progress and go back to M-fourteens.''

"Too heavy." Grove sighed. "I like the M-sixteen's kick.''

"What kick?" Brody laughed as he fired two 5-round bursts using the one-handed pistol maneuver again.

"See what I mean?" Grove pointed at his technique. "Just like the demonstrations in boot camp. *Ti-ti* recoil, man. . . .''

"Shit, in boot," Pasco said, "they made us put the M-sixteen's rifle butt against our groin and pull the trigger, just to prove how little recoil there was. I'll never forget *that*.''

"M-fourteen woulda rammed your balls up through your gall bladder," Brody said.

"My old man used a thirty aught six at Inchon," Grove said.

"Korea?" Pasco asked him, still amazed they were actually holding a semicasual conversation during a firefight.

"Yeah. They had it bad *there*, man: Land of the Mourning Calm, they called it. Weird place. Cold, too. Icy cold. Lotta our guys died from frostbite—nebbah mind the Commies. None o' this hundred-and-twenty-in-the-shade shit. In fucking February!"

"Wake up and smell the piss on the punji stakes, brother—it's March," Pasco reminded him.

"Same-same."

"Just gimme a good well-oiled M-sixteen and five-hundred rounds o' new ammo that ain't been sittin' in some damp Quonset hut in Okinawa for five years, and I'll be happy," Treat Brody beamed as he reloaded a magazine by hand: all tracers. Blood-red tips. "Just me and my main man Mista *Colt* against Void Vicious. . . ."

"Which is somethin' else I been meanin' to ask you *vets* about." Grove spoke before Pasco could, and their expressions told Brody both privates had the same thing on their minds. "Just what exactly is all this shit 'bout some Void? It's all I ever hear the gunnies talkin' 'bout."

"You mean you haven't *noticed* it?" Brody fixed a shocked look on them. His countenance was hard to read—Grove wasn't sure if he was entirely serious or just fifty-fifty, with half the wrinkles at the edges of his eyes the prelude to some sick, only-in-The-Nam punch line.

Pasco popped up and shot a North Vietnamese lieutenant between the eyes. The NVA officer had leaned out only a few inches from behind cover of a thick oak when the cavalryman spotted him.

Brody didn't seem to notice, though he gave a *not-bad* nod before telling Grove, "Void Vicious is the jungle, kid . . . it's the way the trees come to life when you're approachin' the heart of the rain forest on a lima-lima, balls-to-the-wind gunship mission . . . the way their branches seem to reach up for the chopper's landing skids, trying to grab at them, drag the ship down into the triple canopy. . . ." Brody delivered several short bursts with his M-16 as if to break the spell he was trying to weave. Then, back against the log again, he took in a deep chestful of air to dilute the adrenaline surge.

"*That's Void Vicious, man.*" He plopped back down behind the tree and locked bulging eyes with Pasco.

"Sorry I asked." The private's swallow could be heard by all three Americans despite the answering discharges.

"But what about—" Grove began.

"*Don't ask!*" Pasco's head whirled in his direction.

His fellow newby ignored him, however. "What about all this talk I hear claimin' the Void's a slut, man . . . that she's a bitch in heat . . . a real *baaad* mama!"

"Void Vicious is what your head tells you it is," Brody declared after sending two 3-round bursts after a tree monkey scampering through high branches above the NVA positions. He thought at first it was an enemy sniper, jockeying for position. The gibbon escaped unharmed. Brody made a silent wish that the furry critter empty its bowels on the Vietnamese scurrying about below.

"You talk like you're drunk, Sarge!" Pasco laughed as he pulled his second ammo bandolier from around

216

his neck—the smile disappeared instantly, however, when he realized he was down to his last dozen magazines.

"Just so's you understand now." Brody brought the small green army-issue towel up from around his shoulders and wiped a grimy layer of sweat from his forehead.

"That's just it," Pasco replied. "I'm still just as confused as before."

"Then get drunk, too, so we can get on the same wavelength, soldier!" Treat offered his canteen, which Pasco concluded *had* to be spiked with either rice wine or ba-muoi-ba.

"I think I'll stick to lime Kool-Aid." He patted his own canteen.

"Root beer." Brody was still holding his out to the private. "We can get drunk on root beer!"

All three of them resumed laughing as a North Vietnamese sergeant jumped to his feet halfway around the wide crater's rim. He was yelling some kind of unintelligible war cry as he charged toward the three slack-jawed Americans, bayonet fixed.

"Excuse me." Brody did not get up. "Another doper to contend with." Bringing his M-16 almost casually to his shoulder, Whoremonger lined up the front and back sights with the NCO's groin, then jerked on the trigger hard enough to raise the muzzle several inches upon discharge.

"Holy fuckwads!" Grove yelled after watching the ten-round burst stitch the enemy's torso straight up, belly to forehead. Nine of the rounds impacted against flesh. The tenth struck the red star in the belt buckle of a North Vietnamese private emerging from thick foliage behind the NCO.

"Jesus," Pasco muttered as he watched the North

Vietnamese sergeant drop to his knees in a powder-burned stupor, hands cupped beneath his split-open stomach as he tried to keep his entrails sealed up inside. It must have dawned on him that something akin to a sledgehammer had also slammed against his face, for his eyes were lifeless now as he flopped onto his back, cold meat ready for the butcher. And the butcher today was Trick-or-Treat Brody.

"Food for the maggots!" Whoremonger yelled at the other Communists. "You hear me? Your *comrade* is nothin' but worm bait now! Who wants a sample o' the same, huh?" And he sent another few rounds into the opposite bank to emphasize his point.

"I don't get paid enough to put up with all this flak!" Pasco yelled as another stick grenade exploded nearby, showering him with tiny pieces of twisted metal. "How long did it take you to make buck sergeant, Brody?"

Treat glanced at the shattered crystal on his wrist-watch. "NCOs don't make much more than you enlisted men," was the preamble to his answer. "And *nobody* in this man's army gets paid enough to hold down the fort with Arc-Light on the way."

"How much time left?" Grove did not seem concerned. His faith was with the Green Machine. He'd always put implicit trust in the same institution his forefathers had served so well. "Less than ninety minutes." Brody was slowly shaking his head from side to side.

"They *are* going to have the slicks come back down here and extract our asses before the B fifty-twos make their bombing run, don't you think?" Pasco asked.

"Depends on whether or not we come up with some kind of trick to get those troops down at the bottom of the crater—"

"And their cargo," Grove added.

"*And their cargo*"—Brody nodded—"out."

"I think we're up shit creek, guys." Pasco was staring at Brody.

"Without a paddle or a prayer." The cavalryman shrugged, then resumed shooting at anything that dared move in the distant tree line.

CHAPTER 23

Five Hundred Meters to the East

Big Don Wickman's meaty hand shot up. Corky Cordova and the barefooted men following behind him froze in place. Only their eyes moved as they watched Sgt. Wickman drop slowly to one knee to examine a dark shape lying across the trail. A dark, *furry* shape.

A minute later he was waving the men up to his position. "Look familiar?" he asked Cordova.

"Anyone we know?" Corporal Styx jockeyed for position among the grunt gawkers.

" 'And this little piggy' bought the farm." Corky ran his fingers through the thick coat of the wild boar that had nearly run them down earlier.

"And this one, and this one, and et cetera." Corporal Stone lifted several baby pigs from reeds along the trail's edge. He held them over his head like cheap trophies. He expected to see blood dripping down onto the trooper, but strangely enough there was none.

"Don't touch them!" Wickman's voice was low but harsh, and the lifeless bodies rolled instantly from Stone's fingers as he complied without question.

"The gas?" Cordova moved several paces away from the mother hog.

Sgt. Wickman continued to check the adult's filthy coat. "No wounds," he declared, "other than routine scrapes and gouges made by thorns and the like."

"So it *was* the gas." Martinez was standing beside Cordova now.

Big Don nodded somberly. "Appears so."

"Well, then why the hell are we—" Styx began, but Wickman's words silenced him.

"Also appears the gas is gone now. Just like before." He rubbed his thumb and forefinger together, brought them to his eyes for a closer examination, but noticed nothing out of the ordinary. The hogs' odor had rubbed off on him, though, and the Brick's nostrils wrinkled slightly with disgust.

"So what do we do now?" Martinez asked.

A sudden blast behind the men sent everybody but Wickman and Cordova into prone positions. The group soon realized the explosion had actually occurred a considerable distance away—several hundred meters, in fact—but had only now traveled down through the interlocking maze of trails to reach them. Their ears were all perked now, and every soldier present clearly heard the rattle of discharges growing beyond the dense wall of trees.

The trail forked up ahead. If they veered to the right, it would take them away from the shooting.

"The Huey crash site," Styx said, listening to the growing crescendo of rifle fire.

"LZ Sierra," Stone chimed in.

"This way." Wickman rolled the dead hog off the trail, then led his team down the left fork.

"We got trouble." Pasco spoke first, though Brody detected movement through the trees long before.

"Hold your fire," he whispered as the darting shadows moved closer.

"But—" Grove started to whisper a protest when Treat waved him silent.

"They're good guys," he revealed. "Friendlies. Fingers off triggers, guys."

"How can you tell?" Grove strained to see past the stubborn, ground-clinging mist.

"I can smell 'em."

"You can *smell* 'em?"

"Well, they *don't* smell like *nuoc-mam*, first off," he said, "which is what most of the dinks reek of. Two of 'em don't carry no scent whatsoever . . . none that I can pick up at this distance, anyway—that would be Corky and the Brick, who've been eatin' rice and bamboo shoots so long their shit don't stink. But the other three . . . well, amateurs to the hilt: lift your noses, gentlemen, for a lesson in what *not* to wear in The Nam, less'n you're some REMF down in Saigontown, entertainin' the ladies o' questionable virtue. . . ."

"I don't smell nothing," Pasco said, actually sniffing at the air as he kept his rifle trained on the NVA positions but his eyes on the tree line to their right.

"*I* do." Grove nodded. "Old Spice."

Pasco nodded. "Styx and Stone."

"And Martinez," Grove added.

"Yep."

"Shouldn't we signal 'em or something?" Pasco whispered when it appeared the shadows were going to

223

keep moving well beyond the trail that led to their position.

"Wickman knows exactly where we are." Brody grinned. "And exactly what he's doing."

"He's going to try and circle around behind the enemy?" Grove's adrenaline began pulsing through his system again.

"Looks that way, don't it?" Brody removed his half-spent clip and inserted a fresh magazine.

Voices were suddenly yelling among the creeping cavalrymen, however. Voices in English. *"Tripwire!"*

Brody recognized dual warnings by both Styx and Stone.

"We see it," someone else hissed as a loud popping sound reached Brody's ears. Cordova.

"Hit the grou—" Wickman's commanding voice was interrupted by a devastating blast that rolled out to shake the log behind which Whoremonger and his two pogues were lying.

"Jesus." Grove began breathing hard. There was that inevitable anticipation of total doom and pain to come forming in his eyes.

"Claymore," Pasco decided by the force of the blast.

"Yep," Brody agreed. "Train your—"

"What do we do?" Grove cut him off.

"Train your rifles back on the other side of the bomb crater!" He raised his voice until he had the trembling Grove's attention.

"This sucks the big one, man!" Pasco began firing at pith helmets in the distance without further urging.

"Sgt. Wickman!" Brody's sudden and unexpected yell sent a shiver through Grove. "Yo! Hey, Brick! You turds all right out there?"

When there was no immediate response, Brody turned to Grove. "You're gonna be all right," he reassured the private. "You and Pasco hold down the fort, okay? And I'm gonna low-crawl out there to check on 'em."

"You think they've bought the farm, Sarge?" Pasco asked after twenty rounds. Brody watched his spent magazine drop into his lap and a fresh clip appear from somewhere inside his ruck.

"There's no screamin' . . . no groanin'. I've never known a claymore to be detonated, by *either* side, without the whole place erupting into a clusterfuck o' screams and groanin' yells, man. If I know the Brick, he's just lyin' low . . . waitin' . . . makin' sure he knows where Charlie's really at, where the other trip-wires are, and where his own people are. Just cover me while I low-crawl out there to confirm, okay?"

"You got it, Sarge."

"Right." Grove began firing his rifle as well.

Twenty quick rounds later, he glanced over his shoulder while changing ammo magazines, but Brody was gone. The ground-clinging shroud of mist and gunsmoke was still parting where he had dashed between the tree trunks.

"You lookin' to lose your chops, pretty-boy?"

Brody was practically nose to nose with Big Don Wickman before he even knew it—before he was startled into a gasp by the quiet words.

"*Jesus*, Brick! You just about caused me to *shit* a brick in my shorts."

"*You* wear shorts in the Nam?" Wickman, who was lying proned out in the reeds at the trail's edge, produced a testy grin.

"Any of your people hurt?" He did not bother dignifying the remark with an answer.

"Stunned and disenchanted, but still 'live an' kickin,' kid. 'Cept Two-Step. Charlie got him pretty bad. He's still breathing, though."

"I called out to you guys, man"—Brody's eyes darted left, then right, until he spotted the additional four sets of unblinking round eyes trained on him—"but—"

"And we heard you, okay?" Wickman rose into a upper-push-up position. "*But* I wasn't about to give my position away to the dinks before we could—"

"The claymore pretty well gave your position away, Brick," Treat reminded him.

"For all Charlie knows, some wild hog set that sucker off, asshole. We didn't make a sound!"

"Ain't no boars in this stretch o' woods, Big Don—you should know that. Charlie should know it, too. And we heard youze guys yelling a tripwire warning from way over there, so—"

Dual smirks from the unmoving faces lying amidst piles of vines and leaves silenced Brody. "Weren't no claymore neither, Whoremonger." Corky's voice.

"Glad to see you're still low-crawlin' through this crap." Brody threw a handful of moist mushrooms into Cordova's face. His old friend closed both eyes tightly against the harmless assault.

"Satchel charge, jury-rigged monster style to sweep the trail clean, but the other suckers failed to detonate." Corky wiped the purple mushrooms from his face. "Luckily."

"I figure we can take it slow and easy"—Wickman's tone told him it was time to get back to the business at hand—"and circle around behind the bastards. Wipe 'em all out with one mad minute on rock and roll."

"No dice." Brody shook his head.

"And why not?"

"I already thought about that. There's just too many

of 'em, Brick. We must be outnumbered five or six to one.''

"Twenty to one's my guess."

"I see you *bic* what we're up against. . . ."

"Then what do you suggest, pretty-boy?"

Brody hated when Wickman called him that. "I suggest we beat feet back to the east side of the bomb crater. I got two pogues in charge o' fifty feet o' real estate, and I think they'd appreciate a little 'command guidance.' ''

"*Then* what?" Cordova was finally moving out from under cover.

Treat stared at the small pinpoints of blood on his forehead and arms. "We wait."

"Arc-Light's en route, man. We gonna be mashed like potatoes if'n we don't move out soon."

"Our orders are to secure the crash site. . . ."

"Can't get much more secured than it is." Styx's unmotivated voice taunted him again.

"That Huey ain't goin' nowhere, Sarge." Martinez's maturing chuckle.

"Screw the ship and its cargo," Brody said. "There's a crew down there, dammit. If we beat feet and leave 'em behind to fend for themselves, they're cold meat faster'n you can chuck a stick grenade at—"

"He's right." Sgt. Wickman's deep voice was already directing them back to the bomb crater. "Let's move it."

"And keep your eyeballs peeled for tripwires," Brody reminded them.

"No shit." Cordova led the way.

Fire Base Belinda

Snakeman Fletcher leaned into his hatch-60 as Gabriel brought *Pegasus* around hard. One hundred feet below, Fire Base Belinda lay beneath a stubborn blanket of gunsmoke. All he could see were the tops of heads racing about now and then. Asian heads. VC. He would fire down at them, but the Vietnamese usually bent low, just below the top layer of smoke, as he was about to pull the trigger, and he'd never know if he hit his target or not. "What I need is a good stiff mind," he muttered, "to blow this smoke off the flattop. . . ."

He stared at the bobbing heads again. They would appear, then vanish—even before he could swing his M-60 toward them. "If the little shits had any brains, they'd keep their heads down." He fired off a burst. "Course then they'd go bumpin' into stuff, wouldn't they?" He envisioned one of the running insurgents slamming head-on into a gun pit wall of sand-filled oil drums as he charged headlong through the thick smoke.

Fletcher stared down at the gray blanket covering the camp, trying to distinguish the old bunkers and defensive positions, but it was just too thick. He fired off another forty rounds nonstop as two VC bumped into each other near one of the reinforced gun pits. They both dropped, disappearing from view, but a severed arm flew up above the smoke, end over end through the air, and Elliot clicked in with a little cheer.

"Nice shootin', eh?" he asked the two pilots in the cockpit up front.

"Lucky shot," Gabriel retorted.

"How can you miss *anything* when you're usin' an M-sixty?" The peter pilot issued a form-letter laugh.

Snakeman juggled a couple of replies around in his head but concentrated on the smoke screen instead, wanting more Cong for the body count. No enemy tracers from inside the compound. And very little harassment fire from the steep slopes below.

"They must be up to somethin' down there." Fletcher patted his machine gun. "You little fuckers are busy as bees, runnin' around yet goin' nowhere . . . up to no good. . . ." He decided to click in. "I'm startin' to get bad vibes about it, Gunslinger."

"Just hang in there," Gabe responded dryly. "Drop a couple more belts o' seven point sixty-two onto the zipperheads while I make another pass or two, then we're gonna swoop back down to the valley floor and check on the boys dug in at LZ Sierra."

"Hey!" Fletcher yelled into his headset.

His tone immediately worried Gabriel. "Hey *what?*" the AC yelled back.

"Directly below . . . no, back there! Take me right back there, Gabe! Back to port—hard left. *Now!*"

"What *was* it, Elliot?" *Pegasus* was already banking sharply to the left as Gabe brought her around in a tight, flaring hover.

"Pussy, man! That chick everybody's after! I saw her running through the smoke!"

"Where?"

"Okay! Okay, Gabe, *Peg*'s snout is pointed directly at the area I saw her running through, a diagonal southwest-to-northeast sprint."

"You sure it was her?"

"Only saw shoulders and long hair—from the back. It was enough. Drop the snout a couple degrees and *unload* on the cunt, man! Miniguns and rocket pods!"

"No can do, Snakeman!" Gabriel was sounding even more worried now.

"And why the fuck not?" Snakeman began firing his machine gun in wide, sweeping arcs, but there was no way the Hog-60 could match the amount of ground *Peg*'s minigun and nose cannon could cover.

" 'Cause we're pointed directly at the old CP right now—if she's down below that smoke somewhere—and the orders are to try and keep damage to a minimum."

"I thought we gave the place up!" Fletcher made no attempt to conceal his anger.

"You know the game plan, troop. . . ."

"We're gonna retake lost territory." Fletcher did not sound enthusiastic.

"As soon as possible."

"About an hour till Arc-Light arrives," the peter pilot clicked in. "Buchanan wants Fire Base Belinda back in American hands by then."

"Or heads are gonna roll."

CHAPTER 24

Fire Base Belinda

Trinh Thi Kim hugged the earth, completely numb to her leg wound now.

Another U.S. gunship glided over her position, and she did not move despite the protective blanket of smoke cloaking the camp. Now and then machine-gun rounds raked sections of the flattop—mainly far out from the gun pits—so she made a point of keeping close to the cannon.

"Stay close to me." She paused as another Huey floated past above them, then waved the platoon of Viet Cong teenagers away from the perimeter wire and toward the Americans' abandoned command bunker. "Two of you remain here with me," she said. "The rest of you, get over to that far side of the peak. Spread out along the concertina—ten meters between you. Find a foxhole or LP. If you can't, then dig one. I want everyone digging! Check all GIs to make sure they are dead. Now *go*!''

The young VC sappers trotted off through the smoke, and Kim's eyes scanned the eastern perimeter again. There were more of her people climbing up the slopes. More than she would need, probably. But large numbers would perish when the gunships attacked. It would be good to have replacements.

Kim motioned for the two guerrillas remaining by her side to start down into the underground bunker and secure it. Both youngsters produced nervous expressions but did not hesitate in bringing up their rifle barrels and hustling noisily down the steps.

She half expected to hear a volley of shots ring out, but one of the apprentice insurgents sounded the all-clear instead.

Noticing her own frown with distaste, Kim drew the .45 automatic she had captured several campaigns ago and started down the sandbagged steps.

''All dead,'' one of the village recruits advised her. His tone was superstitious, as if he feared becoming possessed by one or more of the dead soldiers' ghosts.

Kim's eyes scanned the corpses, then shifted to the dim shaft of sunlight that dropped through a jagged hole in the ceiling. The CP had obviously suffered a direct mortar or rocket hit.

She did not bother checking biceps for rank but told the nearest buck private, ''Remove all their weapons and boots, and take them topside.'' Then she went about examining the radio equipment.

There appeared to be nothing salvageable: all destroyed. Even the two spare PRC-25s propped in a corner, which might have been utilized to monitor gunship and Blues radio conversations, were riddled with shrapnel. Never mind. It did not matter. They already had enough captured communications equipment as it was.

Kim started back up the crumbling steps. "What do you wish us to do, Commander?" One of the youths rushed after her, less than eager to remain underground with dead men.

"I want you two to remain near this entrance." She pointed at an abandoned machine-gun nest positioned behind a low wall of sandbags topside. "Either of you know how to operate an American-made M-sixty?"

"Yes." The older draftee nodded with narrow eyes. "We are familiar with *all* of the U.S. weapons."

"Good." Kim turned to leave. "Sling your AKs and load that machine gun. And wait."

"Can we fire at the helicopters as they fly over?" the younger insurgent called after her.

"Do not draw attention to yourselves," she responded in a tired and irritated tone.

"But Commander . . ."

"You will have time to engage in gunplay with the imperialists. *Plenty* of time."

"Yes, Commander." The other youth nudged his friend into silence.

They exchanged nervous glances, and Kim vanished in the smoke.

She proceeded to the nearest perimeter LP and checked with the two sentries manning the post. "The entire camp has been secured," they told her. "No American holdouts left."

Kim surveyed the dual lines of black-pajama-clad sappers making their way up through the rocky crags below the mine fields and concertina wire. "Is this the last of them?" she asked, showing no interest in the holdout.

"Yes. The final fifty."

"We have counted nearly five hundred heads," the other guard advised her. "Yet others continue to climb the slopes. Local supporters not on my roster."

"They anticipate a victory," said the other sentry. "Let all the residents join in, for it will be a victory of the people!"

"The long-nosed running dogs will never be able to retake this fire support base," the first sentry assured them both with a confident nod.

"I want to be informed the moment the last platoon of reinforcing troops has arrived," Kim told them.

"Yes, Commander."

Her eyes narrowed as she scanned the procession of out-of-breath climbers. The trek from valley floor to mountaintop had been a treacherous one for them and was now made increasingly dangerous since Kim's perimeter guards had exhausted their supply of smoke grenades. The wind was hitting Belinda from the east and driving all the gunsmoke away from the eastern slopes, toward the west and southwest sides. The open ground between the sparse line of trees several hundred yards down, and the first series of mine fields, offered no cover whatsoever. Smoke grenades set off downslope had afforded moving patches of cover, but now it was open season on the exposed climbers. The Air Cav gunships would soon be taking advantage of the clearing breeze.

"And I want you to remain alert." Kim dropped into a casual squat as a Huey glided past overhead. But the three of them were positioned close to a burning ammo cache, beneath several sheets of drifting smoke, and well hidden. "Do you understand? Ignore the helicopters. Do not draw attention to yourselves."

"Do you think the round-eyes will mount a counter-attack on the ground?" she was asked.

234

"It is very possible"—Kim turned to leave—"but we are prepared for that. I am worried about something worse. Let me know if you sense some other kind of trouble."

"Some other kind of trouble, Commander?"

"Like incoming artillery?" The first sentry's eyes lit up. "You think the bastards up at Camp Buffy would bombard this fire base?"

"I don't know. Keep your ears open for unusual sounds: jeep traffic in the valley below. Airplane engines. Anything different from what we face right now, do you understand?"

"Yes, Commander." They both nodded obediently.

Kim limped back to the eastern edge of the perimeter when she heard the triple pitch of three choppers approaching in typical attack formation.

She began firing on the run even before the Hueys reached the mountain's east slopes. Guiding on the green-and-orange tracers, she lowered her aim, and although several bullets shattered windshield Plexiglas, the helicopters kept coming—straight for the long lines of VC filing forth from the timberline and into the mine fields. "Get down!" she yelled in rapid-fire Vietnamese. *"Get down now!"*

Some who dove for cover were thrust up into the sky like rag dolls—they had triggered mines. Others retraced their steps as fast as they could back to the trees. A few ran for the concertina wire ahead, sprinting across the backs of corpses lined up in neat rows in a last-ditch effort to reach safety, hoping to make the perimeter before the Hueys arrived.

None did.

Geysers of dirt obscured the sagging coils of wire as dozens of rockets slammed into the hillside. Bodies were thrown helter-skelter—severed limbs and decapitated heads made it across with hideous, bouncing rolls; mangled torsos wrapped around the wire's hatchetlike barbs by the cruel impact did not.

Kim turned her eyes away as several dozen comrades were sacrificed for the mission.

She scurried from trench to trench, scooping up ammo magazines for her new M-16, commandeered from a legless corpse. True, they were in semicontrol of the fire base now, but for how long?

She fired five-round bursts at several Hueys as they roared directly above her, ignoring her own earlier directives to the two sentries. Sparks showered down as bullets bounced off the bottoms of landing skids. Once she thought several rounds had struck a ship's underbelly, but she couldn't be sure. The chopper remained airmobile, in any event, and, swerving side to side in an almost comical attempt to evade additional gunfire, disappeared through a high wall of smoke.

It became an endurance contest now. She was finally getting the last of her climbers up onto the mountaintop—positioning them in the various LP trenches, machine-gun bunkers, and howitzer pits. Nearly five hundred strong, they would prove a worthy opponent of anything the Americans could field. The underground bunkers would protect them from artillery barrages and even gunship rockets. She was not sure how they would fare against napalm strikes or strafing runs by the Phantoms—or if the feared jet fighters would even make an appearance. Kim and her Cong would just have to wait and see.

In the meantime, she could sharpen her marksmanship skills by using the low-flying slicks for target practice. Her right eye narrowed as another Huey approached in a swooping dive from several hundred feet up, but before she could pull the trigger, a series of sharp discharges exploded only a few inches from her ear.

More angry than startled, she turned to find a young recruit kneeling beside her and energetically firing off his SKS carbine.

"To the left, to the left," she urged, eyes squinting as she followed the slight smoke trails passing through the ship's rotorwash.

The Huey banked away sharply and climbed almost straight up, turbines straining with a loud, abrasive whine. A lone rocket dropped from the ship's right strut pod and soared out over the fire base, detonating somewhere in the far valley beyond.

"I am sorry." The youth lowered his rifle and shook his head from side to side in self-reprimand.

"Why sorry?" She shocked herself by draping an arm around the seventeen-year-old's shoulder. "You hit it, didn't you?"

"I hit it?" His eyes lit up as they followed the helicopter before it disappeared inside an enormous column of smoke.

"Yes. But we shall have many more chances to shoot down the American gunships, comrade. . . ."

"I want to kill one *hundred* of the Americans!" the youth shouted, raising his rifle over his head.

"And no doubt you shall!" Kim led him over toward one of the gun pits. As another helicopter approached, they hurried down the sandbagged steps and hid in the zebralike shadow of several AA barrels until it passed.

"Are you familiar with artillery or antiaircraft pieces?" she asked the youth as they both took in the heavy cannon platforms and support tarmac.

"No . . ." He was slow in answering, as if his highest priority were to please his commander—but how was one to fake an operating knowledge of a quad-50?

"I have not progressed to that stage of training, Commander."

"And neither have I." Kim produced a rare smile. "Very well. It matters little." She brought up her shiny new M-16. "We will just have to make do with these small arms for now."

"Yes." The tall, slender youth turned away and concentrated on aiming at another gunship hovering over one of the other gun pits. He slowly fired an entire clip of rounds at the helicopter on semiautomatic, missing all of the shots, until the ship finally darted away, out over the steep slopes that dropped to the valley floor thousands of feet below.

"You can operate the M-sixty, no?" Kim asked, patting the boy lightly on the shoulder.

"Of course, Commander," he said quickly.

"Show me you can load it properly." Her voice grew stern.

"First you take this lever and pop the breech cover open, Commander." The youth looked up, but where Trinh Thi Kim had once been standing there was now only a phantomlike swirl of gunsmoke pointing with silver, wispy fingers the direction in which she had fled.

CHAPTER 25

Over Fire Support Base Belinda

"Gimme another belt o' ammo, dude!"

"Here, Snakeman!" The private crouching beside Elliot Fletcher nearly kicked the ammo box out the hatch in his zeal to comply. He pulled the first dozen linked cartridges out of the metal container and fed the first round into Fletcher's M-60 machine gun. Fletch nearly slammed the cover down on his fingers.

"Cam on!" he thanked his ammo man in Vietnamese as *Pegasus* banked hard to the left, circling around for another pass over the artillery camp's western face.

"We gonna *get some* today, Snakeman?" the private screamed in competition with the flapping rotors overhead.

"We definitely gonna *get some,* dude! Just hold on to your jockstrap!"

As if on cue, *Pegasus* dove back down through the top layers of drifting smoke. Gabriel was forbidden from

239

unloading on the ground surrounding the old CP, but he could surely fire some minigun bursts into the ranks of Cong crowding the perimeter trenches.

"You ever seen so many goddamn dinks on an *'merican* fire base, Snakeman?" he called back on the intercom system.

"That's a nasty neg', Gunslinger—but never fear, Super Snake's here." And with that, Fletcher cut the conversation and resumed his peculiar style of leaning hard into the M-60.

"That's what I call *squatters* of the undesirable persuasion, amigo!" Gabriel again.

Snakeman's bungee cords strained against his weight, but the canvas held. Dozens of smoldering, bullet-riddled bodies were left in their wake after *Pegasus* passed over several hundred meters of concertina wire.

"You tryin' for a new record, Fletch?" the peter pilot called back over a shoulder.

"Who's keepin' count?" Snakeman gritted his teeth in anticipation of another low pass.

"I think we oughta be granted permission to zap them AA-pits," Gabriel said, going ship to ship with one of the other Hueys.

"Say again, Python-Lead," came the terse, static-laced reply.

"It's only a matter of time before Charlie mans those AA-guns and quad-fifties, and starts lobbin' heavy ord at our own people, over. . . ."

"I don't think any o' those Charlie-Congs gots the smarts to operate one." A pilot with a deep southern drawl joined the radio net without identifying himself. Gabriel recognized the Delta Company warrant officer.

"Don't kid yourself," he said. "The VC aren't hicks, Harper. They got this weird knack for bein' able to make *anything* shoot."

240

"And they've got hard-core NVA Regulars in their ranks now," his peter pilot added as *Pegasus* banked to the right, swerved in and out of several thick smoke columns, then dropped so low both crewmen were able to see the wild-eyed expressions on a squad of sappers moving between trenches.

One of the NVA responded with several rifle shots, but none of the five or six bullets came close to striking the gunship, and Snakeman responded with an obscene gesture. "Fuck 'em if they can't take a joke!" He glanced back over a shoulder at his ammo man.

"Right!" the private replied, lower jaw dragging.

"Hey, take us around again, Gunslinger!" Elliot called forward, anger replacing apathy.

"Say again?"

"Swing around so I can finish those cocksuckers off, Gabe!"

"No can do, Snakeman. Time to diddy-bop on downslope to check on Big Don and the Whore-monger."

"Shit," Fletcher muttered, upset at having to forgo a good kill. His bad mood didn't last long, though. "This ain't no supply run! Find me some dinks to smoke, Mista Gabriel!" he clicked in as *Pegasus* glided out away from the mountaintop fire base's perimeter and dropped in a sudden, swooping descent toward the Nam Sathay River Valley below.

"That shouldn't be too tall an order, General," the AC replied with the plastic promotion. "You see that B fifty-two bomb crater down there?"

"Shore do!"

"On one side are the good guys"—he spoke in tones of mock patience, like teacher to preschooler—"and on the other side's the *bad* guys. You have to decide which is which, fella."

241

"No sweat." Snakeman chuckled into his headset. "Just keep the action on port side. I don't wanna see that starboard gunny over there chalkin' up all the points."

"Victor Charlie on your whiskey." Gabriel's voice became suddenly serious as they neared LZ Sierra.

"I see 'em, honcho-san." Snakeman leaned out against the front edge of his hatch, body weight into the M-60's butt plate. "Steady . . . steady . . ."

"The bad guys are wearin' the black pajamas." Gabriel's peter pilot giggled, but Fletch was already firing.

The peter pilot's smile quickly faded when he saw the half-dozen heads explode simultaneously—like watermelons struck by an invisible sledgehammer.

"Yeah! *Get some*, Snakeman! Bring smoke down on those mothers!" Corky Cordova yelled as *Pegasus* made her first pass over the NVA side of the bomb crater.

One North Vietnamese soldier foolishly jumped up onto the crater's high rim, perhaps hoping for a better shot at the Huey, and was instantly blow off his feet by an M-16 burst from the crash site below.

"Whoa!" Private Grove lowered his own rifle with surprise after the enemy trooper in his front sight loop disappeared with an unearthly scream. "Those clowns down there aren't pullin' any punches, are they?"

"Just savin' their ammo for sure shots." Pasco brought his own rifle back up and knocked another pith helmet into the air.

Brody's eyes shifted up-valley: two more helicopters were returning to the crash site from Fire Support Base Buffy. "Here comes your equipment!" he yelled over at Cordova, who in turn cast a sideways glance at Martinez, Styx, and Stone.

In less than a minute—while *Pegasus* was circling around and at the apogee of her swing out over the jungle—the first helicopter flared into a hover almost directly over the North Vietnamese position. Both of its door gunners poured an unceasing stream of machine-gun fire down into the NVA's ranks, effectively pinning them while the second gunship swooped in above Brody's people with a slow, sideways glide. Two olive-drab bundles were dropped to the ground, one after the other. Sgt. Wickman reached up and grabbed them both.

Then, in a fury of shifting rotors, the helicopter had ascended out over the trees and vanished.

"Here!" Big Don opened the duffel bags and threw boots to Styx and Stone and Martinez. "If they don't fit, tough shit—just do the best you can. It's lucky they had extras on board."

"Better than humpin' the boonies barefooted!" Brody added.

"Here's two left feet," Styx exaggerated as he threw a pair to his sidekick.

"I thought you were gonna airlift us out." Stone was not amused as his eyes spotted the resupply slick reappear briefly through a break in the trees. It was returning in the direction of the two fire bases—apparently to rejoin the fighting there.

"Are you wounded?" Wickman pulled M-16s from the duffels and gently tossed them to the three enlisted men.

"Well, no," Stone began. "But—"

"But *jackshit*, soldier! Lace them suckers up"—he referred to the jungle boots—"then divide up this ammo." He heaved the second duffle bag at Styx. "If Two-Step can hack it"—he motioned toward a semi-conscious Chance—"so can you two clowns! Cross your legs like ladies," he said, imitating Sgt. Leo Zack.

243

Corporal Styx, who had not been protesting, caught the big duffel the way a boxer in training might latch on to a weight bag, but the momentum still knocked him off his feet.

"Hey, what did *I* do?" he complained at the rough treatment, sending a grin in Treat's direction nevertheless.

Bullets were kicking up dirt clods all around them again, and Marty Martinez ignored the boots, opting to dive for the bagged ammo clips instead. He jerked out three cloth bandoliers and threw his shoulder and side against the crater's edge, slammed a magazine home, and began shooting back with a vengeance.

"*That's* the spirit!" Big Don Wickman joined him.

"I think I'm gonna upchuck." Styx was not impressed.

"Hey!" complained Stone. "They didn't bring us any helmets!"

"You never wear yours anyway, dick-breath!" Styx spat into the elephant grass, then heaved two grenades out at the North Vietnamese position.

"Eat shit and die, you jerk!" Stone pulled on a pair of boots two sizes too small. "How could them bitches steal my helmet if I wasn't wearin' one . . . *huh*?"

"Need I remind you two we're supposed to be fighting?" Brody crouched between them and sent several short bursts out at the enemy.

Grateful for the interruption, it seemed, both corporals joined him in the gunplay, and soon the entire American side of the bomb crater was firing nonstop.

Until two minutes or so later.

Big Don was the first to glance up. Brody's eyes rose at nearly the same time.

"Oh, fuck."

Styx and Stone both heard the low, vibrating drone

a few seconds later. Everyone stopped shooting and glanced up at the high clouds. The earth seemed to tremble with a constant humming underfoot. Everyone stared skyward for a moment—including the VC and North Vietnamese soldiers on the other side of the bomb crater.

Cordova was the first to spot the faint vapor trails. "Into the sun," he told them. "Stare at the patch o' blue just beyond the sun. They swung around . . . didn't come straight north from Saigon, but from the west."

"Utapao," Brody whispered.

"Huh?" Styx and Stone replied in unison.

"Utapao Air Force Base, brothers." Big Don was biting his lower lip. "Kingdom of Siam. . . ."

"Thailand," Brody translated.

"How much longer were we supposed to have?" Grove asked Pasco, who looked to Treat for an answer.

"Maybe it's just a fly-over," said Styx.

"Maybe they're headed north"—Stone nodded his head vigorously—"for Hanoi, man . . . Hanoi!"

"You better get those two Hueys on the horn!" Styx demanded. "You better get 'em back here, and get our asses extracted, *Sarge*! It's your fuckin' responsibility, man! Our lives are in your hands, and they don't appear to be worth a lousy fifty P right now."

Treat Brody stared at the broken crystal on his wrist-watch, then glanced over at the Brick.

"It's still working." Wickman shook his head somberly and held up his own watch for the men to see.

"Arc-Light's an hour early." The look on the Whore-monger's face was that of a man who'd just been screwed by destiny.

"Sixty-*eight* minutes, to be precise." Wickman's eyes latched on to the three helicopters fading in the distance.

Brody was suddenly crawling up along the crater's rim as far as safety permitted. "You guys got commo down there?" he yelled to the men huddled under the smoldering Huey wreckage.

"That's negative!" came the reply in a voice he did not recognize. He stared down at the ashen faces looking back up. Treat knew none of the men. "It was destroyed in the crash! How 'bout you guys?"

"Neg! Lost our commo to an SKS burst during the first inning!"

"Then it's gonna be a helluva no-hitter, Whoremonger!"

"Bases are loaded!" someone else called.

"Strike three, and we're *all* out!"

"Is that B fifty-two we fucking hear, O honorable honcho-san?"

"I'm fuckin' 'fraid you hear right, troop!"

"Well, somebody better get on the horn and either call 'em off or get a slick in here."

"I just told you!" Brody's voice was getting hoarse. We don't have any commo, either!"

From the crewman huddled beside him: "Then we are truly screwed."

"Well, fuck me till it hurts," came the faint reply from below.

Wickman had low-crawled up beside Brody upon hearing the familiar line. "You know them guys down there?" he asked as the North Vietnamese resumed firing potshots at them.

Treat turned a blank face to Big Don. "Never met 'em before in my life."

"You legendary leech." Wickman's grin was one of approval. "I should be as well known."

"But you think they'd make me their beneficiary?" He winked.

246

Both cavalrymen glanced up at the B-52s one last time, then resumed firing their rifles, content in the knowledge that as warriors they would die fighting.

Or some such shit.

CHAPTER 26

Crash Site Sierra

"What's that goddamned whistle?" Brody already knew the answer, but he prayed a second opinion would prove him wrong.

"Sounds like five-hundred-pounders to me . . . maybe a bit smaller." The Brick glanced over at Whoremonger for the first time.

"Bombs."

"*Heavy* bombs. Mean shit, pal. I'd say our mongoose is cooked."

Brody looked skyward again. "Those suckers are pretty far up there, man. Could it be an optical illusion . . . the heat and all? Could it be they're really falling way in the fuck over there, and not just about directly overhead, like it appears?"

"You really want my opinion, Treat?"

Brody was beginning to shake now. His eyes darted

back and forth, from the vapor trails to Wickman's eyes. "What do *you* think?"

"I think you've got about thirty seconds to remove all sharp objects from your pockets, say good-bye to Big Don, then bend over, place your head between your legs . . ."

"And kiss my ass good-bye." Brody finished the overused phrase found on "In the Event of Nuclear War" posters in many barracks of the rear echelon.

"I'd say there just might be one alternative!" Wickman raised his voice noticeably as the whistling sound grew louder and louder.

"We're open to suggestions!" Styx and Stone had both gathered close behind the two NCOs.

"We make a dive for it!"

"A dive?" Martinez asked.

"Into the bomb crater," Cordova surmised. "Down to the crash site with the other guys!"

"Probably the safest place to be, with an Arc-Light bombing run about to pulverize us into smithereens."

"Or, it might be the *worst* place to be!" Styx argued, glancing up. "If one of those suckers explodes down there!"

"Move out!" Brody brought his M-16 up, making the decision for them all. "I'll lay down cover fire, but you've all gotta make the move at the same time. Them dinks'll only let us get away with it one time."

"Are you kidding? They'll probably fuckin' join us down there!" Corky said.

"And call a truce to the war," Martinez added.

"Don't bet your combat pay on it," Wickman told him dryly as he flipped his rifle's safety off and prepared to scramble.

"What about you?" Stone asked Brody, who was

replacing a twenty-round magazine with a longer banana clip.

"Don't worry about the Whoremonger!" But Brody was trembling visibly now. "I'll figure something out!"

"I'll stay up here with you," Styx told him, "and take my chances topside." He readied his rifle as well, but Wickman grabbed his arm.

"Come on, shit for brains. We only need one hero per day. You're comin' with the rest of us and—"

"Bullshit!" Styx jerked his wrist away. "I don't wanna be down in no pit when a five-hundred-pounder impacts down there, man! I'll take my goddamned chances up here with Brody!"

"Suit yourself." Big Don exchanged nods with his fellow NCO, and Brody brought the M-16's butt plate to his shoulder. "But the way I figure it, Arc-Light bombing runs—especially from that altitude"—he glanced up at the vapor trails again—"are kinda like lightning bolts: no two bombs ever strike in the same place twice!" And he took hold of Two Step and slid down the crater's steep rim as Treat unloaded on full automatic.

Styx watched, Stone, Cordova, Martinez, and the others fly over the edge as well. His eyes darted to the other side of the wide crater: the enemy soldiers were all facedown in the dust, trying to avoid Brody's rock-and-roll bursts. He glanced behind him—toward several other bomb crater rims rising in the distance. Could Wickman be right? Was it true no two bombs ever dropped in the same place? Or was that just an old army myth—or worse: something the Brick had just made up on the spur of the moment, to fit their present circumstances.

"Well, help me out!" Brody was yelling in his ear

251

now as his thirtieth bullet slammed into the opposite bank of packed dirt.

"Sorry, Whoremonger!" Styx was on his feet, firing five-round bursts as he stumbled down the rim's side. He kept the NVA and Viet Cong soldiers pinned down long enough for Brody to change magazines.

"*Sayonara,* shit-head!" Brody yelled after Styx, but his bizarre laughter was smothered and consumed by a rolling kind of thunder that suddenly struck the land several hundred yards distant—behind the enemy positions.

Huge geysers of smoke and dust ripped into the air as violent concussions raced toward him, tearing the tops off trees and pushing a wall of swirling debris toward the combatants like a grayish-black whirlwind.

The Communists could not resist staring back at the approaching doom, and Brody leaped after Corporal Styx, firing a last farewell into the enemy ranks an instant before the blast rolled over the helicopter crash site.

Brody slid on his side all the way to the bottom. Trying hard to keep his rifle in the air and out of the dirt, he slammed against the downed Huey tail boom with his right shoulder. The mangled fuselage was already shaking back and forth, side to side, with the explosions raining down on the valley floor, and then bombs were striking all around the bomb crater itself.

Curled up into the fetal position, his folded arms covering a tucked head, Treat Brody resisted the urge to look at the carnage being wreaked on the surface several dozen meters up. He leaned into the helicopter debris, hoping it might shield him from the heat and shrapnel and heart-stopping concussions, and he prayed for the barrage to move on down the valley.

But it refused. Tons of explosives continued to slam

into the earth all around their crash site haven, without letup, for what seemed an eternity.

"Jesus H. Christ. . . ."

Leo Zack did not hear Lt. Vance's words as both men stared out the helicopter hatch, down into the Nam Sathay Valley a thousand feet below at the rolling thunder of B-52 bombs crashing through the trees, clearing a wide swath across the rain forest. White puffs—appearing small as cigarette smoke rings from this distance but actually warehouse-sized—rose from the jungle like ripples from a handful of pebbles tossed into a calm lagoon. Shock waves rushed out in all directions. They looked like rumbling earthquake tremors from the air.

The two cavalrymen were aboard their gunship and hovering above Fire Support Base Buffy—well out of the Arc-Light kill zone. They watched in awe as the numbing barrage moved down along the dry creek bed, passing over the Huey crash site, consuming everything in its path—or so it seemed from Zack's vantage point. "No one could live through that," he said. No one!"

"The bastards were an hour early!" Jacob Vance had tears in his eyes as he referred to the fleet of stratofortresses, as the B-52s were known. "We could have gotten Brody's people out, if only Arc-Light wasn't an hour *early*!"

Peg's pilot, Cliff Gabriel, didn't even bother attempting to rescue the crash site contingent when the B-52 vapor trails were initially spotted. They were just too far away. By the time he got to them, *Pegasus* would also be in Arc-Light's target grid. And she wouldn't have half the time necessary to land and extract all the Americans.

"There's nothing we can do now except wait for the B fifty-twos to move on, then go down and bag whatever body parts we can find." Leo the Lionhearted spoke without emotion, but his head was bowed.

"Any luck, goddammit?!"

Zeke, the Loach pilot, glanced over at Buchanan. "Just now got the bastards on the horn, Colonel!" He nodded.

"You tell them sonsofbitches to knock it off!" Buchanan screamed. Spittle flew across the pilot's black visor. "You tell 'em to abort, and right fucking *now,* or I'll have every last one of 'em makin' cropduster milk runs between Greenland and Antarctica!"

Zeke was listening to the colonel with one ear, concentrating on the B-52 transmissions with the other. "They've finally acknowledged, sir! But it's a miracle we ever got through on this fucking radio net at all."

"Shit, it's a miracle I haven't had a coronary by now!" Buchanan pounded his fists against his thigh. "So what the heck's the skinny?"

"Luckily they flew right over us! But thirty more seconds and I would've missed the window into their net. We were pretty luck—"

"I don't wanna hear it!" Abruptly changing his mind, Buchanan waved him silent. "Take me down there right now, goddammit!"

"LZ Sierra?" Zeke asked unnecessarily.

"Down to the Huey crash site, you idiot!"

"Right. . . . Hold on to your gonads."

The Loach dropped like a rock.

* * *

"I'm ready. I'm ready, I'm ready," Brody whispered over and over as he clutched his Buddha medallion.

Devastating explosions rocking the earth all around him, Treat kept his face against the earth, his head shielded as best he could. But this was the end. He knew it—could feel it in the pit of the gut. Today would see Sgt. Treat Brody's final adventure. The bombing run was not a rapid event. In his mind he had anticipated witnessing the approaching explosions, then a few seconds of bombs falling on either side of the crash site, then the devastation continuing onward as the Arc-Light assault proceeded down the valley. But the bombs just kept on falling all around the crash site—saturating the area—for almost a full minute. The danger quotient had caught up with Treat Brody. This was the end.

Brody felt himself rising out of the dirt as bombs exploded on either side of the crater. And then he was crashing to earth again, nose and ears bleeding, a tooth loose, every bone in his body sending warning jolts to his brain.

He jumped to his feet to find the others—Cordova, Martinez, Styx, and Stone . . . even Big Don—proned out against the wreckage as he had been: eyes closed, heads bowed, bodies curled up into the fetal position as they waited for the blasts to run their course. And, standing now, Sgt. Treat Brody saw something else. Where the steep earthen slope once rose beneath the Americans' former defensive position, what obviously appeared to be an underground tunnel now lay partially exposed.

And the rain of bombs overhead was becoming a paralyzing downpour of shrapnel and shock waves.

"Come on!" Brody screamed, his words mere whispers against the roar of explosions. "Lightning's *gonna* strike!" He raced from man to man, grabbing ears and elbows, pulling them to their feet. "It's gonna strike twice *in the same place!*"

"I'm too short for this shit!" Corporal Styx was yelling. "I'm too short for this shit!"

Sgt. Wickman was already up—he too had sensed something new taking place in their surroundings and was dragging Chance toward the crater's crumbling wall.

Brody's rifle was suddenly barking with rapid-fire speed, right behind him, and the Brick whirled in time to see several North Vietnamese sliding down the crater's opposite wall, trying to find sanctuary from the devastating bombing run above.

Wickman dropped Two-Step, swinging his weapon around, and fired off an entire magazine as well, and half the Communists were dead before they reached the helicopter wreckage. The rest threw down their weapons, refusing to fight. The constant din of explosions overhead was too overpowering to hear what many of the Vietnamese were screaming, but Wickman could read their lips: *Chieu Hoi! Chieu Hoi!* They were surrendering into the amnesty program and apparently expecting to be protected now as prisoners of war—protected from Arc-Light!

Brody and Wickman had no time for them. *"Chieu Hoi* my ass!" The Brick jerked his trigger in.

"Come on!" Whoremonger waved his own people past as Big Don Wickman entered the tunnel without encountering any armed resistance from inside. *"Come on, dammit!"* he screamed at the Huey's crew, who were not anxious to abandon the valuable XM cargo. "Then you're on your own!" Brody wasn't about to sacrifice his life for a bunch of military hardware. And he didn't want to get zapped while the soldiers guarding

256

it were trying to decide what was important in life: one's weapons or one's welfare.

A few seconds after he disappeared into the tunnel, the chopper crewmen all sprinted across the bomb crater's floor and dove in after him.

Good choice! The Air Crew sergeant heard that booming voice inside his head again, and when he turned to look back out the hole in the tunnel wall, he witnessed lightning striking the same place twice. The wild-eyed Communists, scrambling over the scattered helicopter parts and racing after the Americans for the safety of the tunnel, disappeared in a brilliant flash of blinding light.

The explosion tore down more of the reinforced wall and knocked even Big Don Wickman off his feet.

CHAPTER 27

Crash Site Sierra

Bulging red eyes with slashes of vertical yellow through their centers stared back at Treat Brody when he finally came to. The frightening eyes blinked slowly. He noticed his reflection in their depths: ashen-cheeked, face-down in red tunnel dust, helmet askew but still protecting his head somewhat, blood trickling down from his nose and ears, one black eye, and a tooth missing. And then the huge lizard bounded away—frightened off, perhaps, by the incredulous look on Whoremonger's face.

"Well, fuck me till it hurts." He glanced around behind him. Wickman was sitting up, shaking off the stun, but the others—including Two-Step, Martinez and Cordova, Styx and Stone—were still out of it.

And then Brody heard it. Suddenly terrified, he scampered backward on his haunches until his back was against the tunnel's cool earthen wall. And he heard it again: an eerie, total silence.

The bombing run had passed. Arc-Light had moved on.

"You okay, Big Don?" he whispered, glancing around for his M-16.

"Aw, fuck me till it hurts," Wickman muttered, still checking the collection of minor shrapnel wounds across his chest that were coloring his tattered fatigue shirt a purplish crimson. "This ain't no way to make a living."

"Told you we shoulda been gynecologists." Brody forced a slight chuckle.

"You said it, brother. . . ." Wickman still had not looked up, and Brody continued to search for his rifle.

Something gleamed bright silver near the gaping hole in the tunnel wall, and he crawled slowly, cautiously, over to it. "Jesus . . ." He lifted the mangled M-16 for Wickman to see: the entire barrel was missing, and the black fiberglass handguards had been melted down to a shriveled splinter of their former shape.

"That's what you get for losing your weapon, chump." The Brick continued to pluck small bits of iron out of his pectoral muscles.

"It just got away from me, you know?" Treat's words remained a careful whisper in contrast with Wickman's booming, fuck-the-enemy-presence voice.

"Quit making excuses." Big Don was pulling tiny slivers of metal from his scalp now. Rivulets of blood cascaded over his forehead and temples like the chocolate icing on a banana split. Big Don grinned, despite the obvious pain and discomfort, and Brody produced a tight smile as well. "You're a buck sergeant, boy— better start acting like one."

"Hey, what's this?" Whoremonger spotted something else in the scattered debris blocking the hole in the wall. Like his mangled M-16, it sparkled briefly beneath the bright sun sizzling overhead.

"Watch your ass," Wickman warned. "Might be a booby trap, Treat."

"Shit"—Brody laughed aloud for the first time as he glanced at the piles of dismembered NVA bodies littering the bomb crater outside—"them dumbfucks are all dead as they come, Brick. How many bombs you think landed on top o' that Huey wreckage out there?"

"I lost track after the triple crack o' concussions knocked me on my ass." Wickman slowly rose to his feet and began working on his leg wounds. His jungle boots made an odd squishing sound, and Brody knew it was precious blood swirling around inside. "Just simply, fucking lost track, my friend. . . ."

"Yeah, me too." Brody nodded, thankful the storm of shrapnel that struck Wickman had obviously passed him by—even though he had been the last one out of the bomb crater. "Hey, check *this* out!"

Brody slowly pulled a dusty but undamaged XM-148 out of the pile of shredded flesh and twisted helicopter parts. He held the combination automatic rifle and grenade launcher over his head with one hand.

"Check it for a bolt and firing pin," Wickman said quickly, but he sounded unimpressed.

Nodding again, Brody yanked the charging handle back. The dust cover flipped open, and he said, "She's definitely got a bolt. . . ." He broke the weapon down by popping out the frame's center pin and removed the rifle's insides. "Firing pin, too." His eyes gleamed.

"But no magazine," Wickman was swift to point out. "And no ammo."

"No *sweat*." Brody dropped the rucksack from his back—glad to find it was still there—and pulled out a banana clip filled with thirty rounds. He reassembled the rifle in less than sixty seconds and slammed the magazine into its feeder well, jerked on the charging handle again, and basked in the satisfying sound of a live round being chambered. Then he flipped the fire-select switch to safe and locked eyes with Big Don. "Want me to get you one?" he asked.

"First things first." Wickman glanced at the men lying unconscious all around them. Some were rolling over now, returning to a haphazard reality with low groans scratching their throats. "We check on these guys, and do it *rikky-tik*." His own eyes were shifting back and forth along the dark tunnel interiors leading off in opposite directions. "Then we break up into three teams and check out this damn tunnel."

"Three teams?"

"One group stays here to guard the cargo outside there, in the bomb crater. . . ."

"Or what's left of it." Brody did not sound optimistic as he glanced tentatively out into the bright sunlight. "Chance can stay here, too."

Styx and Stone were none the worse for wear, though Stone woke up complaining about his boots being too small for his swollen feet, and Styx's first remark was, "I'm too short for this shit! Four days and a wake-up, gentlemen. I think. . . ."

Martinez seemed to be suffering a slight concussion as well, but Cordova was all right. The other members of Brody's team were stunned and shaken but had not sustained other than superficial shrapnel wounds and would be okay.

The surviving Huey crew members were up and walking within five minutes, except one. Their ranking gunny lay beneath a pile of shattered rifle crates, his head and right arm missing. Brody spent ten minutes searching but was unable to locate the soldier's head.

There were no survivors among the NVA soldiers. Those who were not disintegrated by the barrage of B-52 bombs topside were torn to pieces at the bottom of the crater by the string of three or four 500-pounders that landed atop the Huey wreckage shortly after Brody's people made their hasty exit into the damaged tunnel.

Before Wickman began his tunnel sweep, Brody made a quick check of the bomb crater. There were no signs whatsoever of any of the Communists who had attempted to surrender during the Arc-Light raid. "Well, that solves that," he muttered.

What had once been a crumpled but recognizable helicopter fuselage was now thousands of pieces of scattered fiberglass, magnesium, and electronic parts. The only thing Brody recognized was half of the rotor blade, which was riddled with shrapnel holes and wrapped around a warped M-60 swivel mount. "How many crates did you guys have on board?" he called back to one of the Huey crew members.

"Eight," was the unenthusiastic reply. "Twenty rifles each. Enough for a ragtime company of ARP troopers to play around with for a while."

The distant thunder of Arc-Light, still pulverizing parts of the valley several miles away, remained in Brody's ears. He tried to ignore it, but he found himself constantly gazing up at the calm skies, searching for vapor trails. "Well, there's absolutely *zero* crates left intact." His eyes identified a few planks from former shipment crates. And he was only able to locate one other rifle that was not damaged beyond repair.

"Who wants it?" He glanced at Big Don, who

looked away in silence. Cordova and Martinez also seemed content with their issue M-16s.

"I'll take the sucker." Corporal Styx stepped forward, but Brody ignored him.

"What about you guys?" he asked the Huey crew. "You bled the most for these pricks. Anyone wanna see if they shoot worth a shit?"

"No, thanks," a few men said, with downcast nods.

"Think fast!" With a swift, underhanded toss, Brody heaved the rifle at Styx, who surprised him by catching it with one hand—held out all too casually for what they had just been through together.

"Thanks, Whoremonger." Styx ran his fingers along the XM's slightly pitted barrel, frowning at the damage but smiling again when he examined the grenade launcher attachment.

"Don't give it a second thought, Corp. Oh, and Styx," he added.

"Yeah, Whoremonger?" The corporal did not look up.

"It's *Sergeant* Whoremonger to you," Brody said, his features cold and lineless.

"Sure, Whoremonger." Styx chuckled, eyes still glued to his new weapon. "Say, what the fuck am I supposed to use for frags?" he asked anyone who would listen.

"Stuff your brain down the barrel." Stone fell in step behind Wickman as the Brick started toward the section of tunnel running downslope. "It's small enough to fit."

Eyelids drooping with insult and mock sadness, Styx fixed an unrepentant stare on his partner. "What you got a hair up *your* ass about, fatso?"

"Fuck it," Stone replied.

"You guys come with me." Brody pointed to Cordova and Martinez. "We'll check the other direction."

"Shit." Cordova shook his head from side to side in mild protest but quickly wrapped an arm around Martinez's shoulder, buddylike, and walked him toward the cavalry sergeant.

"Anyone got a flashlight that still works?" Brody examined the shattered red lens of his own. The bulb beneath was also broken.

"Mine's totaled, too." Martinez slowly unhooked the flashlight from his chest harness and let it drop to the ground.

"Here—" Corky threw his light to Treat without checking to see if it worked first.

"The rest of you," Brody said, bypassing the on-off switch and pressing the flashlight's burst button, "stay here and keep an eye on the bomb crater. Styx—you go with Big Don and Stoner." He nodded with satisfaction when the splash of warm light hit him squarely in the face.

"But there ain't nothing left to guard." One of the Huey crewmen dropped his helmet onto the ground and sat on it in mild protest.

"Then climb up to the top of the crater. Keep an eye out for Charlie or the NVA." Brody unscrewed the flashlight's bottom cap and removed a set of thin plastic lens. He inserted the red one inside the bulb housing and replaced the green-and-yellow ones.

"I'll bet it's like the surface of the moon up there." Another man dropped into an exhausted squat. His eyes fell to the dust between his boots, unblinking.

"Well . . ." Brody searched for words and reasons. "Then go up and post a gunship watch. It's only a matter of time before the colonel sends some birds down here to check for survivors."

Three men were already traipsing out into the harsh sunlight. Their heads sifted about, eyes searching for the easiest way up the crater's steep walls.

"I hope Neil Nazi twists some air force wingnuts into an official-fuckin' set o' vise grips over this Romeo-foxtrot," said one of Brody's own people.

"Screw Buchanan," another spat in the dust, "I'm writin' my congressman about *this* clusterfuck, man!"

"You comin' or not?" Wickman called back to Styx, who had paused to listen to the complaints. The dark, downsloping tunnel filled with a red glow as the Brick flipped his L-shaped army-issue flashlight on and off every few seconds.

"I'm your shadow, Big Don," the corporal replied, slapping his XM with renewed pride.

"Then *get* your ass over here, bimbo!" The Brick disappeared around a bend in the tunnel.

"*Right,* oh honorable honcho-san!" And, much to Treat's relief, Styx was gone.

The tunnel was a big one, as guerrilla tunnels in Indochina go—nearly five feet high; the men only had to crouch a little. The walls were a good four feet wide and supported by teakwood beams and, in some places—particularly the bends and forks—sandbags reinforced with packed clay or mud.

"You two know how to do it." Brody locked eyes with Cordova and Martinez before they reached their first bend. Both cavalrymen nodded somberly and waited while Treat advanced up the dangerous turn.

Carefully checking around the wall, he found no hostile activity up ahead and waved Cordova up to his position, then advanced rapidly to the next curve before Corky arrived. Martinez waited where he was until Cordova also disappeared, following after Brody. Martinez would remain flank security during the sweep.

Though it was probably an unnecessary precaution after the bombing, there was always the possibility they might pass a secret side tunnel or hidden chamber from which the enemy could then pop out and terminate them all from behind.

After the second curve, a long, fifty-foot straightaway opened up ahead of them. Brody did not proceed alone but waited for Cordova to join him.

"What do you think?" He gave the cavalryman a moment to survey the situation.

"I'm gettin' bad vibes."

"Me too"—Brody nodded—"but I don't see anything."

"Take off the red lens."

"I don't think so, Gomer. If there's any Cong waitin' for us down there, a white beam of light would—"

"Jesus!" Cordova was fast losing patience. He jerked the flashlight out of Treat's hand and unscrewed the bulb assembly in the dark. "Christ, amigo—ever since they made you a fuckin' sergeant, your brain's been showin' signs of stagnatin' or something."

"Or something," Brody whispered back, grinning.

Cordova's answer was to shine a bright beam of light down the straightaway. "How'd you ever rate such a good set o' batteries, chump?"

"My old man sends 'em fresh every couple weeks from the States."

"Along with those hand flares and CARE packages?"

"Yeah. Ever since we ran into that world o' hurt with the tunnels at Plei Me. . . ."

"Yeah, *that* was a motherfucker. It's nice to have family, ain't it?"

"Yeah."

"You see it?" Cordova's tone changed immediately.

267

It became more businesslike as the nearly invisible strand of wire thirty feet away sparkled slightly in the flashlight beam.

"I see it."

Brody dropped to his hands and knees, then assumed a low-crawl position and started toward the tripwire, flipping the flashlight on and off every few meters to make sure there weren't additional booby traps he'd missed.

When he reached the tripwire without incident, he was quick to locate the satchel of explosives buried in the dirt wall to his right. "C-four," he called back to Cordova. Plastique explosives.

"Fuckin'-A, dude."

"I have nightmares about this shit."

"Just *do it*."

"Kiss my ass, Corky."

"Hey, and Whoremonger?"

"What?"

"Save me some o' that C-four, man . . . I'm out."

Brody knew he was talking about the small supplies every grunt carried for heating C-rations in the field. "I'll think about it."

He quickly determined it was not armed with a pressure-sensitive device. The wire running to his left was anchored to the wall by a railroad stake. On his right, the wire was tied to a primitive nail-and-spring mechanism taped to a dynamite blasting cap. Releasing tension on the tripwire would not cause the satchel to explode—only pulling it farther away from the blasting cap would. He unceremoniously snipped the fishing line in two with the scissors on the Swiss army knife his father had included in his last CARE package.

Brody did not even wince after the job was done but

continued crawling on down the straightaway. If it blew, it blew.

When he finally reached the next curve, he waved both Cordova and Martinez up to his location.

"Well, fuck me till it hurts." Marty sighed.

"Hey, that's *my* line." Cordova grinned at Brody.

"Yo' mama, taco-bender."

"There's two of us taco-benders and one of you loaves of white bread, boy." Cordova bared his teeth with considerable enjoyment. "And we gonna slice you up one side and down the other. . . ."

Brody laughed aloud as they all slapped each other around playfully.

The pressure was off.

Cordova stared at the bamboo ladder rising up from the dead end around the corner, to a trapdoor in the tunnel's sloping roof ten feet above. "Spider hole?" he asked, though it was obviously not necessary.

"Definitely the entrance."

"Probably a jungle trail topside."

"You don't think it might lead up to an NVA camp or something?"

"Or something. I don't wanna find out if that trapdoor's booby-trapped on both sides, brother," Cordova said. "And you know it probably is."

"Besides . . ." Martinez was shaking his head. "Even if there is . . . or was a North Viet camp up there, it's gone now after that Arc-Light bombing run."

"He's right." Cordova locked eyes with Brody.

"Which means Big Don Wickman is headed in the right direction, and we weren't."

"And the Brick is headed for whatever Charlie built this tunnel to hide."

"I'll bet it's an underground hospital complex," Martinez said. "I read in *Stars and Stripes* the brass at

Disneyland East think the Cong got a big one in this valley somewhere.''

"Let's beat feet.'' Cordova started running back down the winding tunnel in the direction of the bomb crater and the unknown that lay beyond.

"Last one there is eligible for a body bag.'' Martinez left Brody the Whoremonger spinning in the dark.

CHAPTER 28

Crash Site Sierra

Big Don Wickman was moving excruciatingly slowly down the dimly lit tunnel. Less than a minute and three turns after splitting up from Brody's people and the contingent left to guard the bomb crater, Wickman's group came across what appeared to be a generator-operated system of sagging wires and bare light bulbs hanging from the ceiling. The lights were not what was providing illumination, however. At each curve in the widening tunnel, lanterns glowed faintly—giving off just enough light for one to safely make it to the next underground bend.

They had already passed four connecting tunnel shafts. Wickman had dispatched a man into each, but they all returned to report the tunnels quickly narrowed into impassable crevices that appeared to shift into nothing more than vertical air shafts.

The flank guard in his team nearly fired a shot at

Brody when a sudden flurry of footfalls announced the unexpected arrival of Whoremonger's team.

"What'd you find?" Wickman asked calmly, eyes darting to the faces of four additional soldiers Brody accrued after passing by the bomb crater again. He recognized only two: the teenaged privates, Grove and Pasco.

"We found the entrance."

"And one lousy tripwire," Cordova added.

"That's what I figured."

"Any contact?"

"None. Coupla air shafts, but that's it. We've been switching on and off every couple turns." Wickman motioned toward his men.

"To keep everybody sharp." Styx sounded skeptical.

"I'm gettin' bad vibes about this place, gentlemen," Stone said. "Bookoo bad vibes. It ain't worth it. I wanna go back to the crater. I wanna go topside and wait for a motherfuckin' extraction slick. This is gonna become our *tomb*, you guys . . . I can *feel* it."

"Stoner, you'd get bad vibes at a free orgy." Cordova dismissed the corporal's complaints.

"I'll take a turn." Brody rubbed his hands. "I'm startin' to get a real feel for this place." He eyed the upcoming bend with some anticipation.

"Be my guest." Wickman held a hand out, palm up.

"Follow the leader." Brody waved Cordova after him, and then the Brick's people fell in step as well, but Treat hadn't gone far beyond the first turn when an unseen plank of wood in the wall to his left—coated with dry mud—popped out and slammed down on the tunnel floor.

"Hit the dirt!" Brody yelled as the Vietnamese guerrilla popped out, brandishing an AK-47 assault rifle.

His men proning-out automatically behind him, Brody dropped into a low crouch and cut loose with a long burst on full automatic at the same time as the VC.

An AK round singed his cheek, but the rest of the green tracer burst flew over his right shoulder and down the tunnel—into the earthern wall at the first turn.

Brody's bullets caught the Viet in the groin and pelvis, and as he flopped forward his assault rifle sent its final magazine burst into several of the men lying in the dark behind Whoremonger.

The tunnel filled with groans as Brody rushed forward, kicking the Viet's rifle away. Then he noticed the Viet Cong's ankle was fitted with a leg iron. A thick chain ran from the manacle to a long iron shaft pounded down into a packed mud base inside the hidden chamber.

Brody had seen it before. The insurgent had probably broken some rule, committed some infraction recently, and his punishment was a couple of days guarding the underground complex's access tunnel. Or the Viet Cong were actually in full retreat now, and this low-ranking private was sentenced to stay behind and slow down the advance of any Americans sent to search the tunnel. The leg iron was applied to ensure the guard didn't bug out when the going got rough.

Brody placed the barrel of his XM against the VC's nose, pressing the guerrilla's nostrils flat, and began to bring in the trigger. The Vietnamese stared up at him, but oddly enough he was not wild-eyed or shaking violently. There was no plea for mercy. Rather, it looked like he welcomed death . . . like he wanted a release from the pain.

"Back off, Whoremonger." It was Corky Cordova, urging restraint, as usual. "We need to talk to the fuckhead, man . . . need to ask him some questions about this hellhole.''

"Shit." Brody leaned into the rifle's butt plate. "None of us speaks Viet good enough to question a northerner, Cork. This jerkaholic probably speaks some Hanoian dialect to boot." But Brody held back. The sounds of Styx and Stone scurrying about, tending to the wounded, made him think. "Aw, screw it." He lifted his weapon. "Better to make the zip motherfucker suffer." And he nudged the Viet Cong's shin slightly, enjoying the renewed grimace of pain on his dark, sallow face.

None of it would have mattered. Brody watched the man's eyeballs roll up into the tops of their sockets. His limbs went slightly rigid. The blood continued to flow from lower torso wounds, but they were no longer gushing with heartbeatlike spurts.

"We gotta carry these guys back to the bomb crater," Styx was telling Stone and Cordova. "We gotta hustle 'em back *now*! And we gotta get a Dustoff slick to beat blades in here an' med-evac 'em out!" But the groaning sounds coming from behind Brody ceased abruptly as well, and he turned to find Corporal Styx suddenly crestfallen, his shoulders stooping heavily, tears dripping from his eyes as he stared down at an unbreathing Marty Martinez.

"Aw, *shit*, kid." Brody rushed over, dropped to one knee beside the private.

Three AK rounds had stitched across the teenager's face horizontally: right eye, dead center, then left eye. Brody turned away and stared at the tunnel ceiling, thoughts cursing Charlie's ghost—who was surely still there, nearby, looking down at them and laughing while he lingered in limbo, waiting for his next life to take shape, form, plop him on his head between the spread legs of some woman lying on her back.

"I'm too short for this—" Styx began, his voice trailing off as Brody checked Martinez for a pulse for the third time but still found none.

Several of the crewmen from the XM cargo chopper were also dead from multiple gunshot wounds to the head and chest. Two of Brody's people bit the dust as well: the cherry boys Grove and Pasco. Treat could not believe it: both killed instantly as a result of tiny, minute slivers of lead that managed to pierce an artery lining the heart muscle.

"You lucked out, motherfucker!" Brody was on his feet again, a blur of motion as he moved through the dazed and shaken troops to the Viet Cong's body. "You really lucked out, didn't you, man?" And he began kicking the corpse's face. "You managed to take out a whole *bunch* o' the enemy with you when you checked out, *didn't* you, asshole? You *proud,* man? They were cherry boys, asshole . . . newbies with no time in grade . . . no Nam under their belts!"

Cordova was behind him now, trying to restrain the Air Cav sergeant. "Forget it, Whoremonger! The gook's dead, man! He ain't worth *this,* man. . . ."

"Sgt. Wickman!" Stone's high-pitched yell startled them both, and for the first time Brody noticed that Big Don was still facedown in the dust, unmoving.

"Yo, *Brick!*" He leaped over the VC's bleeding body and slid up to Wickman on his knees. "Big Don! You okay, brother?! Hey, *Brick!*"

"Aw, mannnn," Wickman groaned as they rolled him over onto his side.

"Christ, someone break out a compress!" Brody muttered as his own fingers fumbled with the first-aid pouch on his web belt. A deep gash ran along the side of Wickman's head, from just above his right eyebrow to a spot directly behind the ear.

"Is that bone?" Cordova was fumbling for the flashlight Brody had loaned him earlier, but Stone already had a pencil-thin beam of light trained on the wound.

"Yeah," he muttered.

"Well, shit. . . ." Brody checked Big Don's pupils. "He's gonna make it, though, man! He's gonna make it—"

"It's just a goddamn flesh wound!" Cordova agreed.

"A flesh wound to the fuckin' bone!" Styx sounded a bit more pessimistic.

"But he *is* gonna make it!" Stone pushed his partner back out of the flashlight's beam.

"No shit," Wickman groaned again. "Would you ladies back off and give a real man some air, for chrissake?"

"Well, all *right*!"

Brody had only managed to wrap the bandage around Wickman's head a few times, and it started to droop down around the big NCO's eyebrows as he moved. Treat resumed the first-aid, and though his hands came up defensively with the first bolts of pain, Wickman allowed him to continue.

"I thought bricks didn't bleed." Stone's attempt at healing humor was met with several glares from the rest of the men. He shrugged and turned away to double-check the other casualties for any signs of life. "I was just trying to—"

But Cordova cut him off. "What do we do now?" he asked Brody. "Can we move Big Don? Can we . . . I mean, should we wait for some medics—"

"I can move," Wickman answered for himself. Brushing Brody away and taking the loose ends of the compress, he tied the knot on his own, then rose to his feet shakily. Cordova rushed to his side for support.

"You shouldn't be standin', Brick." Brody was shaking his head from side to side. "That fuckin' AK round 'bout split your skull, man. We could see the bone. . . ."

"I heard ya," came an irritated reply. Their ranking sergeant was holding his eyes tightly closed. Both hands pressed against his ears now, as if trying to keep the seams of his cranium from splitting apart.

"I say we trot back to the bomb crater," Cordova suggested. "We've cleared this tunnel enough to ensure our safety. We can leave a guard here to make sure that *if* there's any Cong down there"—he pointed down the slope they had yet to traverse—"we'll have plenty of warning if they try anything."

"I think we should post a corporal," Brody agreed. "Like Stoner."

"Or Styx!" Stone was quick to make his own suggestion.

"Now let's gather up our dead and take 'em back to the crater," Brody said. "I'd say them Arc-Light jet-jockies have called it a day."

"We should be able to get Gabriel or somebody to come into the valley and get us the hell out of here." Cordova was shaking his head up and down rapidly.

"You're all wrong." Wickman slowly stooped over and picked up his M-16. With the muzzle, he pointed toward the dimly lit unknown dropping down the tunnel slope in front of them.

"You're shittin' me, Brick." Treat was surprised Big Don wanted to continue the sweep.

"I'm getting a special feeling about this place, Whoremonger. Somethin' in my gut tells me we're gettin' close to an answer. . . ."

277

"You sure it's not shrapnel?" Styx remarked, but Big Don ignored him.

"Let's go." He led the way, still holding his head with one hand, his weapon on the other.

Around the next bend, death was waiting for them.

CHAPTER 29

Over Fire Base Belinda

Snakeman Fletcher was feeling immortal again. This always happened whenever *Pegasus* flew into a firestorm of incoming machine-gun rounds, and bursts of lead passed through the hatch on either side of Elliot, failing to smack flesh.

"Take 'er down, Gunslinger!" he clicked in, knuckles white as he grasped the swinging M-60. "Snakeman *needs* to get some *more*, mister!"

"Bad boys on the starboard side!" Warrant Officer Cliff Gabriel announced. "Attempting to swing around at this time, Fletch."

"Thanks, bossman!" He glanced back over his shoulder at the ship's right side hatch. It was smeared with blood, and the starboard door gunner hung bent over and lifeless from his monkeystraps—the victim of a twenty-round burst from the ground.

As *Pegasus* swung around, Fletcher spotted a platoon of Viet Cong riflemen huddled behind a mound of sandbags, above the perimeter wire on Fire Base Belinda's east slope. Only one VC was using his weapon, and the man was ignoring the hovering helicopter. He appeared to be directing all his shots at something else to the north.

Fletcher leaned into his hatch-60, unloading on the huddled platoon, until some hundred or more rounds tore down into their scattering ranks. The unceasing stream of bullets whipped up a whirlwind of dust and smoke that quickly concealed the two or three survivors sprinting away from each other in opposite directions.

And then Snakeman spotted the target his VC rifleman was shooting at—or, rather, the object's shadow fell across his field of vision.

Sharkskinner II!

"Hey-*hey*! Welcome to the show, Warlokk!" he muttered under his breath, not bothering to click in since his headset wasn't channeled to talk on the ship-to-ship frequency anyway.

A sleek, two-manned Cobra gunship darted between the smoke columns rising up all over the artillery fire support base. It was piloted by Lance "Lawless" Warlokk, the notorious warrant officer who recently crashed the original Sharkskinner into the side of a mountain and lived to tell about it. The ship he now was flying still sported two bullet holes in its side cockpit window—where the craft's assigned pilot was hit several hours earlier, before he could even lift off from one of Buffy's helipads. Warlokk had promptly claimed the Cobra as his own, and the Echo Company old-timers like Snakeman and Gabriel were already calling it Sharkskinner II.

Fletcher dropped one of the sprinting guerrillas with a ten-round burst, and Warlokk's gunship swooped down on the other two, knocking them out with its landing skids, ripping open the flesh along their backbones, flaring into sideways hovers above the whirlwind long enough to drop a belt of minigun rounds into the carnage, then suddenly ascending through the many layers of smoke cloaking the camp.

"Did you see *that*?" Fletcher clicked in.

"Always showin' off," Gabe replied with little emotion, if any.

He wondered who Warlokk's new gunner was. The pilot's last few partners had not fared so well, riding The Nam skies with Lawless holding the cyclic. Snakeman always enjoyed checking out the new gunners and peter pilots firsthand. He'd produce his best wary-eyed thousand-yard stare for them, and they in turn never failed to provide that bewildered, slack-jawed FNG look when he strode by in torn and shredded jungle fatigues, face blackened with charcoal, a ragged M-60 over his shoulder.

"Take us down lower," Snakeman requested urgently. "I wanna find that two-titted sapper with the long hair, Gunslinger!"

"Sorry 'bout that, Snake," came the dull reply, "but we're as low as it goes, now that Sharkskinner two's on-station. You know how Lance is when he's got a newby on board. Always tryin' to get 'em to upchuck all over their chickenplate. I'd just as soon keep *Peg* in the background—can't afford no down time right now. Know you understand, big guy."

"Shit." Snakeman understood, of course, but that was no reason to go with the flow and cooperate with Gabe.

"Fuck it," he muttered, glancing out the starboard hatch as Gabriel swung *Pegasus* around for another pass. He stared down at the smoke-laced valley below, counting the bomb craters visible in several new breaks in the jungle's triple canopy. He thought about Big Don Wickman and Whoremonger and the rest of his buddies shakin' and bakin' down there during the Arc-Light bombing run, and he wondered if any of them had survived.

Small as a black speck against the endless carpet of greens and grays, he spotted Col. Buchanan's Loach circling down through the low clouds below Fire Base Belinda's timberline, with two escorting gunships, searching for the original Huey crash site . . . seeking desperately to locate any survivors of the Air Force's rolling thunder assault.

When the five-hundred-pounders first began to fall, *Peg*'s crew feared Fire Base Belinda, and perhaps even Buffy, might be the intended target—judging by the vapor trails directly overhead. But then the devastation fell upon the Nam Sathay River Valley instead, with an exacting preciseness that was eerie. Too bad they were an hour early.

Fletcher almost wished Buchanan's Loach and the two Hueys riding escort duty were back up here, circling Fire Base Belinda with *Pegasus* and Sharkskinner II and the other gunships trying to retake the mountaintop camp with sheer firepower and pounce-and-strafe tactics. It was time to get to work, sweep up the mess, and wrap up this campaign once and for all.

"Okay, Snakeoil . . ." He heard Gabriel's scratchy voice as the warrant officer clicked in. "Lawless is off on the other side of the hill, takin' a shit. . . . Ready to swoop in and increase the body count?"

"Ready and—" Fletcher was going to say "waiting," but, as he was fond of doing, Gabe the Gunslinger dropped pitch without warning, and *Pegasus* shot nearly straight down on top of the enemy's positions with gut-flopping speed.

"Real funny, Gunslinger," Fletch clicked in after swallowing the morning's C-rations back down, as he let his Hog-60 rip on rock and roll.

In the Tunnels Beneath LZ Sierra

"Is it dead?"

"Well, if it ain't"—Brody brought his rifle to his shoulder—"it's sure *gonna* be."

"Wait." Sgt. Wickman was beside him now, grabbing Treat's other shoulder gently for emphasis. "I've already got a mother of a migraine you wouldn't believe—I don't need you bustin' a banana clip worth o' caps in an underground tunnel to make things worse."

"Then whatta you suggest, Brick?" Stone stood abreast of Brody.

Wickman stared long and hard at the unmoving cobra. Waiting for them around the next turn after their argument over whether or not to continue the tunnel sweep, the snake was a good twenty to twenty-five feet long, but it was not coiled as if ready to strike. The serpent lay against the tunnel wall, belly up, straight, and limp.

"I'll check it." Wickman started forward.

This time it was Brody who did the arm grabbing. "I don't think you should, Big Don."

"Them cobras are sneaky," Styx agreed. "Maybe it's just playing dead."

"Belly up?" Wickman did not glance over at the corporal but continued toward the giant reptile. "I don't think so."

"Suit yourself." Styx flipped his rifle's fire selector

283

to full auto and took a bead on the creature's sparkling eyes—just in case.

"That's the *biggest* goddamn snake I've ever seen in my life." Stone let out a low whistle to prove he was impressed.

"Can it, Stoner," Cordova snapped, staring at the serpent's unblinking eyes.

"Wonder what cobra meat tastes like." Wickman dropped to one knee beside the huge reptile's head and ran his palm along the scales between its lower jaw hinge.

"Probably like every other kind of snake meat," Styx said, offering his culinary expertise. "Chicken."

"Only rattlers taste like chicken," Stone disagreed. "Snakes in The Nam taste weird."

"What would you know about it?" Styx glared at his ex-partner.

"I been to the army's survival school in Panama. They made us catch and eat snakes there."

"I went with you, remember? Those were Panamanian snakes."

"Oh."

"There's a difference."

Brody spoke next. "Tell me somebody shot the thing, Big Don. 'Cause I don't wanna hear that—"

"There ain't a wound anywhere on the monster." Wickman turned the cobra over with some effort.

The self-amused smiles vanished from the faces of Styx and Stone. "You mean . . ." Stone began.

"Poison gas again?" Styx swallowed loudly.

Wickman nodded. "Looks that way. The Cong probably kept this sucker cooped up in this one chamber of the tunnel. . . ."

"You mean"—Cordova stepped closer to the evil-looking serpent—"sort of like a watchdog?"

284

"Sort of." Wickman glanced up at him.

"I'm gettin' *out* of here!" Styx announced. "We've been *wayyyy* too lucky up to now!" He pointed at the snake. "I don't wanna follow *that* damn thing into the hereafter, Sarge!"

"Forget it." Brody remained calm. "If there was any of the gas lingering in this chamber, we'd already be knocked out by now—don't you think so, Don?"

"Sgt. Brody's right." Wickman nodded again. "Come on. Let's see what else there is in this hole."

CHAPTER 30

Fire Base Belinda

"Our intelligence unit advises the Americans are assembling helicopter units at Pleiku and An Khe," Trinh Thi Kim reported to Major Minh as the North Vietnamese officer was escorted up from the frenzy of activity along Belinda's eastern perimeter. "But they will not be able to respond to the Americans' call for help until tomorrow morning, first light, because of a storm in the area around the Air Cavalry camps."

"What about the other firebase?" Lam Van Minh's chin pointed in the direction of the artillery camp less than a mile up-valley.

"The GIs at Buffy are too worried about a People's attack on their own base to cut manpower in half by sending reinforcements here to supplement Colonel Buchanan's small contingent of helicopter gunships. The Seventh Cavalry's Echo Company is on its own."

"So the soldiers at Buffy are too concerned about

defending their own camp to risk leaving it, and the home units are grounded by rain. . . .'' Minh scratched at a cut on his chin.

"That is the runner's report, Commander."

"How did the Americans succeed in getting word to Pleiku and the other division commands? Their radios are not able to transmit beyond the mountains."

Kim lowered her eyes slightly and did not immediately respond.

"Well?" Minh reached forward and grabbed the woman's petite chin, jerking her face back up.

"Intelligence fears we have a spy in our ranks, Commander."

"A spy? *What* spy?"

"They do not know. But it is the only way the Americans could get word to Pleiku—if a Vietnamese relayed it out of the *Chaine Annamitique*, and then our own PRG radio net was utilized."

Minh was fuming as his mind reviewed the possibilities, but he did not continue with the subject—there were just too many "volunteers" streaming up from the villes and hamlets surrounding Fire Base Belinda. The traitor could be any one of them—any *number* of them! He should not have been so careless welcoming all citizens who offered help in overthrowing and chasing out the Imperialists. He should have known the Saigon regime would have informers among them. "What of the B fifty-two attack? What is the latest report on survivors?" He stomped his muddy boots against the earth.

Kim stared at the dirt clods rolling away. "The headquarters bunker has lost contact with the northern contingent charged with escorting the shipment of antihelicopter rockets into the province," she said.

288

"What?" Minh demanded, whirling to face her again.

"We have a man on the way to the crash site where several crates of some new type of weapon were being guarded, but it is doubtful anything remains of that cargo—damage from the bomber strike was extensive, Commander. The fate of the Americans and PRG forces fighting over the downed helicopter transport is unknown, but, once again, it is highly doubtful any of them could have survived such a saturation bombing by the B fifty-twos."

"Agreed." Minh nodded. "Why do you not yet have your people manning these antiaircraft guns?" His narrowed eyes darted about suddenly.

Kim's own sloe orbs scanned the smoke-laced perimeter. Some of the gun pits had Communist-bloc weapons mounted in them—NVA 12.7mm heavy machine guns and even twin-37mm guns, which could fire up to 180 rounds per minute (armament the Americans had no doubt captured from the North Vietnamese and put to good use, she knew). "They are not familiar with the U.S.-made heavy weapons," she began. "But I have them servicing the—"

"Never mind." Minh silenced her with a wave of his hand. "My own people are here in sufficient numbers to take over now. . . ." His nod was most arrogant. Kim felt properly rebuffed, and the flesh stretched taut across her cheeks and forehead began to burn.

"Then, with your permission . . ."

"Your guerrillas are to be commended." Minh's tone softened. "Relay my thanks to them. . . ."

"Yes, sir."

"And return to your duties. Have your people reinforce the trenches between the antiaircraft gun pits."

"Yes, sir. . . ." *Reinforce the shitholes*, Kim was thinking.

"Oh, and Comrade Kim . . ."

"Yes, sir?"

"You've done a fine job." His eyes did not meet hers. "I shall see to it your cell leader is informed. You show potential. Perhaps you would enjoy a trip north . . . for a few months. . . ."

"Sir?" Kim did not immediately comprehend.

"North, Comrade Kim." His tone assumed its superior grating quality again. "Hanoi. A training camp, perhaps. Yes, leadership training. We have many women studying in—"

"My place is here in the south," Kim said quickly. "With my people."

"Ah, yes. . . ." Minh nodded ever so slowly, a mock sadness filling his eyes. "Of course."

"You!" She pointed at a female cadre member standing nearby, manning one of the machine gun nests. "Come over here! *Now!*"

The woman handed the M-60 handle to a young girl who was straightening out a long belt of MG ammunition.

"Yes, Commander?" Obviously intimidated, she bowed slightly in Kim's presence—refusing to look up at Major Minh.

"How long have you been fighting alongside me, sister?"

"Two years this coming month, Commander."

"The girl over there . . . at the machine gun." Kim motioned toward the youngster with the flat chest—who immediately glanced away. "She is blood?"

"My younger sister by four years, Commander."
Both women dropped into a low crouch as two helicop-

ter gunships rushed past overhead, somewhere above the dense ceiling of smoke.

"She knows how to operate the M-sixty?" Kim asked, but her question was answered when the girl whirled around with the swivel-mounted machine gun and began firing at the fading sound of flapping rotors.

"Ah, good." Kim nodded, but the woman beside her unleashed a torrent of rapid Vietnamese at her sister, telling her they must conserve ammunition for now. The gunship continued on, apparently undamaged.

"I must go," Minh interrupted with a smoothly executed pivot of both boots. His back was already turned to the women. "I instructed those captains to place LPs below the wire—looks like I have to do everything myself! You two carry on, please."

Kim watched the major stalk off purposefully toward the fire base's old command post. She spoke as if there had been no interruption. "Who do you know among us," Kim asked the girl, "that might be able to operate the quad-fifties over there?"

"None whom I am acquainted with, Commander. I have never seen such big guns before."

"But a gun is a gun, is it not?" Kim's eyes seemed to boil now. "And are you telling me that out of five hundred freedom fighters, we cannot find someone to shoot it for me?"

"I do not know any such people, Commander"— the woman's lips sought out the right words—"but I know others who might know them. . . ."

"Then find them!" Through a break in the clouds and smoke screen, Kim's eyes spotted movement far below: Buchanan's small helicopter descending in a tight circular pattern toward the recently bombed valley. "I am tired of seeing so many gun barrels sitting idle. The bastard in the black Loach is at the center of all my

291

troubles, and now he sets down his ship amid a barren stretch of bomb craters. Well, we shall give him a taste of the big guns.'' Kim pulled a map wrapped in plastic from her loose-fitting blouse and began to triangulate the colonel's position.

"Yes, Commander!" The woman fled without bowing again. She did not so much as glance at her younger sister but dashed into a rolling bank of smoke from the burning ammo dumps.

"And be quick about it, or when we make it out of this mess you'll be polishing punji sticks along the Laotian border!"

Tunnels Beneath LZ Sierra

Around the next bend the tunnel forked into three smaller tunnels. None were lit with lanterns or bulbs. All were pitch black and damp. "Which one now?"

"I say . . . *left*. . . ." "Left for Lenin," Styx offered.

"That means we go right, Corky," Whoremonger said, charging off into the darkness.

"Shit!" Cordova fell in pursuit after the grinning buck sergeant.

"Hey!" Wickman yelled. "You two watch your butts in there!" He held out an arm, blocking Styx and Stone's path.

"What the fuck, over?" Stone trained a shocked look on Big Don.

"Three's a crowd. Four's a funeral." The stocky NCO left no room in the narrow tunnel for argument.

"Jesus. . . ." Styx bit into his lower lip stifling the protest he knew he would only come to regret later— the Brick was always right.

Brody ran for a full minute before realizing how dangerous they were acting. This tunnel was half the width of the main corridor and sloping gently downward. It was dark as a cellar, and although he was flipping his flashlight on every other second or so, he was still trotting much too fast, outracing the beam. At this pace he'd never be able to stop in time for a tripwire—and that was if he were able to spot it at all.

As he slowed cautiously, Cordova slammed into the back of him. "Jesus, Treat!" Cordova whispered loudly. "Watch where you're stopping, man! Your brake lights is burned out."

"Use your goddamn flashlight, Cork!"

"I can't—you've got it."

"Oh. . . ."

A dim glow appeared in the distance, and both Americans froze, pressing their bodies to either wall, trying to make themselves the smallest-possible target.

Without words, both cavalrymen immediately set about clearing the huge rectangular chamber—it was roughly the size of a four-car garage back in The World. They split up in opposite directions, Cordova checking one way clockwise, Brody counterclockwise.

After they met against the opposite wall a minute later, both soldiers agreed in whispered conversation that there was no other exit or entrance visible. But they also knew no self-respecting Cong would leave such an avenue of escape out in the open. It was no doubt hidden behind one of the many crates crowding the cubicle.

The floor was strengthened with helipad tarmac. "You know all that tarmac that's been missin' from the colonel's private helipad?" Brody nodded down at the metal flooring.

"Yep," Cordova agreed.

"I always suspected his housegirl was Commie to the core."

"Isn't every colonel's?"

Wooden crates were stacked floor to ceiling. The ceiling was ten to twelve feet up and reinforced with teakwood planks and bamboo poles. "Quite a setup," Cordova decided.

"Not bad. But these aren't ammo or weapons crates, Cork."

"And that ain't Chinese script, Ivan." Cordova pointed at the small red letters stenciled to the side of every crate. "Whatta ya say we break a couple open?"

"Sounds good," Brody said, taking out his survival knife to pry open the nearest crate.

As he moved closer, he saw a camou pant leg protruding slightly from underneath it. "What the fuck—"

Cordova helped Treat lift the long wrapped bundle out of the crate. They removed several coils of twine and pulled back the plastic flap.

"Not bad." Brody stared down at the woman's body. She was naked and lying facedown on what appeared to be another body. A man's, fully clothed.

Suddenly the nude corpse rattled from side to side slightly and rose up a few inches, only to plop back down, unmoving again.

"Whoaaaaaa!" Cordova's jungle boots did the ballet of the great retreat, but he went nowhere because Brody the Whoremonger was holding on to his collar.

"Wait . . . one . . . minute!" He didn't sound nearly as spooked as the Cork. "There's something funny going on here." Brody reached down and took hold of the woman's waist.

"Oh . . . Lordy!" Cordova squeezed his eyes tightly

shut when an ugly slurping sound rose from the woman's ripped-open midsection.

"Damn." Brody removed his hands—found that they were soaked with blood. "Help me with this bitch, Corky!" He sounded irritated now, and Cordova slowly complied.

They grabbed her by the shoulders and ankles and gently lifted her off a wide-eyed, bound-and-gagged John Graves.

"Graves!" Brody quickly set the female corpse down, then leaned over the mumbling CIA agent. "What the hell are you doin' down here, man?"

Graves continued to mumble unintelligible exclamations. Brody leaned closer. "What?"

Graves's eyes bulged as if for emphasis.

"Oh. . . ." Brody reached down and ripped the tape from Graves's lips, then pulled the blood-soaked ammo bandolier out of his mouth. "What the fuck, over?" He winced when the agent yelled from the delayed sting.

"Get me outta here!" Graves shook his shoulders, the body language telling Brody he was talking about the bindings and the blood-soaked crate.

"Uh, right. . . ."

"Treat," Cordova said. "Check this chick out, man."

"VC?" Brody was busy untying Graves's wrists and ankles and didn't look down.

"Yeah. But this'll give you some idea of how they treat their own. . . . She's the one we wasted on the trail back there . . . before Arc-Light."

"Holy shit." Brody glanced down at Graves. "Why'd they toss her in on top of you like that, man?"

"Who can tell why these people do *anything* the way they do it?" Graves was free to move now.

"What's Charlie storin' down here?" Cordova asked the CIA agent.

His shirt and jeans soaked with the dead woman's blood, John Graves walked over to the nearest crate and ripped a plank free. He pulled out a small blue canister the size of a beer can.

"Truck oil?" Cordova started toward him.

"Gas," he said simply.

"What?" The cavalryman froze in his tracks and glanced over at Brody for command guidance.

"It's why I'm here in the valley in the first place." Graves began a long explanation. "The North Vietnamese are attempting to introduce a Soviet gas agent to the ground fighting south of the DMZ—at least they were attempting to start experimentation with it. In a highly diluted dose, the gas only renders its victims unconscious. But in larger quantities, or under adverse atmospheric conditions, the gas becomes lethal. We only suspected the Commies were up to chemical warfare for the last year or two, but recently one of our Arvin agents tuned us in to this operation here. That was just before she was killed. My mission was to obtain a sample of the gas—which I did—along with photographs, any applicable intelligence data, and whatever else might support the state department's case when we brought the whole affair to the attention of the United Nations."

"Jesus H." Cordova crossed himself.

"Heavy-duty shit." Brody was shaking his head, too.

"Right. From what I've been able to ascertain by eavesdropping on activities around here, the Air America Loach which I smuggled the sample to either crashed or was shot down by Charlie right after I left the LZ drop site."

"I may be wrong, Graves, but something tells me

296

your boys in the Loach somehow accidentally broke the container's seal. The gas escaped, disabling the pilot, and the Loach crashed back to the ground moments after takeoff. Least that's my theory.''

"Hmphhh.'' Graves contemplated the cavalry sergeant's account of the Loach incident.

"And no sign of enemy activity that might have caused the crash,'' Cordova added. "No bullet holes, shit like that. . . .''

"I see. . . .''

"So finish your story,'' Brody said.

"Right. Anyway, on the way out of the area, I ran into a VC patrol. They were probably on my tail the entire time—and when I tried to flee, they filled my jeep with bullet holes, disabling it, and took me prisoner after a good old knock-down, drag-out fight. . . .''

Cordova nodded. "We found your jeep.''

"D'you bust many noses, Graves?'' Brody sounded somewhat skeptical.

"Damned straight, Whoremonger.''

"Let's get out of here,'' Brody decided.

"What about the broad?'' Cordova motioned down at the dead Viet Cong sapper.

"Pretty face, even in death,'' Graves observed.

"Throw 'er back in the crate, if you want,'' Brody told Cordova. He didn't sound very sympathetic. "Hey, Graves,'' he added.

"Hey what, Brody?'' It was evident everyone was getting irritated—more irritated than usual.

"Is this the only way in or out?'' Brody was standing in the chamber's main entrance.

"Believe it or not, yes . . . as far as I know.''

"He's *always* got a shitload of secret exits in his tunnels,'' Cordova, speaking in reference to all Cong collectively, agreed. "But we ain't got time to search behind every crate. There must be two hundred of 'em.''

"Enough to put all of Saigon to sleep." Treat's eyes scanned the countless rows of Russian writing.

Graves nodded somberly. "The *deep* sleep."

"Permission to enter!" came a gruff voice from the smaller access tunnel outside. Brody and Cordova exchanged worn-out glances: Styx.

"What's the password?" Cordova challenged the corporal.

"Ho Chi Minh's a homo."

"Enter."

Wickman followed Styx and Stone into the storage cache. "Well, well . . . and what do we have here?" Big Don's narrowed, bloodshot eyes roamed the underground warehouse. "Spook's day off?"

"Hello, Don," Graves said. "Long time."

Wickman stared at the open, blood-soaked crate. "Not long enough."

CHAPTER 31

LZ Sierra

Buchanan welcomed his men with open arms when they returned to LZ Sierra, carrying their dead.

"The colonel took a team down in there looking for you," one of the privates assigned to remain behind at the bomb crater crash site started to explain.

"But we took the wrong tunnel when it forked into three." Buchanan frowned.

"By any chance was it the middle one?" Cordova asked.

"Left"—the colonel shook his head—"for Lenin."

Cordova lifted his chin toward Brody and smiled.

Wickman's gaze followed a long, folding ladder up the crater's west wall. The chopper crews had spent the last half hour making it easier for the walking wounded to get up out of the pit. Big Don nodded—it was a welcome relief. Sometimes the small actions were the most appreciated.

Above, the gentle flapping of idling helicopter rotors reached the men's ears. It was a good sound to hear . . . a welcome sound, after Arc-Light's deafening salute.

Wickman waited until all the dead were carried out of the bomb crater before leaving the pit himself. For the time being, the underground cache would be left untouched. It could wait. Right now every able body was needed for the continuing counterassaults against the insurgents atop Fire Base Belinda.

He set the explosive charge that would seal the two tunnel entrances, then scurried up the ladder, his head throbbing from the untreated bullet wound.

Two sharp explosions jarred the ground beneath them as the cavalrymen of Echo Company dragged their boots and their rifle butts and the body bags containing their buddies back to the waiting choppers.

"This is truly a cursed land," Treat Brody told Big Don as they started to climb up over one of the helicopter's landing skids.

"Yeah . . ." Sgt. Wickman seemed to consider his words for a moment. "But somebody's got to give a damn, Whoremonger. . . ." He peeled his sweat-soaked flak jacket off, folded it in two, and fashioned it into a cushion that was designed not for comfort but to protect one's private parts. He propped it beside the snoozing door gunner.

"Uncle Sammy's lucky guys like you and me keep hangin' on here, right, Brick?"

"Got that right."

Brody was first aboard, and when he reached down to offer his fellow NCO a hand, both eyes darted up to movement in a nearby field of charred and blackened tree trunks, all but destroyed by the Arc-Light bombing run.

300

"Look out! Charlie in the trees!" Someone else had spotted the platoon of enemy soldiers as well. Dazed and shaken, some wearing torn uniforms and others nothing at all, faces blackened, arms and legs bloodied, the survivors stumbled from what had once been the edge of the rain forest. Only a few still carried rifles.

Big Don Wickman whirled around, his M-16 already at hip level. His eyes locked on to the unseeing orbs of a shell-shocked North Vietnamese sergeant, but suddenly the Communist NCO realized he had led his bewildered men right up to a contingent of U.S. gunship troopers. And he went berserk, firing his AK-47 wildly, left to right, right to left.

Big Don got off a three-round burst before the single AK slug struck him in the heart, knocking him back into Treat Brody's arms. "Jesus, no! Oh, Jesus Christ, *no*!" the Whoremonger shouted against the roar of rifle fire erupting all around.

Styx and Stone leaped over both sergeants, out the chopper hatch, rifles blazing. The North Vietnamese was blown back off his feet, a shot group of ten or more M-16 rounds between his ears.

"Big Don!" Cordova was beside Brody now, ripping Wickman's shirt open down the middle, hands working frantically with a compress. "Big Don, hang in there!"

The whole area erupted into a thunder of discharges as every breathing, thinking American who could participate joined the fray. One of the gunships rose up above the one-sided firefight needlessly: most of the staggering NVA soldiers were facedown and dead before the Huey's door gunner could even go to work.

A tall shadow fell across Treat Brody. "Is he going to make it? Is there anything I can do?" Col. Buchanan asked Cordova in a fatherly tone.

"Sgt. Wickman fired three times!" a private yelled

excitedly behind them. "I saw it! Three shots, but he knocked down four VC!"

Corky's hands slowed now. They slowed when Buchanan's voice brought a shard of reality back to the nightmarish scene, and then they stopped working on the sergeant's blood-soaked chest altogether.

A weak fountain of blood still spurted from the hole above Sgt. Wickman's left nipple, though. It spurted forth every other second or so, as if the NCO's heart were still beating . . . as if he still had a chance. But Treat Brody was pulling back the Brick's eyelids and trying to examine his pupils but finding nothing but the whites of his eyes. And he heard himself cursing The Nam and telling Buchanan, "No, Colonel . . . no, thank you, sir . . . there's nothing more any of us can do for him."

"Jesus, Brick . . . I'm sorry, man. . . ." Treat heard his voice cracking in front of the men, and he tried to control himself, but the words only came out faster, a flood of emotion. "I don't know how it happened . . . Christ, I'm sorry. . . ." Pushing Corky's interfering arms away, he hugged Sgt. Wickman like a brother. "I love you, man . . . I'm sorry. . . ."

Wickman's lips fluttered for a moment, and blood began oozing from one corner of his mouth. Both Brody and Cordova drew their heads back—a spark remained in the giant NCO's frame. Big Don was still alive! He was trying to speak—trying to tell them something.

"Go ahead, Brick!" Corky had his ears against Wickman's face. "We're listening, brother—we can hear you!"

"Hang in there!" Brody, wide-eyed, hoped against hope.

A harsh, rasping swirl of air left Wickman's lips,

then words slowly formed. "Promises," he said. "Ashes to ashes, tongue to twa. . . ."

"Right, Big Don—we hear you!" Brody yelled. "Hang in there!" Tears filled Treat's eyes now as Wickman's lips curled back away from his teeth in one last, silent grimace of pain. "We're gonna med-evac you out, Brick! *Just hang in there a few more minutes!*"

"He can't hear you, Treat." Cordova wrapped his arms around them both as the clamor of running boots and sporadic discharges and uncertain yells in the distance merged with the flapping of rotor blades overhead, rising to a dull, numbing crescendo. "He can't hear none of us anymore, brother. . . ."

Big Don was dead. He had finally stepped in front of the bullet with his name on it.

Treat Brody and Corky Cordova watched the helicopter carrying Sgt. Don Wickman's body rise up out of the fog and gunsmoke. A patched-up and heavily bandaged Chance "Two-Step" Broken Arrow sat in the open port hatch, legs dangling out above the landing skids, M-16 rifle braced across his thighs—Echo Company's official escort for the dead. Still shaken by his encounter with the VC guerrilla, Broken Arrow was conscious now, however. And his wounds were actually quite superficial. Treat did not doubt the man would be back in battle before they missed him much. The face lacerations and palm punctures were no million-dollar wounds. He brought his gunhand up in a slight semi-salute, but his eyes stared beyond the men waving up at him from the ground. Two-Step had that glassy-eyed, thousand-yard stare.

Brody watched the Huey climb the tree line, then

disappear into several low clouds as it ascended homeward—back to Fire Base Buffy.

"Well, let's get it over with. . . ."

Buchanan had left him in charge of a small squad assigned to search the bodies of the thirty-odd North Vietnamese killed in that afternoon's shoot-out. Their belongings were to be examined. Any diaries—which, unlike the Americans, and despite strict rules prohibiting it, almost every NVA soldier kept religiously—were to be forwarded to MI and the translators at Division on the next ash-'n'-trash out.

Brody was quick to identify this platoon of NVA. His efforts were expedited by the fact eight of the soldiers were still carrying stretchers when they staggered out of the bombed-out forest. Atop the stretchers were cylindrical objects wrapped in waterproof plastic. The objects turned out to be antihelicopter, shoulder-fired rockets.

"This sucks the big one." Styx held his nose with one hand and a dead NVA corpse's ankle with the other as he and Stone helped several other grunts carry the bodies over to a nearby bomb crater after they were searched.

"Dumpin' 'em down into a bomb crater and blowin' the walls in on 'em sure beats breakin' our backs diggin' a mass grave in this heat, though," Stone argued. "You have any idea how bad they'd smell if they lay under the sun until we were done diggin' a hole that deep?"

"I'm not talkin' about that, Stoner."

"Then what *are* you talkin' about, sweetheart?" Corporal Stone cast him an exhausted glare.

"Sgt. Wickman."

"Big Don? Yeah, that was a downer, man. The Brick was the best. Air Cav sergeants don't come any finer than Big Don. I'm gonna miss him, that's for sure. . . ."

"Remember those stories he used to tell?"

Stone laughed for the first time in close to a year. "Yeah," he said. "Ol' Wickman was a real storyteller. I miss the way he always used to use those multisyllabled words, though. That really tends to piss the officers off, when you're talkin' some intellectual shit that's way over their heads, you know. . . ."

"Yeah. 'Member that time he told us 'bout his last wish?"

"His last wish? Naw, man . . . I don't remember nothin' 'bout no last—"

"Ashes to ashes, tongue to twat. His . . . *dream*. . . ."

"Yep. I remember now." Stone nodded. "Big Don wanted us all to promise somehow, some way, we would smuggle his remains into the biggest douche factory in the world where they got these huge vats that produce enough product to fill millions of douche applicators."

"Big Don did research on this." Styx nodded just as seriously.

"And dump his ashes into the vats. Stir it up real good. 'Ashes to ashes, tongue to twat' . . . get it?"

"So a part of Big Don would live on in the private parts and parties of a million women the world over."

But then Styx and Stone fell silent. They stared at each other, and Styx said, "I'm too short for that kinda shit, Stoner."

"That's exactly why we've gotta do it. We owe it to Big Don. Every man's got his dream. We can make the Brick's come true. You're scheduled to DEROS back to the States for ETS next week."

"*This* week!" Styx corrected him.

305

"Right. That's what I meant. This week. And so am I, short-timer."

"But how we gonna get back to Fire Base Buffy and turn Big Don into ashes?"

"We don't have to. Wickman told me a hundred times: it's in his packet. Cremation in the event of death. It's down in black and white, right there in his two oh one file. No next of kin. Burial at Arlington, or whatever the Army deems appropriate."

"And we is the Army."

"Exactly. All we gotta do is arrange to be the ones who escort the Brick's remains back to The World."

"And Buchanan will cooperate on that end." Brody had been listening in. "No sweat. Wish I could join you short-timers."

"You just extended for another six months, didn't you?" Stone asked him.

"Yep." Brody glanced around at the devastation surrounding them. "Coupla weeks back. Before Belinda."

"Bummer. . . ."

"But I want you clowns to write me a letter about it. *If* we survive the next couple days here and you're even able to hitch a hop out of the *Chaine*."

"Don't fuckin' jinx our shortness, Whoremonger," Styx growled.

"Hell, I want some photos, too. . . ."

CHAPTER 32

Fire Base Belinda

Buchanan was alone in his Loach.

Fire Base Belinda extended out below him for several hundred feet in all directions—he was only five hundred feet above the enemy-controlled artillery camp. The colonel had given his pilot, Zeke, instructions to assist Gabriel. Gunslinger's co-pilot had been killed by VC ground fire shortly after the Arc-Light bombing run, and unlike the smaller Loach, Hueys tended to fly a lot smoother when two men were behind the controls.

Buchanan sighed. It felt good to be in control of an aircraft again. He darted about the skyscraperlike smoke columns, plotting strategy: soon he would have enough men and gunships assembled to run the Viet Cong and NVA off . . . soon reinforcements would arrive from Pleiku and An Khe.

But then he spotted something that made his stomach turn. The VC were dragging, pulling, and pushing large numbers of antiaircraft gun bases over toward one edge of the fire base—onto the perimeter overlooking the Nam Sathay Valley . . . positioning them for a heavy-weapons barrage on the Americans down at LZ Sierra. There was no time to warn them by radio—the barrels had already been prepped and rotated to the proper angle and were even now being lowered into firing position.

Buchanan made a decision. Six months down the line . . . six weeks, maybe, the cancer would kill him. He was tired of living that kind of life . . . at playing the waiting game, dying the slow death.

So he made a decision. And he wasn't even sure it was going to work. Suddenly, the heavily sandbagged and reinforced ammo bunker loomed in his sights like a shark's dorsal fin in calm waters. Could a flimsy little Loach penetrate the multiple layers of tarmac, cross-beams, and sandbags? Col. Buchanan was going to find out. His had become a suicide mission. He thought, suddenly, he might now know what a fanatical terrorist felt like inside.

The Loach dropped abruptly into a steep dive, racing toward the mountaintop in excess of one hundred miles an hour, but as he grew closer to the ammunition cache, doubts waved him off, and he flew around for another pass, rationalizing now that it would be better to strike from the opposite angle—there was more chance of causing greater damage that way . . . of setting off the entire dump by burrowing in over the weaker entrance area. "Python-Three-Two, this is Charlie-Six!" he radioed down to the Huey pilot just lifting off from LZ Sierra.

"Yo, Colonel? Send it!"

"Enemy heavy artillery set to fire on our assault group troops. Evacuate them, *now*!"

He brought the Loach down along Fire Base Belinda's steep slopes, granting himself thirty more seconds of beautiful scenery. "I'll probably rate another CMOH out of this one," he chuckled to himself. "Even if they ever figure it out . . . the way it really went down. . . ."

A static-laced reply from Python-Three-Two filled his headset, and Buchanan guided the Loach around the huge hill's lower crest, preparing to ascend through the vast smoke rings once more, rise above the fire base for that final dive into oblivion.

That was until he spotted the NVA officer leading a squad of baby-faced recruits down one of the mountainside trails just below the sparkling perimeter wire.

Lam Van Minh!

Something more powerful than Buchanan's death wish took hold of him: the desire to mount Major Minh's severed head on a high bamboo pole in front of his command post.

He jerked at the controls, nearly slamming head-on into a sheer granite cliff in his excitement, and then he was hovering above the North Vietnamese officer, unloading on the major's people with the grease gun mounted in the Loach's snout . . . blasting most of them out over the cliff . . . scattering the rest.

Buchanan spotted a ledge nearby. It jutted out from the trail only a few dozen feet or so—but it should be enough space to land.

He brought the Loach in with a jarring crash. The port side landing skid collapsed instantly—and both rotors slammed into a slab of overhanging rock the size of a house. He ducked instinctively, but none of the broken blades crashed down into the cockpit. Out the corner of his eye he saw a decapitated NVA head flying through the air.

Flinging the side door open, he jumped from the

309

helicopter just as it began tipping backward from its precarious perch on the ledge.

And Lam Van Minh stood twenty feet away, slack-jawed and unbelieving, a Chinese-made automatic in one hand but lowered by his side.

Buchanan listened to the Loach tumble backward off the ledge and crash down the mountainside. It exploded with several balls of flame that rose majestically toward the fire base above as he ran across the empty space separating himself from Minh. Fists flying, he lunged at the one man on earth he hated with all his heart.

"You are a *dead* man, Colonel!"

Buchanan did not waste energy trading threats or insults. Lam Van Minh was a powerful man for his age and size, and though Buchanan outweighed him, the cancer eating away at his own insides these last several months had also drained him of much of his strength, and the match did not end swiftly, as he had anticipated.

Major Minh had easily blocked his initial blow, pivoting with a martial-arts turn, snatching Buchanan's fist as it came down, flipping the colonel over his back . . . bringing a sometimes lethal heel kick down toward the American's throat, only to have Buchanan slide free at the last moment, rolling away from the flurry of blows and back to his feet.

And Minh had been the one to charge this time, ignoring the sidearm that hung holstered from his hip. "I have waited many years for this day, Colonel Buchanan!" Minh was breathing hard now as they circled each other. Blood ran freely from his broken nose, but he did not seem as exhausted as Buchanan himself felt. "You have no idea how much I have *dreamed* of this day . . . of killing you with my bare hands."

Buchanan answered with his meaty fist, but Minh

310

easily sidestepped the blow, countered with his own swinging kick—which merely glanced off the colonel's thigh harmlessly. Both officers were rapidly running out of punch.

"I tire of these games," Minh growled, and lowered his fists. He backed away several paces and started to draw his pistol again.

Buchanan's gunhand fell as well, and both officers struggled with their rainflaps, minds and reactions shifting to an odd and unwelcome sort of slow motion. The colonel found himself smiling at the strange turn of events . . . somehow he sensed they were both going to die on this mountainside ledge. In an Old-West-style gunfight, two old soldiers drawing down on each other.

But something happened to freeze the arms of both warriors. Their pistols never cleared holster leather.

A clamor of discharges split the air, and high-velocity antiaircraft shells came whistling down on top of them. Minh glanced up, sensing his doom . . . feeling the end of the game, with no winner at all . . . neither man left to boast victory, to tell and retell the tale over campfires to come.

A string of heavy slugs stitched across the hillside above, creating an avalanche of rocks, falling timber, and hot lead. Both men dropped flat against the shale ledge, covering their heads.

"Damn!" Trinh Thi Kim muttered, the anger rising inside her, mixing with anticipation as she watched the two men disappear beneath a rolling cloud of dust and smoke fifty feet below the sagging coils of concertina wire.

311

* * *

"You think it'll work?"

"There's only one way to find out!" CIA agent John Graves gave Brody the thumbs-up after they had loaded two crates of the canisters aboard *Pegasus*.

"You *up* back there?" Gabriel glanced back over his shoulder.

"We're up!" Whoremonger nodded almost casually, and the gunship's rotors shifted slightly, beating at the blanket of smoke with a vengeance. He watched the moonscape of LZ Sierra drop away with dizzying speed as the ship ascended through the fog and mists, climbing the huge mountain's shadow, rising through the muggy skies toward Fire Base Belinda.

"I hope this fucking works," Brody repeated for the tenth time.

"It's gotta work," Graves yelled back.

"It *better* work!" Gabriel told them as Belinda's perimeter defenses appeared suddenly below. "With the troops at Pleiku and An Khe socked in for another twenty-four to forty-eight hours, we're on our own, and Charlie's gettin' ready to make his move on Fire Base Buffy next!"

Brody swallowed hard as they raced over the LP bunkers and concertina wire, drawing intense ground fire from several Vietnamese riflemen. The plan was simple. Graves had it figured that dropped from an altitude of five hundred feet directly over the center of camp, the poison gas recovered from the underground bunker complex at LZ Sierra would have been diluted enough to cause widespread unconsciousness and only a few deaths among the enemy.

"Fucking hotdog," Graves muttered in Gabe's direction. "Why's he takin' us in so low? We don't need no tour of the circus. . . . The hotdog's gonna get us shot down before we can beat blades to the proper altitude. . . .''

But Brody wasn't listening to the spook's complaints. He was going over in his mind the unfolding scenario: they would be able to land *rikky-tik,* without having to fire a shot and with countless prisoners to show the Saigon Press Corps. Fire Base Belinda would be theirs again, and the colonel—wherever the hell he was—would be sure to recommend them all for at least a Distinguished Flying Cross!

"Hey!" Brody dashed to the hatch as *Pegasus* roared above the perimeter at treetop level. "It's her! It's the bitch!" He pointed at the female guerrilla running between the gun pits below, her pistol drawn. "It's the VC bitch, you guys!" He grabbed at the Hog-60, but too late. *Pegasus* had completed her fly-by of the old CP and was ascending almost vertically over the camp, rotor blades and turbines straining against the sudden climb through air so thick and humid it left a saltwater taste on the lips.

"Gabe!" Brody yelled against the downblast, too excited to click in. "Take us back for one more swing, man! Gimme five seconds to blast that bitch to hell!"

"So sorry, Whoremonger." Gabriel spoke over the intercom calmly. "No can do. . . ."

"Mellow out, Whoremonger!" Gabe the Gunslinger added. "If this scheme works, you can go back down there and capture sleeping beauty and do whatever you please with the cunt . . . if you *snatch* my meaning. . . ."

"Nooooooo!"

Brody was hanging halfway out the open hatch without benefit of the monkeystraps or lifeline. Startled, John Graves crowded in behind him.

313

Below, a sleek, two-man gunship with sharks' teeth painted along its snout was darting up and down, all around the woman, forcing her to run behind piles of sandbags, then sprint across open stretches of space again as Warlokk pounced, his gunner spraying the ground around Trinh Thi Kim with minigun fire, but not quite striking the woman yet . . . toying with her only . . . making "the kill" last . . . savoring the hunt.

"Lawless, you *son-of-a-bitch*!" Brody screamed into the rotorwash, and then *Pegasus* banked hard to the right, flipping nearly onto her side with the turn, and the fire base below became the ghost-white, castlelike cumulus of the *Chaine Annamitique*.

CHAPTER 33

Over Fire Base Belinda

"She's all yours, Saint Pat!"

Lance Warlokk grinned. He loved to see his men getting sweet vengeance.

"Take this baby down," Warrant Officer Patterson demanded. "I want it up close and personal!"

"Uh . . . Xin Loi, my man . . . no can do-do! I've already lost one Cobra to Charlie . . . Neil Nazi'd have my ying-yang in a sling if I trashed Sharkskinner two."

"If you wanna have an ass left to trash, you better set this crate down, Warlokk!" Patterson stared back over his shoulder.

Sighing in a mixed vein of resignation and understanding, Warlokk pranged the ship across several Viet Cong bodies, nearly ramming one of the landing skids up Kim's shapely backside. He could have refused, insisting on bringing the new warrant officer up on charges

315

instead, but Patterson was family—First Cav family, from way back—and Lawless understood. . . .

He could still remember the two incidents, long ago . . . the rain forest affair that made Saint Pat notorious among double vets . . . the encounter with a VC bitch who captured Patterson and took his clothes, tied him to a tree, taunted and teased him, then nailed a VC flag patch to his back before setting him free to wander the maze of jungle trails, bruised, battered, and bloody . . . until he was finally found by an American patrol.

Later, he would come face to face with her again . . . at a godforsaken place called Binh Dinh Province. Kim would manage to run him through with a bayonet, but he would survive this nightmare, too.

Over the ensuing months he would recover rapidly, defying the army doctors' attempts to flag him with a medical discharge—what were a few lousy bayonet wounds? St. Pat reasoned.

With the help of Nurse Maddox's father, an MACV general down at Disneyland East, Patterson was allowed not only back onto active duty status, but into an open slot at the helicopter flight school in Alabama as well.

And now he was back. Back in The Nam. A Cobra jockey, hot on the trail to pay an old debt.

Patterson threw the cockpit cover open and leaped from Sharkskinner II as if his flight suit were on fire. Smith & Wesson .38 revolver in his gunhand, he sprinted after Trinh Thi Kim, yelling at her in Vietnamese to stop. "*Dung lai! Dung lai*, you fucking bitch!"

And she whirled, firing chamber after chamber from her own handgun. Startled, St. Pat watched the cylinder turn five times before his own trigger finger went into action.

Kim's chest was heaving from the exertion of limping

316

clear across camp, and all her shots went astray, but Patterson's first slug hit home.

The bullet struck Trinh Thi Kim in the chest, knocking her onto her haunches with a long, painful scream.

Eyes wide, she was still breathing hard when his shadow fell over her. Kim did not look him in the eye—she stared up the gun barrel. But she knew who he was.

"They . . . they are in my pack," she told him slowly, the life's blood draining from her . . . the fight oozing out the dime-sized hole in her chest.

"They?" Patterson laughed, dropping to one knee beside her and pressing Kim's nostrils flat with the pistol barrel. "What could I possibly want besides *you* in this goddamned world of hurt, woman?"

"In . . . my . . . pack," she repeated. "The hammer and nails. . . ."

Patterson laughed again. He threw his head back with the laugh and pulled a First Air Cavalry patch from his thigh pocket. "Oh, you're gonna get worse than a nail through the shoulder blade, cunt!"

"I will see . . . you . . . in . . . hell, Saint Pat. . . ." She tried to spit in his face, but Patterson responded to the taunt by stuffing the First Team horsehead patch into her mouth.

"I'm tired of listening to your shit, bitch!" he hissed. Holstering his pistol, he pulled a long machete from the sheath strapped to his other thigh and placed the machete under her chin. He flipped Trinh Thi Kim over and pulled back on the straight, jet-black strands until the skin along her throat went taut. Without further fanfare, he brought the long, jagged blade up, hard and viciously, until Kim's head parted from her neck with a gush of blood and bile.

Holding the head's face up to his own, Patterson reflected the woman's threat as he stared into her eyes.

317

He basked in the glow of hot vengeance, enjoying the startled expression that seemed to remain on Trinh Thi Kim's features. "Yes, woman . . . I'll see you in hell!"

"Eat shit, Saint Pat!" A jealous Treat Brody yelled down from the hatch as *Pegasus* made one final swoop over Fire Base Belinda after dropping the gas. "You clowns *best* get your buns off that fire base, 'cause we just gassed the whole camp!"

Patterson stood atop the sandbags of a machine-gun nest, godlike, chest out, both arms raised above his head. Enemy bullets danced all around his boots, but none came close to striking the Cobra gunner. He was yelling something Brody could not make out—a Vietnamese war cry, perhaps, judging by his adrenaline-charged gestures. His eyes were bulging and filled with rage and satisfaction. In the smoky backdrop behind him, like shadowy phantoms, terrified VC guerrillas were running about trying to find a way off the mountaintop as their comrades began mysteriously collapsing all around them.

From Patterson's gunhand dangled the severed head of Trinh Thi Kim, blood still dripping from the shredded flesh where her throat had once been.

"Crazy bastard," Gabriel muttered into his mike as Patterson raised the woman's head even higher for them to see.

Brody laughed at his antics, wondering why he himself had never thought of such a display. Gabe the Gunslinger would be talking about it now over First Cav campfires for years to come.

A devastating explosion shook Fire Base Belinda suddenly, and sandbags flew airborne all around him as the ammo bunker disintegrated, but Saint Pat didn't seem to notice.

Standing on the edge of that ledge overlooking the mist-enshrouded Nam Sathay River Valley, he threw the severed head off the mountaintop. He watched it bounce and roll and bounce some more down the steep slopes, flinging a spray of crimson drops into the sun each time it struck a tree stump or boulder.

EPILOGUE

Sgt. Treat Brody sat at the bar of a lounge in Tan Son Nhut Airport's warehouselike terminal, waiting for his flight to Bangkok and working on his Singapore sling. His eyes scanned the *Stars & Stripes* story but kept returning to the free-lance reporter's name: Rusty Stanton.

"Good old Rusty." He nodded, remembering how the kid had lost his arm while serving with Echo Company, only to return to Vietnam as a photojournalist. He'd been meaning to look him up since arriving in the capital three days earlier, but the last seventy-two hours before his R&R to Thailand had been filled with whoring and depression, nightmares and whoring, more whoring, and now the booze to wash out the guilt. He'd meant to check on Em-Ho Lee as well. But when he phoned Third Field Hospital, they could not be sure if the castrated soldier was still in the psycho ward or had been transferred to a hospital in Tokyo. Call back in the morning, he had been told. He never did, preferring not to know . . . preferring to get laid and smashed and laid again instead.

Now he was on his way to the kingdom of Siam . . .

321

land of a thousand temples . . . on his way to the great Chao Phraya River, and *Wat Arun*—the Temple of Dawn—for a long-awaited pilgrimage to Bangkok. Followed by a much earned R&R.

He'd burn a *joss* stick or two in memory of Big Don Wickman at the sacred temple. Maybe one for Snakeman, too . . . and the others . . . all the door gunners who had died before Big Don and would die in the years and battles to come . . . all the warriors fighting beneath the black moon of Vietnam.

He pulled something else from the AWOL bag—a small, brightly decorated package that had been wrapped in plain brown paper, bearing no return address but a New York City postmark.

Inside, taped to the container of douche, was a note from Styx and Stone, in which they swore on their First Team honor and Vietnam Service Medals that they carried out Sgt. Wickman's last wishes and mixed his ashes with the douche formula the company would be sending out to a million women worldwide. "Enclosed is one of the first samples," the letter read. "We were unable to find out whether or not it gets as far as Saigon, so under separate cover and as soon as possible, we'll be sending a whole crate to you douchebags there in The Nam, Whoremonger. Pass some around to the guys, as a souvenir . . . a permanent remembrance of Big Don.

"Then take the remaining hundred or so bottles down to Saigon next time you get a few days in the big city, okay? Just drop 'em off at the black market between Tu Do and Le Loi streets—you know the one. It's sure to get *snatched* up there."

Brody chuckled to himself every time he reread the note, and this was no exception. He replaced the package, glanced at the photo of Styx and Stone posing stone-faced with the Brick's cremation urn, then zipped up the AWOL bag and returned to Stanton's story. It was an account of the battle for Fire Base Buffy.

A high-ranking North Vietnamese officer, Major Lam Van Minh, was believed killed during the vicious fighting to retake Artillery Fire Support Base Belinda in the rugged *Chaine Annamitique* range running through Pleiku and Kontum provinces several hundred miles north of the capital. Minh was the military mastermind behind several recent enemy offensives and campaigns waged by the Communists in South Vietnamese territory south of the DMZ.

Missing in action for three days after the camp was recaptured, Col. Neil Buchanan remains in a coma at 3rd Field Army Hospital, following his rescue from a bomb-caused landslide on the fire base's east slopes. He is not expected to survive, according to MACV sources who requested anonymity.

Sixty-eight Americans died in recent fighting along the mountain range. Over 3,000 enemy soldiers forfeited their lives during the three-month operation.

It was also revealed that several South Vietnamese villagers loyal to the Saigon government sealed off the mountain's base and surrounding slopes during the fighting, thus preventing widespread escapes by the enemy—as is usually common with the Communists' hit-and-run tactics. First Air Cavalry Division commanders were elated to find that the men of the 7th's Echo Company not only succeeded in returning the fire base to American control, but captured some 454 enemy prisoners of war in the process. Among the five soldiers recommended for the Congressional Medal of Honor—America's highest award for valor and heroism under fire—were Sergeants Donald Wickman and Treat Brody, and Warrant Officer Lance Warlok, as well as Colonel Buchanan. Buchanan received the distinguished prize once before—while an infantryman fighting in Korea seventeen years ago.

Brody smiled as he folded up the newspaper and tucked it into the AWOL bag. There was no mention made of the poison gas tactics or the loss of the ammo dump and several antiaircraft emplacements. And Stanton not only left out Gabriel's name regarding the CMOH recommendations, but he misspelled Warlokk's. Boy, were Gunslinger and Lawless gonna have a cow over *that,* he thought.

Treat didn't think he deserved the Medal of Honor, but that was all up to the brass and the politicians, and he would accept their final decision, whatever it might be. It didn't matter. Nothing meant anything. This was The Nam.

He hoped Buchanan pulled through, of course, but the colonel's future didn't look very bright. The guys were shocked to find he was still breathing . . . still hanging on, after they pulled him out from under all that rock and teakwood.

"Flight SQ one, departing for Bangkok and Singapore, now boarding at gate one," came a garbled announcement in heavily accented Vietnamese. But it was a woman's voice, and Brody found himself suddenly aroused. "Repeating, flight SQ one for Thailand and Singapore . . . all passengers are now asked to board at gate one. . . . This is your first call. . . ."

His eyes shifted to the thick envelope lying in his

lap. They focused on the address. Did he really want to do it? Did he really want to answer the nasty letter he'd received a few weeks back from his old English teacher back at Hollywood High with one of his own and ten VC ears he'd collected in-country? What would it prove, anyway?

Brody glanced at the unit patch of the soldier sitting beside him at the bar. He recognized the Combat Engineers' emblem—an outfit currently serving near Nam Dong. . . .

Nam Dong. Snakeman Fletcher was on his way there at that very moment, en route to pick up his mail-order bride. That would be something to look forward to when Brody got back from R&R—to see if she was really as beautiful as Elliot envisioned.

"Another Singapore sling, soldier?" The cocktail waitress was running her fingers through the hair on Whoremonger's arm, and he glanced up to find a beautiful Vietnamese lass batting her dark exotic eyes at him. His own dropped from her high cheekbones and long black hair, down along the tight sarong's sumptuous curves, to her shapely haunches—just the way Treat Brody liked his women. But the intercom was calling to him again, announcing the final call for flight SQ1 to Bangkok and Singapore.

"No . . . no, thank you, gorgeous," he said, "I've got a flight to catch."

"You leave on freedom bird?" She pouted with mock sincerity. "You go back The World, never see Pham Thi Dep again?"

Brody just smiled and patted her cheek. Leaving her a big tip, he zipped up his AWOL bag and left. He was in a hurry but took a second to glance back over his shoulder . . . seeking out the firm, bouncing bottom of

325

the cocktail waitress. He was not disappointed at the exaggerated swish and warm wink she treated him to.

The woman had been waiting for him to look back one last time . . . one final glance . . . that bewitching transfer of mental messages and thoughts, hopes, dreams that they might share just one night below the flares of Saigon, lying in each other's arms, listening to the jets race their engines at Tan Son Nhut Airport, waiting for that solitary VC rocket to crash down in the city somewhere . . . wondering if it might crash down on *them,* yet not really caring—for what better way was there to go than in a blinding flash of shrapnel while making love?

Brody blew the kiss back at her, shaking off the feeling of being mesmerized, refusing to let her weave her magical spell on him as he headed toward a mailbox near the boarding gates, his fingers moist with sweat as they clung to the envelope thick with VC ears.

On the way up to gate 1, Sgt. Brody passed in front of a vendor's stand where plastic bags of iced coffee and steaming sugar-cane cubes and coconut shavings on long bamboo slivers were being sold. He pulled a one-hundred-piaster note from his khaki pants pocket and purchased a package of Vietnamese Blue Ruby cigarettes. Flying on commercial airliners—where there were no doorguns to lean into, no open hatches to spit out, no piles of empty machine-gun brass to stumble through, no monkeystraps to hook to your web belt—made him nervous.

Once again, he started toward the line of anxious soldiers waiting to board the sleek, made-in-America jet waiting outside. But then he hesitated, turned, and walked back to the vendor's stall. Refusing to look at the pretty girl working the cash register, he dropped the envelope of dried and shriveled Viet Cong ears into the trash can, executed a crisp about-face, and rejoined the happy heroes who crowded the boarding gate.

GLOSSARY

AA Antiaircraft weapon
AC Aircraft Commander
Acting Jack Acting NCO
AIT Advanced Individual Training
AJ Acting Jack
AK-47 Automatic rifle used by VC/NVA
Animal See *Monster*
AO Area of Operations
Ao Dai Traditional Vietnamese gown
APH-5 Helmet worn by gunship pilots
APO Army Post Office
Arc-Light B-52 bombing mission
ArCOM Army Commendation Medal
Article-15 Disciplinary action
Ash-'n'-Trash Relay flight

Bad Paper Dishonorable discharge
Ba Muoi Ba Vietnamese beer
Banana Clip Ammo magazine holding 30 bullets

Bao Chi Press or news media
Basic Boot camp
BCT Basic Combat Training (Boot)
Bic Vietnamese for "Understand?"
Big-20 Army career of 20 years
Bird Helicopter
BLA Black Liberation Army
Bloods Black soldiers
Blues An airmobile company
Body Count Number of enemy KIA
Bookoo Vietnamese for "many" (actually a bastardization of the French *beaucoup*)
Bought the Farm Died and life insurance policy paid for mortgage
Brass Monkey Interagency radio call for help
Brew Usually coffee, but sometimes beer
Bring Smoke To shoot someone
Broken-Down Disassembled
Buddha Zone Death
Bush ('Bush) Ambush
Butter Bar 2nd Lieutenant

CA Combat Assault
Cam On Viet for "Thank you"
Cartridge Shell casing for bullet
C&C Command & Control chopper
Chao Vietnamese greeting
Charlie Viet Cong (from military phonetic: Victor Charlie)
Charlie Tango Control Tower
Cherry New man in unit
Cherry Boy Virgin
Chicken Plate Pilot's chest/groin armor
Chi-Com Chinese Communist

Chieu Hoi Program where Communists can surrender and become scouts

Choi-oi Viet exclamation

CIB Combat Infantry Badge

CID Criminal Investigation Division

Clip Ammo magazine

CMOH Congressional Medal of Honor

CO Commanding Officer

Cobra Helicopter gunship used for combat assaults/ escorts only

Cockbang Bangkok, Thailand

Conex Shipping container (metal)

Coz Short for Cozmoline

CP Command Post

CSM Command Sergeant Major

Cunt Cap Green narrow cap worn with khakis

Dash-13 Helicopter maintenance report

Dau Viet for pain

Deadlined Down for repairs

Dep Viet for beautiful

DEROS Date of Estimated Return from Overseas

Deuce-and-a-Half 2½-ton truck

DFC Distinguished Flying Cross

DI Drill Instructor (Sgt.)

Di Di Viet for "Leave or go!"

Dink Derogatory term for Vietnamese national

Dinky Dau Viet for "crazy"

Disneyland East MACV complex including annex

DMZ Demilitarized Zone

Dogtags Small aluminum tag worn by soldiers with name, serial number, religion, and blood type imprinted on it.

DOOM Pussy Danang Officers Open Mess

Door gunner Soldier who mans M-60 machine gun mounted in side hatch of Huey gunship

Dung Lai Viet for "Halt!"

Dustoff Medevac chopper

Early Out Unscheduled ETS

EM Enlisted Man

ER Emergency Room (hospital)

ETS End Tour of (military) Service

Field Phone Hand-generated portable phones used in bunkers

Fini Viet for "Stop" or "the End"

First Louie 1st Lieutenant

First Team Motto of 1st Air Cav

Flak Jacket Body armor

FNG Fucking new guy

FOB Fly over border mission

Foxtrot Vietnamese female

Foxtrot Tosser Flame thrower

Frag Fragmentation grenade

FTA Fuck the Army

Gaggle Loose flight of slicks

Get Some Kill someone

GI Government Issue, or, a soldier

Greenbacks U.S. currency

Green Machine U.S. Army

Gunship Attack helicopter armed with machine guns and rockets

Gurney Stretcher with wheels

Ham & Motherfuckers C-rations serving of ham and lima beans

332

Herpetologist One who studies reptiles and amphibians

HOG-60 M-60 machine gun

Hot LZ Landing zone under hostile fire

Housegirl Indigenous personnel hired to clean buildings, wash laundry, etc.

Huey Primary troop-carrying helicopter

IC Installation Commander

IG Inspector General

In-Country Within Vietnam

Intel Intelligence (military)

IP That point in a mission where descent toward target begins

JAG Judge Advocate General

Jane Jane's Military Reference books

Jesus Nut The bolt that holds rotor blade to helicopter

Jody Any American girlfriends

Jolly Green Chinook helicopter

KIA Killed in Action

Kimchi Korean fish sauce salad

Klick Kilometer

KP Mess hall duty

Lai Day Viet for "come here"

LAW Light Anti-Tank Weapon

Lay Dog Lie low in jungle during recon patrol

LBFM Little Brown Fucking Machine

LBJ Long Binh Jail (main stockade)

Leg Infantryman not airborne qualified

Lifeline Straps holding gunny aboard chopper while he fires M-60 out the hatch

Lifer Career soldier

Links   Metal strip holding ammo belt together
Loach   Small spotter/scout chopper
LP   Listening Post
LRRP   Long-Range Recon Patrol
LSA   Gun oil
Lurp   One who participates in LRRPs
LZ   Landing Zone

M-14   American carbine
M-16   Primary U.S. automatic rifle
M-26   Fragmentation grenade
M-60   Primary U.S. machine gun
M-79   Grenade launcher (rifle)
MACV   Military Assistance Command, Vietnam
Magazine   Metal container that feeds bullets into weapon. Holds 20 or 30 rounds per unit
Mag Pouch   Magazine holder worn on web belt
MAST   Mobile Army Surgical Team
Medevac   Medical Evacuation Chopper
Mess Hall   GI cafeteria
MG   Machine gun
MI   Military Intelligence
MIA   Missing in Action
Mike-Mike   Millimeters
Mike Papas   Military Policemen
Mister Zippo   Flame-thrower operator
Mjao   Central Highlands witch doctor
Monkeyhouse   Stockade or jail
Monkeystrap   See *Lifeline*
Monster   12-21 claymore antipersonnel mines jury-rigged to detonate simultaneously
Montagnard   Hill tribe people of Central Highlands, RVN
MPC   Money Payment Certificates (scrip) issued to GIs in RVN in lieu of greenbacks

Muster A quick assemblage of soldiers with little or no warning
My Viet for "American"

Net Radio net
NETT New Equipment Training Team
Newby New GI in-country
Numba One Something very good
Numba Ten Something very bad
Nuoc Nam Viet fish sauce
NVA North Vietnamese Army

OD Olive Drab
OR Operating Room (Hospital)

P Piasters
PA Public Address system
PCS Permanent Change of (Duty) Station (transfer out of RVN)
Peter Pilot Copilot in training
PF Popular Forces (Vietnamese)
PFC Private First Class
Phantom Jet fighter plane
Phu Vietnamese noodle soup
Piaster Vietnamese currency
PJ Photojournalist
Point The most dangerous position on patrol. The point man walks ahead and to the side of the others, acting as a lookout
PRG Provisional Revolutionary Govt. (the Communists)
Prang Land a helicopter roughly
Prick-25 Pr-25 field radio
Profile Medical exemption
Psy-Ops Psychological operation

PT Physical Training
Puff Heavily armed aircraft
Purple Heart Medal given for wounds received in combat
Purple Vision Night vision
Puzzle Palace The MACV HQ building

Quad-50 Truck equipped with four 50-caliber MGs
QC Vietnamese MP

Rat Fuck Mission doomed from the start
Regular An enlistee or full-time soldier as opposed to PFs and Reserves, NG, etc.
REMF Rear Echelon Motherfucker
R&R Rest and Relaxation
Re-Up Re-enlist
Rikky-Tik Quickly or fast
Rock 'n' Roll Automatic fire
Roger Affirmative
ROK Republic of Korea
Rotor Overhead helicopter blade
Round Bullet
RPG Rocket-propelled grenade
Ruck (Sack) GI's backpack
RVN Republic of (South) Vietnam

Saigon Capital of RVN
SAM Surface-to-Air Missile
Sapper Guerrilla terrorist equipped with satchel charge (explosives)
SAR Downed-chopper rescue mission
Scramble Alert reaction to call for help, CA or rescue operation.
Scrip See MPC
7.62 M-60 ammunition

Sierra Echo Southeast (Northwest is November Whiskey, etc.)

Single-Digit Fidget A nervous single-digit midget

Single-Digit Midget One with fewer than ten days remaining in Vietnam

SKS Russian-made carbine

Slick Helicopter

Slicksleeve Private E-1

Slug Bullet

SNAFU Situation normal: all fucked up

Soggy Frog Green Beret laying dog

SOP Standard Operating Procedure (also known as Shit Output)

Spiderhole Tunnel entrance

Strac Sharp appearance

Steel Pot Helmet

Striker Montagnard hamlet defender

Sub-Gunny Substitute door gunner

TDY Temporary Duty Assignment

Terr Terrorist

"33" Local Vietnamese beer

Thumper see *M-79*

Ti Ti Viet for little

Tour 365 The year-long tour of duty a GI spends in RVN

Tower Rat Tower guard

Tracer Chemically treated bullet that gives off a glow en route to its target

Triage That method in which medics determine which victims are most seriously hurt and therefore treated first

Trooper Soldier

201 File Personnel file

Two-Point-Five Gunship rockets

UCMJ Uniformed Code of Military Justice
Unass Leave seat quickly

VC Viet Cong
Victor Charlie VC
Viet Cong South Vietnamese Communists
VNP Vietnamese National Police
Void Vicious Final approach to a Hot LZ; or the jungle when hostile

Warrant Officer Pilots
Wasted Killed
Web Belt Utility belt GIs use to carry equipment, sidearms, etc.
Whiskey Military phonetic for "West"
WIA Wounded In Action
Wilco Will comply
Willie Peter White phosphorus
Wire Perimeter (trip wire sets off booby trap)
The World Any place outside Vietnam

Xin Loi Viet for "sorry about that" or "good-bye"
XM-21 Gunship mini-gun
XO Executive officer

'Yarde Montagnard

ZIP Derogatory term for Vietnamese National
Zulu Military Phonetic for the letter Z (LZ or Landing Zone might be referred to as a Lima Zulu)

Ride the skies with the First Air Cavalry under new command as Brody and his men defy orders to save Platoon Sergeant Leo Zack from VC torture when he's taken to a secret Cambodian POW camp. Unsupported, they risk their lives in the next action-packed. . .

CHOPPER 1 #9: PAYBACK

ABOUT THE AUTHOR

Jack Hawkins is the pen name of a Vietnam veteran who served with the U.S. Army in Southeast Asia from 1972–75, where he was awarded the Bronze Star Medal. His unit received the Vietnamese Cross of Gallantry and Presidential Unit Citation. He has written twenty-four other Vietnam novels, under several pseudonyms, and alternates between homes in Little Saigon, U.S.A., and the Orient.